Praise for Liane Child

'A glimpse into the world of influencers and their lives which may not be all they seem. A cleverly plotted story which will keep you turning the pages well into the night.'
Catherine Cooper

'I thought it was superb.'
My Weekly

'A page-turning thriller that explores influencer culture, with a shocking twist . . .'
BEST

'Deliciously twisty and diabolically plotted . . . Timely, incisive, and oh so addictive!'
Laurie Elizabeth Flynn

'We read this in one sitting.'
THAT'S LIFE

'A gripping thriller about deception and self-discovery.'
Women's Weekly

'An original, fast-paced and compelling psychological thriller with twists that will give you whiplash.'
Diane Jeffrey

'The addictive plotline sucked me in from the get-go and had me racing through the pages until the nail-biting finale. An easy five stars and more!'
A.A. Chaudhuri

'Gripping.'
CRIME MONTHLY

'It's addictive, with lots of drama, some memorable side characters and a huge twist I for one did not see coming.'
The Daily Mirror

'The absolute definition of a page-turner . . . Perfect for anyone who loves their thrillers to be twisty, mysterious and forever several steps ahead.'
Katy Brent

'Gripping and razor-sharp, this is twisted tradwife lit at its most addictive.'
Heat

'Totally obsessed with this book! So fun, twisty and clever. I loved it.'
Sophie Flynn

'A riveting domestic thriller that rips the filter off an insta-perfect life.'
The Peterborough Telegraph

Liane Child is a writer whose gripping debut *The Tradwife's Secret* was inspired by the #tradwife subculture emerging in the US. Liane loves all things social media, and her second book *Someone Just Followed You* explores the dark art of influencing. When she isn't scrolling Instagram or TikTok, you can find her reading, walking her dog, or attempting to improve her tennis serve. Liane has travelled extensively and now lives in London.

Also by Liane Child

The Tradwife's Secret

SOMEONE JUST FOLLOWED YOU

LIANE CHILD

HQ

ONE PLACE. MANY STORIES

HQ
An imprint of HarperCollins*Publishers* Ltd
1 London Bridge Street
London SE1 9GF

www.harpercollins.co.uk

HarperCollins*Publishers*
Macken House, 39/40 Mayor Street Upper
Dublin 1, D01 C9W8, Ireland
This edition 2026

1
First published in Great Britain by HQ,
an imprint of HarperCollins*Publishers* Ltd 2026

A catalogue record for this book is available from the British Library.

ISBN: 9780008807078

Set in Sabon LT Std by HarperCollins*Publishers* India

Printed and bound in the UK using 100% Renewable
Electricity at CPI Group (UK) Ltd

FSC
www.fsc.org
MIX
Paper | Supporting
responsible forestry
FSC® C013604

For Hannah
My inspiring, cheerleading sister (in-law)

Prologue

Hey guys, so I just had to make this video because guess what? I hit 1.9 million subscribers today! Isn't that cool? Thank you all for believing in me, and hanging out with me, and watching my crazy videos. Honestly, you guys are the best.

Maple's eyelids flicker but she won't open them. She wants to live here, in her happy memory, not in the stifling, claustrophobic darkness that actually swamps her. The door to the outside isn't far away, just a few steps maybe, but it's too far for her. For the shackles on her wrists and ankles, chaining her to the bed.

But the memory has gone now, reality back behind her eyelids, so she gives in, opens her eyes. Takes in her shadowy surroundings. Within seconds the tears start, like always, hot and sticky on her cheeks.

She's lying on her back. There's just enough length in the chains to roll onto her side, but she doesn't. Her whole body feels too heavy, like her muscles are still asleep and her limbs belong to someone else.

She stares at the ceiling. How long has she been here? Her

brain is too sluggish; she can't figure it out. She wants to fight against it, to think straight, to find a way to escape.

To pray for someone to come save her.

But she hasn't got the strength to think. She's too tired.

She closes her eyes again. Drifts off.

Chapter 1

Kirsten

We walk into the arrivals' concourse, and I spot him immediately. A man in a fitted white shirt, black jeans, and thick-framed square glasses. Sure, he looks exactly like I imagine an advertising executive from California to look, but it's the laminate card he's holding that really gives him away. The one typed with my daughter's name. *Maple Clark (talent)*.

Talent.

I close my eyes and savor the moment. Fourteen years of hard work gleaming back at me in shiny black typescript. The clinking and chiming of Harry Reid Airport's slot machines somehow the perfect backing track. With my palm on the small of Maple's back, I maneuver us through the crowd of tourists and gambling addicts toward him.

I smile. I've practiced this a lot, getting the perfect balance between gratitude and expectation, and it seems to pay off because his LA-tanned face lights up.

'Mrs. Clark,' he says, reaching for my hand. 'So great to meet you. I'm Jules, from Studio 88, the lead brand agency on this project.'

'Please, call me Kirsten,' I say, pulling my hand back, vaguely wondering if I retracted it prematurely, then deciding I needn't worry. *Talent*. 'And this is Maple.' I give my daughter the gentlest shove forward.

'Oh, hey,' she says, lifting one hand into an awkward wave. She clearly hasn't been practicing as much as me, which is a little irritating, given the number of times I've talked to her about first impressions, but I don't let my disappointment show. 'Nice to meet you.'

He nods and his eyes linger a second longer than maybe they should, a thirty-something man meeting a fourteen-year-old girl. But of course, Maple isn't any teenager; if she was, we wouldn't be here in the first place.

'Well, welcome to Vegas,' Jules says. 'We're so excited that you were available for today's shoot; I know it can be hard during the school year, but we've got some immovable deadlines; you know how it is.'

'It's fine; we get it,' I say smoothly, pretending that we do photoshoots in iconic locations all year round. Glossing over the fact that Maple skipping school to be here means she will be getting a black mark against her name on the attendance record round about now. 'Luckily Maple's school principal is a fan of her work.'

Jules spreads his hands. 'Well, who isn't?' He laughs, a little falsely maybe, then points to the sliding glass doors. 'I have a car waiting outside, if you're ready?'

I find my best Hollywood smile. 'Lead the way.'

We follow him out of the terminal building, then down a ramp toward a line of luxury cars with drivers sat up front. He pauses at one and gives us a triumphant grin. 'So does this work for you, Maple?'

Maple's jaw drops, literally, turning her mouth into a black hole. 'OMG, Mom!' she squeals. She flicks her face toward me, then back to the car, her golden-brown eyes wide with awe. 'This is for us?'

Jules grins. 'If you haven't cruised the strip in a custom-built baby-pink Cadillac Escalade, have you even been to Vegas?' He opens the door like a chauffeur might, then raises his eyebrows in a way I imagine a chauffeur would get fired for.

Maple giggles, any awkwardness now gone, and climbs in. I worry for a moment that Jules is going to follow, leave me on the pavement – the forgotten mom, even though I do practically all the work. But of course he doesn't. He gestures for me to go next, and so I do, clambering inside as demurely as I can manage.

Chapter 2

Kirsten

Jules is right to brag. The Cadillac looks more like a limo inside, with four huge leather seats facing into each other. Maple has claimed one, her forearms wide on the armrests, the soles of her Nikes visible as she sinks into the deep bucket seat. I sit down next to her, and Jules climbs in, taking the seat opposite Maple.

'As you know, the shoot's happening in Graffiti Alley in the Arts District,' he says as he opens a small fridge and distributes cans of ice-cold water. 'It's got such a cool vibe – perfect for the street-style look that Azione are going for. We've constructed an elevated glass box in front of the artwork, which looks spectacular, and there's security, so you don't need to worry about any snooping fans.'

'But I'll be inside the box?' Maple asks, drumming her new electric-blue shellac nails – a pre-shoot mom and daughter treat – against the can. A note of fear has crept into her tone, and I try not to roll my eyes. Sure, Maple has never liked confined spaces, but the box is made of glass. It will hardly be claustrophobic.

'Exactly,' Jules says with a smile. He seems to have missed

her new nervousness, thank goodness. 'It's the perfect mix of classy and edgy, clean and gritty, you know?'

'Truly perfect,' I agree, although I'm thinking less about the creative direction and more about the paycheck. Azione is an Italian clothing brand that Maddie, our PR agent, told me has been trying to break America since it launched in 2012. They finally struck gold when the eldest Hart child gave them a shout-out across all her social media platforms a couple of years ago – I forget her name now, she hasn't posted for a while, but with eight million subscribers to their @7harts YouTube page, the sales uptick for Azione was immediate.

Having finally caught on to the power of kidfluencing, the brand contacted our PR agency. For a while it was just free clothes in exchange for posts. But then last month, Maddie called to say they wanted Maple to front their digital advertising campaign – a starring role for Maple's very first modeling gig. I was ecstatic for her, and I can still remember her face when I told her the news. Making your child's dream come true is so special.

The strip is just beyond the airport, so we're there in no time, and I turn toward the window to soak up the view. The Eiffel Tower statue at Paris Las Vegas, more beautiful than the original, I've heard people say. And the Bellagio opposite, unashamedly opulent with its iconic fountain and grand entrance.

I've only been to Vegas once before, a long weekend with Garrett over ten years ago. We were celebrating my first brand deal for Mom & Maple, the original name of Maple's YouTube channel, and we stayed at the Four Queens on Fremont. It was a nice enough hotel, but it wasn't the Bellagio. I wonder if that was the moment I redefined my ambition.

We pass other world-famous landmarks, places that make

me feel proud to be American, like Caesars Palace and the Venetian, before the Boulevard starts to slip downhill. Not in topography, but the polish leaves the pavements. Tourists are replaced by workers, or worse. I feel a waft of disappointment that the photoshoot isn't taking place somewhere more glamorous; that even in Vegas, a European fashion brand can choose grunge over glitz. But if they're willing to pay twenty-five thousand dollars for Maple to spend a day in Graffiti Alley, who am I to complain.

I reach for her hand and squeeze it. 'You excited?' I murmur.

'Yes, I think so,' she whispers. 'Maybe a bit nervous. First time, you know. Don't want to get it wrong.'

My eyes dart to Jules, but he's hunched over his phone, thumbs jerking against the screen, so I reach out, stroke her long chestnut hair, inhale the scent of Verb shampoo. 'You will be awesome, my Maple honey,' I promise. 'The best model they've ever used. And you know why? Because you have been preparing for this moment your entire life. You perform for the camera every single day. And now it's time to reap the rewards.'

Chapter 3

Maple

This has to be the wildest day of my life so far, for sure.

I'm in a glass box in the sky when I should be in math. Finally proving that filming all those videos for YouTube was worth it.

'You okay up there, honey?' a voice calls out. It's the woman with cropped blond hair and loads of tattoos. Lois. She's the creative director from Studio 88 and seems to be the person in charge. It's crazy to me that someone who's surrounded by gorgeous models all day makes zero effort herself, and I can't decide whether that's super rogue in a good way, or bad.

'I'm great, thank you.' I smile, follow Mom's rules: look pretty, act grateful. But the truth is I've spent nearly four hours in and out of this box and I'm kinda done now. Hungry, thirsty, tired. Six outfit changes feels like a lot, especially as it's hot as hell in here and my head's hurting. There may be four men on scissor lifts holding diffusers and strobes to even out the light, but the Nevada sun is still finding its way through.

'You know, the shots look amazing,' Lois goes on. 'Exactly what I was hoping for, and the client absolutely adores you.

Another twenty minutes and we'll have everything we need. You can cope in there okay? You don't need another break?'

I eye Mom, pick up the subtle shake of her head. And I suppose if the client really does adore me, this could be the start of something bigger. Maybe a commercial for TV. The Superbowl even. I can't wreck my chances by being all needy now. 'No, I'm good, thank you.'

She nods, smiles, then turns to the cameraman, Paul, and starts a conversation I can't hear. Paul has a bald head and a goatee so black it must be dyed. He barely comes out from behind his camera – his assistant is right next to him, also taking photos, but I haven't seen them interact once – and I can't help thinking he's a bit creepy. In fact, if I think too much about it, it's lowkey freaky that he's looking at me through his zoom lens. He could be staring at my knobbly elbows, the pimple on my chin that Destiny, the makeup lady, promised she could hide, or even my . . .

It's crazy to think I have tits now. And proper ones with cleavage. This time last year I barely needed a bra, but a lot can happen in twelve months, I guess.

'Hey, Maple, could you lie down on your front, then lift up onto your elbows?'

I do as Lois says, even though that means most of the top I'm wearing is now hidden. Except the straps are super cute – cream lace with a vintage vibe – and the cut of the neckline is low and curvy. I guess that's enough to sell it.

'Beautiful, I love it,' Lois calls up. 'Now dip your head to one side, no, the other side. That's so much better. Let your hair fall over that shoulder. Wow, Maple. You're a natural!'

There's a sudden clatter to my left and I jump at the sound. One of the men in the scissor lifts has dropped the piece of equipment he was holding.

‘Shit, sorry, man,’ he shouts down, grimacing. ‘My hands are so sweaty, it just slipped out.’

He does look sweaty. His dark hair is wet at the edges, and there’s lines of it running into his beard and down onto his Raiders T-shirt. His eyes are blinking unnaturally fast too, like maybe he’s high.

‘For fuck’s sake,’ Paul grumbles from below, his toe nudging the diffuser now lying torn on the ground. ‘That cost me a hundred fucking dollars.’

I don’t know why, it’s not like I’ve never heard people swear before, maybe it’s the heat, but from nowhere, I feel a giggle work its way up from my belly.

Lois watches me crack. And it must be infectious because she starts giggling too. Mom picks up on the vibe and follows suit, and then Jules joins in. Soon the whole production crew is laughing except for Paul; even his assistant’s sniggering, I think, although he’s doing a good job of hiding it behind his camera. I sense the man who caused this mayhem looking at me, and I instinctively turn toward him, expecting gratitude for the distraction. But his expression is weird. Super intense. The giggle inside me dies, and my smile drops. My stomach clenches and I have a sudden urge to throw up.

Because this middle-aged guy with a sweaty head doesn’t look grateful. He looks hungry.

Chapter 4

Maple

I click the seatbelt and lean back against the headrest. It's a ninety-minute flight to Salt Lake City, and I want to use the time to forget about that guy's disgusting expression. At least he lives in a different state from me. Unlike that creepy guy who tried to give me chocolates outside school a few weeks ago. I don't actually know where he lives, but I figure he's local, and every day I go to school, I lowkey freak out that he'll be back with more unwanted gifts.

Or maybe a gun, like Taylor, my best friend, suggested when I told her about him. I remember wishing she was joking but knowing she wasn't. Too many famous people have been shot at lately for people to make those kind of jokes anymore. The only good thing to come out of it is that Dad drives me all the way to school now. And I'm trying to believe that Mom's right when she says weird guys like him are almost always harmless.

The other thing I need to do on the flight is prep more social media posts about my day, ready to upload as soon as the plane lands. I managed to get a TikTok and a reel up before the shoot started – with lots of cool content from that epic car ride, and me getting my best ever glow-up from Destiny – and

Mom nudged me to make another video on the car ride back to the airport. But she has airdropped loads more photos and video clips from the day, and I want to share them all.

I lift my phone and start swiping through. Mom is great at filming content, which isn't exactly a surprise when she's been doing it for forever. Maybe I should post something on my Instagram story before we fly, crediting her, of course. I usually spend more time on TikTok, but Instagram is where all the models post their content, and I guess I'm a model now. The airplane's PA system has told us to turn our phones to flight mode, but Mom is still scrolling through hers so I should have time.

I click into the app but then freeze. Because my numbers are slaying it. I blink, but they don't change. I have got twenty-two thousand, four hundred and sixteen likes on my reel, and double that number of views. And more than that, most of them are from accounts who don't follow me. *Don't follow me yet*, I think. Because that's what Mom would say.

A grin spreads across my face, so wide it makes my cheeks ache. I turn to tell Mom my good news, but she's put her phone down now and is lying back against the headrest, a mask pulled tight over her eyes. 'Do not disturb' etched into her cheekbones. I bite my lip. I should turn my phone off too, I guess. Maybe try and nap like Mom's doing. But I'm too excited to sleep; I need to tell someone my good news.

Taylor. My best friend. At least, most of the time. Sometimes she gets jealous of my numbers, or how kids talk to me in school but ignore her, but then I just tag her in a few posts and we make up pretty quick. I click into Snapchat, go to her contact, but then pause, my thumbs hovering. Because there's a snap from her that I haven't seen until now – *you're not gonna like this* – with video content attached.

My stomach contracts.

'Miss?'

I flick my head up, look at the air steward. 'Yes?'

She glances at Mom, clocks that she's sleeping. 'You need to put your phone on flight mode now,' she says in a quiet – but firm – voice.

I turn back to my screen, the unwelcome message. I feel frozen. Like ice-cold dread has immobilized my bones.

'We'll be taking off in minutes,' the air steward continues, her tone becoming sterner, like she's done with teenagers and their phone addictions. 'You don't want to interfere with the frequency, do you?'

I look up at her and jerk back to the moment. 'Sorry, no.' I swipe my screen and tap on the airplane symbol.

And spend the next hour and a half in the air, wondering what it is that I'm *not gonna like*.

Chapter 5

Kirsten

Block. Sigh. Block. Block.

I tap my forefinger on the mousepad of my laptop. Luckily there are only three creeps to deal with this morning. Three unwelcome subscribers who think it's okay to talk about panties, or body parts, on a child's YouTube page. It's disgusting for sure, but it doesn't even raise my heart rate anymore. These anonymous men think they can get a reaction with their gross language, upset Maple or enrage me, but they forget who has all the power. The power to oust them with one click of my dainty finger.

Task complete, I slide my laptop away – the smooth metal on new quartz making a satisfying swish – and reach for my coffee. Yes, it's caffeinated, but some rules of our church are just not for me. I take a long sip and eye the calendar hanging on the wall. It's the public-facing one for fun activities like Aspen's gymnastics classes and Ash's bug club, rather than the work diary, which frankly wouldn't fit in those little boxes.

And for Maple, I suspect the work side of life is going to get even busier after yesterday. That lesbian creative director, Lois, waxed lyrical about Maple's potential, and the skinny Italian woman from Azione who, in my opinion, looked laughably off brand with her Fendi handbag and Gucci heels, was super complimentary too. I left a few messages for Maddie at the PR agency yesterday, telling her all the good news, so I imagine she'll call me back soon, hopefully with some positive feedback of her own.

Tomorrow's scribble on the calendar makes me smile. Friday June 5th, the day school breaks up for summer. Which means in a couple of days I will have my three beautiful babies all to myself for two whole months. I love family time. And not having to fit Maple's filming around the school day will be a welcome relief too. Especially when school does nothing but interfere with the education that's actually going to make a difference in Maple's life.

But we won't have to worry about that ever again, thank goodness. I haven't told Maple yet, but I'm moving her to homeschooling. Yes, Maple is the most popular girl in her school – 1.9 million YouTube subscribers, 400,000 TikTok followers and a growing Instagram profile can do that, I suppose – so I get that she may be reluctant to leave. But she turns fifteen in October, and if she wants to be a successful influencer, capitalize on the impressive start she's made, she is going to have to make some sacrifices.

I eye my phone and notice the time. Shit. Garrett normally does the school run – he's been at a loose end since he lost his job last year – but he's gone fishing on the Provo River this morning; for a man who loves animals so much, he seems strangely keen on killing them. He left before sunrise, promising to be back by lunchtime with a bucketful of rainbow trout. My first instinct was to tell him he couldn't go, that he was needed here – I've got so much to do after yesterday's shoot – but then

I considered how cute a video of the twins helping him gut the fish might look, and waved him off with a reluctant smile.

But it does mean the school run is down to me today. And with Maple still insisting on being driven all the way to the gates, just because of that one sad man and his cheap box of chocolates, I need to get things moving.

I slip off the kitchen stool and enjoy the feel of the smooth cherry wood flooring beneath my feet. We only moved into this house last December, just in time for Christmas, and I still thank the Lord for it every day. It's modern, airy, sparklingly new, and three times the size of our old place. The big windows and swathes of light make it perfect for filming. And the swimming pool has brought us – and our subscribers – hours of fun already. Sure, it was expensive, and it took some sustained effort to convince Garrett to buy it, especially with him not working, but I talked him round eventually. And the bank practically bit my hand off when I applied for the loan. They know income potential when they see it.

At the bottom of the stairs, I rest my hand on the square oak newel post. 'Hey, guys!' I call upwards. 'We need to leave for school in twenty minutes, so come get some breakfast!'

Chapter 6

Kirsten

There's shuffling, whispering, and finally a door slamming shut. A moment later, the twins appear at the top of the stairs, and I feel my face lift into a smile. Aspen has already got something about her. She's fairer than Maple, more like Garrett, and has developed a few freckles on her nose over the last month or so. Her green eyes – another gift from her father – have a gorgeous habit of changing color with her mood, and her grin looks so cheeky on camera that it's perfect for pranking. Ash is a little different. He's a sweetheart in so many ways, but his online presence needs some work.

'Hey good morning, my babies,' I say in the singsong voice I perfected a long time ago and now feels as natural as breathing. 'Go grab some cereal and fill your water bottles. Is Maple coming?'

'She's in her room,' Aspen says, flicking her hand as she half walks, half slides down the wooden stairs. 'And I don't want cereal. Can I have one of those new smoothies instead?'

'Shit, the smoothies,' I mutter. After all the excitement of the Azione photoshoot, and the fishing curve ball Garrett threw at me last night, I've forgotten all about that job. Did I even add it to the schedule in the first place? I grimace. This is so unlike me. But there's no need to panic. I can set it up tomorrow and still meet the deadline. 'No, leave those,' I say. 'I need to do the filming first, and we don't have time for that this morning.'

Aspen's eyes narrow in annoyance, but Ash cups his little hand around her ear and whispers something. I don't hear what he says, but Aspen's expression clears, and they skip off together toward the kitchen. Unlike his twin sister, Ash is a rule follower, so I'm comfortable leaving them to it. I walk upstairs and knock on Maple's door.

'Come in,' she says, her voice more deflated than I'd expect from a rising star in the world of streetwear.

'Morning, my Maple honey,' I say, as I walk into her bedroom. 'Are you nearly ready to go?'

Maple shrugs. 'I guess.' She unfurls from the bed and gives me a weak smile. She's wearing light wash barrel-leg jeans with a tan and brown asymmetric scoop-necked top. Her long hair is hanging loose on her shoulders, and her skin is shining with freshly applied moisturizer. In other words, she looks amazing.

'Did you do a "get ready with me" video this morning?' I ask, almost rhetorically – she knows the schedule as well as I do. 'Can you airdrop it to my laptop, and I'll edit it when I get back from the school run?'

'No, I didn't.'

'Sorry?'

'I haven't done any filming this morning,' she adds in a mumble.

I feel an odd mix of fury and concern. Because Maple did seem exhausted on our car ride back from the airport last night, her head hanging low over her phone the whole time. It's not a good enough excuse – this pace is something she needs to get used to – but I also can't roll back time and make her get ready again.

'Okay. Should we do a quick short?' I suggest. 'You look so beautiful.'

'I'm not really . . .'

'Just a quick TikTok then, ten seconds max.'

'Jeez, Mom, can you give me one morning off?'

Her words are so shocking that I flinch. 'Can we take a moment to remember who's helping who here?' I shoot back. 'I work around the clock for you, Maple! I shouldn't have to deal with this attitude too.'

Slowly, she lifts her eyeline to mine, and thank goodness, she looks contrite. 'I'm sorry.'

I take in a deep breath. Remind myself that she's a teenager, that her period is probably due or something. I hold up my phone again. 'So you can find a smile for me?'

She sighs. 'I guess.'

I ignore her reluctant tone and open the camera app. And luckily, Maple switches straight to performance mode – pout, eyebrows, giggle – and gets it perfect on the first go. 'Should we head downstairs now?' I ask, feeling a rush of relief that I've got my daughter back.

'Mom, would it be okay if I didn't go to school today?'

I frown. Maple is usually desperate to catch up on her schoolwork after a day playing hooky. 'Why?'

'Everyone's just waiting to break up and it's so boring. There's honestly no point.' As she stares furtively at the floor, I think about the school run, and how bad the traffic always is. And how her being around would give us more time to film the smoothie content. 'Well, I guess you could stay home, if that's what you want.'

Her face breaks into a big smile. 'Thanks, Mom.'

I kiss the top of her head. 'I'll tell the twins,' I say. 'No point tackling the traffic just for them.'

Chapter 7

Maple

I listen to Mom's footsteps on the stairs, and then the twins squealing at her no-school news. It makes me smile, my first real one since I watched the content Taylor sent me yesterday. I still feel so sick about it.

How can a video of people watching another video be so excruciating?

But that's a stupid question when the video they're all watching is two-year-old me in a leaky diaper. And the audience is my classmates, laughing so hard that half of them are bent over with it. Worst of all is that Theo Williams is there. We were on an eleven-day Snap streak before yesterday and I was thinking maybe . . . but how can anything happen between us now, when I'd rather die than face him?

Oh God, the shame.

Even Taylor, my supposed best friend, was giggling silently. I could tell from the way the footage jerked up and down.

I pick up my brush and run it through my hair. When I was little, I hated my hair, wanted it to be blond like my mom's. But everyone goes on about how gorgeous it is now. Rich, warm, red tones, gold tones. The compliments keep coming. And it's true that brunettes are owning it on Instagram right now. Maybe I need to start liking it too.

Eventually I place the brush back on my vanity and eye the door. I know I need to go downstairs. That if I don't, Mom will be back here, reminding me what a beautiful day it is, how the light is just right for filming, and how much my subscribers will love to see some new content from me. But I'm not in the mood to pretend life is perfect today. I don't have it in me to smile for the camera.

Which I know is how quitters talk. If I want to be a famous influencer, I need to put content out every day; it's like the first amendment of the social media constitution. And I have to expect some rough treatment too – from people who are jealous or attention-seeking or just plain mean.

But it's still a lot, that video, especially when I wasn't at school to defend myself. Except, what would I have done if I had been? Screamed at Tabitha – the girl who shared it, according to Taylor – to fuck off and die, then watch that scene back on TikTok? Because someone would film it and post it, tag me in it too probably. And everyone who watched it would share it. And I doubt Maddie, or Studio 88, or Azione would want to work with me after seeing that.

At least I don't have to face anyone at school today. I won't go in tomorrow either – Mom won't care; she never does – and then eighth grade will be over, and middle school will be done, and hopefully everyone will have forgotten about it by the time we start high school in August.

That thought lifts my mood enough for me to pick up my phone. My mom still runs my YouTube channel – she set it up when I was a baby, back when it was called Mom & Maple instead of Maybe Maple like it is now – and no one has ever suggested that she lets go of that control. I supposedly run my own TikTok and Instagram accounts, but Mom has all my login details and seems to interfere on a daily basis.

Which is why I click into Snapchat instead. The platform which is all mine. There's a load of messages from my so-called school friends – Taylor, Scarlett, Milly, Martha – but I slide to delete them all. If they've sent me apologies, it's too little, too late. And if they think I'll see the funny side, well, they're too dumb to be friends with anyway. I know I'll forgive them at some point because I can't do school without them. But right now, they are part of the problem, and I'm not ready to move on.

And anyway, I have other friends. Online friends like Coco. It's crazy, but I sometimes think I've become closer with Coco than my girlfriends in real life over the last few months. I guess she understands me better because she's trying to build her profile on social media too. And luckily there are five new snaps from her.

Chapter 8

Maple

I read Coco's messages, a mix of goofy and sweet, then send her a selfie. She sends one back straight away. Coco's roots are Mexican, and she has curly black hair, these amazing brown eyes, and tanned skin. She never seems to overthink stuff, so she's always good with advice too. She has maybe five thousand subscribers to her channel, which is a lot less than me, of course, but her reason for wanting to build up her following is way cooler.

Coco wants to be a filmmaker, and nothing glitzy or commercial like Disney movies. She wants to make true crime documentaries. A fifteen-year-old girl from her neighborhood in Miami was raped and murdered three years ago. Sophie Lyle. Her killer still hasn't been caught, which shows how crap the police are. But Coco is telling Sophie's story via her @CocosColdCase channel and hopes to get justice for her that way. Uncover her killer. She knows it won't be easy, but she's determined to find a way. And knowing Coco, I bet she does.

We share a few more silly selfies, and I giggle at her weird expressions. Mom would freak out if she knew I was taking ugly pictures of myself, but luckily, she'll never know. That's the beauty of disappearing messages. Thank you, Snapchat.

'Maple honey!' Mom's voice drifts up the stairs and I know my time is up.

'Coming!' I call back, while sending a final message to Coco and clicking out of the app. Then I take a deep breath, practice smiling in the mirror, and head down to the kitchen. The twins are already in the pool, splashing around, and Mom must have been filming them because her blouse is covered in splash marks.

'Ah, you're here,' she says. She looks me up and down, then nods slightly, as though I've passed some mystery test. 'I'm glad you're feeling better. Now, we've got that Verde Fresh smoothie filming to do, so let's get that set up.'

God, not this. 'Do we have to?'

'Well, three grand says yes we do, actually.'

I feel my cheeks heat up. 'I just mean, can we do it later? I'm so tired after yesterday; I'm not in the mood right now.'

Mom doesn't say anything, but even her silence makes me feel guilty. Like she's using some weird telepathic messaging to remind me how much she does for me. Maybe I should just get the filming over with. But then she drops her head to one side. 'What's wrong, Maple honey? You're not yourself today.'

'It's nothing,' I mumble.

She shakes her head. 'It's not nothing.'

Her tone is so soft that my eyes grow hot. Mom and I used to be really close, but it hasn't felt that way lately. Last year she was all caught up in buying this house, and more recently it's been about getting my YouTube channel to two million subscribers and signing new brand deals. I know it's for my future; she reminds me of that regularly enough. And I do see how hard she works, for me and the twins. But it's all we ever talk about, work. Like she doesn't care about the other stuff going on in my life.

But she seems to care now, so maybe I've got that wrong.

'Honey?' she presses gently.

'Maybe there's something,' I finally murmur.

'Can you tell me about it?'

'Maybe.'

'How about I make you some eggs while you talk.' She turns to open the fridge, then takes two eggs to the opposite counter and starts cracking them into a bowl. Without her eyes on me, it feels easier, and I tell her what Taylor told me. How Carmella was giving a presentation on the classroom screen yesterday afternoon when Tabitha airdropped a video to her laptop. And when everyone chanted at Carmella to open it, she did.

'And what did the video show?' Mom's tone is light and soothing.

'It was from the old days of our channel,' I murmur. 'It was called Poop Scoop, and I was about two, racing around our old kitchen in a dirty diaper. You were chasing me. There were brown patches, Mom. Disgusting shit smears on my stupid fat thighs.' I drop my head to hide my tears, but I can't stop my shoulders convulsing.

Mom leaves the eggs and walks over, puts her hands on my arms. 'Now, you know I don't like to hear you swear, honey,' she says. 'But I'm sorry. That's not kind of your classmates.'

I look up. 'So can we take the video down?'

'Of course we can.'

'And could we maybe take all the content down of me when I was little?'

Mom bites her lip. 'We could, yes. But you know what we should do first?'

'What?'

'Go shopping. Life always feels better in a new outfit.'

Chapter 9

Kirsten

I listen to Garrett's truck roll onto the driveway and breathe a sigh of relief. Because it means I can get on with taking Maple to the mall, getting her out of this black mood, and then back in time to film the damn smoothie content with her actually smiling.

But it also means I need to leave Aspen and Ash, who are now upstairs doing God knows what, to Garrett's supervision. And their YouTube channel really needs a new post today. I'm proud of the 2AStarz name I chose a few years ago, and of course everyone loves the twin thing, but the space is so competitive now, much more than when I started Mom & Maple in 2011, and Ash isn't a natural performer. Of course practice makes perfect, so he'll get there. But only if he's filming regularly, and I'm struggling to fit it all in.

'Hey, how was fishing?' I ask, pretending to care.

'Yeah, good.' Garrett strolls into the kitchen. He reaches for a glass and holds it against the water tap on the fridge. Even from here, I can see that his hands are grubby, that he'll leave smudges on my shiny fridge, but I manage to control my annoyance.

'I went down to Provo Canyon,' he goes on. 'Trout are bigger on that stretch. Caught three beauties.'

'Right, great.' I push up to standing and drop my phone into my bag. That's plenty enough conversation about fish. 'Listen, I'm taking Maple to the mall,' I continue. 'So you're in charge of the twins.'

His face scrunches in confusion. His handsome, chiseled, Chris Hemsworth-like face – otherwise I'd probably have kicked him out years ago. 'Aren't the kids at school?'

'No. But I don't have time to explain it all now. Oh, and can you get the twins to help you gut the fish? And film it? Ash will love it so we might even get a smile out of him, and I'm hoping Aspen will hate it, because that will make great content too. All the squealing.'

'But if she hates it . . .'

I huff out a sigh. 'I can't do everything, Garrett. Can you just help me out this one time?' Then I head toward the front door, calling for Maple as I go.

Five minutes later, the two of us are on the road. Provo Towne Centre is our closest mall, but it's been a while since Maple was happy shopping in JCPenney, so I'm making the forty-minute drive to Salt Lake City instead – which isn't exactly a chore in my beautiful new Lexus. Hopefully Urban Outfitters or Zara will take Maple's mind off the Poop Scoop prank, and maybe there'll even be time for me to stop by Anthropologie. Personally, I think Maple's being overdramatic about her classmates' antics – it was only kids having fun after all – but who knows where her hormones are at right now; it's always safer to act sympathetic.

And her sadness is a gift in a way because girly shopping trips always make great content. Our posts about yesterday's photoshoot in Vegas have got her thousands of new followers, and I really want to keep the momentum going. With her not doing the scheduled 'get ready with me' video this morning, I need to find something to fill the gap. I've set my phone up on the dash to capture our drive, and I'd love to suggest carpool karaoke – those videos always get a crazy number of likes, and luckily Maple inherited my singing voice – but I get the impression she won't be up for it today.

In fact, Maple waits until we're beyond Utah Lake before speaking at all. 'Thanks for this,' she finally says, her body shifting slightly toward me. 'I know how much you've got on, so thanks for making time for me.'

I turn to look her. She's curling her hair around her ears, and the sight makes my heart melt. 'Don't be silly. I love spending time with you. Of course I adore the twins, but we were the originals, weren't we? Mom and Maple forever?'

Maple gives me a small smile. 'I guess so, yes.' But then she blinks, and her eyes narrow. 'Hey, Mom.'

'Yes?'

She nods her head in the direction of my upright phone. 'Are you filming us?'

I tap the steering wheel. Wonder why I feel guilty when Maple knows creating content is literally our job. 'Of course I am,' I say, calm but firm. 'Every day is a work day for an influencer, isn't it? And you've got other things on your mind today, so I'm doing the thinking for you.'

'Wow, thank you so much,' she mutters before turning to stare out of the window. Which would be nice of her, if the words weren't drowning in sarcasm.

Chapter 10

Kirsten

I take a long, quiet breath. Remind myself that mothering is about sacrifice. 'Remember, Maple, I'm doing all of this for you. You haven't posted anything on YouTube yet today, so we need to film some content.'

'But I thought you said this trip was about making me feel better?' she counters. 'Not building my brand.'

'It's both, Maple,' I say, gritting my teeth, wondering why she still doesn't get this. 'It's *always* both.'

Maple doesn't respond, just continues staring out of the window like I've betrayed her. Injustice seeps through me and I feel my grip tighten on the steering wheel. Because I am so loyal to her, always thinking of ways to make her more popular, to grow her brand. It infuriates me when she suggests otherwise.

But Maple is a fourteen-year-old girl, I remind myself. Pushing the boundaries is normal at her age. My own parents encouraged my rebellious streak, which is why I blame them for a lot of what came next, but it will be different for Maple. And I know deep down that she'll thank me for it one day, maybe even apologize for being a brat. I inhale, hold oxygen in my lungs, and stare at the view through the windshield.

It's a perfect summer's day – the sky cornflower blue and cloudless – and I can see for miles. I was born in Utah, and the Wasatch mountain range that runs from our home up to the Idaho border feels like the backdrop to my life. Glowing white in winter, casting shadows in summer. For a time, I felt locked in by their presence – back when I was young enough to think moving to New York, breaking into the music scene there, was a good plan. But now I like having the mountains this close and feel grateful for how uniquely Utah they are. It helps that our subscribers love them too, of course.

When I can see the City Creek mall up ahead, I know I've only got a few minutes to get Maple back on side, which I need to do if this day is going to be any fun at all, so I swallow my pride and break the silence. 'By the way, I've got a surprise for you.'

'Yeah?'

'We've got someone coming to stay Monday through Wednesday. And you're going to love me for it, because he's got half a million followers on Instagram and over a million on TikTok.'

Maple's head whips around. 'He? Who?'

I feel a swell of triumph for getting a reaction. 'Dylan Dope, you know, the skateboarder?'

Her eyes widen. 'Dylan Dope? Of course I know him,' she stutters, her cheeks turning pink. 'I mean, I follow him. Everyone does. But he's coming to our house? How do you know him well enough to sort that? And jeez, Mom, why would you want to?'

Her frenzied stare does not look attractive, but I hold back from telling her. I pull into the mall parking lot and cut the engine. 'Well, Dylan lives in Utah too, although in St George in the south. His mom has set up this amazing online school, very exclusive, just for successful influencers like you and Dylan. And we got talking about other opportunities.'

Maple screws her eyes, then shakes her head. 'Why are you talking to anyone about an online school?'

'Well, you're starting there in August,' I say, making sure it sounds final. 'And Mrs. Jones, Dylan's mom, is super excited to have you. Isn't that great?'

'But I'm starting high school then,' she says, her pitch rising even more. 'With my friends.' But she hesitates over the last word, which I take as a good sign.

'But this is going to be so much better for you,' I say. 'You can study whenever you want, have a dip in the pool, or time on your phone, in the middle of the day. I promise you'll love it, and you don't even have to take my word for it because Dylan will be able to tell you all about it. He's a year older than you, so he's just finishing ninth grade.'

Maple drops her face in her hands. 'Oh God, you're actually doing this.'

'I'll do anything for your future, Maple.'

'But I don't know Dylan Dope!' she wails, her voice cracking at the top. 'And he's a boy, and fifteen, and has the coolest drip. And we've never chatted, or swapped snaps, or jeez, I don't even know if he's liked any of my posts.' She's running out of breath, but she keeps going anyway. 'How can he possibly be staying with us? Please, Mom, can you quit filming!'

'Hey, calm down, honey,' I say, reaching for my phone and stopping the recording – I've got enough to make a great YouTube short anyway. 'You'll get to know him, won't you? You can hang out around the pool, take him to Provo skate park. Maybe even get him to teach you a few tricks. These collabs are working so well for other influencers on socials right now. I honestly think your follower numbers are going to skyrocket after this.'

'But Dylan Dope?' she whispers in horror.

I smile. 'He's hot, right?'

'Yes, but . . .'

'So we better get you the hottest outfit we can find. Come on, honey, it's time for some retail therapy.'

Chapter 11

Maple

I stare into the fitting room mirror. How can I look this normal? It makes no sense when my heart is bouncing out of my chest and my stomach is twisting like a pretzel.

Dylan Dope is coming to stay with us. To hang out with me. What the actual fuck?

No. I need to get Mom to change her mind.

But Mom never changes her mind. Whatever I say, however hard I might beg. At first, she'll try to convince me that it's the best idea ever. And if I manage to swerve that, then she'll remind me whose house it is. And that I'm a child who doesn't get to make decisions.

There's nothing I can do about it. Dylan Dope is coming to stay in my house.

Oh God.

I'm itching to check out his socials, to see if there's anything I can pick up that might make this nightmare just one percent easier, but I'm not doing it with Mom around. Looking over my shoulder, giving me advice. I'm stressed out enough as it is.

How do I even act around him? It takes me ages to figure out what to say to Theo, and that's on Snap where he can't even see me. I'm going to have to think of funny, or cool, or clever things to say to Dylan in real time, *and* look good while I'm doing it.

I grab my hair from behind, bunch it on my head, and pout into the fitting room mirror like those OnlyFans models do on Instagram. Then I lean forward, let my hair fall loose, watch my cleavage deepen. But it looks weird, not hot. Embarrassing, not cool. I'm not ready for all that stuff yet.

Especially when I have weirdos staring at me. Like that freak in Vegas, or the creep outside school a few weeks ago. That's what I hate most about being famous on YouTube. The gross, old Stans who watch me. Mom blocks the ones who give themselves away, but I know there are others. Sick pedos who just lurk like ghosts.

I straighten up.

'How are you doing in there?' Mom calls out, her voice floating over the curtain. 'Do you need any help?'

'No, I'm good.' I quickly pull on one of the tops she picked out for me. It's embarrassing that Mom still chooses my clothes, even worse that she's better at it than me. My girlfriends are always falling out with their moms over what they wear – their skirts are too short; tops too low, or too high, or too tight or too something. But my mom never raises an eyebrow.

'I think that baby-blue gingham crop top is super cute,' she continues. 'Those puffed off-the-shoulder sleeves are gorgeous. And wow, that red halter-neck top.' She attempts a chef's kiss. 'And after yesterday's paycheck, you've earned them both, honey. And the denim miniskirt; that's one hundred percent you.'

I pull on the skirt with the red top and assess myself in the mirror. 'Do you think the buttons down the front of the skirt give me bop girl vibes?' I ask, while wondering why I can't tell if clothes make me look hot or trashy.

'Wow, Maple, there is nothing sleazy about you!' Mom exclaims, her volume making me cringe. 'That's why people love you, because you're so wholesome and pure. As soon as I saw that skirt on the rack, I knew it was perfect. Like everything else I found for you. You know what, let's stop talking and take it all to the cash register.'

I take one last look in the mirror – maybe it does hit right after all – then wriggle back into the clothes I arrived in. In truth, I way prefer shorts and T-shirts to skirts and fitted tops, but I keep quiet about that. I mean, what woman got famous wearing comfortable clothes?

With my new purchases folded inside an Urban Outfitters bag, we head back to the parking lot and climb into Mom's new car. It's a big, boujee SUV and judging by Dad's face when Mom came home in it last month, it probably cost a heap of money we can't afford.

'Hey, how about we stop at Swig on the way home for a dirty soda?' Mom asks.

I turn to look at her. I'm still lowkey mad that she invited Dylan without asking, but she has just spent two hundred dollars on new clothes for me. And the thing is, Dylan Dope is crazy popular right now, so maybe – even though it makes me feel sick to think about it – him coming to stay is good for me, like Mom says. I find half a smile. 'Yeah, sure.'

A trip to Swig is always weird because Mom hates soda, but she pretends to love it. I used to think it was because dirty sodas are a Utah thing, and filming us drinking them strengthened my brand. But my grandma told me that Mom's been this way since she was a little girl. Like she's been trying to fit in here her whole life – and just because Grandma and Gramps moved here from Chicago.

We park outside the soda shop and head inside. I order

a Raspberry Rodeo and Mom chooses an Eagle, probably because its blue color complements her nails. But as soon as we sit down, Mom's phone rings and Dad's face lights up on her screen.

'Hey,' she says, answering it while gesturing for me to film our sodas. I'm still not really in the mood, but I pick up my phone anyway. I try to film Mom too – she usually loves being part of my videos – but she backhands the air and twists away from me.

'Jesus, Garrett, you had one job,' she mutters into the handset, and I feel my shoulders tense. I hate it when my parents fight, and it seems to be happening a lot lately.

'I don't care that Aspen didn't want to do it,' she goes on. 'She's eight. She doesn't get to decide. And of course Ash wouldn't know to wait for you to set up the camera. But you're their father, Garrett. You're supposed to be the one in charge.' She lets out a long sigh. 'Look, it's fine. I get that gutting fish isn't so fun for eight-year-olds. But we need something.'

She looks at me over her shoulder, like she's just remembered I'm here. 'Actually, hold on.' Then she covers the mouthpiece. 'I'm going to take this outside,' she tells me. 'Come meet me in five minutes by the car and we'll head home?'

'Sure,' I say nodding. 'Hey, do you want to take your soda with you?' But she's already walked out.

Chapter 12

Maple

Forty-five minutes later, we pull onto our drive, and I jump out of the car. I'm desperate to lie on my bed and scroll my phone. Check out Dylan's grid and text my friends without Mom peering at my screen. Taylor will freak out, for sure, but she'll be jealous too, which might just make me feel better. Coco will be chill about it, maybe even have some advice on how I should handle it.

The front door flies open before I have chance to turn the handle.

'Oh hi, Maple.' Aspen grins at me.

Mom walks past us, ruffling Aspen's hair as she steps inside, but otherwise ignoring her. Not that it seems to bother Aspen, whose excitement only seems to ratchet up.

'Hey, what's up?' I ask her. 'What's with the grinning?'

'I saw something really cool,' she says, grabbing my hand. 'Wanna see?'

'Well, I was going to . . .' I eye the stairs.

'Please, Maple?'

I look at her earnest, cute face. 'What did you see?'

'There's a chipmunk in our yard!' she yells.

I blink. 'Wait, really? A chipmunk?'

'Come on!'

I let Aspen lead me through the house and then out through the back door, but when we reach the deck, she pulls up abruptly.

'Woah!' I call out, almost knocking into her. 'Why d'you stop?'

'Do you think he might bite me?'

'The chipmunk? Of course he won't,' I say, while considering how much I know about chipmunks, which is basically nothing. 'But how about I go first, just in case?'

Her face lights up. 'Thanks, Maple! He's over there in the bush.'

I follow Aspen's pointed finger with my eyes, then step off the decking toward it. But I stumble slightly as I catch my foot on a bit of rope. Shit. I'm going to fall. But no, I steady myself. I'm fine. Except . . .

I scream as a bucketful of water empties on my head. Ice cold. Heavy. Soaking. I shudder as it runs down my back and fight the urge to cry. Aspen squeals with delight. Then Ash appears from behind a tree, also giggling.

My little brother and sister. They must have rigged the prank up with Dad while I was at the mall, then coaxed me out here with their fake chipmunk story. 'You little . . .'

'No swearing, Maple honey!' Mom calls out. 'Remember this is a kids' channel!'

And it's Mom, not Dad, who emerges from behind a camera that's attached to a tripod. So she was in on the prank too. I think about her phone call with Dad in Swig, how she walked outside in the middle of it. Is this what they were talking about? A plan for their youngest kids to prank their eldest?

Tears smart my eyes and I flick them shut. Silently tell my

family that I hate them all. I know that's not fair – we've always been into pranking, like pretty much every kidfluencer on YouTube. I was lowkey obsessed with it when I was younger. One time when the twins were toddlers, I swapped their clothes around to see how long it would take my parents to notice, and it's still one of the most popular videos on my channel.

But today has been a lot. The poop scoop cringe fest followed by the Dylan Dope bombshell. And Mom knows this, so how could she think it was okay to add to the shit pile with an embarrassing prank?

'Ah, don't look so sad, honey,' she says, handing me a towel. 'You did great. Honestly, your face was a picture. But cute too, I think you're going to love it. And your subscribers definitely will. It'll do wonders for the twins' channel too, so it's a double win.' She puts her arm around my shoulder. 'Thanks for being such a sport about it.'

Like I had a choice.

I push my lips together – I don't have the energy for a fight. Then I wrap the towel around my shoulders and head inside.

'Hey, remember to take your sneakers off!' Mom calls after me. 'I don't want wet patches on my cherry wood!'

I pause in her kitchen, consider my options. Then I wring out my hair, watch droplets splodge on her precious floor, and squelch in my shoes all the way to my room.

Chapter 13

Maple

I flop onto my bed and stare at the ceiling.

I bet Mom is already on her laptop, editing that prank video, adding cute stickers and emojis that make me look even more stupid. One minute she's buying clothes that make me look hot for Dylan, and the next she's setting me up to get tricked by a couple of eight-year-olds. It's like I'm a lump of Play-Doh that she shapes into whatever she wants.

I send Taylor a message, asking to video-call.

Can't babe. Got swim training
Missed you today 😞

I'm not sure if I'm pissed that she can't talk, or that her sad-face emoji reminds me of the video she sent me, and how it wobbled with her laughter. But either way, I don't respond. Instead, I send Coco a snap, asking the same question, and she comes back with a thumbs-up. But then she adds another message almost immediately:

Wait, gimme 5.

So I click into TikTok, take a second to prepare myself, and search for Dylan Dope.

The first thing I do is check that he's following me – he is, that's something I guess – then I scroll through his profile page, clicking on random TikToks, sinking further down the bed with each one. Because in every video, he looks so good. Natural, confident, like he actually likes himself. His style is awesome too. In some posts he's wearing brands I know, like Vans and Supreme. Then there are others I don't recognize, but seeing how he wears them makes me want to buy them. Which I guess is the point.

He's got over a million followers, an agent, and a sponsor. He is the guy every boy wants to be. And the evidence is there. Thousands of reposts, everyone loving his content. I swipe through his followers at dizzying speed, then catch my breath, like I've been running.

Am I being super lame about this? Is a collaboration with Dylan actually an amazing opportunity, like Mom said?

I imagine dropping into my group chat with my girlfriends, calmly mentioning that Dylan Dope is coming to hang out at my house. They will all be crazy jealous. So why am I so stuck on how awkward it will be?

Except I know why. Because I'm the one who's going to have to make conversation with him. To think of things to do together, knowing every moment will be filmed and posted. And all this while knowing the visit wasn't his idea either. Our moms organized this. And he's probably lying on his bed right now, praying for a meteorite to drop on him before Monday.

I need a better distraction while I wait for Coco to come online, so I open the video I took in Swig earlier. I cut it, stitch it, and add the Barbie track 'Pink' by Lizzo. I've been doing this stuff for so long it's as natural as breathing now, but when

I start to type a comment, I can't think what to say. I always tag Mom when I'm with her, but I'm not in the mood to be nice to her today. Eventually I choose a raspberry and pink hearts – everyone knows less is more – and post it to TikTok and Instagram.

Then I stay on Instagram, scrolling through my grid. I haven't done this for a while, and it's good to remind myself how far I've come since I opened an account on my thirteenth birthday. Over a hundred and twenty thousand followers now. There's been so much bad stuff going on recently – gross men getting in my face, Tabitha sharing that nightmare video, Mom seeming to care more about my channel than me – that I've started to question whether I even want to be an influencer. But these Instagram stats, alongside close to half a million followers on TikTok and nearly two million subscribers on YouTube shout loud. Most girls would kill for these numbers. I can't give up on this dream because of a few bad experiences.

I'm watching one of my first reels – a dramatic Sabrina Carpenter lip synch – when Coco's face finally pops up on my screen. I flip over onto my belly, rest my phone against the headboard, and accept her call.

Chapter 14

Maple

Coco is sitting at her desk, leaning forward over crossed arms. Her face is so close to the screen that it's shimmering, and I feel an urge to reach out and touch it. Except it quickly folds into a frown. 'Hey, babe, what's up? You look sad.'

'Do I?' I feel self-conscious, like she can read my mind as well as my face.

'Sorry, that came out wrong. I guess I just thought you'd be super happy after yesterday,' she explains. 'Your posts made it all look amazing, by the way. I can't believe they built a glass box just for you!'

'It was pretty cool,' I admit, reminding myself how I felt being the center of attention, Lois giving me loads of compliments. 'But there was this one gross guy.'

'Eurgh.' Coco sighs. 'What did he do?'

Coco's question makes me realize that he didn't actually do anything. 'I guess he just looked at me funny,' I mumble. 'But a ton more bad stuff has happened since then.'

Coco tips her head. 'Oh?'

'You know Dylan Dope?'

She looks at me, confused.

'Yeah, you do,' I tell her. 'The skateboarder; does all those tricks. You must have seen his content?'

Her face clears and she smiles. 'Duh, Dylan Dope, of course. What about him?'

'Mom has invited him to stay with us. He's coming on Monday.'

'Woah.' Coco leans back in her chair. It's a gaming chair, but not because she's into gaming – she really isn't – but because her dad got it for her at a garage sale. She says she likes it because it's super comfy, but I think it's more to do with it being a gift from him. He's not that interested in Coco usually – something else we have in common – so she takes the scraps, same as me. 'Have you met him before?' she asks.

'Nope. Haven't chatted either. I don't even have his snap.'

'So this is another one of your mom's crazy plans?'

'She wants us to create content together,' I explain with a sigh. 'She thinks collabs are good for my channel.'

'Well, I guess she's right there,' Coco says. 'And Dylan Dope is huge on TikTok.'

'Yeah, and he's a year older than me, and a boy, and his style is so gas. And worst of all, he'll be hating this idea even more than me.'

'You don't know that,' she counters. 'You are the girl who's just been to Vegas, remember? Azione is a huge brand, and it's got skateboard vibes. And jeez, Maple, you have like two million subscribers on YouTube! You've been famous since you were a baby. Maybe he's the lucky one, getting an invite?'

My mouth lifts into something close to a smile. I don't believe her, but it's good to hear her say it. I wish it was Coco coming to stay next week, not some stranger. We would never run out of things to talk about.

In fact, maybe she could come to stay, later in the holidays.

She might not have as many followers as me, but she's got plenty. And if Mom thinks collabs are such a great idea, then she should be up for me organizing another one.

'Hey, do you have much on this summer?' I ask.

Coco shrugs. 'Not really. Why?'

'I just wondered if you wanted to come and stay with me for a while?'

She blinks, and for a moment I think she's going to say no. But then her eyes widen. 'In Utah? Oh my God, yes! When?'

Shit. Maybe I didn't think this through. Of course she would be excited. 'Um, I'm not sure exactly, but I'll check with my mom.' I watch Coco's enthusiasm fade as she realizes it isn't an actual invite. 'But I guess you'll be busy investigating the Sophie Lyle murder anyway?' I say, trying to change the subject.

And it works because her face brightens a notch. 'Yeah, I want to use school break to do more digging. The police are so shit; they've done absolutely nothing for her. While that man is still out there, free, doing anything he wants. Killing other girls for all we know.'

I think about the man with the chocolates, Taylor's comments about him carrying a gun. 'Was Sophie on social media much?'

'Why d'you ask that?'

I shrug. 'You hear stories, don't you? Stans online becoming psycho stalkers for real. And school is always going on about online predators.'

Coco sighs. 'I know what you mean. That stuff freaks me out sometimes too. But then I remind myself that there are thousands, probably millions, of influencers out there who are safe, and getting to do what they love without any hassle.'

'Yeah, you're right. I'm being stupid.'

'And if it helps,' Coco adds, 'Sophie Lyle wasn't on social media.'

'What, not at all?'

Coco shrugs. 'Maybe her parents were super strict. She didn't even have a phone. So he can't have found her that way.'

'Thank you,' I whisper. 'I think it does help.'

She beams. 'Anytime, babe. But sorry, I need to go now. You'll be okay?'

I nod, smile. When I cut the call, my phone drops back into Instagram, and I notice that Mom has a new reel up on her own channel. I wonder if it's content from our shopping trip and whether I feature.

But when I click into it, I see it's Mom in our kitchen, talking direct to camera. I hit the unmute symbol and hold my breath.

She's talking about parenting. How tough it is to see your child upset when she's the butt of a classroom joke. But how hormones and menstruation and neural pathways all play a part in making teenage girls overdramatic or morose or too emotional. How she's learned that the most important thing is to just be there for me.

I confided in her, and now she's telling the world about it.

I scream and throw my phone across the room.

Chapter 15

Him

He leans forward over his phone, hunches his back. He doesn't want anyone to see what he's doing. To judge him for it. Because he knows what they'd think, his workmates. They wouldn't understand. He should wait until he gets home where it's private, but he doesn't have the willpower for that. He needs to see her now.

He presses play on the YouTube video, watches a commercial for hair loss treatment, hits 'skip' as soon as he's able. He runs his hands down his grubby jeans. How long since he washed them? He doesn't like being dirty, but stuff like that, he finds it hard to prioritize.

It's childish, the film, all those sounds and stickers, and he likes that, he thinks. Although it is confusing, lots of different feelings prickling his skin. But he likes the innocence of the bright colors and bubbly music.

And she's beautiful. God, so beautiful. He fights the urge to stroke the screen, to pretend he's touching her hair for real. It's so rich and warm. It reminds him of his mother's and for some reason that makes this thing he's doing, connecting with her in the only way he's able, feel right somehow.

She's standing on a deck overlooking a garden. Not a big backyard, but neat and lush with a swimming pool in the distance. He wonders if she likes to swim. He used to swim too, but that was years ago. Not sure he'd even remember how to do it now.

She's holding hands with her little sister, Aspen it says in the comments. A twin. She's cute, but too young to be interesting to him. She backs away as Maple takes a step forward. Or Maybe Maple. Her handle is so perfect that it speaks to him on an almost spiritual level.

He watches the bucket above her tip, the water flood out, splatter her head, drip down her face. Soak her white T-shirt. He runs his tongue over his lips.

He wonders if she knows that the water has turned her top see-through, that her lilac bra is now on show. He feels bad for her. Like it's his job to protect her but he can't do that because he's not there, just watching on a tiny six-inch screen hundreds of miles away. Sat in the back of a work truck on his lunch break, workmates in scruffy clothes milling around.

Maybe he should just go see her. Fuck it. Jack in this job and drive to Utah. He doesn't know where she lives, but he's sure he could find her if he put his mind to it. A girl with millions of followers leaves her mark.

But is that really what he wants? Or does he prefer to look at her like this?

When she doesn't know he's watching.

Chapter 16

Maple

There's a rap on my door and I twitch at the sound, but otherwise don't move.

'Come on! Wake up!' Mom hollers. 'We need to be there by eight and I want you looking your all-American best!'

I groan into my pillow, then prise my eyes open. I check the time on my phone, groan again, and fall back against the mattress. It's Sunday. I will be spending the whole day stressing about Dylan arriving tomorrow, and now, thanks to Mom, I get to do that from six a.m. Awesome.

But what else would I expect from the woman who invites a famous TikToker to stay without asking me, and then tells all her Instagram buddies my deepest darkest secrets?

'I'm not going!' I shout back, even though I don't actually know where she wants me to be by eight. But then my door flies open, and Mom is standing there. She claps her hands, and I flinch, the sound like firecrackers in my ears. She marches up to me, her face glowing with self-righteousness.

'Come on, get up,' she instructs, flicking her hand over my bedsheets. 'I do not have time for teenage dramas today.'

'I don't even know where you want me to go,' I mutter, but

I can already feel myself wobbling. And it's like she can smell weakness, because her vibe changes too. Suddenly she looks like the cat who's drunk all the milk.

'I'm sorry, that's my bad,' she says, her voice almost purring now. 'I wanted to tell you yesterday, but you didn't seem in the mood to talk.'

Of course I didn't after her Instagram reel. And I still don't. But I'm not sure I've got the energy to keep fighting her. Especially when I feel like I don't have anyone else.

Yesterday I decided that I needed my friends back, so I forgave them for the video nightmare, and we met for sodas in the afternoon. But all they talked about was the amazing summers they've got planned. Taylor's going to a swim camp in Canada, then to Vancouver Island with her family for a vacation. Martha and Scarlett are going on summer camp together in Arizona, and Milly's going to visit her cousins in Montana. While we're staying in Utah because, according to Mom, there's no window in the schedule for a vacation.

Coco understands a bit more, but she lives six states east, so it's not like I can hang out with her. Anything that might have been starting with Theo is over now because of that video, and while I love the twins, they're only eight. Dad never has time for me, so it looks like Mom is all I've got.

'It's the Freedom Festival's baby contest today,' Mom explains. 'It's the first Independence Day celebration in the calendar, and they've asked me to judge the twins' category. I feel very honored, of course, even though it means missing church, which you know I hate to do. But I need your help.'

I screw my nose up. 'Babies? How is that going to help my profile?'

'Oh, Maple honey. I actually love how self-absorbed you

can be; it's an important trait in our world. But this time, it isn't about you.'

I bunch my fists. 'Mom, what are you talking about?'

'I thought it would be obvious,' she says with a sigh of disappointment. 'I'm taking Ash and Aspen with me because I want to create a film of them playing with each of the sets of contestants. Honestly, it will be so cute. But I'll be too busy judging to film the content, which is why I need you there.'

I shake my head. 'Sorry, I can't. I need to get ready for Dylan arriving tomorrow, and I've got my own content to create. That's what you keep saying, isn't it? That if I want to make it as an influencer, I have to post, post, post.'

'Which is why I got you up early enough to film a "get ready with me" video before we leave,' Mom says, without missing a beat. 'They are so popular right now – I've noticed Bella Tells is doing three a week – and you haven't done one since Tuesday. Oh, and I have a new lip gloss for you to promote, shea butter and caramel. Honestly, it's so good. And it's discounted at Walgreens this month, so it's time-sensitive too. Come on.'

She hands me a pink tube, and for some crazy reason, I take it from her. I even feel an urge to put it on my lips. And this fucked-up impulse seems to have some major g-force, because it also powers me out of bed, out of my room, and into the shower.

Chapter 17

Maple

Less than two hours later, Mom has edited and uploaded my 'get ready with me' video to YouTube and created a teaser from it for Instagram and TikTok. She has persuaded the twins to dress in red, white and blue (luckily, I escaped that) and has still found the time to look amazing herself. I should be impressed, but it's this crazy work rate that makes my life so exhausting.

We climb into her Lexus. Me in the front, the twins in the back. Dad has already left for church, as though him going early to help set things up might absolve the rest of us for the sin of not attending.

'Watch your skirt, Aspen,' Mom calls backwards. 'Don't rip that tulle on the seatbelt.'

'I don't know why I can't wear my stars and stripes shorts,' she grumbles. 'I hate skirts.'

'The skirt's prettier, sweetie,' Mom says, peering through the rearview mirror. 'It'll look better in the photos.'

'I like my shorts,' Ash offers. 'But this shirt is super itchy.'

Mom tuts. 'Will you quit complaining, please? It's only three hours and then we're going to Nana and Papa's for lunch, so you can choose what to wear for that. Deal?'

'Three hours?' Aspen wails.

Mom presses a button on her steering wheel, and Taylor Swift bursts into the car. It's loud enough to drown out any more complaints, and I spend the rest of the journey staring at the mountains. Ten minutes later, we pull into the parking lot of Hillcrest Park community center. There are red, white and blue balloons around the door, and already loads of buggies lined up.

Inside, it's manic. There are toddlers dressed as soldiers, and firefighters, and (I think) cows, racing around the hall. Chubby babies wearing old-fashioned outfits are pulling at the straps of their bonnets and screaming, and there are a few skinnier, smaller babies wrapped in stars and stripes blankets, somehow fast asleep. The adults are mainly in twos, moms and dads here to prove their child is the cutest in Provo, while sweating under the photographer's lights.

A little boy zooms past me on a wooden tricycle, then clips Mom's ankle, which makes me smile. A pacifier drops from a baby's mouth onto the floor, and she lets out a howl.

Aspen's eyes light up. 'Maybe this isn't so bad,' she says. 'Come on, Ash!'

'Hey, wait,' Mom calls after them. But it's too late.

'Mrs. Clark?'

We both turn toward the voice. It belongs to a woman with badly dyed hair and chipmunk cheeks.

'We are so excited that you accepted our invite to judge the twins' category,' she says in a fake-posh voice. 'A real celebrity mom. Can I show you to the judge's chair?'

Mom beams at her, then hisses, 'Find the twins,' at me, and floats off after the waddling woman.

As I scan the room for Ash and Aspen, my eyes land on a man holding a baby. He's got longish hair and is wearing slouchy jeans and a white T-shirt that looks grubby from sweat, or milk, or baby puke; it's hard to tell. His face is wearing a stupid grin and he's staring at me. I shift my gaze away, but still catch him passing the baby to someone else, his wife I guess, then start walking toward me.

I turn away, but not in time, because his hand lands on my arm.

'Hey,' he says. 'You're Maybe Maple, right?'

I take a breath and turn back. Remind myself that this is the price of being famous. 'Yep. My mom's a judge here, so . . .' My voice drifts off. 'And you? You've brought your baby along?'

'What?' He starts to laugh. 'No, she's not mine. I'm here with my sister. And my niece. I'm too young for kids. And single – I should add that.' He smiles again, and it's like he's flirting with me. I feel a retch build in my chest. He's doesn't have the intense stare of the guy in Vegas, or the freaky excitement of the creep with the chocolates. But he's still old, mid-twenties at least, and smells of cigarettes.

'Any chance I could get a selfie?' he asks.

The thought brings another wave of nausea, but I swallow it down. Remind myself that I should be celebrating getting noticed, not gagging. 'Sure.'

He wraps his arm tight around my shoulder, then butts his head against mine and stretches out his other hand, his phone held between nicotine-stained fingers. 'Smile!' he calls out, and somehow, I do. Then his hand drops down my back, and it brushes my ass before he pulls away. Vomit reaches my mouth.

'I better go,' I blurt out, stumbling backwards. But there's nowhere *to* go in this big box of a community hall. So I take the only option I can think of, and walk outside.

Chapter 18

Maple

I feel giddy with a sense of freedom. It's crazy – I'm in a dusty parking lot in Orem – but it feels like I've broken out of jail and the cops don't know about it yet.

I walk fast, out onto the main road. Getting far away from that gross flirty guy, and those crying babies, and Mom's constant demands. And with every step, I feel better.

I can go anywhere I want, and no one will know.

But the only place I really want to go is home, to be in my house without my mom following me around with a camera and a schedule, or the twins squealing, or Dad shuffling from room to room not noticing me. I want to swim in my pool, lie on the couch with my sneakers on, eat a snack without having to record the moment.

I check the walking route, then set off down University Parkway. The sun is warm but not hot, the air is dry, like always – no frizzy hair in Utah – and the UV is only three today, so my skin isn't even aging. It's weird, because I have a lot of stuff going on right now, but I think this might be what contented feels like. I can literally feel my shoulders dropping.

Yeah, Mom will be mad when she gets home. But what will

she do? Confiscate my phone? Send me to my room? Right now, both those things feel like bliss.

Google Maps takes me off the highway and past a couple of fast-food places I recognize. I think about grabbing some fries, mainly because Mom hates me eating fried food in case I get too fat to be photogenic. But the only bank card I have on my phone is my mom's, and she might get a notification when it's used. I don't want to risk this feeling by getting caught, so I walk on instead.

The road is quieter now; I can even hear birdsong. I look up at the mountains ahead of me and get a bit mesmerized because sunshine is reflecting off their peaks. They're such a permanent feature of my life that I rarely notice them. But it's nice to have some time to properly look. To appreciate how majestic and special they are.

'Maple!'

I close my eyes, like it might block out my dad's voice. But I can hear the familiar groan of his truck too. Slowly, I turn toward him. 'Hey, Dad. I thought you were at church?'

'I was,' he says, emphasizing the past tense. 'Now get in.' His arm is hanging outside the open window, and he knocks his hand against the metalwork twice, like a rider tapping a horse with his heels to make it run faster.

'I was on my way home,' I say, resisting, trying to make it sound legit. 'And I've got stuff . . .'

'Mom messaged me,' he interrupts. 'Told me to find you and get you back to the baby contest. I missed most of the sermon, so please don't put up a fight.'

His expression is something between desperate and angry. I push out a long sigh, then climb, defeated, into the truck. Dad's old Ford is the opposite of Mom's Lexus – noisy, polluting, exposed metal edges – and I have to yank the seatbelt to get it to move.

'So you ran out, huh?' he says, his expression clearing now he knows he has me trapped.

'I was going home,' I correct. 'And I'm fourteen. I'm allowed to make decisions about my own life.'

'You also have responsibilities,' he reminds me, unimpressed. 'Like helping Mom out when she asks.'

'But I'm busy,' I counter. 'I don't have time to film babies.'

He nods, quiet for a while. 'I saw some photos of Vegas,' he eventually says. 'The whole glass box thing, and that Cadillac, wow. It must have been an amazing experience.'

I smile, my mood lifting an inch. 'Yeah, it was fun.'

'And Mom said they adored you?'

My smile grows. I can't help loving it when Dad takes an interest in what I'm doing. For as long as I can remember, my family has been split by an invisible line: me and Mom on one side, Dad and the twins on the other. Maybe it's a legacy from our Mom & Maple channel when Dad was working long hours as a ranger in Wasatch Mountain State Park. Or it might be because Aspen, the most adventurous and outdoorsy of the three of us, gravitated toward Dad, and Ash followed. But whatever the reason, any attention Dad gives me is so rare that I feel the need to treasure it.

'Lois, the creative director; she called me a natural,' I say proudly. 'And Jules, the account guy, was funny. And the Azione client said I was perfect for their brand.'

'That's honestly great, Maple. And you deserve it. All the hard work you've put in.'

My cheeks are actually aching now. 'Thanks, Dad.'

'The thing is, you're not the only one who works hard, are you?'

My smile fades. I should have known it was too good to be true.

'Think about it. I only saw those photos of you in Vegas because your mom spent the entire day taking them. Like she does every day, working on your schedule, filming content, editing footage, posting it at just the right time. Seven days a week.'

I stare out of the window, see Hillcrest Park community center loom closer. 'I know.'

'So when she asks for a few hours of your time, would it not be kind to oblige?'

I turn to look at him. I could tell him how Mom demands all my hours, never a few of them. Or how she breaks my trust, railroads my privacy, always puts my stats before my happiness. But he would never take my side over hers, so instead, I climb out of his truck and head back inside to the soundtrack of babies crying, knowing exactly how they feel.

Chapter 19

Kirsten

I take a sip straight from the bottle like I'm some kind of alcoholic. It's crazy, thirty-six years old and having to hide in the pantry to enjoy *one* glass of wine. But that's Utah, I guess. I learned soon after starting kindergarten that my mom and dad were different from my friends' parents. That sleeping in on Sundays and drinking merlot with dinner was not normal behavior here. And that if I wanted to make friends, I needed to start acting like someone else.

I joined the church when I was thirteen, when my best friend at the time, Janie, was so concerned for my soul that she invited me to go with her family. I'd get picked up by Janie's dad every Sunday morning, much to my parents' bemusement. I lapsed for a while, rebelled maybe, when I thought my future belonged in New York. But Garrett made me realize that Utah was home, and I've been faithful to the church ever since.

Loosely speaking.

It's only one drink after all.

And I need it tonight after the day I've had. The baby contest was exhausting, having to choose a winner from those six sets, while twelve pairs of eyes dared me to reject their precious children. And on top of that, I had to convince Garrett to drag Maple back, him fretting about what the bishop would think of him leaving church early, her sullen and unapologetic when she finally reappeared. I still can't believe she abandoned me like that. I should be punishing her really, but I don't have the bandwidth. I've still got the baby contest content to edit, an unboxing video to film, and Dylan Dope is arriving tomorrow.

And then there was lunch at my in-laws to get through. Trying to be sociable while not letting the opportunity to create good content pass me by – all while being judged by the other women in Garrett's life. His mother and sisters-in-law who pretend to have concerns about Maple's schoolwork, or Ash's language development, when it's so clearly the green-eyed monster at play.

The thing is, I can brush off their criticisms easily enough. But what I really want is their admiration. I am director, producer, prop manager, cameraman, child psychologist. All the children do is smile and follow direction, and that's fine; they're kids. Garrett, on the other hand. I take another large gulp, then twist the aluminum lid back on and stash the bottle behind the sack of potatoes. Garrett was let go from his park ranger job last September, and he still does nothing to help. In fact, he does the opposite a lot of the time. Obstructs. Questions. Acts like I'm the problem.

I crunch a mint, then head back into the TV room. The twins are fast asleep in bed, and Maple is in her room, doing whatever fourteen-year-old girls do. Scrolling, messaging, lip synching, who knows. As long as she's not damaging her brand, I don't really care. And she's too smart to do that.

I flop down on the sofa.

'What a day,' Garrett says, his eyes not leaving the TV, a documentary about tigers. 'But fun, right?' he goes on. 'It was great to catch up with my brothers; it's been too long.'

'I thought you hated your brothers,' I murmur, closing my eyes. Garrett is the youngest of four boys, and the only one born without the sports gene. From how he's described his childhood, it sounds like he spent most of his spare time in the car with his mom, waiting for one or other of his brothers to finish whatever sports training they were at. He says he's not bitter about it, that it was because of those stretches that he got interested in wild animals – his mom would give him nature books from the library to keep him quiet. But I always notice some tension when they're all in a room together.

Garrett clicks his tongue. 'I don't hate anyone, especially not my family. I'm just not into talking about football twenty-four-seven.'

'Yeah, sorry. I'm tired.' I shift closer toward him, and he winds an arm around my shoulder. I snuggle in. Garrett might be crap at sport, and social media, and making money for his family, but he's good at this. Being physically present.

'Why don't you sleep in tomorrow?' he suggests, kissing the top of my head. 'You haven't got school to worry about now.'

'Nice idea,' I murmur. 'But the twins will be up early, racing around, making a racket like usual.'

'Not tomorrow they won't.'

I open my eyes. 'Why do you say that?'

'Well, I've booked something. A surprise.' His demeanor has changed, from relaxed to an odd mix of apologetic and belligerent. I narrow my eyes, push forward on the sofa and twist to face him.

'Garrett, what have you booked?'

He takes a deep breath, then looks me straight in the eyes. 'I'm taking the twins camping for a few days. And we're leaving tomorrow at dawn.'

Chapter 20

Kirsten

Garrett's palms lift in the air, as though he thinks he might need to defend himself from me. Which he just might. 'Sorry not to mention it before,' he says. 'It was an impulsive thing, a few nights camping at Bear Lake.'

'Without running it past me?' I ask. 'Did you not think I deserved that?'

'Well, I figured that you've got your hands full with that Dylan kid coming to stay and might appreciate the twins not being around.'

Maybe he's right that it'll be good to have the twins out of the picture. But Garrett is crap at lying, so I know this has nothing to do with him wanting to make my life easier, and everything to do with him getting what he wants. And I won't give him the satisfaction.

'I'm sorry, you can't this week; the twins have a deadline.'

'A deadline? Listen to yourself, Kirsten. They're eight!'

'Oh, stop being so dramatic. They're unboxing free toys not working a factory line. And they love it.'

'Aspen might love it, but Ash gets freaked out. And anyway,

they're both too young to understand the pitfalls. I listened to this podcast the other day . . .'

'You mean with all your free time since you lost your job?' I throw back. 'Let me guess. Those poor kidfluencers are being exploited by their moms and preyed on by online predators. Their schoolwork is suffering; their mental health is spiraling. They have no time to play, no real friends. In fact, all those overworked, mistreated children have is huge online popularity, heaps of media interest, a pile of free products, higher earnings than most college grads, and a foothold in one of America's fastest growing industries. How terrible for them.'

Garrett sighs. 'Look, I'm not saying we should stop doing it completely.'

'Well, that's lucky because last time I looked, the kids' income is the only money we've got coming into the household right now.'

'But it's not from all three kids, is it? Not really. Maple makes ninety percent of what comes in right now. She's the one with the big brand deals. The two million subscribers. And she was telling me today about how much she loved the Vegas shoot. It's Maple who's smashing it, not the twins.'

I huff in protest. One minute the guy wants to take the twins camping, and the next he's complaining about them not earning enough. But this, I can handle. 'Aspen and Ash are just starting out,' I explain. 'And it's a competitive space. But I've shown what I can achieve, haven't I? The twins will do just as well as Maple in time.'

Garrett shakes his head. 'No, you don't understand. I'm not questioning your commitments; I'm just saying that Maple's success is enough for all of us. That's how it started, isn't it – Mom & Maple – and you've both proven how amazing you are at it. It's exhausting trying to create content for all three of them, so why don't you concentrate on managing Maple, and let the twins take a step back?'

I shake my head. 'I love my kids equally, and the twins deserve the same opportunities that Maple has enjoyed over the years. You think I'm going to put all my effort and expertise into my eldest daughter's career and ignore theirs? Do you really think they'd thank me for that when Maple is famous and earning hundreds of thousands of dollars, and they're . . . what? Park rangers on thirty grand a year like you?'

'I'm a big-cat specialist,' he reminds me tetchily. 'I had a job lined up at Zion National Park if you remember, but you wanted to stay in Provo. I compromised my career for you.'

I stare into his green eyes, darker now because he's mad, more sage than honeydew, and consider my response, whether to escalate or de-escalate. But it's been a long day, so I choose the latter. 'Look, I know the internet can feel like a scary place to our generation at times,' I say, forcing some softness into my voice. 'But it is the future for our kids. So the best thing we can do is to teach them how to be winners on there. Maple, Aspen and Ash.'

'But they're so young.'

'And kidfluencing is a whole lot less dangerous than ice hockey, or skiing, or camping near bears.'

He narrows his eyes. 'I'm still taking them camping. It's all booked.'

I release a long sigh. 'Fine. I'll talk to Maddie, try and get an extension on that unboxing video. But make sure you film lots of content while you're away. Melting marshmallows around a campfire means guaranteed clicks.'

Chapter 21

Maple

The doorbell sounds. Oh God. It will be him. Jeez, why is my heart pumping so fast? It's hardly a life-or-death situation. But now my armpits are clammy. If I get sweat patches on my top, I will literally die of embarrassment. I eye my vanity, grab the body mist, spray it liberally. Watermelon explodes in the air.

Should I go downstairs now? Or wait for Mom to call me?

I hear her welcoming him inside. Dylan Dope is in my house. His mom was dropping him off, but she couldn't stay; that's what Mom said. It's a long drive back to St George and she needed to get going.

He'll be in the kitchen now. Mom will be asking if he wants a glass of homemade lemonade. She cursed and bitched about it earlier, the acidic citrus juice stripping her nails, but now she'll be pretending we drink it all the time. What else will she be saying to him?

I can't avoid this any longer.

I take a deep breath and head downstairs.

'Hey,' I say, but it's a squeak, so I quickly ram my lips closed. I select the best angle to assess him from, one where I can check him out without accidentally making eye contact. He's slim, long-limbed, with a puff of dark blond hair that hides half his face.

'Maple honey,' Mom says, her makeup perfect, her white smock dress giving me tradwife vibes. 'I was just telling Dylan how much you want to learn to skateboard, and he offered to give you a lesson. Isn't that kind of him? We can go to the skate park this afternoon.'

This doesn't slow my heart at all. I follow some skateboarders online – like that cool British-Japanese girl Sky Brown – and I've seen the injuries. 'Sounds good,' I hear myself say.

Dylan nods but doesn't make eye contact. Then he turns his attention back to Mom. It's too quick. It's obvious that he doesn't want to be here, which makes me feel even more sick. 'You have a nice home,' he says. 'And a pool – that's amazing.'

Mom puffs out her chest like a peacock. 'Thank you, Dylan, that's sweet of you. It's nothing special really, but we love it, don't we, Maple?'

'Um, yeah,' I say, feeling my cheeks heat up. Mom's making an effort to include me in this conversation, while Dylan clearly doesn't want me involved.

'Do you mind if I take your photo, Dylan?' she goes on. 'Show Maple's followers you've arrived? They're so excited about you coming to stay, they'll want all the gossip.'

She's raising her eyebrows. Oh God. Please make this stop.

'Sure,' Dylan says, like people ask him this all the time. Which of course they do.

'Hey, Maple, get in shot too,' Mom casually demands.

I knew this was coming. Mom's been posting about Dylan's upcoming visit for days, and now he's here, I doubt she'll let him breathe without her declaring it a photo opportunity. But the thought of getting physically close to him makes my pulse race.

I shuffle toward him, place my trembling hand on the back of his barstool, lean in, smile at Mom's phone lens. And crazily, it helps. My heart thump reduces to a regular beat. As though smiling for the camera, making content, is so familiar that it actually relaxes me.

'Beautiful,' Mom says as she finally lowers her phone. 'The twins will be so sad to have missed this.'

'It's Aspen and Ash, right?' Dylan says, earning himself more brownie points. 'They're not around?'

Mom's jaw sets. I slept through Dad and the twins leaving this morning, so the first I heard about their adventure was from Mom when I came downstairs. She pretended it was her idea – getting the twins out of the way so she could concentrate on me – but I could see she was mad about it really.

'Their dad's taken them camping,' Mom says, with the same fake smile she used on me. 'Those three love the great outdoors. Garrett will have them hunting with him next.'

'You didn't want to go?'

I jolt as I realize Dylan's question is aimed at me.

'Oh. No.' I shake my head. 'Camping isn't really my thing.' The words come easily, but his question sticks. Because it's true that I'm not into camping like they all are, but if this is a dad and kids' trip, why wasn't I at least invited?

Maybe I was though. And Mom vetoed it because Dylan was coming to stay. Of course that makes sense. I manage half a smile in Dylan's vague direction.

'How about we go to the skate park now?' Mom suggests. 'It's a big one, Dylan, I think you'll like it.'

'Provo skate park gets a lot of love in the community,' he says, his voice lower than the boys' at school. 'I'm excited to see it.'

'But I don't have a skateboard,' I say. My final attempt at not completely embarrassing myself.

'Oh, you do now,' Mom says with a bright smile. 'Amazon delivered it an hour ago.'

Great.

Chapter 22

Maple

I stare down the ramp. Jeez, it's steep. My knees start to shake so I look away, at the mountains in the distance, trying to find my inner Sky Brown.

The skateboarding actually started much better than I thought it would. It turns out I'm pretty good at riding on the flat, and it didn't take me long to figure out stopping and turning. Dylan has warmed up a bit too, now that he's talking about his favorite subject, and my nerves have gradually settled over the two hours we've been here, even with Mom sitting on a bench like ten feet away taking photos and videos.

But then Mom suggested Dylan teach me a trick, something intrepid and cool. And yeah, she actually used the word 'intrepid'. And that's why we're here. At the top of a ramp with no way out except down.

'You've got this, Maple honey!' Mom calls out unhelpfully from her bench.

'You sure you want to do this?' Dylan asks, with a kind of morbid curiosity. 'I mean, you'll probably be fine. But you've only been skating for an hour or so. And with your mom forgetting to get you a helmet.'

When it comes to my channel, Mom doesn't forget anything, so I know her selective approach to protective clothing will be about aesthetics. The wrist guards and elbow pads make me look like a serious skateboarder, while a helmet would flatten my hair and add shadow to my face, so it's conveniently forgotten.

But that's not what sticks in my mind. *I mean, you'll probably be fine.* Dylan Dope believes I can (probably) do this. And he's the expert, isn't he?

'I'm good,' I say, with more confidence than I feel.

Dylan nods. 'Okay, cool. I'll go first, so watch me. You keep your knees soft the whole time, but the move has got to be decisive. Lift the board by pushing down on your back foot to clear the lip, then lean forward and go.' He disappears over the ramp, then slows to a stop in the dip. It looks so easy, it's almost an anti-climax. Of course I can do that.

I step onto my board. The grit on the grip board is sparkling in the sunshine, and I use it to lift my mood. *Come on, Maple. You've got this.*

Knees bent, lip cleared, bodyweight forward, go!

The board disappears from under my feet. I'm flying in the air. I flail my arms; one hand hits the concrete, then my shoulder joins it. And whack, my head slams down. Smooth, hard, unforgiving. Pain ricochets around my body. I screw my eyes closed, beg them not to leak tears.

'Fuck!' Dylan crouches down next to me. 'Are you okay? Shit, I should never have let you try that without a helmet.' He shakes his head.

'It's not your fault,' I manage, still not daring to open my eyes, nausea rising in my belly. 'And I'm good, honestly. I just need a minute.'

'Oh, Maple honey, are you okay?' Mom's voice filters in. I

test one eye, then the other. She's leaning over me, her white dress floating in the breeze. Concern is etched into her face, but is it real or fake? I have no clue anymore. 'Did you hit your head? Can you see straight? How many fingers am I holding up?' she asks in quick succession. 'God, why did I forget the helmet! This is all my fault!'

I gingerly curl up to sitting, blink a few times. 'No, it's not, Mom,' I say, my instinct always to make her feel better. 'And I'm fine, I think. I hit my head, but my shoulder took most of the impact.' I touch my scalp. There's a lump forming, but I think that's a good sign.

Mom lets out a long sigh of relief. 'Thank the Lord for that. I have some Tylenol in the car, so let's head there now. You poor thing, falling like that, but I may have something to cheer you up.'

'Oh yeah?'

'The way you hung in the air for a second before you fell? It was so dramatic. This video is totally going to go viral.'

Chapter 23

Kirsten

When I first contacted Kayleigh Jones, I didn't have an ulterior motive. I'd just heard good things about the online school she'd set up for child influencers and wanted to discuss the possibility of Maple joining. But when I realized that she was the skateboarding sensation Dylan Dope's mom, it didn't take me long to come up with a side hustle.

And I'm so pleased I did, because him coming to stay is proving even more effective for our social media stats than Maple's photoshoot. The post I put on Maple's socials when Dylan first arrived was only a collection of stills of the pair of them, but it has already generated thousands of likes, comments, reposts and shares across the different platforms. I just knew this collab would cause a stir.

And that's from one post. I took lots of footage of Maple and Dylan skateboarding this afternoon, so I'll be able to create a great film for YouTube, and then use the best bits to make TikToks and Instagram reels. Really keep the momentum flying.

The highlight will be Maple's fall, of course, but there were other moments that might prove more valuable in the long term.

The way Dylan held Maple's forearms when she first stepped onto the board. And his energy as he demonstrated the basics to her, his expression so encouraging. Two beautiful young people doing something cool and edgy, but also wholesome and supportive. The kids will love it for sure – Dylan Dope and Maybe Maple hitting it off. But I think the moms will like it too. The big sisters, the grandmas.

And yes, some weirdos, of course. The pedos and incels, and assholes. But I know how to deal with them, which means they're not a threat, despite what Garrett might think after listening to those left-wing podcasts. Pious, jealous cat ladies blinded by self-importance. Believing they know what's best for my children. It might be funny if it wasn't so rude.

I hear footsteps on the stairs and look up. Maple is still wearing her skateboarding outfit, but she's accessorized it with a forlorn expression. I concentrate on not rolling my eyes. 'Oh hey, honey. How are you feeling?'

Maple slides onto the kitchen barstool. 'The Tylenol helped, I think, but I still feel a bit weird.'

I give her a sympathetic smile. 'That's probably the embarrassment of falling more than anything. Not that you should feel bad – you were great out there, for a beginner. Hey, why don't you go in the pool?' I suggest, sensing that a change of subject might be good. 'The cool water will take the sting out of your grazes. And a swim will be nice and relaxing.'

'Is Dylan out there?'

'By the pool? Yes, I think so.'

'Hardly relaxing then.'

Wow, teenagers can be annoying. Maple knows the single reason I invited Dylan to stay was to build her profile. 'Maple, I can't film collab content if you're not together,' I tell her, as calmly as I can manage. 'And no content means no engagement.

And all this discomfort you tell me you're feeling . . .' I draw a circle in the air for emphasis '. . . will be for nothing. And anyway, the boy spent two hours teaching you to skateboard this afternoon. The least you can do is provide a little entertainment now.'

Her eyes widen. 'Entertainment?'

'Conversation,' I clarify.

'But we have nothing to talk about,' she moans. 'I don't see why I couldn't have had one of my own friends to stay instead, like Coco.'

'Who?'

'Coco. I told you about her.'

A vague memory fails to form properly. 'Remind me again?'

Maple shakes her head, then turns away from me. The proceeding silence seems to thicken the air, and I'm trying to work out how to loosen it when my phone vibrates against the kitchen counter. I pick it up and accept the call without looking at the caller ID – grateful for the interruption, I suppose – so my heart sinks when I realize who it is.

Chapter 24

Kirsten

'Oh, hey, Maddie,' I say, adding a fake smile in case she can hear it.

'Hi, Kirsten!' she fizzes back. 'Thanks so much for picking up. I thought you might be busy today, with you not responding to any of my emails.'

I close my eyes, hold in half a dozen swear words. 'We just got home; we've been out filming content.'

'That's so awesome to hear,' she says in the patronizing tone she uses when she's pissed. 'But hey, listen, Kirsten. Those airplane launcher toys. The client really wanted to see that unboxing video go up online in time for summer break.'

'Yes, I'm sorry about that.' Heat rises in my cheeks. God, I hate being on the back foot. 'It will go up soon, I promise.'

'And you know, the fee was paid in advance, like you requested. We don't normally do that, but I appreciate you had some costs come in, and of course I'm sympathetic to that, but it does compound things.'

The second payment on my car. My chest feels tight suddenly. Full to the brim with animosity for my ignorant, selfish, jobless husband, stealing my children away before dawn.

I grip the phone tighter. 'I'll talk to Garrett,' I say, trying to sound calm. 'And the video will be up before the end of the week, I promise.'

'That's great, Kirst . . .'

I cut her off. Stare down my daughter.

'Maybe I will go for a swim,' she says. Maple has always been good at picking up on my mood. 'And hang out with Dylan for a bit. I'll go and get changed.'

I give her a grateful smile. Of course it's normal for teenage daughters to test their parents. But we'll always be Mom and Maple, two sides of the same moon, when it matters. 'Thank you, honey,' I say softly. 'And can you do me a favor?'

'Um, sure.'

'Can you wear the Abercrombie Kids two-piece that Maddie sent the other day?'

Maple's face clouds over. 'Can I not just wear my regular swimsuit?'

I glower at her. 'Please, Maple?'

She bites her lip, but eventually nods and heads upstairs. She returns five minutes later wearing the sky-blue floral two-piece underneath a white minidress. Maple's skin tone is slightly darker than mine and Garrett's, more like my dad's, which gives her a light tan all year round. Couple that with a sunny June, and her legs are contrasting nicely against the white cotton.

'You look gorgeous, Maple honey.'

She gives me a tentative smile, then disappears through the glass doors. I'll give them ten minutes, then head outside myself. If Maple has coaxed Dylan into the pool – and in that bikini, how could he resist – then there could be some good content to film.

But first, I have something more urgent to do.

I call Garrett's number, silently rehearsing what I'm going

to say, but it clicks into voicemail. I swallow down a gallstone of annoyance. Did he not think that I might want to contact him, to talk to my precious children? After all, it's me who carried those twins in my belly for nine months, who's got stretch marks and wrinkles to prove it. But now he thinks he's their big protector. The one who knows best. Keeping them away from their mother.

From their responsibilities.

I leave a message – short and sweet; get the hell home – then walk into the pantry and reach for something sharp and revitalizing behind the bag of potatoes.

Chapter 25

Maple

Why do boys make life look easy?

Dylan is lying on a lounger, wearing nothing but beach shorts and fat headphones. His eyes are closed, his head faintly nodding along to whatever tune he's listening to. I'm willing to bet there's not one self-critical thought moving through that prone brain right now.

In contrast, I can't even work out which foot I prefer to put my weight on, rocking between the two like I'm trying to stay upright in a storm. I want to get in the pool – wash off the memory of my fall at the skate park like Mom suggested – but that brings a whole load of awkwardness with it. Like disturbing Dylan, then finding something to talk to him about. It's true that he had stuff to say earlier, but skateboarding is his passion; of course he can talk about that. It's my turn now, and I can't think of a single interesting subject to bring up.

I also have to strip off my dress. The bikini is gorgeous, sure, but it makes my boobs look even bigger than they really are, and exposes my tummy, and with Dylan watching on, it feels too revealing. Dylan, whose whole chest is bare.

Boys. Life. Easy.

But I know Coco would tell me to go for it; remind me that I'm beautiful and should quit questioning myself. So that's what I'm going to do.

I take a deep breath, walk up to the lounger next to Dylan's, and drop my towel. He must notice my shadow because his eyes open, and he slides his headphones down to his neck.

'Oh hey, how's your head?'

'Oh, all fine now,' I say, flicking my hand. 'What are you listening to?'

It's not exactly a controversial question, but he looks awkward, like he's a hardcore Swifty and doesn't want to admit it. 'Oh, nothing much,' he says. 'You going for a swim?'

'Yeah, I think so.' I stroke the front of my dress, like it might settle the churning in my belly. 'You coming in?'

'Sure.'

He removes his headphones and unfurls to standing. We catch each other's eyes, and I nod, smile, wonder whether my heart rate has a max speed or if it moves straight to cardiac arrest without warning. But then Dylan breaks eye contact and jumps in the pool. A few drops of water splash on my arm and it gives me the reset I need. I pull off my dress, force my shoulders back, and curl my toes over the edge. He's looking at me, my almost naked body, but that's okay, I remind myself. He's not leering like that weirdo with the chocolates, or staring intently like the man in Vegas, or smiling stupidly like the guy at the baby contest. He's not grossly old either.

I dive in. Feel the instant hit of cold, fresh water. But shit, my top has slipped down. Fuck, my nipple is out! I wrench at the fabric frantically, get it back in place just before I rise to the surface. Did Dylan see? But no, he's facing away from me. Swimming toward a ball bobbing in the corner of the pool.

'Wanna play some volleyball?' he shouts, twisting to face me.

My heart is still hammering. And after what's just happened, I'm scared about leaping around the pool. But I've already proven how crap I am at skateboarding, I can't refuse to play this as well. 'Yeah, cool,' I call back, trying to keep my voice level.

He grins, chucks the ball in the air. It lands on my splayed fingers, and I push it back. I've played plenty of volleyball over the years – my cousins are all sports mad, so there's often a game during family get-togethers in summer – and I fall into the back-and-forth rhythm easily enough. A few throws veer off course, meaning I need to dive underwater, but luckily there are no more clothing disasters. I even find that I'm enjoying myself. Squealing when I slip backwards, cackling when Dylan misses the ball and slaps his face on the water.

'Hey, kids, you look like you're having fun!'

I catch the ball and turn toward Mom who's standing on the edge of the pool.

'You know, I think this game you're playing would make great content,' she goes on, as though she's just thought of it, instead of having orchestrated the whole thing. 'You both okay with me filming?'

Chapter 26

Maple

I was having fun for a moment then. I'd almost forgotten that Dylan Dope is only here because his mom made him come.

But creating content is what this whole visit is about. And as Mom said, if I don't get something out of it, then all this excruciating awkwardness that she's caused (she didn't mention that part) will be for nothing.

'Yeah, sure,' I answer.

'Good with me,' Dylan adds.

'Fantastic,' Mom calls back, attaching her phone to the tripod that's permanently at the side of the pool. 'Go ahead and pretend I'm not here.'

Dylan and I do as she asks – we're both pros at this after all. But the spontaneity has gone, and I feel body-conscious again, wondering what my figure looks like in profile, whether my bikini will keep me covered. I jump up, slam the ball, celebrate when I outplay Dylan, giggle when he mucks up. But it's a performance now, staged for the camera. I wonder if Dylan feels the same.

'Hey, I've got an idea,' Mom says after a while, still pretending like this is all organic. 'Why don't you guys play a game of tag?

It'll be mayhem with you both trying to escape each other in the water! And so fun for our subscribers to watch.'

I imagine Dylan lunging forward, his arm outstretched, trying to tag me. And me curving and writhing to avoid his touch. I inwardly shudder.

'I don't know,' Dylan says nervously. 'I'm not sure that kind of thing fits my brand.'

I feel a surge of relief, but Mom's face darkens.

'I'm sorry, Mrs. Clark,' Dylan goes on, clearly noticing Mom's reaction too. 'But my dad has strong opinions on what works and what doesn't.'

'And I've been doing this for quite a while too now,' she counters, her voice clipped. 'What's the problem with tag? Or is it playing with Maple you're not happy about?'

Oh God, did she really ask that? I look down at the lapping water, feel my cheeks burn.

'What?' Dylan's pitch rises. 'No, I just mean that Dad might think it's too childish. He wants my content to be mainly skateboarding and fashion work. I think volleyball will be okay because it's sport. But playing tag is more kids' stuff, you know?'

Kids' stuff. He thinks I'm a baby, into stupid games.

'Oh, I see,' Mom says, her annoyance deflating like an untied balloon. 'Actually, that's a good point. Maple is in that transition period between child and young adult, you know? We probably need to focus on maturing her content too.'

Dylan gives her a weak smile, his expression a mix of relief and unease.

'How about I get you guys some lemonade instead,' Mom says, her sunny disposition already back. 'You can just hang out together, listen to some music, do whatever young adults do.'

I freeze except for my eyes, which risk darting toward Dylan, to check how he's read Mom's comment. But his expression is fixed.

'Thank you, Mrs. Clark,' he says.

Mom turns to head inside, and Dylan climbs out of the pool. Once he's settled on his lounger, and not looking in my direction, I do the same. As I sit on the edge of the bed and lean forward to wring out my hair, my necklace tips forward.

'That's a cool necklace,' Dylan says, leaning toward me to read the engraving on the slim oblong pendant. My instinct is to pull away – he's so close now that his breath is tickling my chest – but that might seem rude, or childish, so I hold my position. The necklace was a fourteenth birthday present from my Nana and Papa, a platinum chain and pendant engraved with my initials. I remember Dad clasping it around my neck, the pride on his face as he did so, and I've worn it every day since.

'M-L-C,' Dylan reads. 'I'm guessing that's your initials. What does the L stand for?'

'Lily,' I manage.

He rolls back on the lounger. 'That's my sister's name. Well, one of them. There's Charlotte too, but they're both older, so it's just me at home now. No one to hide behind.'

'Oh, hiding is overrated in my opinion,' Mom says, appearing by our beds. Her face is beaming now, like she's hit some jackpot, and I eye her suspiciously as she hands us both a glass of homemade lemonade.

Chapter 27

Him

He should have gone to Utah to find her. Packed up his stuff and just driven there. He's a pussy for not doing that.

She might want him to save her. And even if she doesn't, he should have gone anyway.

He wonders whether she'd put up a fight. The image makes him feel conflicted. Sad and excited. Hard done by, but lucky. He pushes his laptop away for a moment, catches his breath.

At least there's nobody's around him this time. No nosy workmates asking why he's watching a kid's YouTube channel. He's alone in his trailer, work done for the day, a four-pack for company. Just how he likes it.

He drags the video back three minutes. He's watched the film from the start – the skateboarding crash, the water volleyball – and it was good to see her smiling and giggling in the water. But he doesn't need to see that a second time.

This is what he needs to see again. The kiss.

Although is it even that? The sticker appearing at the wrong moment, hiding their faces as the boy leans toward her, teasing their audience.

Maybe, Maybe Maple.

His palms are sweaty, so he picks up his drink, uses the chilled aluminum can to cool his hands. He takes a long swig, feels the cold liquid swill in his gut.

Did she kiss him? Did she fucking kiss that dude? He crunches the empty can.

He needs to see her, really see her. Not her kissing some skateboarding jerk with cartoon stickers flying around. But the true, whole Maple Clark.

But how?

Maybe the mom could offer a way in.

He's heard the stories, how money talks with moms like her. He's broke, of course, barely has a pot to piss in. But maybe the promise of wealth and glory will be enough if he aims high. And the sky's the limit when it comes to fake promises.

He clicks on the @_MaybeMaple_ channel profile. There's an email address there, an opportunity to connect privately. He can't use his own contact details; that would be stupid. But there are ways to stay anonymous. A VPN and a new email address is all it requires.

He opens another can and sets to work. He makes up a name, one that gives nothing of his identity away, and crafts a message that he imagines will seduce a woman like her.

Because if the mom is going to agree to this, he needs her defenses right down low.

Chapter 28

Maple

I know I look a mess. I don't need a mirror to show me that my skin is blotchy, my eyes puffy and bloodshot. But at least it's just me out here in the darkness, plus a few long-legged insects, skittering across the pool like anorexic ballerinas.

It's freezing cold, so I slide my feet up the lounger to my backside, pull my bare legs into my chest, and then cover them with my hoodie. The sky is clear, showing off its mass of sparkling stars. I usually love stargazing, but tonight I can't even look up. As though uninhabited planets from light years away are going to judge me – like everyone else will.

I bury my face in my knees.

How could she do that to me? How fucking could she?

I close my eyes to trap the tears, but then the images come. The content Mom put on my YouTube channel. I don't know if it was the angles she used, the filters, the exposure. But the way I'm jumping around the pool, giggling, adjusting my bikini. It makes me look sexy, like I'm performing for Dylan. When the only person we're both trying to please is my mom, like always.

But the ending is by far the worst. The big fat lie that brought me out here at two in the morning, alone, too embarrassed and ashamed to even look at the stars.

Dylan and I are sitting on the loungers. I lean forward and he moves toward me. Then a sticker appears between our heads – FIRST KISS!! – with tiny love hearts raining down the screen. Mom knows damn well that Dylan was just reading the engraving on my necklace, but instead of sticking with the truth, she made up some fantasy story for clicks.

And I know that this is only the beginning. And not just for me. Whatever happens now, the rumors will always be there. Dylan Dope and Maybe Maple. *Are they? Aren't they? WTF is he thinking? He could do SO MUCH better.*

I get that Mom's ambitious for my channel, and yeah, stuff like this always blows up. But I'm her daughter; how could she do this to me?

I run my fingernails across the palm of my opposite hand, digging hard into the flesh, soaking up the relief that physical pain brings. I slice a line on my hand, and it gives me some resolve.

Because Mom *has* crossed a line. And this time, I am *not* going to let her talk me around.

I've let her off so many times. Like when she insists on filming even though I'm exhausted, or ill, or busy with my schoolwork, or just not in the mood. And how she pretends to care, when it's really just manipulation. The only thing she actually cares about is creating content. It's not just me – she wants to make the twins the most adorable double act on the planet – but it's mostly me. Because I'm the one who brings in the big bucks for her.

'I hate you.'

I say it quietly, testing the words in the anonymity of darkness. It feels good to let them out.

'I'm done with you,' I go on, getting louder. 'With your demands, and your fake love, and how you always claim you know what's best for me, but never bother to ask me what I think. Did you hear that, Mom?'

I feel a smile form. I know it's pathetic. Pretending to call her out when she's fast asleep in bed and I'm out here, freezing my butt off. But still, it feels good. Before tonight, I couldn't stay mad at her. Because every time she let me down, she'd twist things, make me feel like I was the one at fault – too lazy, or ungrateful; too stupid or selfish to see what we were building. And then I'd blame myself.

But I'm not doing that anymore.

She doesn't love me, not unconditionally like parents are supposed to. So why should I listen to her?

'I don't think she did hear you, actually, but I did, and I think that's a fair call.'

My head whips around. It looks like I'm not alone anymore.

Chapter 29

Maple

'Shit, Dylan,' I say, wiping my eyes, hoping the cold air has taken the red blotches out of my skin.

'Sorry,' he says. 'I couldn't sleep, and I saw you through the window. Mind if I join you?'

'Um, I guess.' I watch him walk over to the lounger next to mine and drop down. I can't help noticing that it's exactly how we were sitting earlier, when Mom took that video. My heart starts to thud at the memory. *FIRST KISS!!*

'You're pissed off with your mom, huh,' he murmurs, looking out at the pool. 'Guess I can't blame you for that.'

I nod, drag my bottom lip with my teeth. 'Did you . . .'

'Yeah, I saw it,' he interrupts. 'Couldn't avoid it really; your mom tagged me.' He shrugs. 'Well, actually you tagged me, your account, but I figured your mom was behind it.'

'On YouTube?' I whisper.

'On everything.'

'Oh God, I'm so sorry.'

'It's not your fault.'

'But she's my mom – it happened at our home. You must hate us.'

'I don't know,' he murmurs. 'I have pretty low expectations as far as parents go.'

I think about how Mom came across Dylan via the influencer school his mom's set up, the one I'm supposed to be starting at in August, something else she didn't bother to discuss with me. 'Is your mom as obsessed with clicks as mine?'

He sighs, half smiles. 'Nah, she barely understands social media. But she pretty much does what my dad says. I'm sure she'd prefer to still be teaching elementary school if he'd let her, but Dad decided a senior school for kidfluencers has better earning potential.'

'And your dad always gets what he wants?' I ask.

'Our family is traditional that way.'

'Skateboarding sensation on TikTok doesn't sound that traditional.'

Dylan laughs, which makes me feel a tiny bit better. But the sound quickly fades. 'Providing for your family is the traditional part,' he goes on. 'Dad works in real estate, but the money's up and down. He heard through church how much influencers can earn and figured we should start monetizing my skateboarding.'

'At least you've got an actual skill to earn from,' I mutter. 'And my friend Coco's channel is about trying to uncover a real-life killer. While I just make lame "get ready with me" reels and do stupid pranks.'

'I'm not that good a skateboarder,' Dylan counters. 'Yeah, I can do some tricks, but so can lots of riders. They just don't make a big thing of it on social media.'

'Well, you look pretty good to me.' I cringe as I realize how that sounds, then quickly start talking again. 'And I guess sponsorship must bring lots of opportunities.'

'Yeah, but not the ones I want.'

'How's that?' I ask, genuinely curious.

'Sponsors want me to win skateboarding comps. Brands want me to wear their clothes, or eat their snacks, or drink their rancid protein shakes. Everyone wants to throw money at me, so Dad's happy. But it's not my dream.'

'So what is?'

He hesitates, like he's not sure whether to trust me. I can't blame him for that, I suppose. I do share DNA with my mom. 'Can you keep this between us?' he eventually asks.

'One hundred percent.'

'Okay so my dream is to go to Columbia University to study law. I want to be a human rights lawyer.'

'Wow.' So he's hot, sporty and clever. 'That's really cool.'

He sighs. 'Maybe, but I doubt it will happen. My mom's knowledge of the senior school curriculum is pretty sketchy. I'm trying to do stuff myself – there's resources online, that's what I was listening to when you asked earlier; dull, hey? – but it's hard to find the time with all the filming Dad makes me do.'

'Can't you just tell him that? That you've got other, worthier, aspirations? I mean, a human rights lawyer?'

'He tells me to be grateful for what I've got,' Dylan says, shrugging like it's not a big deal, but also looking away, like it is. 'That we need the money now, and being a lawyer takes too long, end of discussion. But I've got a few years to figure it out; I'm not giving up yet.'

'It's funny,' I murmur. 'I never think about dads being pushy too.'

'So yours isn't?'

'God, no. He's not a fan of social media, period. But he doesn't dare cross Mom.'

Dylan looks thoughtful. 'You're his little girl though, aren't you? And your mom's latest post, I dunno, it's pretty suggestive, isn't it? Everyone's got a breaking point; maybe this will turn out to be your dad's.'

I lie back, absorb Dylan's words, and wonder if he's right. If Dad might finally decide to fight for me. Or if he'll even bother to watch it.

Chapter 30

Kirsten

I had a feeling that inviting Dylan Dope to stay would turn out to be one of my better ideas. And when I saw the two of them lying next to each other on the loungers, I knew the moment was worth recording. But I could not have predicted that they would lean toward each other like that, or how wild the response would be to my little stretching of the truth. The video has gone viral on every channel. And especially TikTok where there are already thousands of memes mimicking their FIRST KISS!!

I'm so proud of myself. Spotting the opportunity. Tweaking the narrative to give it some clickbait spice. I just hope that Maple is pleased too, that she doesn't go into a hormone-induced sulk about me adjusting reality. But she knows we're in the post-truth era now, that if we limit ourselves to fact, we'll always be at a disadvantage. Anyway, no one cares whether Dylan and Maple are actually dating – it's the drama that matters, and if we do this right, we can keep it going for months, maybe even years.

I reach for the coffee pot and pour myself a second cup – life is good this morning, and I need to celebrate somehow.

Even Garrett's bringing the twins home early. After my voice message yesterday, he sent me a curt text agreeing to cut his trip short, while warning me that we needed to have a serious conversation. It's a win in my book. I can film the twins opening those airplane launcher toys this afternoon, which will keep Maddie quiet. And Garrett's serious conversation will just mean listening to him whine for ten minutes, then reminding him that he's unemployed and doesn't get a vote.

I scroll through the comments on YouTube, but there are so many exclamation marks and emojis that it's dizzying, so I give up, and click into my email instead. Considering Maple has almost two million followers, I get very little email traffic from YouTube – I suppose that mode of communication is as outdated as actual mail to Gen Alpha – and the ones I do get are generally trying to sell me something. But this morning there's one with a subject header that gets my attention.

Modeling opportunity.

I open the email.

Hey Kirsten,
Thanks for your time; I hope you're having a good day.
I run a modeling agency with my business partner, and we represent some of the world's most successful models, both photographic and catwalk. I came across your daughter, Maple Clark, via her Instagram profile, and noticed that she has recently worked on a campaign for Azione. I appreciate she is a minor, which is why I am contacting you rather than Maple directly, but if Maple is keen on developing her modeling career, could you please

send four or five profile pictures, so that I can discuss her future representation with my business partner?
Please send these via Telegram (details below) to protect Maple's privacy.
I look forward to hearing from you.
Blake

My skin tingles. I read the email a second time, feel the corners of my mouth stretch high and wide. This good day is getting even better. Maple is going to be a model! I always knew she had the potential, but there are so many beautiful girls out there, I wasn't sure she'd rise to the surface. But she has. It's there, in black and white.

Azione was only the start for Maple, just as I predicted.

I pick up my phone, hover my finger over the Telegram app. Telegram isn't my usual messaging app, but some of our followers prefer it, all the talk of mainstream platforms scraping private data getting into their heads, I suppose. And to be honest, the thought that those power-crazy tech bros are watching us all the goddamn time has started to creep me out a bit too. So if professionals like Blake prefer Telegram, I'm more than happy to follow her lead.

But I realize I need to choose the right images first, so I open my photo library instead. My face breaks into a smile as I start scrolling through pictures of my beautiful daughter, wondering which ones I should send, which show her off in the best way. Or maybe I should take some new ones specifically. Opportunities like this don't come around often, and Maple is becoming more striking, less childlike, every day.

But before I have chance to decide anything, I hear the front door opening.

Chapter 31

Kirsten

'Ah, my gorgeous kids!' I hold out my arms, then feel my jaw tense as both twins pretend not to notice.

'Hi, Mom,' Aspen says with a sigh.

I lower my arms. 'How was camping?'

'It was amazing,' Ash says mournfully.

'Until you made us come home,' Aspen adds.

'See?' Garrett mutters, walking past me without even a kiss on my cheek.

Annoyance rises in my chest, like stomach acid, and I swallow it down. Two minutes ago, I was on a high and now that's gone. Trust my sanctimonious husband to kill the mood. I bend my knees until I can look into the twins' eyes. 'Why don't you two chill out in your room for a bit,' I suggest, giving them my best mommy smile. 'I bet you've missed your cozy beds, haven't you?'

Aspen shrugs, non-committal, but Ash nods and smiles back. He is always so easy to get on side in real life; it's a mystery why I can't persuade him to perform for the camera. I watch them traipse upstairs, then I follow Garrett's path into the kitchen, trying to relax my bunched fists as I go. Reminding myself that life is always easier if I keep him on side.

‘Thanks for bringing them back,’ I say sweetly. ‘I was not Maddie’s favorite person yesterday, so I appreciate you getting me out of trouble.’

‘It’s fine,’ he says, his voice a little clipped. ‘As long as you appreciate that a favor deserves a favor.’

My skin prickles. Garrett is not usually this assertive. ‘Go on.’

‘Well, I brought the twins back so that you could keep your promise to Maddie, and now I want you to make a promise to me.’

I place my palms against the cool quartz countertop. ‘Oh?’

‘I want you to stop this.’ He lifts his hands. ‘The brand deals, the YouTube channel, all of it. I want the twins to grow up without the world watching on, and don’t try and talk me out of it, because I’m putting my foot down.’

Inside I baulk at his blatant patriarchy, but I worry this is down to my Chicagoan heritage, so I pretend to take it in my stride. ‘And have you thought about how a ban might affect them?’ I ask instead, because prioritizing the children is always my first instinct.

‘It will give them the chance to make mistakes without consequences,’ he says, without missing a beat. ‘Time to figure out who they are without hundreds of comments telling them what to think.’

‘And when they see their competitors doing brilliantly?’ I ask. ‘Getting loads of free gear, and heaps of compliments. How do you think they’ll feel then?’

Garrett sets his jaw. ‘They won’t know. Because I’m banning social media in this house for anyone under thirteen.’

My eyes widen. I feel dizzy. I curl my fingers around the edge of the countertop to keep myself upright. ‘Excuse me?’ I say, something between a whisper and a squeal. ‘Social media has been our lifeline! Since you stopped bringing any money in, those payments have kept us going.'

'I'll get a job,' he says, his voice still resolute. 'Work at Walmart if I have to.'

I start laughing, and it's manic and ugly but I can't stop. 'You think Walmart can pay this mortgage?! Have you completely lost your mind?!'

'Hey, Dad.'

I whip around. 'Maple,' I blurt out, heat flooding my neck. 'Dylan. I thought you guys were watching a movie in the den.'

'How was camping?' Maple asks, ignoring me, just like her siblings did. The vein in my neck starts to throb.

'Short but sweet,' Garrett answers. Then he shifts his gaze. 'And you must be Dylan.'

'Nice to meet you, Mr. Clark. Thank you for letting me stay in your beautiful home.'

Did you hear that? I want to scream. *Our beautiful home, Garrett. The one I've worked so hard for, that YouTube has made possible.* I push my lips together.

'The pleasure is ours,' Garrett says. 'Are you enjoying your stay?'

Dylan blinks, gives Maple a sideways glance, then blinks again. 'I am, yes,' he finally says.

Garrett nods, but there's an edge to Dylan's tone, and he must hear it because his face tightens. 'Why don't you kids take a day off filming today,' he says. 'Give yourselves a break and do something fun instead. After all, Kirsten will be too busy filming the twins' last ever video, won't you, hon?'

Chapter 32

Maple

The twins' last ever video. Dad's words bounce off the walls. Was Dylan right last night? Is Dad so mad about the kissing video that he's finally standing up to Mom? 'What do you mean their last ever video?' I ask.

'The twins are stopping the paid brand work going forward,' Dad explains in a voice I don't recognize, all authoritative and clear. 'And they're taking a break from YouTube in general.'

My eyes widen. 'No YouTube?'

'No more social media until they're thirteen. I've made my decision.'

I look at Mom. I promised myself I wouldn't – that I would never engage with her again after her latest betrayal – but I wasn't prepared for this news.

'We're still discussing it,' she says, her voice somehow both breezy and furious. 'Personally, I think they deserve the same opportunities as you've had. But Dad seems happy to decimate those.'

Opportunities? Like being lied about, made to look sleazy, for a few extra clicks?

'It's not up for discussion,' Dad says decisively. But then he turns to look at me, and his voice softens. 'Look, I get that there are positives to being an influencer, and you and Dylan are great examples of that. But it's different for the twins. Ash is camera-shy, and Aspen . . .' His brow furrows. 'Well, she's impulsive. She might do something one minute and regret it the next. She needs her privacy too.'

'And what about me?' I ask, trying to keep my voice steady. 'Do the same rules apply to me?'

He smiles. 'No of course not. I see how much you love it. And how much your subscribers love you. And I know how hard you've worked for this, how you've set yourself up for an amazing future as an influencer. I would never take that away from you.'

I nod. I don't know why. Inside I'm screaming to tell him that no, I don't want this anymore. That I hate how Mom lies about me, and how those gross men make me feel, and how embarrassing being filmed in a bikini is. And that if he took an ounce of interest in my content, he might hate it too.

But then, how would I feel if he banned me from social media? Because there are things I love about this lifestyle too. Like riding the Strip in that pink Cadillac in Vegas, and posing in a glass box, getting all those compliments from Lois and the Azione client. And the buzz I get out of how many followers I have, all the likes and comments, how my subscribers want to wear what I wear, use the products I promote.

Could I live without it? Or is a regular, normal life already too late for me?

'You know, I might go get some fresh air,' Dylan says. 'If that's okay with you all?'

'Of course it is,' Mom says, her sunshine smile back in place. 'Why don't you go with him, Maple honey? Leave me and Dad to talk some more.'

I glance at Dylan. I understand why Mom wants me out of the way, and that definitely works for me too. But Dylan probably wants time out from all of us, and I owe him that at least. But he gives me a tiny nod, and I take that as permission.

'Yeah, okay.' I gesture for Dylan to head to the front door and follow him out onto the sidewalk. 'Do you want to go to the park?' I ask.

'Will it be busy?'

I shrug. 'I guess. A lot of kids hang out there on school break.'

He doesn't respond, but in the silence, I realize why he's asking. And that makes my lungs feel like they're shrinking. I focus on breathing, trying to inflate them.

'D'you mind if we go someplace else?' he finally asks.

'Um, sure,' I murmur, my mind scrabbling for ideas. One comes to me, but I can hardly believe I'm suggesting it; I'm supposed to be a young adult. 'There's a tree on the corner,' I tell him. 'It's fat and flat, so I guess there's room for two.'

His forehead smooths out. 'Sounds perfect.'

We walk toward it without talking, but the noise in my head is deafening. We are famous now. We may be able to hide from it online – turn our phones off, our laptops, pretend it's not happening. But offline it's different.

We can't control what happens out there.

Chapter 33

Maple

'Hey, is this a maple tree?' Dylan asks, inspecting the jagged edges of the leaves as he shuffles back against a thick branch.

My face blushes. I don't know why. It's the only tree at the intersection of our road. But now that he's noticed, I feel like I'm aura farming.

'I don't know,' I lie. 'Maybe.'

He smiles. 'Nature really isn't your thing, hey?'

'I guess not.'

He laughs. 'So what is your thing, Maybe Maple?'

The bark on the tree is smooth, almost shiny, and as I lean back against the branch to consider Dylan's question, I feel its warmth on my back. It's true that maple trees don't usually require much skill or nerve to climb. But there was one in the park near our last house, and I would love climbing that when I was a little kid. Does that mean I was into nature like the twins back then? Did we all miss that about me?

'I guess clothes mainly,' I say, knowing it's not true. My mom provides my wardrobe – with Maddie's help. 'Makeup, skin products, jewelry, you know,' I continue, as though it might help convince us both.

Dylan nods. 'Well, I guess that makes sense, with how your channel is.'

His words are neutral, but he looks disappointed, and it makes me want to tell him the truth. That I don't really care about any of that stuff. But then he would ask what I do care about, and I'd have to admit there's nothing. That I'm so busy being Maybe Maple for my subscribers, and my mom, and Maddie, and our mortgage payments, that I don't have time to think about who I really am.

'How do you think the twins will take the news about their social media ban?' Dylan asks, reading the silence – correctly – as a sign to move on. 'Not sure I'd have loved a no YouTube rule when I was their age.'

'If it gets that far,' I say. 'In our family, Mom always gets her way.' I think about that video again, the sticker – FIRST KISS!!

'Well, I hope your dad gets a win on this,' Dylan says quietly. He drops his head forward, ruffles his hair. I've noticed he does this when he's embarrassed, or unsure about something, like when he told me he wants to be a human rights lawyer. I built up a certain picture of Dylan Dope from his Instagram posts, but he's not really that guy at all.

'Are you going to talk to your dad?' I ask. 'About making less content and having more time to study?'

He shakes his head, then looks up at the higher branches and smiles. 'Sadly, my dad is nothing like yours. Not exactly the introspective type. He'd never think about how social media could be damaging, especially not when there's all those dollars to be made. Shit knows what he's going to think about your mom's latest prank. He might love it; he might hate it. Either way though, he's gonna have an opinion.'

'You make out like my dad's a saint,' I say. 'But I'm in the same boat you are. And at least your dad has a job. I'm the only one earning anything in my family.' From nowhere, I feel my eyes grow hot and I blink to fan them cool. 'You know, it's weird,' I go on. 'Hearing him so desperate to protect the twins when he said nothing like that about me when I was their age.' I swallow. 'It's almost like he loves them more than me.'

Dylan drops his gaze to look at me. 'Listen, it won't be that,' he says. 'Remember, six years ago, when you were eight, kids being on social media was only about the upsides. The fun, the popularity, and the "oh wait, we can make money out of this too?" Your dad had no reason to worry back then, did he? No context for it.'

'And now?' I push.

'Well, you're older now. And you heard him. He thinks that you love it too much to stop. He probably thinks you're a pro too, that you can handle the bad shit.'

'I'm not sure I can,' I admit in a whisper.

'No, of course you can't. Because it's impossible to. Social media is a colossus. No one can control it or outsmart it, and especially not a bunch of minors. Just look at what happened to Ella Hart.'

Ella Hart. I know the name, of course, but I haven't heard it spoken in a while. Ella is the eldest child of the Hart family, who are huge influencers on YouTube – their @7Harts channel has got over eight million subscribers. They live in Austin, Texas, and are all blond-haired, blue-eyed and super cute. Ella's a talented dancer, and she went to London in England to follow her dreams.

'What do you mean?' I ask. 'What happened to Ella Hart?'

Chapter 34

Maple

Dylan raises his eyebrows. 'She couldn't take it anymore – that's what they say. And now she's missing.'

'But Ella went to England,' I say. 'Her mom made a short about it, how she'd been selected by some fancy dance school.'

'Yeah, the Royal Ballet School in London,' Dylan says, nodding. 'That's the official line. Except apparently, it's complete bullshit.'

'What? No.' I shake my head. 'I remember her mom talking about how proud she was of her beautiful firstborn, blah blah blah.'

'Yeah, but the rumor is her mom made the whole thing up. To cover up the truth.'

'Why? What is the truth?'

'They had a huge fight, and Ella ran away. Lots of screaming and shouting, then Ella spun off in her car and no one has heard from her since. At least, none of her friends have, and no one believes anything her family says. Loads of people think she's dead and her mom's covering that up too.'

'What people? Where are you getting this from?'

Dylan shrugs, dips his head, ruffles his hair. 'A couple of gaming groups I'm in.'

‘Gamers? What the hell would they know about it?’

‘Ella’s neighbor in Austin is this guy called Tommy G. He’s big into *Grand Theft Auto* and livestreams on Twitch the whole time. Rumor goes that he heard the argument, then watched Ella drive away super-fast through his bedroom window. He says her mom made up the ballet story as a way of explaining why Ella had gone AWOL on her socials.’

‘And you know Tommy G?’

Dylan shakes his head. ‘Not personally, but some of the guys I game with do.’

I give him a skeptical look. ‘Sounds like bullshit to me. I mean, yeah, Selena Hart does come across pretty fake. But no mom would make up a story that wild about their own daughter.’

‘Your mom told the world that we kissed, and that’s pretty fucking wild.’

A mix of shame and embarrassment and, for some weird reason, guilt, blurs my vision. Shit. I need to bring the conversation back to Ella. ‘Well, it must be easy enough to find out,’ I say. ‘I mean, if Ella’s in London, people will have seen her there.’

‘Yeah, I guess.’

I expect him to say more, so when he doesn’t, I try again. ‘So have they? Have people seen her in London?’

‘I don’t know.’

‘You haven’t checked?’

‘Sorry, but why would I check?’ Dylan asks, looking genuinely confused. ‘I don’t know her.’

‘So you’re happy to spread rumors about her, but not find out if they’re true? Listen, if she’s run away, and no one’s seen her for eighteen months, and her parents don’t care, then it could be bad. Especially if no one’s looking for her. Your friends are gossiping about her being dead, but what if she really is? Or what if she's alive and in trouble?'

'I guess I haven't given it much thought.'

He looks embarrassed now, and I feel an unfamiliar sense of power for causing it. I've listened to Coco talk about getting justice for Sophie Lyle loads of times and have felt really proud of her. But what's stopping me from doing something similar?

'So we should check, right?' I press. 'Because if she is in London, we have nothing to worry about.'

'I guess, but how? I don't know anyone in England.'

I sigh. 'Me neither. Farthest I've traveled is Nevada.' I twist my heel against the trunk's bole and try not to think about the camping trips to Colorado and Montana that my dad's taken the twins on. And whether social media might one day break me like Tommy G said it did to Ella. And if it did, whether my mom would be cruel enough to cover it up. 'But I do have nearly two million followers on YouTube.'

Dylan's face lights up, but slowly, like it's on a dimmer switch. 'Maybe some of them live in London,' he says.

'Yeah. And Austin. Maybe someone who even knew Ella.'

'Her mom's gonna get mad if we start asking questions.'

'Only if she's got something to hide.'

Dylan nods slowly. 'You think we can find Ella?'

'I don't know,' I admit. 'But wouldn't it be wild to use social media to get to the truth, rather than to tell a bunch of lies?'

Chapter 35

Kirsten

My head hurts. Why does my head hurt? I try opening my eyes, but bright sunlight floods in, so I screw them closed again, roll onto my side, away from the window. My brain throbs. What the hell is wrong with me?

But slowly, it starts to make sense.

Garrett took the twins to his parents for a sleepover last night. He said they'd invited him, but I knew that was bullshit. He was just scared I'd make him fold like a pancake on the twins' social media ban if he stuck around, which I totally would have done. I guess that's why his absence was so frustrating. Frustrating enough for me to drive over to a liquor store and buy myself a bottle of wine, as it turned out. Maple and Dylan were hanging out downstairs, so I was forced to sit on my bed like a broke student. And somehow, drink the whole bottle.

And what the hell was Garrett thinking anyway, telling those two teenagers they didn't need to do any filming when practically everyone on the internet was salivating for more content from them? When they got back from their little outing, hungry, because of course Maple still expects me to stock the fridge twenty-four-seven, they point-blank refused to do any filming. If Dylan wasn't here, I'd have made Maple see sense, but it's more delicate when there's a guest in the house. Which meant I had to get all my footage covertly. I filmed just enough to keep the story alive I think, but they didn't make it easy for me.

I spent the rest of the day getting the twins' unboxing video filmed. It should have been a breeze – the airplane launchers are a great toy – but Aspen was still angry about missing out on camping, and Ash was tired and emotional. After a few aborted attempts, I called time-out and suggested we bake cookies instead (which of course I filmed and uploaded because fuck you, Garrett), and that put smiles on their faces, thank goodness. I think the sugar rush helped too, because the next attempt at the unboxing video went like a dream.

'Daddy, where's Mommy?'

As Ash's voice floats up the stairs, I realize it must be late, the three of them back already, so I reach for my phone: 9.13 a.m. Damn, it is late. Especially in hardworking, God-fearing Utah. I push up to sitting and release a groan. Why do I think drinking is the answer when it so clearly isn't? This is my mom's fault for being a bad role model.

As I unlock my phone screen, I notice there's a new message on Telegram. I hesitate. Did I message Blake from that modeling agency last night? Yes, maybe I did. My heart clicks up a gear as I try to remember what I said, how I worded it. I have the tendency to overshare after a couple of drinks.

With growing unease, I click into the app and see that the message is indeed from Blake. But instead of reading it, I scroll up to remind myself what I wrote. There are five photos of Maple. Two of them are from last week in Vegas, and the others are photos I've taken at home when she's looked particularly gorgeous, the last one in that Abercrombie Kids bikini. Stunning.

Nothing to regret so far. I read the message I sent with the photos.

Hi Blake,
This is Kirsten, Maple Clark's mom. It was so good to see your email – thank you so much! Yes, Maple is absolutely looking to further her modeling career, and your agency sounds perfect for her. I am including 5 photos of Maple, but I have thousands of others, of course, so please just ask if you'd like to see more. What are the next steps? Would it make sense for you to meet Maple in person? I really think you'll fall in love with her if you do!

I grimace a little at my last sentence; maybe 'fall in love' sounds a bit desperate. But then again, isn't that how everyone in the fashion industry talks? No, this is just my hangxiety. I shake the worry away and scroll down to Blake's response.

Hi Kirsten,
Thanks for the photos. These are perfect, although feel free to send more anytime. I think it would make sense for me to meet Maple. Thank you for offering that. I just need to figure out how best to arrange it. I'll be in touch again soon.

Perfect. She thinks the photos are perfect! I throw back the duvet. Dylan is leaving this morning, and I'm impatient to have Maple all to myself again. Having him here has been amazing for Maple's profile, but she has become even more classic teenager since he arrived, and I'm feeling a loosening of control that I'm not really enjoying. So it's time he left. Especially now I've had this good news from Blake.

Chapter 36

Him

He can barely climb into his truck, he's so tired. But he's got a new job starting today, and he can't afford to be late. He hoists himself in, then leans back against the grimy headrest to catch his breath. As his heavy eyelids droop, he sees the images again, and despite how he's feeling, they make him smile.

Because they're the reason he stayed up most of the night staring at his laptop. The five photos that he couldn't drag his eyes away from. He enjoyed zooming in on the bits he wanted to see more of, stroking her young, fresh features through the screen. Yes, it had made him yearn for things beyond his grasp, and that had brought a certain amount of frustration. But it was worth it.

She is worth it.

He drops the old Ford into gear and pulls out of the trailer park and onto the I-11 highway. His life wasn't supposed to turn out this way. He had dreams once. Ha! Imagine that. A fuck-up like him believing he could make something of himself in Vegas. He'd known within a year that it wasn't going to happen, but he'd kept pretending for another ten or so. Drugs are good like that, making you think that anything's possible when evidence to the contrary is staring you in the fucking eye.

He's done with that now though. Moved on. He knows who he is, what he's capable of, and what he isn't. He's got weaknesses, yeah, but there are worse men than him out there. So if everyone just leaves him alone, doesn't question why he goes straight home after work every night, except that one night a week when he feeds a habit too good to break, then life will be fine. Not perfect, but fine.

Except now he knows it could be more than fine.

He grips the steering wheel, fights the urge to press hard on the accelerator.

Jesus, he wants access to her, real physical access.

I think it would make sense for me to meet Maple. I just need to figure out how best to arrange it.

Really, he should have thought of an actual plan before responding, a way to see Maple without her mom asking questions or getting in the way. But he was too excited about the photos, too impatient to download them to his computer so he could study them in detail. So he wrote the first thing that came to mind, a holding message to give himself time to think.

Because does he definitely want to see her? He has the photos now. Maybe they could be enough. He knows that anything more brings risk, the potential for things to go very wrong. The thought makes his cheeks feel hot behind his beard, despite the aircon blasting in his face.

But he's been choosing the easy option his whole life, hasn't he? The coward's way out. Isn't it time for him to be brave? To go the fuck out there and grab what he wants for a change? And it might not be that hard, anyway. When he sent that first email, he knew it was suspicious. No name or address for his fake modeling agency in case she Googled it. A gender-neutral name, no surname. Requesting the photos via Telegram and pretending it was for Maple's benefit not his. But that woman still fell for it all.

Maybe setting up a face-to-face meeting wouldn't be that hard either.

Of course that wouldn't be the end of it. There would be a rocky road ahead, lots of decisions to make, and plenty of convincing to do. But it might work. Maybe – some fucking sliver of a maybe, for sure – Maple would learn to love him like he has already learned to love her.

I really think you'll fall in love with her if you do!

Oh Jesus Christ, if she only knew the truth.

He pulls into the staff parking lot of the MGM Grand. Drops his eyelids again. Sees her pretty face, her caramel eyes and bright smile.

He'll think of a plan to get her back out to Vegas. He has to.

Because whatever risks lie ahead, there's no turning back now.

Chapter 37

Kirsten

'Thank you for your hospitality, Mrs. Clark.'

Dylan's words are polite, but his tone is ice-cold, and for the first time, my conscience wobbles a little about that first-kiss video. But no. Maybe I've made an enemy of Dylan, but the level of engagement we've had shows it was worth it. Maple has had a big presence on YouTube for years, but getting that same recognition on TikTok and Instagram has been difficult. Until now. Yes, the modeling for Azione got her noticed, but it's this thing with Dylan that's taking her viral.

And how could I regret that?

'Not at all, Dylan,' I say with my brightest smile. 'The pleasure is all ours. I hope you can come again one day.'

He gives me a tight smile and turns to Maple. Without saying anything, she follows him through our front door, as though they can read each other's minds now. I watch them walk down the drive together, then stop a few feet away from Dylan's father's Subaru. I film them saying goodbye, just in case, but there's nothing exciting about it, so I delete the video.

Finally the car speeds off, and my excitement grows again as I picture Maple's thrilled expression when I tell her about

Blake's modeling agency. But before I get chance to say anything, she brushes past me and mumbles something about going for a swim. I feel a stab of frustration – but the twins are in the pool with Garrett; it makes sense that she'd want to join them.

In fact, maybe I should get in too. Some fresh, cool water to wash away the remnants of that wine. And it might provide the perfect opportunity to get Garrett back on side; he's never been able to resist me in a two-piece.

Ten minutes later, I slip my robe off and slide into the water.

'Mommy!' Ash shouts, twisting around as he notices me. 'Help me get up!' His skinny arms are curled around Maple's sparkly pink float, and his legs are causing an almighty splash as he tries to create enough momentum to lift himself up. My heart tugs a little and I swim over to hoist him on top.

'Yay!' he shouts out, before toppling over the other side. He comes up giggling. 'That was so fun! Can we do it again?'

Suddenly a head pops out of the water. Slicked-back blond hair, jade green goggles to match her eyes, and a cheeky grin. 'No, it's my turn.'

'Hey, no!'

Ash and Aspen both grab the float and start climbing onto it. Of course Aspen gets there first, but then she reaches for her brother's hand, and he slithers up the wet plastic.

'Let's pretend it's a canoe!' Ash suggests. 'And we're on the Green River.' He straightens his arms, like paddles, and pushes them through the water. 'Look, there's an otter!'

'Is that a golden eagle in the trees?' Aspen asks, curling her fingers into makeshift binoculars.

God, how I ache to film this. To show the world how wholesome, imaginative and truly wonderful my family is. How can Garrett not get that? He has got it so wrong with all that nonsense about the kids needing privacy, or how filming content causes them stress. Sure, there are downsides, but what lifestyle choice doesn't have those? Why can't Garrett focus on all the good things that come with being popular on YouTube?

With a new sense of resolve, I shift my gaze toward him. He's standing at the shallow end playing skip ball with Maple, a smug smile on his face as the ball bounces across the sparkling water between them. He thinks he's won the argument, I can see that. And while that's aggravating, it also means his guard is down. Which everyone knows is the perfect time to attack.

I swim slowly toward him, close enough that our bodies touch as I rise out of the water.

Chapter 38

Kirsten

'See, isn't this more fun than worrying about camera angles or catching the right light?' Garrett asks. 'Actually being present with the kids?'

I feel a vague urge to slap his face, but I give him my best Mormon smile instead. 'It was a great idea of yours,' I say. 'Some family time, having a break from filming.'

The skip ball lands on the water in front of him, and he picks it up, but doesn't throw it back to Maple. Just squeezes it hard. 'It's not a break, remember,' he says. 'This ban is permanent. The twins are not going to be influencers like Maple. And you know, after seeing how much Maple enjoyed her day off yesterday, I even wonder if this lifestyle choice is right for her.'

Despite my best efforts, rage bubbles. I know what he's doing. By bringing Maple into the argument, raising the stakes, he's giving himself a negotiating position, hoping I'll settle with just the twins missing out.

'I don't see why you get to make that decision,' I say cooly. 'When our entire income comes from the kids' social media earnings.'

'Because I'm their father,' he answers. 'And the head of this household.'

'So you're spouting some priesthood bullshit at me now?'

'Kirsten!' he admonishes.

A loud splash distracts us, and I turn toward it. The twins have jumped off the float and are swimming toward the steps, fast.

'I'm gonna get out now too!' Maple calls out. 'Thanks for the game, Dad!'

I watch our three children vacate the pool like it's a fire drill, desperate not to hear us argue, and it makes me sad. Our family life was supposed to be perfect; that's how I planned it, right from the moment I found out I was pregnant with Maple. There were obstacles along the way, for sure, and Garrett knows the sacrifices I've made, yet he's still prepared to pull patriarchal rank.

'YouTube paid for this pool,' I remind him softly. 'Our mortgage payments are significant, and social media pays generously. The twins will earn two thousand bucks for that unboxing video, which will cover all our groceries for a month, with change.'

'It's their money,' Garrett mutters. 'We shouldn't be spending it.'

'You want to pick up the Smith's tab next time I go for groceries?'

He glares at me. 'Actually, I might have a job interview soon,' he finally says.

'What?' I scoff. 'You've been out of work for nearly a year, and you magic up an interview on the first day of the twins' ban?'

'At Zion National Park,' he continues, not rising to my bait. 'My old manager moved there and said he'd make sure there'd be a job for me if I wanted it. I didn't follow him up on it at the time because I thought the move wouldn't be good for the kids. But you've enrolled Maple in online school anyway. And I think a big change is just what the twins need right now.'

I clench my fists to cope with the rising panic in my chest. 'You can't make me leave this house. I love this house.'

'And its significant mortgage payments?' he throws back. Then he sighs. 'Look, I think this will be good for all of us, our marriage included.'

'Not Maple,' I counter. 'She'll hate you for making her leave her friends.'

'But that's what you want, isn't it? For Maple to drop her school friends and build connections with other influencers online – which she can do from anywhere. Dylan lives close to Zion, and they seemed to be getting on pretty well yesterday.'

I'm not leaving this house. And Garrett is not making these big life decisions for me. Only right now, I can't figure out how to make that clear. 'I'm getting out,' I declare. Then I wade to the edge of the pool and climb the steps.

I grab a towel, pick my phone off the garden table, and drop onto a sun lounger, taking care to look at my screen, and not my husband. There's a new message on Telegram and I click straight into it.

Hi Kirsten,
We're still very keen to meet Maple. We're based in New York, but I'm flying to Vegas next week, which I think is closer for you. I don't have much time between meetings, but I do have two front-row tickets to Cirque du Soleil at the MGM Grand next Tuesday evening and I was hoping Maple could join me. It's always helpful to get to know our clients before we sign. I hope she can make it.
Blake

I lurch forward onto my sit bones. Excitement explodes in my belly. It looks like fame and fortune are heading Maple's way despite her father's meddling. And front-row seats at Cirque du Soleil? Blake must really want to sign her. Except there are only two tickets, which means it will just be Blake and Maple. I frown. Is that safe?

But it's a theater, I remind myself. Not a private office or hotel room. I can deliver Maple to the door, then collect her when it finishes. And in between, she'll be surrounded by all the other theater-goers. Of course it's safe.

I send a quick message accepting, then stand up. I want to tell Maple we're heading back to Vegas. But my head is pounding again; I need a nap first.

Chapter 39

Maple

I pull the door quietly behind me and tiptoe down the drive. It's early – I think everyone else is still asleep – but I've been awake for ages. Too excited to sleep maybe, now that I have a purpose. Because I spent most of yesterday researching Ella Hart, and it is kind of a head-fuck that she seems to have completely vanished. I'm hooked on finding her now.

I reach the maple tree and climb up. Since Dylan and I hung out here on Tuesday, it's become like my personal retreat. I came yesterday, after Mom and Dad started fighting in the pool, and it was so peaceful. No one nagging me to film a reel, or a short, or do a prank, or an unboxing. In fact, no one noticing me at all.

So I'm back, with my phone and a notebook. Ready to do more research into Ella Hart.

Yesterday, I checked out the Hart family socials, both refreshing my memory and picking up some new stuff. Ella has two brothers and two sisters. Her mom, Selena, was a model before she had kids, and her dad, Bodi, was in a boy band called Crush. They described themselves as a west coast NSYNC, but it turned out Bodi was no Justin Timberlake because his singing career was crushed – of course that's how TMZ styled it – after one album.

Still, the Harts live in a huge ranch-style house in Austin now, with a pool, and stables, and a totally lit games room, so I guess he bounced back. And I'm pretty sure that's courtesy of YouTube because their @7Harts<3 channel – five kids, two parents, seven hearts – gets wild stats. Ella started her own TikTok and Instagram accounts when she was thirteen, same as me (although I'm trying not to think too hard about our parallels), and her last post on both channels went up two weeks after she turned eighteen; two days before Dylan says she ran away.

Ella is an amazing dancer, and a lot of her posts are of her doing some form of that – ballet, contemporary, hip-hop, street dance. In her early posts she looks happy and bouncy, a bit extra maybe, but like she's loving life. But something changed about a year before she disappeared. She dyed her hair, and started dressing kinda emo, with heavier makeup in some posts, and none at all in others. Her dancing style changed too. Still beautiful, but slower, and to sad Billie Eilish tracks rather than more upbeat hip-hop stuff.

Her last post was a reel on New Year's Eve 2024. Ella deciding what to wear for her night out. But her back is to the camera because she's facing her closet, commenting on different outfits. And that's it. She still has over a million followers, but nothing new on her grid.

Then there's one more post about her. Selena's YouTube short – posted on January 4th, 2025 – where she explains that Ella has won a place at the Royal Ballet School in London. She says they're all super thrilled, but Ella's intense schedule along with the school's strict phone rules, means that she won't be on social media for a while. The post finishes with a collection of photos of Ella to a schmaltzy Mariah Carey song, and the last shot is Ella standing on a bridge with a backdrop I recognize from *Heartstopper*. The show that's filmed in London.

But of course it doesn't really mean that she's there because everyone knows how easy it is to edit a photo. And there's nothing about Ella on the Royal Ballet's website. Except maybe they don't showcase dancers until they finish training?

My phone buzzes. It's Coco FaceTiming me and I quickly accept the call. It's not the best signal up here, but I can still tell that she's frowning.

'Hey, babe,' she says. 'Are you in that tree again?'

I smile. 'Is that bad?'

'I guess it depends whether you're doing it because you identify as a monkey now, or because you're hiding from your mom.'

'Definitely the second one,' I promise. 'I've been looking into Ella Hart some more.'

'Oh, right. That's great, babe.'

I feel a swell of relief. When I first told Coco about Dylan's take on Ella's disappearance, and how I felt this compulsion to find her, she seemed a bit salty, like I was treading on her toes or something. So I explained how she'd inspired me, and how good it felt to finally have something to focus on. She warmed up after that, and it's good to know she's still feeling the same way.

'Have you found out anything new?' she asks.

'Not yet,' I admit. 'But there's definitely something weird going on. For one, the only picture I could find of Ella in London was the one her mom put up. And also, she totally changed her vibe in the year before she disappeared. I'm sure she was freaking out about something.'

'Sounds like her mom's worse than yours,' Coco says. 'Are you sure you want to prod that bear?'

I consider that, and how my gut is telling me that Selena Hart's lying to protect herself without giving a shit about her daughter. 'Yeah, I'm sure. I just don't know exactly how to do it. I want to use my platform, but Mom runs my YouTube channel, and there's no way she'd let me go that far off brand. I could do a Live on Instagram or TikTok, but I'm just a kid who does stupid lip synchs on there. Who would take me seriously, or even bother to watch?'

She tips her head in thought. 'Why not set up a new YouTube channel? Maybe brand it to show you're serious. Maple Uncovers or something like that.'

I kick my foot against the fat branch. 'You think I could?'

'You're Maybe Maple. You can do anything. You really need to start believing in yourself more.'

Chapter 40

Maple

I snap Dylan.

I think we should do this.

It's funny. A week ago, I was freaking out about him coming to stay. Now, it doesn't feel like a big deal to ask for his help.

I think Coco's right about setting up a dedicated channel to search for Ella, but I don't want to go it alone. I have decent numbers on social media, but not enough to get the traction this will need. But if I join forces with Dylan, maybe together we will. When that fake kiss was just for clicks, or brand deals, it felt gross and embarrassing. But if we could use the gossip it caused to get people caring about Ella's welfare, maybe it could be worth it.

He responds with a lightbulb emoji, and I roll my eyes. This feels too important to communicate via snaps.

Can you FaceTime?

A minute later, his face appears on my screen. 'Hey,' he says. 'How's your crazy mom?'

I click my tongue. 'I don't know; I'm keeping out of her way. How about your dad?' I look down to avoid eye contact. 'Was he mad about the whole first-kiss bullshit?'

'Nah, it wasn't too bad.' Dylan ruffles his hair. 'He said the mind-blowing stats made up for me behaving like a dick, just about.'

'But you told him it wasn't real though? That Mom made it up?'

'Honestly, there's no point. Laying low is always the best way to handle him.'

My shoulders sink. 'I guess you're probably not going to be into my idea then.'

'Try me.'

'You know how we were talking about Ella Hart the other day? And how we could use our platforms to find her?'

'Yeah.'

'Well, I want to go all in,' I say, trying to make out like it's the best idea ever. 'Start a new YouTube channel, maybe interview people close to her, or her family. Kinda crowd-source information so that we can work out where she is.'

'Sounds cool,' he says, but his tone doesn't give much away. I take a breath.

'And I want us to do it together,' I say. 'Reach out to both our fan bases, you know? Plus, if we start a joint channel, and maybe keep the reason vague at first, well, all those people gossiping about us; it might get their attention.' I scrape my lip. 'And anyway, it was you who told me about Ella going missing in the first place, and you seemed up for helping then.'

He nods but doesn't speak so I keep going. 'Coco thinks I should call it Maple Uncovers. But if we're doing it together then we'll obviously need a different name and . . .'

'Wait, Maple Uncovers?'

'Um, yeah.'

'Isn't that for a different kind of channel? You know, like OnlyFans or something?'

I think about it for a millisecond and then it hits me. Oh God. Maples *uncovers*. Heat surges into my cheeks and my vision blurs; I think I might faint. It's only a stupid name, a silly mistake, but it's like the whole of last week has built into this one tsunami of embarrassment. It must show on my face too, because Dylan's eyes widen.

'Hey, I'm sorry,' he says. 'I didn't mean . . .'

'It's fine,' I say, trying to breathe. 'You're right; it's a stupid idea.'

'No, it's not,' he says quickly. 'It's a good idea. A great idea. Like you said, Ella doesn't have anyone looking out for her, so we might actually do something good.'

I risk looking straight at him. 'You think?'

'For sure. And it'll expose Selena Hart as a liar. Get one back for the kids.'

'Does that mean you'll do it with me?'

He ruffles his hair, sighs, then looks away.

'Your dad won't like it,' I murmur. 'I shouldn't have asked.'

'My dad will hate it,' Dylan says, nodding thoughtfully. 'But how can I say I want to be a human rights lawyer and then be too scared to help someone who might be in trouble?'

'Because he's your dad, and you live in his house.'

'Yeah, and I'm sixteen soon, and stronger than him, and maybe it's about time I built a spine.'

I feel the pull of a smile, but I resist it. I need Dylan to be certain. 'Are you sure about this?'

'I'm bored of Dad telling me to jump and me asking how high, sometimes literally. I want to skateboard at the weekend, when it's sunny, with my friends. Not every day. Not do the same trick a hundred times over because the light is wrong, or whatever. I want to study, make an actual difference. So yeah, I'm sure. Fuck him.'

I feel a swell of something like pride or power or shared endeavor in my chest. 'What will we call it? Our channel?'

'How about just Maple and Dylan?' he suggests. 'Then people can think what they want.'

'Maple and Dylan,' I repeat slowly, as though I'm considering it. When actually I'm just trying to hold my shit together. *Because he said my name first.*

Chapter 41

Kirsten

I hear the front door swing open, lay my palms flat on the counter, and wait for Maple to appear. She has been either moody or absent since Dylan left, and I have zero patience left. Everyone has off days, sure, but I need her to refocus now on what we're building together. Especially with Garrett getting on his high horse about the twins, and then threatening to stop Maple too. And now he's talking about us moving away. Honestly, it's so tiring being the only one who knows what's best for this family.

I managed to film enough covert content on Tuesday to pull together a reel of Maple with Dylan that was just about suggestive enough to keep followers' tongues wagging. But there's been a content drought since, and we're starting to lose followers. It's so frustrating. This collaboration with Dylan is Maple's best chance at making it into the super league and she's throwing it away. Well, I'm not letting it happen. Especially with a new modeling contract in the balance.

'Oh, hey,' Maple says with as much energy as a corpse.

'Hi, my gorgeous Maple honey,' I respond, injecting enough sparkle for both of us. 'You went out early. What have you been up to?'

'Um, I was at Martha's.'

'No you weren't. I looked on Find My iPhone. You were up the street somewhere.'

Her eyes narrow. 'Why are you tracking me? I'm nearly fifteen!'

I could remind her that it's my job to keep her safe, and that there are real dangers out there. But that's not the message I want to be conveying this morning. 'I'm sorry, honey, you're right. But listen, I've got some exciting news.'

'Oh yeah?' Maple pulls open the fridge door and grabs a slice of cheese. She peels away the plastic cover and folds it into her mouth – like it's a stick of sugar-free gum, and not a slab of saturated fat. I breathe out, tell myself that it's only one slice. And if the worst happens, there's always Wegovy.

'An international modeling agency has been in touch,' I say. 'They've seen your Azione work, and they want to sign you. Isn't that amazing?'

Finally, she looks semi-interested. 'Like a proper one?'

'Yes!' I walk closer, stroke her hair. She leans back against the countertop. 'They're based in New York,' I say. 'Which is obviously quite a trek for us, but Blake, who runs it, is going to be in Vegas next week. She asked if you'd meet her there.'

'Meet her in Vegas?'

'Exactly. And she's got front-row tickets to Cirque du Soleil at the MGM Grand on Tuesday evening and wants to take you as her guest. Isn't that so cool?'

'It is cool, I suppose,' Maple says, her forehead creasing. 'But I don't really want to go back to Vegas right now. Can we not just have a meeting on Zoom or something?'

'No, Maple, we can't.'

'Why not?'

'Well . . .' I stutter to a stop. Because I'm not totally sure why not. Blake has Maple's photos, and I offered to send her more. And modeling is all about photos, isn't it? But you don't offer a child amazing tickets to a Vegas show for no reason, and the last thing we want to do is disappoint her, especially with Garrett making things so difficult. I already feel like I'm hanging off a precipice and it's Blake who's holding the rope.

'Modeling isn't just about how you look, is it?' I continue, finding my groove. 'They'll want to know you're a hard worker, disciplined, ambitious. And that you eat and drink healthily,' I add pointedly as she opens the fridge door again.

She sighs, closes the fridge, and turns back to me. 'What's the agency called? I'll check them out, then decide if I want to go.'

I feel a sudden flushing in my cheeks. I don't know the agency name. Why didn't I ask Blake that? 'I can't remember it right now,' I say, flicking the question away. I'm not letting an inadvertent oversight get in the way of Maple's future. 'I'll check the email and let you know. But you don't want to miss this opportunity; they don't come around often.'

Maple straightens up, and I suddenly realize that she's as tall as me. It's unnerving, this aesthetic of equality. 'Like I said, I'll check them out,' she mutters. Then she grabs another slice of cheese before I can stop her, and walks out of the kitchen. I blow out a long, loud sigh, which helps more than I'd expect, and pick up my phone. I message Blake first – *Could you remind me of your agency name please?* – then do my usual checks across our various social channels. There's a new reel on Maple's TikTok and Instagram. I narrow my eyes, tap the screen to play the video. And it's Maple telling the world she's starting a new YouTube channel with Dylan.

What the hell is this? I manage Maple's YouTube content, not Maple. I lean back against the counter, play the reel again. How dare she do this without checking with me first?

Except.

Maple & Dylan is a genius idea. And the reel is eye-catching; Maple looking gorgeous and also a tiny bit in love. I feel a smile edge its way onto my face. I thought Maple's recent reluctance to film was about laziness, or hormones, or just being a stubborn teenager. But is it actually about ambition? And wanting more control over her career direction?

I feel an unfamiliar sense of admiration as I leave the kitchen, climb the stairs, and knock on Maple's door, impatient to find out more about this new channel. Because maybe we're finally becoming equals in more ways than our height.

Chapter 42

Him

He stares at the message, feels an unnecessary surge of rage. Of course she would ask this. She's a shit mother; he's pretty sure of that. But even a shit mother gets curious eventually.

He just wishes it had happened after Tuesday. When it was too late.

It would be easy to make up a name for his fake modeling agency, but then she'd search for it. He could probably pull together a website – he's got no qualifications, but if you spend a lot of time online, you pick things up – but that wouldn't be enough. Instagram, Facebook, LinkedIn, Substack. Press articles, photos, models, clients. He doesn't work for the NSI for fuck's sake; he can't create a fake digital footprint overnight.

He kicks the box in front of him. Turns out it's metal and his foot screams in pain.

'Hey! What the fuck are you doing?'

'Sorry, man.' He shuffles off the stage, behind the scenes, where he feels safer. He got this job as a favor, and it's a sweet gig, part of the lighting crew for the new Cirque du Soleil show. It's grunt work really: changing bulbs, fixing stuff, keeping the lights clean. But the pay is decent, and no one hassles him for

more effort. He'd be crazy to piss his manager off, at least right now, with no upside to it. Of course, if by some miracle Maple comes on Tuesday, he'll do whatever it takes, use his access-all-areas pass however he needs, if it means getting some private time with her.

But that dream is slipping away now. Because he doesn't know what to say to her mother, Kirsten. How to answer her question and still stop her becoming suspicious.

He sets the ladder against the wall and climbs. He likes being up here, staring down at the stage, no one realizing, or caring, that he's there. He's seen things in his time. Arguments, romances, deal making, some legit, some less so. And stuff the left-wing media would get all righteous over. The #metoo rulebook playing out between directors and actors, choreographers and showgirls. He knows it's wrong, if he takes a moment to think about it, but there's no way he's getting involved. Him taking some kind of moral stand? It makes him laugh just thinking about it. And anyway, the last thing he needs is scrutiny.

Especially now. If she comes.

But she won't come, will she? Not without a name for his stupid fake modeling agency.

He grimaces, fights the urge to punch the gloomy light he's up here to fix.

Why did he come up with such a crap plan? Of course it was never going to work.

But he can't fail, not now, not after thinking about her constantly, after spending every spare moment staring at those photos or her YouTube channel. He needs to see her in the flesh. To talk to her, touch her. Be alone with her. And then, who knows. But something good, he hopes. Something life-affirming.

Which means he needs a better plan.

Chapter 43

Maple & Dylan

Maple: *Hey, everyone! Welcome to our new channel. I'm Maybe Maple, talking to you from Provo.*
Dylan: *And I'm Dylan Dope, down in St George in south Utah.*
Maple: *Now, you're probably wondering why we've set up a channel together.*
Dylan: *And news flash, it isn't what you're thinking.*
Maple: *No, we've got a much more important reason than that. You guys all remember Ella Hart, right? Maybe you heard that she went to London in England to train to be a ballerina? Well, we've been told—*
Dylan: *By a very credible source.*
Maple: *Yeah, someone who actually knew Ella and her family, that the whole ballet story is fake news. And that the truth is Ella had a big fight with her mom in early January last year and ran away. But Selena Hart, her mom, didn't want to admit that, so she made up a bullshit narrative about ballet to cover up why Ella stopped posting on social media. And no one has seen Ella since. Which we think is very sus.*

Dylan: *But we don't know any of this for sure. I mean, they could have had a fight, and Ella still made it to London. Or there's a chance our source could be wrong. But if she did take off by herself, where is she now? That was eighteen months ago. It's one thing to want a break from social media, but who stays offline for that long?*

Maple: *And so we've started this channel to find Ella in case she's in trouble. And we need your help.*

Dylan: *Yeah, we want this to be a community thing. So if you know where Ella is, or have something you want to say, jump into the Live Chat and we'll talk about it. Also, if you are Ella, and you want us to quit looking for you, just tell us and we're gone.*

Maple: *But for all the rest of you, in case you can't remember what she looks like, we're showing some pictures of her now.*

Dylan: *Okay, guys, we're loving the chat, but remember this is about finding Ella, not about whether Maple and I are dating, which we're not, by the way.*

Maple: *No. Definitely not. Okay, anyway, hey look Dylan, LoobyTrue101 has said something interesting. She met the whole Hart family at a YouTube meet-and-greet event in the summer before Ella disappeared. She says they all seemed super nice, but Ella had some bruises on her arm, like someone had gripped her really hard.*

Dylan: *Bruises? Wow, that's not cool. AngelicaTombes11 has commented too. She says her cousin went to elementary school with Maia, one of Ella's younger sisters, and that her aunt didn't like Selena at all. Apparently, she'd invite Angelica's cousin for playdates, then feature her on their channel without asking her mom's permission.*

Maple: *Permission to be filmed? I mean, that's overkill, isn't it?*

Dylan: *Not to Angelica's aunt, I guess. Anyway, it seems a lot of you noticed how Ella's vibe changed in the year or so before she left. We picked up on that too and have been wondering why that was. Does anyone watching today know Ella directly? Could you give us any insight into what was going on with her?*

Maple: *It looks like lots of you have opinions, and we're grateful that you're engaging with this. But NachosandCheese99, do you have any proof that Ella was taking drugs? And Hideout482, I think abortions are against the law in Texas now, so don't say stuff that could get Ella into trouble unless you're really sure, okay?*

Dylan: *Look, LucyStarkBalletDancer has got involved. She says she's studying at the Houston Ballet School, and she doesn't think Ella would get into the Royal Ballet School in England. She thinks Ella's a great dancer but isn't committed enough to ballet. Jealous maybe?*

Maple: *Or the best evidence so far that Selena Hart lied. Oh wow, look. Ruby Marshall is watching us from London. She says that she follows a few Royal Ballet dancers on Instagram, and they post content all the time. So why hasn't Ella?*

Dylan: *You know, my gut is telling me that she's still here, in America. And your comments back that up, I think.*

Maple: *Which means her mom totally lied about her own daughter.*

Dylan: *So much for being the perfect family.*

Maple: *You know, to me, it makes sense that Ella would want to get away; having eight million subscribers watch your whole life playing out must be intense. But why hasn't* *she shown up anywhere else? We've had over three hundred comments, and no one says they've seen her, or know anyone who has.*

Dylan: *No one's got anything good to say about her parents either. It's funny. None of you seem to like Selena and Bodi Hart, or how they raise their kids, or how they post so much content about their family life. But millions of people watch their channel every day. Go figure.*

Maple: *I reckon DaisyfromSeattle has got it right. She says it's the same reason why everyone slows down for a car crash.*

Dylan: *They want to watch the trail of destruction.*

Maple: *But has Ella's life been destroyed, or has she escaped destruction? That's the question we want to answer. We really hope that she's safe and living her best off-grid life. But we're worried she isn't. That she's in trouble, or worse. We think she was struggling with something before she disappeared, and she hasn't been online since, or been spotted in the real world. Worse than that, her parents seem to have put their own reputation before Ella's wellbeing, which says a lot about what kind of parents they are.*

Dylan: *So we are going to continue reaching out to people who know Ella, and we'll post on our socials when the next live Maple & Dylan show will broadcast, so make sure you're following us both, and subscribing to our channel.*

Maple: *And get in touch using the hashtag 'Find Ella'. Thanks, guys.*

Chapter 44

Kirsten

What the actual fuck?

No, no, no, this can't be happening.

I push my laptop away, as though that might stop the live stream, then pull it back in case I miss something. What the hell is Maple doing? She told me this new channel was just her and Dylan hanging out, talking about stuff that interests them both. I thought she meant skateboarding, or music, or cool clothing brands, while keeping the romance drama on a simmer. Not this. Not making accusations about one of America's most-loved influencer families.

I mean, I know true crime is popular, but there are other YouTubers who focus on it. The ones with nose piercings who wear black and aren't blessed with Maple's looks or talent. Maybe this kind of content will get her some new followers in the short term – everyone loves a missing girl, especially a famous one – but it will also make her a target, divide opinion, scare brands away. And what then?

She'll fade away. Become just another shouty TikToker that people will grow bored of. And the effect on her earning potential will be devastating. Maddie is probably having a heart attack right now, and then she'll recover just enough to fire us from her hospital bed.

God, I want to run into Maple's bedroom this second and shut it down. But I know how that will look, how it will draw more attention, not less. I need to wait this out.

But why on God's Earth is my daughter risking her career, her whole life, for a girl from Texas who has got nothing – nothing – to do with her?

Even if it does sound a bit suspect. Which of course it does. I remember at the time being surprised that Ella had been accepted into the Royal Ballet School – TikTok is one thing, but *Swan Lake* is something else. And her not posting for eighteen months does make you think. But she's their problem – Selena and Bodi Hart's – not Maple's.

Why didn't I interrogate Maple more about the show? I just took her words at face value, jumped to the conclusion that everything I've taught her over the last fourteen years was finally paying off. When did I become so gullible?

The live stream finally finishes, and I stare at the thumbnail – Maple holding a photo of Ella – with YouTube's familiar promise underneath, that the video is processing. In minutes it will be uploaded. Available for anyone to watch, forever. A video of my daughter saying it makes sense that Ella ran away from home, comparing the Harts' channel to a car crash, and calling Selena Hart a liar. It will ruin us, for sure. After everything I've done.

A jet of rage floods through my veins. I spin off the barstool, storm upstairs and push open Maple's door. It slams against the plasterboard, and I just know the handle will have left a dent, which only enrages me more.

'Mom?' Maple is sat on her bed now. She pushes up against the headboard, like she's scared, which gives me a tiny jolt of satisfaction.

'What have you done?' I ask, trying to sound more betrayed than furious. 'Do you realize how much damage you will have caused?'

'The Maple and Dylan thing?' Her voice is high and timid. 'Are you mad because we said we're not dating?'

'No, Maple,' I say, gritting my teeth. 'I'm mad because you blindsided me. Made out like it was going to be some cute chat show, then went all Nancy Drew on me!'

'I'm looking out for another influencer,' she mumbles. 'And you're always saying that mutuals are the best relationships to build.'

I tut so hard it feels like the roof of my mouth comes loose. 'Honey, Selena Hart is the absolute queen of influencing, and you called her a liar. And made out that she doesn't care about her daughter's welfare. Do you really think someone like her, who has built her entire multimillion-dollar brand around being the perfect mother, is going to accept that without a fight?'

'But if the whole perfect family thing is fake . . .'

'No one cares! Practically everything we watch on social media is fake. That doesn't stop us enjoying it, does it? Post and let post, Maple; that's always been our motto. We create content and let others – the less talented – make their snidey comments about it.' I inhale, then release a long sigh. 'Look, if you take the video down now, maybe it'll be okay. It was your first live, and you've only got a few hundred subscribers, so if you remove the channel, I'm sure people will forget about it pretty quickly.'

Then a new thought comes to me. I drop into her desk chair and snap my fingers. 'Or better yet, film a different kind of video with you and Dylan to replace it with, one where I write the script. I promise, no one will be thinking about Ella

Hart after that.' I look at her curled on the bed, mute, her lips pressed together. 'Maple, come on! This requires some urgent damage control, and that's a good idea, isn't it? A great one maybe?'

'No.'

'Sorry, what did you say?'

Chapter 45

Maple

@BrookebabeNYC, TikTok
So, guys, I have got something JUICY for y'all today. I just watched this YouTube Live with those kids Dylan Dope and Maybe Maple talking about Ella Hart. I'm gonna put a longer post out soon, but some TikTokers are already saying that they know Ella is DEAD. Fuckkkkkk! – I've put a link to their live in my bio. Thank me later #findElla

'I said no, I'm not taking it down.' I try to sound confident, even though Mom looks like a vampire craving blood. 'We've already had heaps of new comments about Ella. How everyone is worried about her, and that they're grateful we're doing this. We can't stop now.'

I shuffle along my bed until I'm facing Mom, then risk making eye contact, reminding myself that Dylan is probably facing worse from his dad right now. 'Look, I get why you're freaking out,' I say. 'It is different to my usual stuff. But you've always said that success comes from getting noticed. Well, this will get me noticed, and maybe, hopefully, do some good alongside it too.'

'Not when you're being noticed by Selena Hart, or Maddie, or that skinny Azione woman with her colossal budget, or that modeling agent Blake, or any of the other brand managers we've been working with.'

'They'll be proud of me for helping out another influencer.' I try to sound convincing, but I'm pretty sure I don't.

'What? When you compared one of the most-watched kidfluencer channels on YouTube to a car crash?'

'That wasn't me; I just . . .'

'And said that it made sense to you that Ella ran away?'

'I don't think I said . . .'

'Brands choose to work with you because you're so good at making our lifestyle look amazing,' Mom interrupts again. 'They slot into the nirvana we create, and suddenly they're perfect too. So what do you think happens when you rip away that filter?'

'I know there's risk involved, Mom, but life isn't just about brand deals. I have a platform now, and I want to use it for something better than selling rank smoothies or crap toys.'

'I'm sorry, but when did you become such a self-serving little bitch?'

My whole body feels the impact of her words – Mom never swears at me. My muscles tense and my eyes burn. But I mustn't cry. Mom has always been so good at redefining the truth, and convincing everyone else to believe it too. But I need to push back, to keep remembering how good it felt to be doing this for Ella.

'I'm just doing what the church teaches us, helping others in need.'

I watch her expression darken. Mom has always been insecure about not being raised Mormon, and I know I've prodded her weak spot. I feel bad, but I need to do something to get her out of my room. Because the truth is, I am feeling a bit wobbly now. About how powerful Selena Hart is, and what she might do to us.

'Well, if you think that ruining our reputation, bankrupting your own family, is God's work, then I have no words.' Mom twists to go – thank goodness – and I twitch as she slams the door behind her.

I snap Coco.

Did you see it?

She responds instantly.

Of course! You were great :)

Relief floods through me and I type again.

Bit worried I'll get in trouble for saying that stuff about Selena.

I stare at my phone. Nothing. It's nearly a minute before Coco responds, and my palms are sweaty when she finally does.

You're on the right side of history, babe. So brave. I'm proud of you.

I know she's trying to make me feel better, but it's not working. Because I'm not sure I am that brave.

She snaps again.

Hey, have you seen TikTok? Your content is going crazy on there right now.

A mix of excitement and fear dance in my belly. I open TikTok and scroll through my For You page. At first, it's the usual content – makeup sessions, dance routines, skateboarding tricks (okay, that's new) – but then there's a reel by an influencer I love, BrookebabeNYC, and she's got a split screen with our YouTube video playing. She's talking about Ella, and our new show, which is so cool. But she's also saying that she's heard Ella's dead, maybe killed by Selena and Bodi.

I shake my head – Brooke is crazier than I thought; no one's going to believe that – and swipe on. But a few videos later, there's another one talking about me, Dylan and Ella. A guy I've never seen before. He believes Ella's dead too, except he thinks she was killed by a stalker, a stalker who'd been freaking her out for a year before she disappeared, which is why she'd changed her style. But how the hell does he know that? He lives in Canada and records his content in a creepy-looking basement.

I keep swiping. More reels about our search for Ella pop up, plenty claiming she's dead, but others just keen to get to the truth, like us. I read the comments too. Ella spotted in Mexico, Panama, Wisconsin, Alaska. It's exciting, I think. All this interest, a sign of how much people care.

Exciting, for sure. So why is my stomach churning like an out-of-date milkshake?

Chapter 46

Kirsten

@Anonfrom>>0, TikTok
I live in Austin, and I heard that's Ella's dead, and that her parents know about it. But why keep that secret unless you're the guilty party?

I lean over my vanity, wonder if the faint lines around my eyes now classify as wrinkles. Christ, I'm only thirty-six. But keeping this family in check is taking its toll, especially after the stunt Maple pulled yesterday. *I'm looking out for another influencer.* Honestly, how naïve can a nearly fifteen-year-old be? Although not so much when it comes to insulting me. Thinking to throw that church comment in my face.

And she's still refusing to take the video down, a full twenty-four hours later, which is a lifetime on social media. Of course I've tried myself, but I can't figure out a way of doing it. Which also feels wrong. Maple is a minor, for Christ's sake; shouldn't I have some kind of parental control over her new channel?

The bedroom door opens halfway, and Garrett's face fills the gap. 'We need to leave for church in five minutes; you'll be ready?'

‘I will,’ I snap back. I know Maple’s rebellious behavior isn’t his fault, but it has distracted me from the conversation we need to have about getting the twins back online, so it feels like he’s complicit. Alongside Blake, who’s also let me down, ghosting me since I asked for the name of her modeling agency.

Garrett backs out of the room, the classic wounded animal, and I pick up my lip liner. But then my phone rings. I eye it suspiciously. It’s an unknown number, which means it will be a spam call, but maybe I am in the mood to be really shitty to someone, so I press to accept. ‘Yes?’

‘Oh, hey there, am I speaking with Kirsten Clark?’

My eyes narrow. The voice is too creamy, too self-assured, to be some loser sat in a soulless call center in the Arizona desert. ‘It is, yes. And who’s asking?’

‘This is Selena Hart.’

‘Oh.’ I drop the lip liner.

‘You’re probably wondering how I got your number.’

I wasn’t, but only because my brain had frozen before she finished saying her name. ‘So how did you?’ I manage.

‘Kayleigh Jones has been sweet-talking me for months, trying to get my kids to join her online school. She gave me your number after we had a little chat ourselves.’

‘Right.’ My lips look weird in the mirror, pale against my made-up face. ‘I guess you’re calling about Maple’s new channel?’ I finally build up the courage to ask.

‘Well, you guessed right,’ she says, her Texan drawl still managing to sound clipped. ‘It was a shock, watching that video, and you know, a little hurtful too. I’ve followed Maple’s journey since she was a baby, and I suppose I felt a kind of kinship with you both, our content being so similar. So for Maple to say these things about me, well, I feel betrayed.’

Do I say that it was a shock for me too? Confide that Maple

has suddenly developed this extra head, one that makes stupid decisions and won't listen to reason, and I don't know what the hell to do about it? Or do I pretend that Maple and I are as close as ever and face Selena's wrath as a co-conspirator?

'Anyway,' she goes on, before I have to choose between two equally unappealing paths. 'I'd appreciate it if she'd take the video down asap and stop accusing me of lying about my daughter's whereabouts.'

'So Ella is in London then?' The words spill out before I can stop them – my desire to be in the know has always been my downfall. 'Maybe if you got Ella to create some new content from there,' I continue, 'this would all be over in an instant.'

But Selena doesn't rise to the bait. She releases a soft laugh, like she finds it cute how dumb I am. 'Here's the thing, Kirsten – and you know, I mentioned this at a speech I gave at the Meta annual conference just last week – we don't owe the public anything. It's important to remember that. Ella isn't a politician, or a judge, or a public figure of any sort. It's no one's business if she's in London, or Paris, or here with us in Austin.'

'But wouldn't it make your life easier?' I ask, still feeling like there's mileage here.

'Maybe so, but it's the principle that matters,' Selena replies. 'I have eight million followers, and I don't say that to brag, but a number that large brings a weight of responsibility. Because they follow my lead for how to behave online, as do lots of younger, less experienced influencers. I'm not going to let public pressure force Ella into anything she's not comfortable with.'

'But you're happy to pressure Maple into deleting her content?'

'That's not true. I have a soft spot for Maple; she's beautiful, cute, likeable. She could go far in this crazy, awesome world of ours. Which is why I want to give her the chance to reverse what she's started.'

'And if she doesn't?' I ask, forcing my voice to sound steady.

'Well.' She sighs. 'I imagine she'll be learning the true meaning of regret very soon.'

Chapter 47

Kirsten

@JoelMTBchamp, TikTok
You know, my question is, if Selena Hart is capable of killing her own child, what is she going to do to the two kids who exposed her? #findElla

Almost everyone you meet in Provo is a member of the Church of Jesus Christ of Latter-day Saints, or Mormon if you don't want to get out of breath saying it, and there are dozens of churches, stakes and wards in the city. Our ward meets at a modern church by Rock Canyon Park. There's an hour of chapel, then the kids disappear off to children's classes, and every second Sunday, Garrett and I go to Bible study.

Church usually falls somewhere between soothing and dull for me, but today I'm mainly agitated, Selena Hart's words on repeat in my head. I know exactly what a woman like her is capable of – it takes one to know one, I suppose – but how do I make Maple understand the dangers? She's being so rebellious right now, I can't get through to her.

'Hey, Kirsten,' Belinda sings over my shoulder as Garrett and I walk from the chapel to the classroom. Belinda is our old neighbor, and still salty about us moving to a house three times the size of hers. 'What's with Maple's new YouTube channel?' Her eyes are wide, like she's horrified for me. 'It seems so out of character?'

Luckily, we reach the classroom door before I have chance to respond. As I'm ushered inside by one of the men in suits, I give Belinda an apologetic look, a silent *I'd love to give you the full scoop, but rules are rules*.

'What did she want?' Garrett whispers as I sit down next to him.

'What do you think?' I whisper back. 'Maple and Dylan's YouTube video has gone viral, and now half of TikTok seems to think that Ella Hart is dead, either directly or indirectly by Selena Hart's hand. Of course everyone's got the popcorn out.'

'Shit.'

'And it gets worse. Selena Hart called me this morning and practically threatened to ruin Maple if she doesn't take the video down.'

'What?' Garrett twists in his seat.

'Right, everyone,' a voice rasps from the front of the classroom. It's Tom Dixon, a counselor in our ward who can recite whole chapters of the *Book of Mormon* by heart. 'This week we're going to take another look at the Book of Ether, so settle down.'

Garrett turns to face Tom, like the good Mormon he is, while I stare at the milk stain on Tom's lapel and daydream about smashing every one of Maple's devices with my bare fists.

An hour later, Tom dismisses us and we all file back into the hallway.

'Selena Hart must be some kind of monster if she can threaten a child,' Garrett says as soon as there's a hum of conversation to hide behind, making me wonder whether he was concentrating on Tom's monologue after all. 'I might not be a fan of social media,' he continues, as though I need reminding, 'but seeing Maple do that video with Dylan, I was actually proud of her. Forget about the crazies on TikTok, but it is weird that Ella Hart has dropped off the planet. And if Selena really did make up that story about her going to London, she deserves to be exposed as a liar. I think we should support Maple in this.'

'But Ella might not want to be found,' I point out. 'And Selena might be protecting her daughter. I mean, think about it. You want to take the twins off social media; how would you feel if everyone started accusing you of killing them when they go offline?'

'They wouldn't. The twins are eight, not eighteen; everyone will assume – correctly – that they're having some time out. Five years' worth.'

I shake my head. 'Social media doesn't work that way, Garrett. Logic and sense don't get clicks. It's the extreme, the just about possible, and the outright lunacy that goes viral.'

He scoffs. 'And you wonder why I don't want the twins to have any part of it?'

'Well, they're not going to have much choice now.'

His eyes narrow. 'What does that mean?'

'Do you really think Maple's going to get brand work after practically accusing one of America's favorite moms of abusing her child, then igniting some conspiracy theory about her being a murderer? I'm surprised Maddie hasn't called me yet – maybe she's still in shock – but I am fully expecting a call from her tomorrow morning. And if Maple stops bringing money in, then we'll have to double our efforts with the twins.'

'No,' Garrett says, shaking his head. 'I'm not changing my mind on this.'

'God, why are you being so stubborn?!' A dozen eyes turn to

look at me. I smile brightly, then lower my voice to a murmur. 'This is about survival right now, Garrett. Save the parenting awards for another day.'

'Look, I'll talk to her.'

'Who?'

'Maple. I'll ask her to take the video down and explain why. Nice and calm.'

'But I thought you were a big fan of her new venture?'

He twitches slightly, like I've made a direct strike with a pea shooter, then straightens his face. 'I didn't have all the facts then.'

I follow Garrett out of the church and let the warm breeze float over my cheeks. He's never been as close to Maple as I am, which may be my fault; she was such a gorgeous baby, I did pretty much claim exclusive rights to her as soon as she was born. But maybe a little distance is exactly what this problem needs.

Chapter 48

Maple

@Tellatttale, TikTok
Guys, I know something about Ella Hart that explains A LOT, I think. And when I get to ten thousand followers, I'm going to tell you everything, so get sharing this #findElla

Mom and Dad are silent on the drive back from church. Aspen gabbles to Ash the whole way, something about Joseph Smith being a badass. And I try to not feel guilty.

Because I know this atmosphere is my fault. The video Dylan and I recorded for YouTube yesterday has turned into a lowkey TikTok meltdown. Everyone's accusing Selena Hart of being America's worst mom, and some are calling her a killer. But I will not feel bad. Because making sure that Ella's safe is the most important thing. And if she is in England, like Selena claims, she just needs to say so online.

Dad pulls into our drive, and I jump out, desperate to get back to my room. But as I reach for the front doorknob – we never lock up for church, like we assume Provo thieves must be church-going Mormons too or something – Dad's hand falls on top of mine.

'Could we take a walk?' he asks gently.

I can guess why he's asking, so my instinct is to say no. I don't want to fight with him about this too. But the feel of his warm, rough skin on mine is so unusual that I find myself nodding. And when he looks grateful, my stance softens even more.

'How about I take you for a soda?' he asks as we hit the sidewalk.

Fifteen minutes later, we're sitting outside a soda shop drinking dirty Diet Cokes – coconut syrup, lime juice, and a dash of half and half (I know, weird).

Dad takes a long suck on his straw then leans back. 'So I saw the video you made with Dylan.'

'And?' I ask, holding on to the possibility he might follow up with something good, like he's proud of me for holding Selena Hart to account. 'What did you think?'

He sighs. 'I really need you to take it down.'

It's supposed to be boys who break your heart, but I'm not so sure. Boys make my tummy squirm, and my lungs malfunction, and okay yes, my heart hit the accelerator sometimes. But it's Dad who shatters it. 'No. I won't. Sorry.'

He nods, like he was expecting pushback. 'You know, Selena Hart called your mom this morning.'

I look up, because this is news.

'And I don't want to scare you,' Dad goes on. 'But she's not happy. And she's a powerful lady, you know. I'd hate to see you lose everything you've built over something like this.'

I think about Coco's snap, how she called me brave, and even though it freaked me out a bit, it made me feel good too. 'Sometimes taking a risk is worth it,' I point out.

'Yeah, and sometimes it isn't. You told me how much you loved that Azione job. And Mom says that your engagement stats tripled after Dylan's visit, the fun content you put out. You're flying high right now, honey. The world is yours for the taking. Now is not the time to be ruffling feathers and risking it all.'

'I don't even know if I want it anymore,' I admit in a whisper, wondering whether he's seen the fake kiss video yet, if he approves of it. Or if he's got no idea how badly Mom lied.

'You don't mean that, not deep down. Being an influencer has been your whole life; it's who you are.'

I want to say that I'm only fourteen. That I'm not fully formed yet. But maybe he's right. Maybe it is too late for me.

'And if you threw it all away now,' Dad continues, 'I promise you'd regret it.'

'What about if Dylan and I found Ella?' I ask. 'Saved her from some kind of trouble? Would I still regret it then?'

Dad sucks hard on his straw, then pushes the soda away, the ice cubes clinking in protest. 'There isn't just you to think about, Maple.'

'Huh?'

'Look, I hate that I'm not contributing at the moment, but park ranger jobs are hard to come by.'

Slowly, it starts to make sense, and my heart fractures again. 'So this is about the money?' I say. 'You don't want me to piss off Selena Hart in case brands stop working with me?'

'I wish things were different.'

I dig my fingernails into my palm. 'So everything you've said is a lie. This fake concern for my future is actually about Mom's fancy car and our big house.'

'No, it's not like that.'

'You've never asked about Maybe Maple before, or told me you were proud of me, or thanked me for bringing in thousands of dollars. But now that it might all come crashing down, suddenly you've got an opinion.' Tears burn my eyes. I feel physically wounded, but the pain makes me want to fight back. 'Well, no. Fuck you. I'm not listening.'

Dad leans forward, his face pinched. 'I wanted us to do this together, as a team. But I will not have you swearing at me, disrespecting me, Maple. I order you, as your father, to take that video down.'

I push to standing. The chair tips, falls backwards. I set my jaw and stare at him. 'And I am telling you, as your daughter, that I won't.'

Chapter 49

Maple

@Amelieeeetalking, TikTok
Guys, I've heard there are heaps of media trucks outside the Hart house. This story is so blowing up right now #findElla

I stare at Dylan on my phone screen and feel a sense of panic, like I want to run away but all the exits are blocked.

'What happened to your face?' I ask, hearing the tears pool in my throat. Today has been too much already, and now this.

'Nothing,' he says, shrugging. 'I'm learning this new trick, but I messed up, and my skateboard flew into my cheek.'

'You're sure that's what happened?'

'Yeah, course.' Dylan fixes on a smile. I'm almost certain he's lying, that the purple bruise is from a punch, his dad punishing him for making the video with me. But I don't know that. And maybe I don't want to know. It's hard enough dealing with my own parents right now.

'Things have gone pretty crazy, hey,' I say instead.

'Off the scale. There are thousands of comments on our page, and jeez, so many TikTok creators have picked up the story. A lot of crazies, I guess, but some decent posts too.'

He pauses. 'You know, Selena Hart called my mom. Made her cry.'

'She called mine too. Seems she's got a lot to say to us, but there's nothing on her socials. No denial, or proof of where Ella is. She's gone dark.'

'Which shows she's got something to hide,' Dylan points out.

'So it's a good thing, what we're doing. Trying to get to the truth.'

'Are you telling me, or asking me?'

I look down at my hands, embarrassed at how easily Dylan has read me. 'My parents want me to take it down,' I say. 'Mom wants me to replace it with a video of us pushing the whole dating thing again. And Dad wants me to just delete everything and shut the fuck up so I don't miss out on those big bucks.'

'Your dad said that?' Dylan looks surprised and it makes me feel devastated all over again. 'But I thought . . .'

'Yeah, well. Seems he saves the protective dad routine for Aspen and Ash.'

'So what are we going to do?' Dylan asks.

I go quiet as I try to figure out how to answer. Because if Mom's right, and doing this thing for Ella is going to mean an end to my influencing career, I need to work out if I'm okay with that. I did love the Azione modeling work. And having nearly two million followers is cool. But working every day, keeping up with Mom's crazy schedule, is exhausting. And the way old men think it's fine to stare at me, or give me crappy gifts, or grab me for a selfie, is totally gross.

But more importantly, I loved doing the show with Dylan. Responding to comments about something that really matters. Exposing liars. Taking a few baby steps toward finding the truth. And Dylan's right – Selena Hart is mad with us for a reason.

‘We’re going to keep going,’ I say. ‘I mean, if that’s okay with you?’

Dylan smiles. ‘Totally okay. I haven’t felt this good in ages.’

Suddenly I’m imagining his dad getting all mad while Dylan keeps his cool. His dad throwing a punch, and Dylan matching it with an unbothered stare, despite the exploding pain in his cheekbone. I bet his dad would have hated that.

I smile. ‘So what next then?’

‘Well, I’ve run the comments on the video through a key word tool, and there’s one that jumps out. Someone called MaisieMDanceTX. She says that she was Ella’s dance tutor for three years and knew her really well.’

My eyes widen. ‘Wow, that’s amazing, Dylan! We should talk to her. Hey, do you think she’d come on the show?’ I push off my bed, start pacing. ‘The Hart house has a dance studio in the basement – they film heaps of content in there – so I bet she taught Ella at their house. She’ll know so much!’

‘Well, she’s on Instagram,’ Dylan says, half smiling, like he thinks my sudden burst of energy is weird, but good-weird (I hope). ‘Why don’t you drop her a message and ask?’

I finish the call with Dylan and tap into Instagram. Maisie’s profile is easy to find, and she’s already following me, so I tap out a DM, explain how much of a difference she could make, and send it. Then I lean back against the pillow and think. I think about Dylan’s face, and Dad’s mandate, and Mom’s shock, and Selena Hart’s threats.

And I think about how good I feel.

Chapter 50

Maple & Dylan

@CateShakey2006, TikTok

Okay, I have a public announcement to make, guys. Dylan Dope and Maybe Maple are doing another YouTube Live tonight at six o'clock, mountain time. Do NOT miss it! #findElla

Maple: *Hey, everyone, happy Wednesday, and welcome to the second episode of our Maple and Dylan show! Thank you so much for all your comments, our thousands of new subscribers, and all your interest in this story. We have been blown away by your support.*

Dylan: *But we know you're not here for the gratitude. Well, maybe you are. But we have got something much more exciting for today's show. And hopefully we'll get a bit closer to working out what might have happened to Ella.*

Maple: *That's right. All of you putting Ella's story on your socials has paid off, because someone very close to the Hart family has been in touch.*

Dylan: *And more than that, she has agreed to be interviewed on this show.*

Maple: *So please welcome Maisie, Ella's personal dance tutor.*

Maisie: *Hey guys. I'm not actually Ella's dance tutor anymore. I mean, of course I'm not now, with her not being around. But what I mean is I left before Ella did. In the February of 2024, so maybe ten months before.*

Dylan: *Do you mind me asking why? I mean, was it your choice or Ella's?*

Maple: *Or Selena's maybe?*

Maisie: *It was Ella's. Selena wasn't happy about it actually. She wanted the lessons to continue, but Ella was adamant that she didn't want to be a dancer anymore.*

Maple: *And this happened less than a year before Ella was supposedly accepted into the Royal Ballet School?*

Maisie: *Yeah, I was pretty surprised when I heard that. I mean, Ella was a talented dancer, and she'd practiced ballet from when she was tiny, so with some intense training, I guess it's possible that she could have passed their auditions. But she was not in the right headspace when I last saw her.*

Maple: *Had something happened to put her off dancing?*

Maisie: *Umm. You know, it's funny. I never signed an NDA or anything, but I guess there's an understanding when you work in someone's home, isn't there? Like some level of discretion?*

Dylan: *We get that this is difficult for you, Maisie, and we really appreciate you coming on to the show. But nobody has heard from Ella in a year and a half. Anything that might help us find her is a good thing to share.*

Maisie: *Yeah, you're right, sorry. And I want to help. Ella was always so sweet-natured. At least, she was until the argument.*

Maple: *You mean the fight between Ella and her mom?*

Maisie: *No. I mean, that might have happened, but I'd left by then. I'm talking about an argument between Selena and Bodi around Christmas 2023.*

Dylan: *Oh? What happened?*

Maisie: *Ella and I had been in the dance studio in the basement, but we came upstairs to grab a drink. All her siblings were out, at a rehearsal for a nativity show, I think, and we heard them fighting. I mean, not physically, but they were really going at each other. All screaming and swearing and throwing their phones around.*

Dylan: *Was that normal for them?*

Maisie: *Not at all. They were always so smiley and affectionate whenever I saw them together.*

Maple: *Maybe that was an act for you, and they thought you were downstairs, out of the way.*

Maisie: *Maybe, but Ella seemed as shocked as me. Selena and Bodi were too mad to even notice I was there, but I could tell that Ella wasn't comfortable with it, so I left pretty quickly. I figured I'd be back the next day, like usual, but she messaged to say she was sick. And then it was Christmas break. I started back in January, but Ella was like a different person by then. Quiet and self-critical. And maybe six weeks later, she quit altogether.*

Maple: *Did you ever ask her what was wrong?*

Maisie: *Of course. I'd been teaching Ella for three years by then, and I loved her, so I hated seeing her sad. But every time I asked, she said the same thing. She had some stuff to work through, but she'd be fine.*

Dylan: *And she never told you what that stuff was?*

Maisie: *Nope. And then I was gone. When I heard that she was moving to London, well, I was surprised, like I said. But I was also relieved, I suppose. And happy for her. I wanted to believe it was true. That she was getting a fresh start.*

Maple: *And how do you feel now?*

Maisie: *Like maybe I should have trusted my instincts more.*

Chapter 51

Him

Look at her. Acting all grown up and independent on her new YouTube channel. He likes her asserting herself, he thinks, finding a cause to get all hot under the collar about. It shows passion. And passion is important in life.

But she'll need to be careful, he thinks. Making accusations like that could land her in trouble.

Although maybe that means she'll need saving. He smiles. He'd like that.

In fact, maybe this could be an opportunity for him.

The thought makes his heart race, and he drums his fingers against the table, sticky with sugary coffee and whatever else builds up when you don't clean stuff. As he contemplates what grime is made of, he notices the date on his computer screen, and it makes him sad. Wednesday. If things had gone his way, she'd be in Vegas by now.

Of course, he never answered the mother's question about the name of his fake modeling agency. He still hoped she'd come though, like an idiot. Got all dressed up, his best jeans and a shirt he bought for the dates he's never been on. Spent the evening at the MGM Grand, lurking, watching. But she never showed. Of course she didn't.

He leans back against the sofa cushion and scans his trailer. Would he have brought her here if she'd come? Or would that have been too big a risk? He considers the small, untidy space, the grease-stained Burger King boxes from last night's dinner, and empty soda cans stuffed with cigarette butts.

It's no place for a lady. But maybe she'd be past caring about decor by now.

The noise of a car backfiring outside makes him jump. PTSD, that's what the doc called it. But that's bull. He's been navigating bad shit all his life. He's a pro now.

He leans forward over his laptop, the only thing he owns that's worth something, that and his truck, and thinks. It's easy to set up a new account, but what should he write? He'll be one of thousands; he knows that. He barely goes on TikTok, but even he's seen content about the missing Ella Hart. If he wants to get Maple's attention, he needs to choose his words wisely.

He thinks about the desperate girls he's met over the years. How they're polite at first, always trying to negotiate. Until they realize it's a man's world, that they have no power. Then they fight. They know they're gonna lose; they're half the size, for Christ's sake. But that doesn't stop them trying. Bad odds don't seem to intimidate.

And it's brave. Whatever he's done, whatever he might do in the future, he'll never stop believing that. So is Maple brave too? He guesses it's time to find out.

He spreads his fingers and hovers them over his keyboard. Then he thinks up his best lie, and lets them fall.

Chapter 52

Kirsten

@hereforthedrama09, TikTok
So what do we think the argument was about? I heard that Bodi was having an affair, and Selena found out. Thoughts, guys? #findElla

This spa bed is ridiculously soft, so why can't I settle? I force myself to snuggle deeper, listen to the soothing music, breathe in the jasmine fragrance, let the gentle fan waft cool air over my skin. This is costing a hundred and fifty bucks after all.

The beautician – Louisa, I think she's called, she's new – goes through the motions. Cleanser, toner, peel, moisturizer. My skin tightens, tingles, burns with cold, and heats up with expensive antioxidants. Forty-five minutes later, Louisa informs me that she's done. My face feels raw and naked but hopefully the wrinkles have faded.

'Thank you,' I sigh as she steps away.

'You're so welcome. Now, you take as long as you need; I'll see you out front when you're ready.' She backs out of the room, the door barely making a sound as it dinks shut.

I take Louisa at her word for a while, stretching and pulling my face, but I can't hide away in here forever, so eventually I curl up and climb off the bed. I glug a glass of cucumber water, then turn my phone off silent and scan my notifications – there are lots of them, but nothing from Maddie. The only person I actually want to hear from.

She called first thing Monday morning but didn't drop the guillotine then. She'd seen the content about Ella, she said, and needed clarification because Maple's profile would have to be updated. I spun it as well as I could – the popularity of true crime online, the explosion in Maple's follower numbers – and Maddie seemed satisfied, if not ecstatic.

But then she called again yesterday, after Maple's second show with Dylan. The team had decided the content was too hot, too adult, for how they were positioning Maple in the marketplace right now. That if Maple wanted to continue her new channel, they sadly couldn't work with her. But we should for sure get back in touch when Maple turned eighteen.

I didn't handle it well. I mean, how was I supposed to stay calm when Maddie was taking a sledgehammer to our income? But I followed it up with an apologetic, slightly begging, email, so there's still a chance she might change her mind. A sliver of a slim chance.

Of course the way to get back into Maddie's good books is glaringly obvious – Maple needs to stop her ridiculous show. Garrett promised he'd sort it last Sunday, and after being in church, surrounded by powerful, dominating men, I'd allowed myself to hope. But all I got was a daughter charging upstairs and refusing to leave her bedroom, and a husband who spent the rest of the day – and pretty much all days since – holed up in the office, searching for jobs that might pay him slightly higher than minimum wage. Pathetic.

I pay for my facial with a credit card and leave the salon.

My phone buzzes, but when I check the number, I let it ring out – there are too many outstanding bills this month for me to accept 0800 calls. I head toward my car, but slow as I see someone leaning against the hood. A woman. Copper-red bob and scuffed trainers.

'Can I help you?' I ask while giving her my best 'get off my car' stare.

'Kirsten Clark?' she says, peeling off the hood and twisting to face me. 'I'm Meg Jackson with the *New York Times*.'

'Right.' I pause, conflicted. The *New York Times* has a reputation around here, and not a good one. But still, they don't visit often. I stand a little straighter. 'What do you want? Because if it's to talk about this Ella Hart stuff, then the answer's no.'

'I wanted to ask about Maple, actually.'

'Well, that's a bigger no.'

'How she's coping with being in the spotlight.'

'Maple loves the spotlight, so she's doing just fine. Now, would you mind stepping back from my car?'

'Would you mind if I quoted from her channel?' Meg parrots back. 'Because I thought it was interesting that she said, "To me, it makes sense that Ella wanted to get away; having millions of subscribers follow your whole life is intense." That sounded like a cry for help to me.'

'That's complete bullshit!' I ram my lips together. I mustn't lose control, especially with my face this bare, no makeup, no camouflage. I find a smile. 'Maple is just a normal teenager who loves to share her life with her friends online,' I go on. 'It's as simple as that.'

'So you're not worried about the stats then,' Meg says, not missing a beat. 'That a third of teenage girls say Instagram makes them feel worse about their body, and half have received unsolicited sexual content. Or the risk that Maple's online fame might spill into the real world, like it did with Ava Majury. Kirsten, do you worry that Maple will blame you for monetizing her childhood later in life?'

'No!' A bright light flickers in my eyes, sunrays bouncing off the windshield maybe, and I blink. 'Maple and I are the closest mother and daughter you'll ever meet.'

'So you support her takedown of Selena Hart then? Are you worried how Selena might react?'

I shake my head at the subject swerve. 'What? No! Please, leave me alone.'

She steps back, and I whip open my car door and tumble inside. But her smug smile remains in front of my eyes. Alongside an image of the guy across the street with a big camera and a matching grin.

Chapter 53

Kirsten

@feministrageclubTX, TikTok
So my question is, why is it always the mom's fault? Where's the dad? #findElla

'Maple!' I shout as I walk into the house. 'Get down here!'

'What's wrong, Mommy?'

I look into Ash's questioning face, his worried eyes. 'Nothing's wrong, sweetheart,' I say, trying hard to hide my anger. 'So what have you been up to this morning?'

'Um, me and Aspen made lemonade with Maple. It was really fun.'

'You did, huh.' Another wholesome activity not captured, not shared. God, this is so frustrating. Maple is sabotaging everything I've built over fourteen years, and Garrett is behaving like a dinosaur about the twins. How the hell have we got here?

I look up to the sound of footsteps on the stairs.

'Yeah,' Maple says. 'What's up?'

What's up. Like she doesn't know. Rage bubbles through my every pore.

'We need to create some content for Maybe Maple,' I say in my most professional director's voice. 'You know, the channel you've been dedicated to your whole life? We haven't put a video up since Dylan left, which is so off-schedule I can hardly bear to think about it.'

'I've been busy with my new channel.' Maple's voice is quiet, but there's a steeliness there I don't like. 'And keeping up with all my new followers on TikTok. I hit half a million this morning.'

I waver. Those kinds of numbers are what we've been aiming for since Maple joined TikTok a year and a half ago. But what's the point of popularity when the content that got her there also got her fired from our PR agency? It's like me being approached by a journalist from a national newspaper; it should be something to celebrate, but it's not.

'Even more reason to show them the real you then,' I say. 'You don't want to only be known as the girl who brought down the Harts.'

'Ella's missing, Mom. Can't you be proud of me for trying to find her?'

'I'm proud of you, Maple,' Ash pipes up.

'Go find your sister, sweetheart,' I say. 'Before she drinks all the lemonade.'

Ash's eyes widen as he realizes that's exactly what Aspen would do, and he scuttles off toward the kitchen.

'I know you think you're helping,' I start. 'But Ella Hart isn't a girl, she's a nineteen-year-old woman. And she's not your problem. Why would you ruin your career for her?'

'I'm not ruining it,' Maple mumbles. 'I'm evolving it.'

'Well Maddie called yesterday. She's fired you.'

'Huh?'

Maple looks so shocked that I feel the slightest ripple of

guilt for breaking the news so bluntly. But this is her doing; why should I sugarcoat it?

'Yep. Which means no more modeling work with Azione.'

'Okay.' Maple drops her gaze to her feet, and I sense an opportunity.

With gargantuan effort, I soften my voice. 'Listen, we've been working with Maddie for a long time. I'm sure I could get her to change her mind if you dropped this "find Ella" stuff. And Azione did love you, didn't they? It feels a shame to miss your big chance.'

Maple looks up. 'But I'm doing something good, Mom. And all the comments we've had point to Ella being in real trouble. I can't just abandon her now.'

'Of course you can!' I take a breath. 'I mean you're not a detective, or a social worker, or even a friend of Ella's. And you're a kid. Your content should be about having fun, showing your followers how awesome the world is, not how scary it can be.'

'But that all feels so fake now.'

'Oh, Maple!' I wail. 'We've been over this! Brands don't want regular or normal. They want thrill and pizzazz, just dressed up as authentic.'

'Like Dylan and me supposedly kissing, you mean? Pretending we're dating when it's all complete bullshit and the most embarrassing thing I've ever had to go through?'

'Exactly!'

The sound of the study door slamming open against the wall grabs both of our attention. Then Garrett appears in the hallway, his fists clenched.

'What's happened?' I ask.

Garrett scowls. 'Who the hell is Meg Jackson?'

Chapter 54

Maple

@Taylrtrix666, TikTok
Anyone else think it's weird that the Harts have said literally nothing about this whole shitstorm? Just turned off their comments and carried on like they live in a fucking bubble. Although I guess they do live in a bubble, looolll

Mom throws me one final dagger stare, then sighs and turns to Dad. 'She's a journalist with the *New York Times*,' she mutters. 'She just accosted me outside the salon after my facial.'

Even in this crazy tense atmosphere, I feel a jolt of excitement. A journalist from New York is talking to Mom. It must be about Ella. And if they run her story, then a whole load of new people – the old people who read newspapers – will find out that she's missing. And maybe even Ella will see that we're looking for her too.

'Did you give her my number?' Dad asks, giving Mom an accusing stare. 'Because she's just called me. Throwing all these personal insults at me.'

'Of course I didn't,' Mom spits back. 'What insults?'

'Questioning my parenting! When this shitstorm is nothing to do with me!'

Slowly, quietly, I back away. Maybe this isn't such great news after all.

Mom throws Dad a dark stare. 'You better not have told her anything, because they're snakes, those kinds of journalists. They hate people like us.'

I start climbing the stairs.

'People like you!' Dad throws back. 'And she made out like Maple's going the same way as Ella, all rebellious now, and then AWOL later, because she's so famous and so young and this is your doing, not mine!'

I reach the top of the stairs without either of them noticing, then creep into my bedroom. I close the door behind me – silently – then lean against it and close my eyes. I can still hear them arguing, but at least it's muffled now. The volume just low enough for me to think.

Because that's what I need to do. I want to be proud of what I'm doing with Dylan. Enjoy the momentum we're creating together, my profile ballooning but for an actual cause, not because I query-kissed a boy. But I hate the arguments it's causing. I can handle Mom and Dad being mad with me; I deserve it, I guess, throwing a hand grenade on the family income. But watching them fight with each other over something I've done is so much worse.

And there's Maddie firing me. It's a relief in some ways. No more drinking gross smoothies for hours, or applying some greasy face cream, or dealing with Mom stressing about new content every minute. But there were some amazing moments, like working with Azione. It made Mom proud too, and it was something we did together. If I reject it all now, what have I got left?

My phone buzzes, and it's Coco requesting FaceTime. I haven't spoken to her for a couple of days, and I click to accept like I'm underwater and she's an oxygen tank. 'Hey,' I breathe.

'Hey, babe. Sorry I've been offline. I've been super busy.'

'Oh?'

'Yeah, I've been going door to door on Sophie Lyle's street to see if anyone remembers anything new.'

'And any luck?'

'Hmm, maybe. A lady across the street says she remembers a guy hanging around outside quite a bit before Sophie was murdered. That she had a bad feeling about him. She told the police, but they weren't interested, which is so negligent. I mean, bad feelings are really our subconscious telling us something, aren't they?'

'I've never thought about it that way,' I murmur. 'But it makes sense, yeah.'

'Anyway, enough about me. I loved your show, babe. Honestly, you are kicking up a storm. What do you think Selena and Bodi were arguing about? Everyone on TikTok is saying that Bodi's a secret psycho, and that they're always fighting when the cameras are off. But I don't know. What's your take?'

I listen to the argument still going on downstairs, Mom's screeching and Dad's hollering. 'Maybe they were arguing about Ella.' I drop into my desk chair and wiggle my mouse. I was looking at the comments on our latest video when Mom summoned me downstairs, and the page is still open. I roll my finger over the mouse wheel.

'But why?' Coco asks. 'She was such a good girl back then. What would she have done to cause an argument?'

I sigh. 'Yeah, I don't know.' A comment catches my eye, and I lift my finger off the wheel. I read the words and my stomach twists. 'Oh,' I say, and it's loud, like a pop.

'What?'

'This is bad, Coco.'

'What's bad?' Coco asks. 'What's happened?'

Chapter 55

Maple

@MollyMarch14, TikTok
Sorry, but why is no one talking about Ella's siblings? They must want to find their sister too #findElla

'There's a new comment on our video,' I tell Coco. 'From someone called Anon357.9.'

'That sounds legit,' she murmurs sarcastically.

'Yeah, but he's saying – I mean, I'm guessing it's a man – that Ella's some star on the dark web. A porn star.'

Coco sucks in a breath. 'What the fuck?'

'I suppose that means she's alive, which is good, but she must be in trouble if she's doing that. No one chooses that kind of life, do they?'

'No,' Coco says. 'I mean, some actors claim they do, but they're all exploited, one way or another.' Her eyelids blink super-fast, like she's trying not to cry. It makes me wonder what's behind her desire to get justice for Sophie. Whether bad stuff has happened to her too. Maybe one day I'll ask her.

'So why would Ella leave her family for that?' I ask now.

'Remember this dude could be lying,' Coco points out. 'Which feels pretty likely to me, with a handle like that.'

I think about Coco knocking on strangers' doors to get to the truth. And Dylan, willing to take a punch from his dad to help find Ella. 'You're right; we shouldn't take his word for it,' I say. 'Which means we need to go onto the dark web and find out for ourselves. I just know that's what Dylan would do.'

Coco gives me a weak smile. 'And I'm sure he'd appreciate you saying that, but do you even know how to get on there?'

'Well, no,' I admit. 'But I guess it can't be that hard to figure out?'

'I heard that you need to download a special browser,' Coco says. 'But if my parents found that on my computer, they'd kill me.'

'Well, luckily, my parents couldn't get any madder with me than they already are.'

Coco shrugs. 'It's up to you, babe. But there'll be some gross stuff on there.'

'I'm sure.' I want to sound chilled, but it's hard when my heart is thudding like a jackhammer on steroids. I understand enough about the dark web to know it's where people buy drugs, and order hits, and watch snuff films, and stare at gross pictures of children. But I'm doing this for Ella.

I look up how to get onto the dark web on ChatGPT, then follow the instructions. But everything's so slow that it's excruciating. I want Coco to distract me as my computer whirs, but it's like she's weighed down by the stress of what I'm doing too because she barely speaks.

Eventually I get to a webpage with a list of categories. The page design is dark and cluttered, like it's been built by people who don't give a shit about aesthetics, and every category name feels like an unexploded bomb.

'What should I choose?' I ask, hearing the rising panic in my voice.

'Well, is there anything about porn?' Coco's voice is weird too, like she's being half strangled.

'I mean, yeah, but there's too much. So many categories. Loads of different websites with bonkers URLs and .onion domain names.' I see now how stupid this is. Of course there would be thousands of images on here, millions probably. How did I think I was going to find Ella in this massive disgusting underworld?

'I don't know,' Coco says. 'I'm not sure if this is such a good idea.'

My heart is still racing, but my breathing slows. 'There's a category called "Private Dancers",' I whisper.

'Jesus,' Coco exhales.

My hands are shaking so much that the link opens, closes, then opens again. I expect to see photos, videos, but there's just another list of websites with gross names. When I read 'Dancing Tweens,' I almost vomit. I'm not sure I can do this. 'There's one here that she could be on,' I tell Coco. 'It's called "Ballet Babes". But I'm scared of what I might see.'

Coco swallows, loud enough for me to hear. 'It's your call,' she says softly. 'But once you see it, you can't unsee it.'

I take a breath and click into the website. But then I gasp so loud it's like an inverse scream.

'What?' Coco asks. 'Tell me!'

'It's Ella,' I whisper. 'There are loads of thumbnails of different girls, but the biggest picture is of her, like she's the star or something. A porn star, like that comment says. And she's naked.'

'Oh my God.'

'Well, maybe not naked,' I stutter. 'It's only her top half. But there's a slogan about clicking for a thousand more images.'

'Eurgh, so gross. Fucking men,' Coco spits out.

'But there's something even weirder about it,' I say, my heart thudding so hard my chest hurts.

'What do you mean weird?'

'Ella is nineteen now, right? But in this picture, she looks younger. A lot younger. More like our age.' Acid rears up into my mouth. I scrabble with my mouse. Click, click, click until it's all gone and I'm back on YouTube.

'Are you okay, Maple?' Coco asks quietly.

'Sure,' I answer quickly. But I don't dare close my eyes in case I see that image again.

Chapter 56

Kirsten

@Tellatttale, TikTok
So I got to ten thousand followers. Honestly, you guys are the best. I guess I owe you some intel now, huh? #findElla

I put my car into gear. I wish it was dark, to match my mood, but the evening sun is still shimmering, so I drop the visor and press down on the accelerator. I turn right at the intersection. I have nowhere particular to be, but I just need to get away for a few hours. To pretend my life isn't collapsing around me.

Because it's been a very long week. And then Meg Jackson's article came out today. And it's not just a piece in the regular paper, but a whole feature in *The New York Times Magazine*. The story claims to be about kidfluencing in general, but it's really about Maple – illustrated with a very unflattering photo of an angry me. It seems that Meg Jackson thinks we should all celebrate Maple's newfound agency, that it just might save her from a hellish future as a bop girl, or washed-up ex-celebrity with zero work skills.

Well fuck you, Meg Jackson. Get your judgmental claws out of my family.

I might have been spared the shame of the article if it wasn't for Belinda. It's not like I ever buy that newspaper – or any newspaper actually; who needs to when everything gets shared online – but there's no way Belinda was going to give up the opportunity to gloat. She grabbed me outside church this morning, told me about it with such joy. It was excruciating. Especially as I then had to sit through a whole hour of chapel, followed by a relief society meeting about Pioneer Day, before I could get hold of a copy.

The news had reached Garrett too, so we sat in stony silence on the drive home from church, and then he went straight back out to buy the paper. We both read it, him first, then me. Then I threw it in the trash, and Garrett went out hunting with his brothers, but I don't think either of us felt any better.

I pause at the stoplight, and my eyeline drifts right. I thrum my fingernails against the steering wheel. Look straight ahead again.

The light turns green. Fuck it. I spin the wheel, cross over to Freedom Boulevard. Maybe I was heading somewhere particular after all.

I park, and with my head lowered, push open the door to NBG's Bar. I draw in a long breath and feel my whole body relax as I exhale. It's dark, and musty, and seedy. The lit-up signs in the window cast shadows over the handful of drinkers hunched over beers or glasses of liquor. I smile. A Mormon woman in a dive bar on the Sabbath. This is so much more rejuvenating than a facial.

I order a vodka soda and take it to a small round table at the back of the bar. It's cool and sharp, and it's not long before my glass is empty. I shouldn't have another – I need to drive home for one thing – but God, it tastes good. And I like being here, amongst strangers who are too busy anaesthetizing their own problems to wonder about mine.

I catch the attention of the bartender, and he must be a mind reader because he nods, and a minute later, places a new glass in front of me. I tap my card against his machine. Luckily I have a secret bank account – one I set up when Maple's checks became big enough to hide money – but it's a booze fund, not a new life fund, sadly.

Except. I take a sip of the cold drink, and with the buzz that freshly consumed alcohol always brings, an idea starts to form. There's over two thousand dollars in that account now, so enough to fund some clandestine activity. And maybe there is a solution to this problem after all. Maple's right that her follower numbers are sky high, but Maddie's also right that this obsession with finding Ella Hart has caused Maple's earning potential to nosedive. But maybe there is a way to bridge the gap.

I pick up my phone and start a Google search. I find five possibles, then cross-check those against online reviews. I choose the second one – no point overthinking it – and send an email to Stu Miller. Then I smile at my own brilliance, at the chance that I might have found a way to survive this. But as I click back to my home screen, I see there's a new message on Telegram. My stomach lurches. Has Blake finally responded to my request for more information? Is that door still open for Maple after all?

But no. It's just a message from the app, telling me about a new privacy feature. My heart sinks. But with the app open, I can't help clicking on my chat with Blake anyway. I wonder why she never responded. Was I too demanding? Too needy?

I take a long sip of my drink. Blake runs an international modeling agency; of course she doesn't have unlimited time for Maple. Maybe my message just slipped under the radar. So where's the harm in following it up?

I send a quick message.

Hi Blake, how are you? Just reaching out as I haven't heard from you in a while.

I'm not really expecting a reply, especially not on a Sunday evening, but when I look back at my screen, there's one there. Finally, some good news.

Chapter 57

Kirsten

@redheadsrockkk, TikTok
Is it just me or is Ella Hart's later content way cooler than all those embarrassing dance routines she did before? #findElla

As I read the new message from Blake, I imagine a door opening, and a glimmer of sunlight shining through the gap.

> *Sorry, totally my bad. Crazy busy with Berlin Fashion Show. I can't remember where we left things. Is Maple still keen to meet in Vegas?*

So Blake had forgotten about my request. I obviously need that information before Maple can meet her in person (especially with Maple being so demanding about that), but I don't want to sound all officious by repeating the question straight away. Maybe I should suggest doing our first meeting virtually, like Maple said, and get those details more organically. I start to type.

> *Maple would LOVE that, but she has a sinus infection at the moment and can't fly. Could we do a Zoom thing instead?*

The response is instant, but it's not what I was hoping for.

Sorry to hear that, please give Maple my best. And there's no hurry – we can arrange something when she's better.

Dammit. I click my tongue so loudly that the bartender looks up. He must think that I'm trying to get his attention, because he nods at my now-empty glass, and for some reason I nod back. I watch him place a third vodka and soda in front of me. This will get me drunk. There will be consequences if I drink it. But Maple and Garrett have already caused terrible consequences for me, so why should I hold back?

I take a gulp and refocus on my phone.

I need to get Maple in front of Blake, somehow. And Jesus, my daughter owes me after all the trouble she's caused. But it looks like it's going to take time, especially with all this Ella Hart drama going on, which means I need to keep Blake sweet. I type again, the new message looking blurrier than the last.

That's kind, thank you. Hopefully she'll be better soon. I'll be in touch, but do let me know if there's anything I can help with in the meantime.

Blake doesn't respond so quickly this time, and I wonder if this is it. If she's already lost interest again. I stare at my phone and sip my drink and pray for it to light up. And finally, it does.

We would like some insight into how Maple's bone structure will develop in the next few years. Could you possibly send some photos of Maple growing up? Unfiltered, natural. Holiday snaps would work. Thanks.

Bone structure? Wow, modeling is so scientific these days. And holiday pictures are easy; I've got albums for all our different trips. I switch to photos and choose a selection. Camping in Zion National Park when Maple was seven and eight, Oak Creek Canyon at nine, then Bear Lake when she was eleven and twelve. I send them over to Blake, a little giddy now, or drunk maybe. And I get a two-word message back – *Thank you*.

I sit back, pleased with myself. For taking the initiative.

But suddenly I remember that I still don't have the name of Blake's modeling agency. I quickly type another message, my fingers more slippery on my screen now, and wait.

But it seems that Blake's gone dark on me again.

Chapter 58

Maple & Dylan

@Unicornsarereal<3, TikTok
Maple is SO into Dylan, you can tell. And that kiss they had was so cute! Not gonna lie, I think them doing this thing together is SO romantic #findElla

Maple: *Hey, everyone, thanks for, um, you know, coming.*
Dylan: *Yeah, thanks for watching our live stream. There are literally thousands of you this time, which is wild, isn't it, Maple?*
Maple: *Huh? Yes, amazing. So cool.*
Dylan: *Anyway, we've got a lot to share with you tonight, so we should start. Do you want to go first?*
Maple: *No, you go.*
Dylan: *Right, okay. So after our last show, we had a comment from someone called Brandoninthesky. Now we've had lots of people say they've seen Ella over the last eighteen months, but this guy, well he claims to know where Ella is right now. But he doesn't say where that place is. I guess you could say we're skeptical, but Brandoninthesky, if you're watching today, will you get in touch please? DM*

either of us on TikTok or Instagram. We'd really love to hear what you know.

Maple: *We really would. Unless it's bullshit, of course. Because while we love that you all care so much about Ella, we're both getting heaps of really sus DMs. I know we can delete them so it's not that deep, but it still takes time away from what we're trying to do. Which feels more urgent now.*

Dylan: *Yeah, because Maple discovered something pretty bad last week. Can you tell everyone about it?*

Maple: *I can, yes. Sorry, give me a minute.*

Dylan: *Sure. No stress.*

Maple: *So yeah, last Friday I was tipped off, by an anonymous account, that Ella was working in the porn industry. And that her image was on the dark web. I was happy that she was alive, of course, but freaked out about what state she must be in mentally to do that. I also didn't know whether to believe it or not. It's not like an account that starts 'anon' screams genuine.*

Dylan: *So you did what any decent investigative journalist would do.*

Maple: *Well yeah, I found my way onto the dark web. And the tip-off proved to be right because Ella was there, on this website, and it was a photo of her topless, plus the chance to click for a thousand more photos. Except . . . well, except it wasn't Ella now. Sorry, guys, this is rough, but the photo was from when she was younger. More like my age, I guess.*

Dylan: *Which is both shocking and illegal. We've talked about it, and we think that this could have been what Selena and Bodi were arguing about that day. Because if they'd just found out that their daughter was on the dark* *web, it makes sense that they'd be mad as hell about it, throwing their phones, blaming each other. And if they then told Ella, her reaction fits too.*

Maple: *Her content became darker after that. She changed her style, dyed her hair, used makeup like a mask. Maybe that was her first way of hiding. And then ten months later, she did it for real.*

Dylan: *Scatsforbratz is asking whether that means we think she ran away, and if so, if it was her choice to go, shouldn't we let her stay hidden.*

Maple: *You know, I do think she ran away, but I don't know what's happened since then. Maybe she's happy somewhere, enjoying her privacy. But she was eighteen. She doesn't seem to have any friends or family to rely on. Naked images of her were probably on the dark web back then, and they're still there now. How much more vulnerable can you get?*

Dylan: *Which is why we still want to find her.*

Maple: *She shouldn't have to hide away from the world; none of this is her fault.*

Dylan: *GemmaPopsicle55 wants to know who took the photos, suggesting the obvious answer is one of her parents. While RickyDetroit18 takes it one step further, saying he thinks Bodi sold those photos of Ella on the dark web, and that's why Selena was so mad.*

Maple: *I hope not, because that's pure evil.*

Dylan: *Well, however they got there, we've reported it to the ICAC Taskforce via the NCMEC cyber tipline, so hopefully someone will be working to take them down. And yeah, Jeffersondopeski, we know they pop back up as quickly as they're taken down, but we've got to do something.*

Maple: *And we're doing something else tonight. Giving*

you another way to find Ella. I was sent a post that @Tellatttale made on TikTok yesterday. Her actual name is Tamsin, and she's a tattoo artist in Austin. Maybe she's online now, so hi Tamsin if you are. Tamsin inked a tattoo for Ella on her eighteenth birthday, just two weeks before she disappeared, and she's posted a picture of the design. So here it is for you guys too. A lotus flower, inked right in the center of Ella's upper back.

Dylan: *If you don't already know, lotus flowers are a symbol of overcoming adversity, because they begin life in mud but grow on the top of the water.*

Maple: *Which is beautiful symbolism, but we need to find Ella before she drowns.*

Chapter 59

Him

He clicks out of YouTube. Brandoninthesky, loud and clear out of Dylan's mouth. Fuck. Unreal. He wonders about the message he sent. Whether now's the time to send another. It's hard to decide; the stakes are so high.

He pushes his laptop away in frustration and scans the photos spread across the table instead. Ghosted for a week was all it took for that woman to fold like limp linen. What a terrible mom she is. And he feels bad about that, the crap hand Maple has been dealt. But also, good. Because maybe there's hope there too.

Except she's still not willing to bring Maple to Vegas.

He feels an urge to pick the photos up, but he doesn't want them spoiled by his sweaty hands. Not after the stress he went through getting them developed. He should have sent them off somewhere, kept it anonymous, but he went to PhotoShack instead, stood at the machine, listened to it drone and whir. It only took a minute to print the thirteen photos – five original, plus eight new – but he spent every second thinking that someone was going to look over his shoulder, accuse him of something terrible.

But no one even noticed him. Which shouldn't be a surprise because it's a skill of his, being invisible. There was a time when it bothered him, made him feel worthless. But then he discovered its advantages, and he's not sure he'd change it now.

He rubs his hands on his jeans and collects the photos up. Maple in a swimsuit as a little kid, splashing around in a river, then a little older in a two-piece, looking more pensive. At first, he wondered whether he had a favorite age, but he likes her in all the photos; it's too hard to pick.

His mind floats back to their YouTube show. Fuck it. He should throw caution to the wind.

Hopefully she's so desperate to find this missing girl that her guard will be down, like the mom's seems to be permanently. Maple did seem different tonight, both wound up and wounded. Maybe if he puts in more effort with his wording this time, more than comes natural to him, he'll convince her to come.

It'll be seeing that girl Ella all over the dark web that's got to her. He imagines Maple sinking, click by trembling click, into the murky depths of those underground websites. Seeing the face of another child, a girl she recognizes but more than that, who shares so many parallels with her. Of course that would scar her.

Then a new thought hits him. He leans back in his chair. Balls his fists. Grimaces.

Because maybe Maple saw more than she's letting on.

There's so much AI-generated porn these days; that's what he's heard anyway – real faces on AI bodies. And Maple is all over the legit internet. What's the betting she's on the dark side too? His jaw aches with tension as he reaches for his laptop again and opens the Tor browser.

He needs to know. To see for himself.

Chapter 60

Maple

@DebsfromDetroit, TikTok
OMG that sick and twisted motherfucker. How could Bodi put photos of his own daughter on the dark web? He was a shitty singer and now we know he's a disgusting human #findElla

I lean against the crinkly bark and close my eyes. It's weird. When I'm here, halfway up a maple tree, sunshine sneaking through, I can do this. Close my eyes without that image of Ella appearing. So why can't I do it in my bed at night?

But I know why. It's because the darkness seeps into my imagination. And then it's not Ella on that gross website, it's me. My photos being dribbled over by disgusting men.

When I read that comment from @anon357.9, I thought he meant that Ella was a porn star now, that it was her job. I didn't think it could get worse than that, but then it did. Either someone took those pictures of Ella when she was young and posted them there, or some pedophile has pulled a regular photo off her socials and used AI to create porn. Either way, she's been exploited and abused. Of course she'd want to run away.

And it all makes sense now. The argument, Ella struggling

with who she is, that lotus flower tattoo and what it symbolizes. But none of this gets us any closer to figuring out where she is now. Still the only person claiming to know where she's at is Brandoninthesky. And he's gone dark since leaving that comment, so it's probably bullshit anyway.

My phone vibrates and I look down. It's a snap from Dylan, but without words, just a link. I click into it and see that it's the Harts' YouTube page. There's a new short, the first they've posted since we started our channel. Selena and Bodi are sitting close together, face-on to the camera. Both wearing white linen, like they're a gift from God.

I play the video, and it's Selena who does the talking.

Some of you may know that there have been rumors abounding about our beautiful daughter Ella. Until now, we've chosen to stay silent, to respect Ella's right to privacy. But no longer. We could cope with the lies, the crazy gossip, the fake news and loud opinions of people who don't know us and have no right to judge. But these recent allegations, that Bodi – who, by the way, is the best father in the world – was involved in something as despicable as child sexual abuse. Well, we had to speak out.

So yes, it is true that Ella's not at the Royal Ballet in London, and I apologize with all my heart for not being honest about that. But we didn't do it to protect our brand, like the haters are saying. We did it to protect our daughter. To honor her request for anonymity as she worked through some things.

Because it is also true that some evil creature has used Ella's beautiful face and new AI technology to create disgusting images for depraved perverts on the dark web. Ever since we discovered this, we have been working tirelessly with the ICAC Task Force to get them taken down, and to find the perpetrators in this horrific crime. But it is not easy.

And do you know what? It will be so much harder now that this terrible truth has been shared so widely. So shame on you, Maple Clark and Dylan Jones. Maybe it's too late for Ella to come out of this unscathed, but please remember, actions have consequences.

The video ends, but I continue staring at their faces, the gut-punching mix of purpose and accusation frozen in time. *Shame on you, Maple Clark*. Is Selena right? Have I made things worse for Ella by telling the world what's happened to her?

My eyes sting with tears, and I screw them closed. I wasn't supposed to feel like this. I was doing something good. But now my parents hate me. Selena and Bodi Hart blame me. Maddie's rejected me. And my followers only care about the drama I'm creating.

I replay the video. Listen to Selena's apology for lying again, then her promise that it was for the right reasons. Her talking about the work she says she's doing to reclaim her daughter's dignity. She doesn't mention anything about where Ella is now. She makes out like that's about respect for Ella, but I bet it's because she doesn't actually know.

My phone buzzes in my hand. It's Dylan trying to FaceTime. For some reason – him caring enough to call maybe – tears threaten again. I quickly blink them away and accept his call.

'You know it's basically bullshit, right?' he says as soon as we connect.

I nod, try to smile, but my lips feel stuck together.

'Selena Hart has been performing for her adoring fans for twenty years, remember. She knows exactly how to manipulate an audience.'

'But she's right about that last thing though,' I manage to whisper. 'We have told the world about Ella being on the dark web. Well, I have,' I correct. 'It was me, not you.'

Dylan shakes his head. 'No way. All of this, we've done together. Collective responsibility. We're a team, right?'

Jeez, I'm definitely going to start crying now. I blink madly, nod, smile.

'And what's the alternative to speaking out?' Dylan continues. 'Staying quiet? Protecting the disgusting men who commit these crimes?'

I feel my shoulders drop an inch, then draw back. 'You're right,' I murmur. Then my voice strengthens. 'I mean, why should Ella be ashamed of something that's not her fault?'

'Exactly.' Dylan smiles, relieved. 'Selena Hart is just doing that classic thing of finding a scapegoat to hide her own fuck-ups. Don't let her get to you.'

'I'm glad we're doing this together,' I say quietly, not quite making eye contact.

He smiles again. 'Yeah. Me too.'

Chapter 61

Maple

@BrookebabeNYC, TikTok
Anyone else feeling a bit shitty about this Ella Hart thing now? I've always loved that family, so Christ knows why those teenagers made me look at things differently. It's so obvious they're just trying to build their profiles. Urgh

It's crazy. Life has been so shit lately, but hearing Dylan remind me that we're in this together made me feel good for a second. Like all the bad stuff is worth it because it's made us tighter. I love Dylan being my friend, and maybe I'd like it to be more than that. One day. Maybe. But maybe not, I mean, who really knows these things?

I wish I could talk to someone about this. Discuss, dissect, whatever.

I open Snapchat and notice a new symbol next to Coco's name. A red one hundred, signifying a one-hundred-day snap streak. Of course I can talk to Coco.

'Oh, babe, I'm so happy you called,' she says, sounding relieved as she accepts my video call. 'How are you doing?'

'I'm good, thanks.'

'You are?' She looks confused. 'I thought that post from Selena Hart might have sent you spiraling. Not that it should,' she adds quickly. 'But she's such a manipulative bitch.'

'Yeah, well, it did throw me a bit when I first saw it,' I admit. 'But Dylan made me see things differently.'

'Oh?'

'He reminded me that the alternative was letting pedos get away with their gross behavior.'

'Well, he's a smart guy.' She tips her head. 'You like him, don't you?'

I shrug, look away. But the smile creeps back. 'Maybe. I mean, he's cool, isn't he? And gorgeous. And a genuinely good person. But the really crazy thing is that he seems to like me too.'

'Sounds like someone's got a crush.'

I risk looking at the screen and see that Coco's eyes are shining with a mix of humor and pride. 'Do you think I've got a chance?' I ask in a whisper.

'A chance?' She shakes her head. 'Damn, you're so pookie. The dude would be lucky to have you.' Then her expression softens. 'I'm really happy for you, babe. I think you'd make a great couple.'

I curl my fingers into a heart in gratitude. 'Not that anything's going to happen anytime soon, with Dylan in St George and me in Provo. But we're finding Ella together, and that's making us closer. Especially now Selena Hart's trying to invent a whole new truth.'

At that, Coco's expression changes. She suddenly looks sad. 'What did I say?' I ask.

She sighs. 'Listen, Maple, there's something I need to tell you.'

'Oh?'

'After our call the other day,' Coco goes on, her voice more muffled, like her hand is covering her mouth now. 'You know, when we found Ella's pictures. Well, I guess I couldn't stop thinking about it. About how AI means that just being known on social media puts you at risk of gross stuff happening to you.'

'Why are we talking about this?' My heart is booming, but my voice is tiny.

'Because I went on the dark web this morning.'

'But your parents . . .'

'This is more important.' Coco exhales and it judders out. 'Looking out for my friend.'

'Ella's not your friend,' I whisper.

'I found your image on some of those sites, Maple. Your face anyway. On naked bodies. I'm so sorry.'

I feel a strange sensation, something vile and disgusting, like a million eyes stripping away my clothes. I drop my face into my knees, pull myself into the smallest ball, feel hot tears against bare skin. I can hear Coco saying my name, asking if I'm okay, apologizing, over and over.

I should say something. But I can't speak.

I rip out my AirPods, feel them slip through my fingers, then listen to them skitter along the sidewalk below me.

Chapter 62

Maple

@RubyRoccsVox, TikTok
Me, I love that tattoo, but Selena Hart would have hated it, don't you think? Tainting her sweet little girl with black ink like that? Maybe that's what they were fighting about on the night she left #findElla

I stare into the mirror of my vanity and wonder about going back to bed. But I'm not sure I even have the energy to do that. Since that video call with Coco two days ago, I've barely done anything. I make food I can't eat, spend hours in bed but can't sleep. I scroll through my phone without even noticing the content. All I can think about is Coco's words. And how her sympathy somehow made it all worse.

I found your image on some of those sites, Maple. I'm so sorry.

When this was about Ella, I felt sick. Now that it's about me, I want to die.

I drop my eyeline, catch my forehead in the heels of my hands. My phone is glowing beneath me, never far away, like a conscience, always judging. And even though I hate it right now, I pick it up.

There are thousands of comments, and hundreds of messages. But they're not about Ella now; people want to talk about me instead. How I'm a liar, aura farming, a heartless bitch for exposing Ella's shameful secret. And the thing is, they're right. I deserve their hate. Because now I know that I've been abused in the same way Ella has, I can't bear the thought of a single person knowing.

Still on autopilot, I scan my message requests from people I don't follow. It's more of the same, but then one handle catches my eye. Brandoninthesky.

The guy who said he knows where Ella is.

I open the message, expecting something equally cryptic and unhelpful. But this one is different.

Hello Maple, I'm sorry it's been a while since my YouTube comment. I had started to question whether the girl I see at my favorite bar is the same one you're looking for. But I had a eureka moment during your most recent show, because I recognized her tattoo. I seem to have caught the sleuth bug too, because the next time I saw her, I followed her home. So now I have her address as well.

However, that's the good news. The bad news is that your friend is not in a good way. I don't want to say too much – this is Ella's story to tell, not mine – but I believe she is being mistreated by an abusive man. And I'm worried that, as a man, she would not trust me if I tried to help her.

Sadly, the police won't get involved because she's an adult. And it's clear that her parents are lying to protect themselves, so I wouldn't advise you contacting them. My suggestion therefore is that you come here. I will take you to Ella, and you can tell her about your show, and how much everyone wants to see her safe. I think you might be the only person who can persuade Ella that she deserves better.

Ella is living in Las Vegas, in a rough neighborhood close to downtown. There are direct buses from Provo into Vegas, and the journey takes approximately seven hours. If you let me know which bus you get on, I can pick you up from Bonneville Transit Center – it's the downtown stop. Meet me at the circular seating area underneath the clock.

I think what you're doing for Ella is amazing. She's lucky to have you looking out for her.

See you soon, Brandon

Wow. I blink. Read the message again. Take a photo, then delete it from TikTok – I don't want Mom seeing this. A man suggesting I cross the state border.

But Ella is in Vegas – the same place I modeled. While I was dreaming about being rich and famous, she was alone and desperate.

Brandon sounds so certain that I will come, so efficient with his bus timetable and pick-up plans. But isn't it a crazy idea? I rub my eyes. Shit, I'm so tired. I want to help Ella, and I owe her now, for sure. But going to Vegas by myself, meeting up with a guy I don't know? Brandon could be a psycho, a pedo. This whole story could be pure fantasy, just a way to lure me to Vegas so he can do whatever he wants with me.

I look down at my phone again. I should tell Dylan. We're a team; that's what he said. But he'll insist on coming to Vegas with me, to look out for me. And Dylan is a man, or almost one, and Brandon thinks a guy would scare Ella off. If we lost our chance to save her, then it would be my fault for not being brave enough to go it alone.

Brandon is right that the police won't care. And Ella's parents are willing to lie about their daughter rather than see her safe.

I think you might be the only person who can persuade Ella that she deserves better.

Maybe Brandon's right.

And more than that, maybe Ella is the only person who can save me.

Chapter 63

Kirsten

@USarmyvetAfg2018, TikTok
Y'all can say what you want. Selena Hart is a good Christian mother, and those two teenagers will go to hell for making up shit about her daughter

I was so excited when we moved into this house. It was beautiful, of course. Spacious and light. But more importantly, it represented how successful we'd become. Well, me; it was my hard work that got us here. But the house was also about the future. A palace fit for a family of YouTube millionaires.

With a mortgage to go with it.

So what am I going to do? The twins' channel is dying from lack of content. Maple's isn't far behind. And no one has made me a dollar since that Azione check came through.

I eye the store cupboard. I have never sneaked a sip of wine before lunch, and I will not start now. I have standards. But God, how nice it would be to take the edge off. To be able to forget about the outstanding bills, the anger and impotence frothing under Garrett's skin. The twins acting like they don't have a care in the world, and Maple refusing to leave her room.

I wouldn't let loose like I did on Sunday, of course, recklessly drinking, acting like a woman with nothing left to lose. I was lucky to get home without a DUI, luckier still that Garrett was already asleep, and that he preferred to give me the silent treatment on Monday morning rather than ask why I slept in the guest bedroom. Stu Miller turned out to be a good call too, I think. In fact, the only fallout from my boozy night was that message exchange with Blake.

I may be overthinking this, but I feel a bit uncomfortable about sending those holiday snaps now. Especially with all these rumors flying around about kids' photos getting onto the dark web. But I'm sure it's nothing like that. It's about bone structure.

My phone buzzes on the kitchen counter. I assume it will be another call I don't want to take, so I only glance at it. But shit no, it's Maddie. I grab it.

'Hey, Maddie.'

'Oh hey, Kirsten. How are you?'

'I'm good, thank you. Great. Life is great.'

'Yes, I imagine things must be very exciting for you right now,' Maddie says. 'All this change. Maple making waves on TikTok. I saw that she forced a reaction from Selena and Bodi Hart too. That's impressive. Although Selena is a pro, isn't she? She might just have done enough to turn the tide. What do you think?'

I close my eyes and visualize the bottle of wine behind the potatoes. 'Did you want something, Maddie?'

'Oh yes, sorry. I have a brief for you—'

'You do?' Desperation spills out before I can stop it.

'Yes, and it's a good one too. Quite heavy content requirement, but they've got a lot of money to spend.' The words have a soothing effect, a bit like wine. 'It's for an outdoor activity brand,' Maddie goes on. 'They like how the twins are into camping, and swimming, and handling dead fish and stuff.'

'Wait, it's for the twins?'

'Yes, who else would it be for?' Maddie asks, genuinely confused, like she's already forgotten she represented Maple for eight years.

'Right, of course. They'd love that, Maddie, thank you,' I say, pushing thoughts of Garrett's diktat away. We need this. 'So what's the schedule?'

'Oh, I'm so pleased. If you could send over a ninety-second showreel by three today, I'll put the twins in the mix, and we'll confirm by close of play tomorrow.'

'Wait, this isn't a done deal?'

'Don't worry, Kirsten. You get the twins doing something cute in that gorgeous pool of yours, and they will totally be the front runners.'

They've got a lot of money to spend.

I hold my tongue, finish the call and check the time. Four hours to create a winning reel. 'Aspen!' I call out. 'Ash! Get down here!'

Half an hour later, the twins are in the pool, the tripods are in situ, cameras recording, and I feel like I've returned to my natural habitat.

'Okay, kids, get back on the float; I want to see that paddling move again; it's so cute when you do it in synch. Hey Aspen, take the goggles off, they make you look like a snake.'

'But my eyes are stinging!'

'It's one take, Aspen. Quit being a princess. Okay, Ash, listen up. You're going to fall off, then I'll throw the crocodile float in, and I want you wrestle with it until Aspen comes and flips it off with her paddle, okay? Hey, not yet, Ash!'

'But I fell in, it's not my fault!'

‘Wow, you guys do not make this easy. Quickly, climb back on.’

‘But I’m tired. And hungry.’

‘And my eyes are still stinging,’ Aspen adds. ‘Can we do this later?’

‘You’ve been in the pool for twenty minutes!’ I shout. ‘You usually spend hours in there! Are you doing this to spite me? Is that it?’

Aspen screws up her face. ‘What?’

‘Well, I have news for you two. I’m in charge here. And you will damn well climb back on that float. Quit crying, Ash!’

The crash of a door slamming makes me jump.

‘What the hell is going on here?!’ Garrett shouts.

Chapter 64

Kirsten

@Jessiewantsapuppy, TikTok
You know, I feel sorry for Maybe Maple. I get that she's a bit of a social media whore, but who made her like that? Her mom put her on YouTube from when she was a baby. Of course she chases likes to feel good about herself

'Garrett, I've got this,' I say, forcing authority into my voice. Because we're broke, and I'm done with his macho bullshit.

'Ash, Aspen, get out of the pool,' he says, ignoring me. 'Go inside and get dry.'

I watch my children splash toward the edge like they're being chased by a bull shark and decide to stay quiet. It's never smart to fight a battle you can't win.

As the children slide the glass door into the kitchen closed behind them, Garrett turns to me. 'What are you doing?' he asks accusingly. 'Why are you filming them?'

'Because we need to eat. And you don't have a job. And it's a sweet gig to be able to earn thousands of dollars from playing in the pool.'

'A sweet gig? Being eight years old and having your self-worth defined by likes?' He tuts, shakes his head. 'You put Ash and Aspen's whole life on social media, but have you ever thought about who's watching them? How many disgusting old men are getting off on our children?'

'None, that's how many,' I throw back. How dare he suggest I don't look out for my kids. 'I block every weirdo who's ever commented.'

'And what about the ones who don't comment? Wise up, Kirsten! Some of their videos get millions of views. How can you possibly know that none of them are weirdos?'

Urgh. It's like he's vomiting up those podcasts. 'Jesus, Garrett, so what if there is!'

'What did you say?'

I take a breath. 'Listen, I agree that what those men do is gross, disgusting. But really, what difference does it make to the twins? Of course I wish that every one of their subscribers is a kid like them. But if a few of them don't hit that profile, then what does it really matter? It's those men who are the losers, their lives so fucked up that they choose to watch eight-year-olds on YouTube. The twins are oblivious, aren't they? Which makes them the winners, Garrett, the ones earning money, getting famous.'

'We're talking about child abuse, Kirsten! What the hell kind of person are you? No one thinks about their kids that way!'

'I'm a pragmatist, Garrett. And do you know what, maybe you should try it sometime. Get a job that actually pays well instead of following some stupid passion for big cats.'

'I'm trying to get a job,' he growls. 'You know that.'

'Well clearly not hard enough. Which is why you need to step aside and let me save this family from ruin.'

'You're not saving anyone,' he says, his voice rising again. 'You're destroying our kids! And I won't allow it. Not anymore.'

I shake my head in disgust. 'You can't even get a fourteen-year-old to fall in line,' I remind him. 'So why the hell do you think you can control me? When did I become a softer touch than Maple?'

'You?' he throws back. 'You're nothing but hard edges! I just don't understand why I didn't see it before. Right back when you came to visit me in college.'

'See what? That I'm ambitious? Resourceful? That I want the best for my children but am also smart enough to know the difference between actual child abuse and woke bullshit?' My voice is loud now, possibly in range of our neighbors' garden. I should lower it, but I can't; I'm too mad.

'That you don't give a shit about other people,' Garrett says. 'And you'll do anything to get what you want.'

'Why should I apologize for being strong-willed? Look around you, Garrett. I did this. I gave you this beautiful home!'

He cracks out a laugh so bitter it hurts my head. 'I didn't ask for this house. Neither did the twins. This is your vanity project, Kirsten. Perhaps Maple wanted it too – you've always worked so hard to reproduce her in your image – but even she's had enough of you now!'

'And look how much good that's done her,' I throw back. 'All those new followers who were drooling over her content last week are turning on her now. And Selena Hart was always going to win; she's been the queen of this for twenty years. If you'd stopped Maple when I asked you to, she wouldn't be suffering now.'

'It's always my fault with you, isn't it?' he hisses. 'Like you had no hand in it.'

'It was you who refused to father Maple properly,' I spit back. 'It was as though the day she told you she was scared of spiders, you backed off, like it gave you the excuse you were looking for. At least I loved Maple from day one, and never stopped. I'd do anything for her.'

'Except be honest!' he shouts back. 'Except tell her that we'd been apart for over two years when you knocked on my college room door that night, begging for my help!'

'Shut up, Garrett.'

'And that the man she calls Dad is just some schmuck who fell for her pregnant mom's fake charm!'

Chapter 65

Maple

@BrettSmith2504, TikTok
Yeah, Maple's been going after the wrong YouTube mom IMO. She needs to look a little closer to home

The world around me is shifting, spinning. I catch eyes with Ash, then whip my head away like it stings. I thought things couldn't get any worse. But I can't catch my breath; can't think straight.

The man she calls Dad is just some schmuck who fell for her pregnant mom's fake charm.

Did I hear him right? Dad isn't my real dad?

This, on top of all the shit I'm already dealing with?

And if Dad isn't, then who is?

I think of those images on the dark web. My face on a stranger's body. Being watched by gross men, fantasized about, jerked off over. Me, but not me.

That's what I feel like now. I look like me, but it's all fake.

'Maple?' Aspen whispers, her voice shaky too. 'What's Dad shouting? What does he mean?'

'Nothing,' I fire back. I don't know who I'm trying to

protect: myself or my siblings. Jesus, my half-siblings. All this time, wondering why Dad has more time for the twins than me, why he seems to love them more. Always blaming myself for being too girly, not daring or outdoorsy enough. When the truth is, this all started before I was even born.

My face starts to crack, and I force myself to smooth it out. I can't let the twins see me cry, but I can't leave them alone here either. I need to get them away from the glass doors with their shit sound insulation. 'Let's go watch a movie,' I say. 'Come on.'

I grab their hands and pull them out of the kitchen and into the den. I close the heavy wooden door. Shut out the noise. I put on *Zootopia* 2 and turn the volume up. We all lower onto the big couch in silence, like we're counting the seconds until we can get transported to a different world. But that's not how it is for me. I want to be alone – to have space to think – so as soon as the opening credits are done, I mumble an excuse and head upstairs.

I walk through my room, into my bathroom, and lock the door.

My dad is not my dad.

I sink down to the floor, pull my knees into my chest, rest my head on the edge of the bath.

We'd been apart for over two years when you knocked on my college room door that night, begging for my help.

I have always known that Mom and Dad – maybe I should call him something else now, but I don't know what; I can't go there yet – dated in high school. Then Dad went to college in Colorado and Mom stayed in Provo, doing babysitting work, singing in her spare time. She was just waiting for Dad to graduate; that's what they always said. But it's not true. They'd broken up. Mom slept with a different man who made her pregnant.

Did my biological father reject me? Is that why Mom went running to Dad? Or did she never consider my bio-dad husband material?

Fuck. Does he even know I exist?

God, I have so many questions! But I can't ask any of them because I don't want to talk to either of my parents ever again. Dad has always made me feel second best and now I know why. Mom tells me I'm special, that it's Mom and Maple forever, but she's kept this huge secret from me. I guess I know that Mom lies, all the fake stories she posts about me. But lying about who my father is? How could she do that?

And I would still be in the dark if I hadn't got thirsty enough to drag myself out of my room and go downstairs for orange juice. Aspen and Ash would know and I wouldn't – by overhearing their mom and dad shouting. Shit parenting 101. Jesus, I can't believe I was feeling bad about causing their arguments when they've kept this huge dark secret about me.

There's the other stuff Mom said too. How she called child abuse woke bullshit. I wonder whether she'd feel that way if she knew what I know. That all those cutesy pictures and videos of me when I was two, three, four, five, every fucking age, might now be fair game for tech freaks to make AI porn from. Would she finally feel guilty?

But maybe I'm giving her too much credit. Maybe she already knows and doesn't give a shit.

I'm a pragmatist, Garrett. What difference does it really make?

That woman does not deserve to be anyone's mom.

I push up to standing, my fists clenched. I'm not spiraling anymore. Not shocked, or sad, or broken. I'm just angry. Pissed off that I've spent fourteen years listening to my mom, believing that she loves me, that she's sacrificing her whole life for mine.

I grab a warm jumper from my cupboard, pull on my most comfy sneakers, and shove the money I've been saving – a few hundred dollars – in the pockets of my jeans.

Because I might have nowhere to go, but I'm not staying here.

Chapter 66

Maple

@JoJoPiper12, TikTok
Hey, do any of you guys know where Maybe Maple gets her clothes? She always looks so cool. They're probably gifted though, right? What kind of numbers do you need for free clothes?

'Mall closes in five minutes, so if you could head for the exit, miss.'

I nod at the security guard, then walk toward the semicircle of glass doors that will take me outside. He doesn't need to know I've got nowhere to go. Mom and Dad have both messaged me, but only to ask where I am. It means the twins can't have said anything – either out of loyalty to me, or because their brains haven't processed it yet – but that doesn't change the truth. I've sent a few words back – *I'm fine, I'll be back later* – and they've left it at that. More proof that they don't care. That I'm just there to pay the bills.

I push open the door and stare at the dimming sky. It's not night quite yet, only eight o'clock, but I know it's coming. Darkness.

When I left home over seven hours ago, I walked around my block for a while, trying to get my head straight. But then I saw on Snap Maps that Milly was back from Montana. I messaged her, suddenly desperate for some normality, and she invited me over to her house.

Milly's an only child, which is rare around here, and her house is always super quiet. I thought I'd like that, some calm, but it just made the noises in my head louder. Milly poured us lemonade and talked about her cousins' amazing ranch, and going horse riding, and how bright the stars are in Montana. And I thought about how I don't know who my dad is, and that my face is on porn sites, and my mom is an even bigger liar than Selena Hart.

And I still haven't found Ella.

God, I want to go to Vegas. Do something risky and stupid that just might turn out to be the bravest and most important thing I've ever done. And Brandon could be a stand-up guy who just wants to help me save a girl in trouble.

But he could also be one of those men who fires up the Tor browser every night and looks for naked pictures of me.

And then what? He gets to go one better?

Acid surges in my belly, and I reach out for the barrier at the parking lot exit to steady myself. But then it lifts, a car driving through, and my hand slips off. The mall parking lot is almost empty now, the last few cars heading out, back to their families maybe, or cozy apartments, or student houses. Somewhere.

I left Milly's around four, when I couldn't stand her not knowing what was in my head, but also couldn't find the words to tell her. I walked south, downtown. I hoped I'd get that same sense of freedom I felt when I escaped the baby contest. But that was before my life turned into a car wreck.

I was tired and thirsty when I reached the mall, so I went

straight up to the food court and ordered a thirty-two-ounce soda. I messaged Coco from there. It was always going to be Coco I told; I don't know why I left it so long. My phone battery was in the red by then, and anyway, I didn't want to say it out loud, so I just typed, snap after snap, all too fast for her to respond to until I was done. My parents' argument. The look on Ash's face and wobble in Aspen's voice. How I've been lied to my entire life. And how I now have no one.

Of course that's when Coco told me that I had her.

'Hey, you got somewhere to be?' a voice calls out, making me jerk at the sound. 'Because this parking lot closes soon. You can't be hanging around here.'

'Oh, sorry,' I mumble. 'Yeah, I'm just leaving.'

The security guard nods, but slowly, like he hasn't decided whether to believe me yet. 'Someone picking you up?'

'I'm getting an Uber,' I improvise.

'Okay, well I'll wait with you until it shows. Not a great idea, you being out here on your own.'

I can tell he's not going to leave until a cab arrives, so I open the app. I don't want to go home yet, but I can't think of another destination, not with the security guard staring at me. So I tap on my address and hate myself for it. How my resolve seems as firm as Jell-O.

Five minutes later, a black sedan draws up next to me. I give the security guard a half-smile, then slide quickly into the back seat. But when the driver swivels round to check I'm in okay, our eyes catch. And hold; a few seconds too long. Eventually he turns back, starts pulling out of the parking lot, some woman singing raspy love songs through the speakers.

But I'm frozen. My breath caught in my chest.

Because in that moment, I saw it.

Recognition. The slimy kind.

Chapter 67

Maple & Dylan

@TommyInfluenza, TikTok
Technical problems??? I bet her evil momager locked her in the basement lollll. Who's with me, guys? #findMaple

> ***Dylan:*** *Hey, everyone. Thanks for joining us again today and happy Friday. Sorry Maple isn't with us yet, I guess she's having some technical problems, but I'm sure she'll be here soon. Anyway, I know Maple wouldn't want me to go ahead and talk about Ella without her, but this little bit of a delay does give me an opportunity to address something else. And you probably know what I'm going to say, because if you've been following this story, I'm willing to bet that you've watched Selena and Bodi Hart's YouTube short from earlier this week. Well, I just want to say that they may have finished with some big line about how Maple and I should be ashamed of what we've done, but let's not forget who lied here. Who supposedly protected their daughter by making up some big bullshit story that just happened to complement their brand identity perfectly. Now, I know there'll be a range of opinions on this, and yeah, I can see*

there are loads of comments coming through on the chat. Listen, I will address them, but I might not be able to read all those while I'm flying solo, so if you could just be patient on that, wait for Maple to come online, that would be great. In fact, do you know what, I'm just going to message her again now, check how she's getting on. Don't go anywhere. I'll be right back any second. And with Maple too, I'm sure. Hold on.

Chapter 68

Kirsten

@TyroneMB05, TikTok
I don't know about you, but I am sniffing the sweet smell of bullshit from every single one of those social media whores

I frown. Why isn't Maple online with Dylan?

And also, why is my heart pounding? It's not like she's missing. She just hasn't shown up for her YouTube Live – the show I keep telling her to leave. Maybe she's finally wised up, listened to my advice for a change. But my palms are clammy as I slide my laptop away. And when I knock the barstool over with my foot, my gasp sounds more like a scream.

But why am I being so dramatic? There is nothing to worry about. Maple is upstairs, in her room, where she spends most of her life these days. And this anxiety I'm feeling will be the stress of yesterday's argument with Garrett and the hellish migraine that came after. I right the barstool and draw my shoulders down.

Except, it's also true that I didn't see Maple last night – the migraine getting so bad that I crawled into bed with two double-strength Advil around eight o'clock. Which means I haven't seen her since yesterday morning.

Which isn't ideal, I realize now.

I head for the stairs. Slowly, as though I'm not sure I want to know what's coming.

After my fight with Garrett, I was grateful when I discovered Maple had gone out. I needed a moment to reset, to remind myself that Garrett is absolutely her father, whatever he says to the contrary. It's a truth I decided on a long time ago, and I'm not changing it for anyone.

But now I'm suddenly desperate to see her. And more than that, to see myself in her, to remind myself why I chose my husband. Who I did it for.

When Maple didn't show up for lunch yesterday, I tracked her location and found that she was at Milly's house. A while later, I checked again, and she was at the mall, clearly enjoying some retail therapy with her friend. Then when Garrett announced he was taking the twins to his parents for the night, my migraine swelled and throbbed so badly that Maple's text confirming that she was fine felt like enough reassurance for me to crawl into bed.

But as I knock on her bedroom door now, then push it open, my nerves tingle. It looks exactly like it always does. Her vanity covered in beauty products, clothes spilling out of her closet. Chargers like spaghetti slithering out from plug sockets. But no Maple.

I roll my shoulders.

She must have slept over at Milly's. Yes, that makes sense. That's why I didn't hear her come back in. I whip out my phone. I have all of Maple's friends' numbers stored, partly because I'm a hands-on mom, a vigilant mom. But also because they've become like friends over the years, all the fun content they've helped create for our Maybe Maple channel, and the gratitude they've shown me for giving them a tiny taste of fame. It's created bonds that not many moms can claim.

I send Milly a message:

Hey sweets, is Maple with you?

And I get a reply in seconds.

No, sorry. She came over yesterday but left around 3 or 4. I saw she wasn't on her show. Is Maple missing?

My stomach lurches. No, Maple is not missing. She's just not here right now. I don't bother replying, but I send messages to Taylor, Scarlett and Martha, Maple's other good friends. They all come back quickly – it's an undeniable fact that teenagers are glued to their phones; this is why I'm right about influencers ruling the world one day – but with nothing helpful. Taylor's in Vancouver on a family vacation, and the other two are on a summer camp together in Arizona. None of them have heard from Maple in days.

I feel a bit sick, but I can't work out if it's from fear or annoyance. My migraine faded overnight but it's left me with a headache, and I really don't need to deal with this drama too. I check Find My iPhone – I'm not sure why I didn't do this first – but after whirring for a while, it places Maple close to Provo Towne Centre mall. Fourteen hours ago.

I drop onto her bed.

Maple was in here yesterday morning – she gave me a few monosyllabic words while I waited for the twins to get changed into their swim stuff. She'd left by the time I found Ash and

Aspen watching a movie in the den, but she was at friend's house, then at the mall. Normal places for a fourteen-year-old girl to hang out on her summer break. There was even a message saying she was fine. I had no reason to worry.

Except Milly didn't go to the mall with her. And Maple didn't stay over at Milly's house. And I've no clue where she's been since 8.35 p.m. last night.

Chapter 69

Kirsten

@ClarissaBobcat, TikTok
You know, the girl just didn't show up for a YouTube Live. It's not that deep, guys

I yank open Maple's closet doors. I need to work out what's missing. Because there must be something. Maple wouldn't run away without taking anything with her, and that is definitely what has happened. Because no one could have taken her. Harmed her. This is Provo, not Chicago, for God's sake.

I rifle through her clothes. Her big hoodie has gone, which is a good sign because it was hot yesterday; she'd only need a thick jumper if she was planning on staying out after dark. Those rancid sneakers aren't here either, the ones she claims are too comfortable to throw out. It's the uniform of a runaway, for sure.

I quickly turn to her vanity and pull open her drawer. Her money has gone too, all those twenties that I've given her over the years that she never spends because she gets everything she wants for free. She could have taken it for her trip to the mall, but my gut says something different. That this is the final act of a teenage girl who's been getting more rebellious with every passing hour.

And with that thought, a fresh wave of anger builds in me. Does she not realize the fallout this will cause? A girl with her profile choosing to leave her family? Especially with her current content being all about another missing girl!

I blink back tears. We have always been close, Mom and Maple, forever. But no one will believe that now, or ever again. This one thoughtless act of hers will destroy everything I've built.

I need to get her back. I mean, she's fourteen, of course I do; she can't survive out there alone. But I also can't let this become a story for our followers to devour.

The slam of a door downstairs makes me jump. Garrett and the twins are home. My heart speeds up again at the thought of the inevitable confrontation. But this is his fault too, I remind myself. Alongside Maple's. He's responsible for the killer migraine that floored me last night.

'Mommy?' Ash calls out.

'Maple!' Aspen shouts.

I close my eyes, transport myself to a tropical beach for a few blissful seconds, then take a long, slow breath and head downstairs.

'Hey guys, how was Nana and Papa's?'

'It was good,' Aspen says, but her tone is cold, dismissive. It would be typical of Garrett to have spent the evening poisoning them against me. 'Papa made a fire, and we ate smores,' she adds matter-of-factly.

'Wow, sounds fab,' I say. Then I turn to Garrett. 'Can I have a quick word?'

I close the kitchen door before the twins can join us. 'I think Maple's run away,' I say, making sure I don't sound defensive.

His eyes widen. 'What? How long ago? Is she on foot? Will I go find her?'

I lean against the counter. 'I got sick last night. After how you spoke to me. A terrible migraine – I honestly thought I might die from the pain of it. I had no choice but to go to bed.'

He's quiet for a moment as he processes my words. 'Are you saying she's been missing all night?' he finally asks, a tremble in his voice. 'Have you called the police?'

'I've been contacting her friends. Trying to find out what they know.'

'And?'

'Well, no one knows for sure, but Milly thinks she might have gone to Dylan's.' The lie comes easily, not because I don't care, but because I feel like that's the most likely scenario; he has become her partner in crime after all. I mean, yes, he acted surprised about her absence on their Live this morning, but isn't that the most obvious way to throw me and anyone else who's interested off the scent?

God, if only I'd known what this would turn into when I first organized for him to come and stay. It was supposed to be a simple crush, a first kiss with a hot skateboarder and a springboard to new heights of fame. Not teenage mutiny.

'So have you called him?' Garrett asks.

'I was just about to when you distracted me,' I say.

'I assume you've checked her location, and whether she's used our Uber account?'

Shit. Uber. 'Her location isn't showing,' I say. 'Either she's turned it off or her phone has run out of juice. And I'll check Uber now.'

But Garrett is already ahead of me, opening the app on his phone. 'Yeah, she booked one,' he says, nodding, a look of relief crossing his face for split second before it vanishes. 'At half past eight last night. The driver has marked it as complete, with our address as the destination.' He looks up. 'So why didn't she come inside?'

I swallow. Possibilities rush into my head, but I can't let myself catastrophize. Maple has run away, caused a fuss for me to resolve, like always. That's all. She's not in danger, not hurt. No one has grabbed her from our doorstep.

I'm not sure I want to speak to Dylan now, to hear a truth I can't handle. But then my phone starts to ring, and as I look at the screen, I see that he's calling me.

Chapter 70

Kirsten

@RubyRoccsVox, TikTok
It's funny how no one's talking about Ella anymore. The poor girl is all over porn sites and still missing, but suddenly all the tea is about why Maple didn't show up for a Live. Honestly, you guys have the attention spans of jellyfish #findElla

'Hey, Dylan, we're really worried about Maple,' I say quickly, needing to control the conversation. 'Is she with you?'

'Me? No,' he says, his voice rising. 'That's why I'm calling you. She didn't show for the Live, now she's not responding to my messages, and her Snap Maps hasn't updated since last night.'

'And you're not lying to me?' I ask. 'Because if you're covering for her.'

'I'm not!' he calls out. 'I haven't heard from her since yesterday, around mid-morning, I think. She sent me a voice note about today's show. She sounded a bit quiet maybe, thinking back, but she was totally up for this morning. She had some new information about Ella but wasn't sure that she should share it after Selena Hart's latest video.'

'What new information?'

'That's the thing: she wouldn't tell me either. And now she's missing. I guess I was hoping she'd decided to keep it to herself, and that's why she didn't come online. But if you're worried about her too . . .' His voice trails off. 'I mean, have you spoken to her friends? Could she be with one of them?'

'Of course I have!' God, why is everyone acting like I'm either clueless or heartless? 'They don't know anything.'

'Have you tried Coco?' he asks. 'Maple tells her everything.'

'Coco?' I frown. The name is familiar, but I had no idea they were close. 'No, because I don't have any contact details for her. Do you?'

'No, sorry. She has a YouTube channel, but I'm not even sure what it's called. Something about searching for a killer.'

'Wait, what?' Now I think about it, Maple has mentioned Coco a couple of times, but I assumed she was a typical teenage YouTuber, trying to make it big by pouting into a mirror like all the others. But searching for a killer is something entirely different. Almost like searching for a missing teenager. Is it actually Coco who's to blame for Maple's new wayward behavior? And why am I only finding this out now?

'Mommy.'

I twist at the sound of Aspen's voice. She's standing with her brother – Garrett must have let them into the kitchen, pushover that he is. And actually, he must have done more than that because the two of them are holding hands and blinking a lot.

'Please just find Coco for me,' I bark down the phone at Dylan. Then I end the call and turn to my youngest daughter. 'Yes, sweetie?'

Aspen bursts into tears, which is so out of character that the sight makes my stomach clench. I look at Ash.

'Daddy said you don't know where Maple is,' he mumbles, bowing his head.

I throw my husband a death stare, then turn back to Ash. 'Well, we don't right now,' I say, trying to keep my voice light. 'But we're sure she'll be home soon. She's probably just visiting a friend.'

'But what if she doesn't come back?' he murmurs.

'Of course she—'

'She knows Daddy's not her real dad!' Aspen bursts out. 'We all do! We heard you say it yesterday!'

Her words bounce off the walls like a sonic boom. I feel instantly sweaty, like every pore has leaked simultaneously. I shake my head, but in a manic way, like a crazy person. I try to slow it down, but it won't stop. 'No,' I say. 'No, Daddy was pretending. Weren't you, Garrett?'

I beg with my eyes, but Garrett's face is so white, his expression so fixed, that I wonder for a moment if the shock of Aspen's outburst has killed him. Do I wish it had? This man who I thought would be my rock in a good way, but who seems to have done nothing but weigh me down?

'It doesn't matter,' he says, finally coming back to life. 'Maple heard that I'm not her father and so that's what she believes now. And she's out there, alone, with that news spinning around her head. I'm calling the police.'

'No, wait,' I say on instinct. 'If we tell the police, the world will find out, and the internet will turn on us, and there'll be so many lies, because people have such crazy theories – you know that.'

'Are you seriously putting your social media image before our daughter's safety?' Garrett spits out.

'My daughter!' I shout, beating my chest, suddenly furious with him. 'And her running away is your fault! Your big mouth!'

'Don't you dare lay this on me!' he spits back. 'It wasn't me who started the lies.'

I catch sight of Ash's bugged-out eyes. I can't have this conversation now. 'Look, at least this means that Maple will have run away, not been taken,' I say, forcing my voice to soften. 'Dylan is tracking down Coco, who will probably know where she is. And I'm going to call Uber now about her trip. If that doesn't help, I'll call the police, I promise.'

'You promise?' Garrett throws back. 'And since when has your word meant anything?'

Chapter 71

Kirsten

@Flossythemermaid, TikTok
OMG Maple Clark is actually missing!!! This is like a plot twist from a Freida McFadden novel, and I am here for it! #findMaple

I walk outside, hoping the fresh air will calm me. But the sun's too strong, the air too accusing in its stillness. Maple knows that Garrett isn't her real father. Fuck, fuck, fuck. That was never supposed to happen. We have been so careful, for so long.

I walk around the side of the house and into the shade of the roof overhang. I lean back against the cool render, and finally I'm able to breathe.

Garrett was my childhood sweetheart. The two of us getting married was meant to be; everyone said so. But when he went off to college, instead of missing him, I found that I liked my freedom. Suddenly my dream to be a singer, to move to New York, felt more like an ambition than a fantasy. I started a YouTube channel (long since deleted now) and recorded a demo of my favorite songs. Eventually I got offered a weekly gig at Kilby Court in Salt Lake City. It was a Tuesday night, and sometimes the audience might only be a dozen students, but I was performing. Singing my own songs. And people loved me.

People like him. The man who kept catching eyes with me one night when I was singing, and then asked me to join him for a beer after my set. It's not like he was the first guy to hit on me in that place, but there was something about him that drew me in. Him coming all the way from South Dakota maybe. The guys at Kilby Court knew I wasn't twenty-one, which meant we couldn't get a beer there, so we left. Found a bar a couple of blocks away. Dark and intimate, the kind of place where time stands still.

It took me three years to get pregnant with the twins. With Maple, it was around eight minutes in the back of the guy's truck.

But I couldn't bear to be that woman, that cliché. A single mother singing in dive bars. I had spent my entire life trying to be better, to fit in with all those doe-eyed girls who could trace their lineage back to Joseph Smith. I wanted a big family to sit with in church, a fat CTR ring on my finger, my hymen still intact on my wedding day. So when I missed my period, and a pregnancy test confirmed the worst news, I drove to Colorado State University in Fort Collins and begged.

I loved Garrett so much in that moment. How he looked sad at first, then stoic. And how, before long, his expression turned to pride. I thought it was aimed at me, that he was proud I'd chosen him to spend the rest of my life with. But I've come to realize he was proud of himself. For doing his Christian duty to save a fallen woman.

And now my beautiful, rebellious, bastard child has run away because of it.

I open the Uber app. I can't find a phone number – of

course there's not an actual human who gives a shit about the millions of people who take Uber rides every day – so I navigate to the chat function. There's a dropdown box, and I wonder for a moment if 'I left an item in the car' might work, but of course that's not what happened, so I keep scrolling, looking for some way to ask for help to find a missing child.

As I concentrate on the task, a notification appears at the top of the screen. That's not unusual, and flicking them away is as natural as breathing, but as soon as I do, a new one appears. And another, and then another. Suddenly I can't get rid of them fast enough. What the hell is going on?

So I look. And I see that Dylan has tagged me in a post shared to TikTok and Instagram. This can only be about Maple. I click into the reel, and as I watch it, I have the strange sensation of slipping underwater.

Hey guys, you might have seen that Maple didn't turn up for our YouTube Live this morning. Well, I've spoken to her mom, and the really bad news is that they don't know where she is either. I know that Maple going missing probably feels like some crazy plot twist to you, but she's my friend, and I'm really worried about her. I'm trying to get in touch with Maple's friend, so if you're listening, Coco, please DM me. Or if any of you know Coco, or the name of her YouTube channel, drop me a message. Her content is about trying to find the killer of a teenager in her neighborhood, but that's all I know. And Maple, if you're watching this, please get in touch. I know life hasn't been great lately, but I can't believe that you've run away, not with everything we've been doing to find Ella, so now I don't know what to think. Please let me know you're safe.

I stare at the now-still image of Dylan, his hand over his tousled hair, those sad puppy-dog eyes that were supposed to seduce Maple, not condemn me to a public shaming. But that's what he's doing by creating this post, because everyone always blames the mom. Just ask Selena Hart.

It also means I'll have to call the police, right now, this second. Answer their questions. Weather their judgment.

I slide down the wall and slump forward. My Maple honey has left me. And I've never felt so alone.

Chapter 72

Kirsten

@BillieEsuperfan16, TikTok
You know how Maple found out that Ella Hart was some poster girl on the dark web? Well, Maple's been on YouTube since she was a baby too, right? What if she found herself on the dark web, and that's why she's gone AWOL? #findMaple

I offer Officer Browne a glass of water, but he refuses. The man is about fifty, thickset with an overgrown buzz cut of silvery gray hair and a closed-off demeanor.

'So Maple didn't come back here last night,' he says, repeating what I've told him. 'But you only realized this around eleven o'clock today because you'd gone to bed early with a migraine and then assumed Maple was sleeping in this morning?'

'That's right, yes,' I murmur, trying not to look guilty. It sounds so much worse the way he says it, so I tell him a white lie. 'Maple was at the mall yesterday afternoon, and when I saw that she'd booked an Uber back home, I relaxed and let the pills knock me out.'

'Right,' he says, nodding. 'We'll contact Uber; find the driver.' Then he turns to Garrett. 'And you, sir?' he asks.

'I spent the night at my folks' house with our youngest two. I only found out Maple was missing when I got back this morning.'

The officer nods again, but more vigorously, and I can tell he's a man's man. That he instinctively wants to cut Garrett some slack while holding me to account. 'Has Maple run away before?' he asks, still looking at my husband.

'No, never,' Garrett says.

'And has anything happened recently that might have caused her to go?'

This question is directed at me. I sense Garrett try to make eye contact, and of course I know that what Maple overheard yesterday is relevant. But I can't do it. I can't let this officious man with his wide stance and narrow eyes think I'm some kind of whore.

'No, nothing,' I say. 'Maple has a great life. She's an influencer, and her YouTube page – Maybe Maple, you might know it? – has nearly two million followers. She's a model too; she did a shoot recently in Vegas. And we're really close as a family; she adores her younger siblings.'

I'm expecting to see some admiration in Officer Browne's expression, a softening at least, but he looks alarmed. 'So Maple has a public profile on social media?' he asks. 'And do you know if she's been communicating with her followers online?'

I wonder how to answer such a stupid question. 'Well, that's how being an influencer generally works,' I choose.

'Give me a minute,' the officer says gruffly, then speaks into his radio. 'Dispatch, I'm with the parents of the missing girl. I've carried out a risk assessment, and I'm going to need a detective to come by here. Also, look up Maybe Maple on

YouTube for a description, yeah, it's her, and send out a BOLO asap. Great, thanks.'

'You make it sound like Maple's in real danger,' Garrett says, his voice gravelly. 'BOLO means what exactly?'

The detective gives him a sympathetic smile. 'Be On the Look Out. We would always treat Maple's disappearance as urgent due to her age, but it's true that her having a public profile does increase the risk that this is more than a teenage runaway situation.'

The room seems to sway. 'You think someone's taken her?' I whisper.

'No, I don't,' he says. 'I just can't rule it out, not with the growing evidence of how many predators operate online. Especially around child influencers.'

I feel the stain of his judgment like an oil slick. 'I am aware of the dangers,' I say with all the authority I can muster. 'That's why I have access to all of Maple's social media accounts and check them regularly.'

'Well, that's good,' he says, his expression softening a notch. 'Because I'm going to need details of all her devices and social media handles. TikTok, Instagram, WhatsApp, Snapchat. Did Maple have any other apps like Discord or Telegram?'

'Of course she didn't,' Garrett says, affronted. 'Telegram's for drug dealers and conspiracy theorists, not happy-go-lucky teenagers like Maple.'

I push my lips together, remind myself that Garrett has always been ignorant about these things.

'Well, some of its users are suspicious of the mainstream apps, yes,' Officer Browne says, nodding. 'And online predators generally fall into that category, so it's a relief to know she doesn't use it.'

I feel my neck flood with heat. But Blake runs a modeling agency, I remind myself. And anyway, she's a woman, like Blake Lively. Not a man, like Blake Shelton. I blink. Why exactly did I assume Blake was a woman?

'Now, I appreciate that there will be lots of accessible photos of Maple online,' the officer continues. 'But I'd be grateful if you could provide one that we can use officially with your consent.'

Consent. Is that what I gave Blake when I sent those photos via Telegram? And consent for what? I'd love to find out for sure, to prove the police officer wrong, but Blake has gone dark on me again. That's twice now. Both times when I ask questions, and after I've sent photos of Maple. At all ages, and in not many clothes.

Nausea balloons inside me, pushing against my rib cage. God, I'm going to be sick.

'I'll get a photo,' I blurt out. Then I rush out of the kitchen.

Chapter 73

Kirsten

@Gabbythemakeupartist, TikTok
I say let the poor girl run. I mean, we've all seen those Netflix shows about kidfluencers and their psychotic moms, right?

I lean over the toilet basin and vomit up a disgusting mix of coffee and eggs. Then I slide my cheek down the cool porcelain, and curl into a ball on the floor of my en-suite. I usually love the muted stone tiles, but right now they feel cold and unforgiving.

I'm sure Maple has run away – the clothes she wore, the money, overhearing our argument. But the police officer has put horrible ideas in my head, like poisonous maggots. And there's the Uber she booked home.

Cold sweat runs down my temples.

An obsessive stalker could have been watching the house last night, then pounced when Maple got out of the cab. It would have been dark by then. And she was on her own. Her head spinning after Garrett betrayed us both with his outburst. Maybe she even went willingly, feeling upset, easily drawn in.

Was it Blake? Did I treat Maple like bait?

But my daughter is famous. She has 1.0 million subscribers.

It could have been anyone. Like the guy who hassled her outside school a few weeks ago. I brushed it off as nothing at the time, just the price of celebrity. But it was weird, a grown man trying to give a child a box of chocolates. Why didn't I make more of it? Report it to the police?

Except, maybe this is me clutching at straws. Because Blake has to be the prime suspect. The evasiveness, the unanswered questions, the preference for Telegram over email. How he – because shit, I think maybe Blake is a man – wanted Maple to join him at the theater without me there, then wanted holiday snaps from when she was younger.

I mean, bone structure. What a fucking fool I've been.

I retch, lurch forward again, and bring up more breakfast. I should tell Officer Browne about Blake, which means telling Garrett too. But God, I don't want to. I can already see the looks on their faces. Disgust mixed with horror mixed with a misogyny neither of them think they feel. *But how could you? You're her mother! Where was your mother's instinct?*

I open the Telegram app to check how bad our conversation is, but it's bad, and that brings on another rush of nausea. And tears too. For how he duped me, and how I let him. *I really think you'll fall in love with her!* They were just words to me, a way to show how excited we were about the modeling opportunity. But how would a pedophile have taken them? Would he have got excited in a different way?

My stomach clamps, but I ride it this time. I need to be stronger, to think clearly.

And it's not like I know for sure that Blake has taken her. Or even that she's been taken. Maple did discover that Garrett's not her biological father yesterday. It makes sense that she'd want some time to herself to process that kind of news.

I mean, of course I'd sacrifice my reputation if it was

guaranteed to help save Maple. But I'm not convinced it is. Not yet at least.

I click out of Telegram and open TikTok. There are thousands of comments on Dylan's post, mainly from accounts I don't recognize. I scroll through them at pace. Capital letters and emojis and exclamation marks blurring. I'm sure some of them must be kind, hopeful, maybe even helpful. But every time I slow my scrolling enough to read one, I wish I hadn't. Insult after insult.

How they're not surprised Maple has run away, because who would stay with a greedy ruthless bitch like me. A mom who treats her daughter like a slave, who uses her for monetizing content, period. And that the signs of Maple breaking were always there, just like they were with Ella. Maple's vibe changing, her new content, a cry for help through a different lens.

I click out of my account and into Maple's. I'd already know if she'd posted since she went missing, but I want to see her. Remember her how she was before her obsession with Ella Hart. I check her messages too, including new requests, but there's nothing interesting there either.

My phone starts ringing. It's a number I don't recognize, but it could be Maple on a borrowed phone, so I quickly accept the call.

'Kirsten Clark?'

I close my eyes as I recognize the woman's New York accent. 'I don't want to talk to you. This has got nothing to do with you.'

'Listen, I'm writing a piece about Maple's disappearance,' Meg Jackson says. 'I'd love a comment from you, but it'll be on *The New York Times* website in the next hour or so with or without your contribution.'

'Well, my comment is that I miss her desperately,' I spit out. 'And I would do anything to get her back.'

'Anything, Mrs. Clark? Like take her off social media?'

I cut the call and slide back onto the floor.

Chapter 74

Nikki, West Virginia

@Lilyput<3, TikTok
You know, I can't help thinking that there's a serial killer of kidfluencers out there and he's murdered both Ella and Maple. Am I losing my mind or is anyone with me on this? #findElla #findMaple

Nikki Herrera looks at the only kid left sitting on the bleachers, his back folded over his knees and his shoulders hunched. 'Hey, Ryan!' she calls out.

The boy's head tilts up, but the rest of his body doesn't move, like he's in training to be a turtle. 'Yes, Coach Herrera?'

'Did you not hear me when I called you down here?' Nikki shouts. 'Come on, we're doing high jump now. Your mom didn't pay for sports camp so you could sit around all day!'

'Coming,' Ryan calls back. But then his head lowers and he stays put.

Nikki swears under her breath. Her parents were both teachers, and she remembers long family vacations with her two brothers every summer. Taking their RV on the road, West Virginia to Florida, six weeks exploring the Sunshine State. So it kinda pisses her off that she can't afford to do the same. That if she wants to live in a half-decent neighborhood, she needs to top up her school coach salary by working most of the summer break at camps like this.

'Ryan!' she calls out again, but this time he doesn't even acknowledge her. Even though camp rules state that all tech needs to be kept in the kids' bags until home time, she just knows that he's nose-deep in an iPhone. She turns to the nine other twelve-year-olds in her group. 'Wait here,' she instructs. 'If anyone touches anything,' she adds, wafting her hands toward the high-jump bar and the giant blue cushion beyond it, 'it'll be twenty push-ups, no arguments.'

Nikki strides over to the bleachers and stands, hands on hips, in front of the errant kid. 'Ryan,' she says for the third time. 'What are you doing?'

He looks up. His eyes squint in the sunshine that's leaking over her shoulder, and he lifts his back just enough for her to spot the rectangular contraband in his hands. 'Nothing.'

'So what are you watching?' Nikki asks, nodding at the phone that he's now failing to cover. 'Come on, what TikTok video is more fun than me teaching you high jump?'

Nikki expects Ryan to look down at his clean white Nike trainers, finally chastened after being caught in the act. But instead, he beams, his eyes glinting, like he's excited to find a fellow TikTok fan. 'Maybe Maple's gone missing,' he announces. 'And Dylan Dope is trying to find her.'

'Okay,' Nikki says, wondering who the hell these people are, and how badly it will affect her cool teacher status if she admits ignorance.

'But do you know what's crazy?' Ryan goes on.

'You showing no remorse for being on banned tech when you should be Fosbury flopping over a high-jump bar?' she asks.

He looks puzzled for a moment, but he mustn't have learned sarcasm yet because his face quickly clears. 'No, not that. Dylan is asking if anyone knows Maple's friend Coco, or the name of her YouTube channel, and the crazy thing is that I do! It's called "Coco's Cold Case." Do you think I should tell him?'

Nikki crouches down until her face meets Ryan's. Then she finds her hardest Coach Herrera stare. 'Do you know what I think, Ryan?' She points a finger at him. 'I think you should spend the next ten seconds putting your phone in your bag and running as fast as you can to join your group. Then you'll get to hone your high-jump skills, and I won't have to tell your mom that you misbehaved today. How does that sound to you?'

'It sounds good, Coach Herrera,' Ryan whispers, understanding finally landing.

'Great.' Nikki stands up, claps her hands, and watches with satisfaction as the boy leaps into action.

Chapter 75

Maple

@Anonfrom>>0, TikTok
I told you that Ella was dead. What did Maple expect if she was willing to play with fire?

Why did the Uber driver look at me like that? Like he knows me, all of me. I feel sick. Slutty. Even though I've done nothing wrong.

When that weirdo shoved chocolates at me, and that sweaty man in Vegas looked at me grossly, and the handsy guy at the baby contest put his arm around me, I assumed they recognized me from YouTube.

But maybe that was wrong. I mean, why would grown men watch a kid's YouTube channel anyway? Especially when they can see me, all of me, at least a body they think belongs to me, someplace else.

'Hey, actually could you drop me here?' I blurt out, suddenly desperate to get away from this dirty old man in his Toyota Prius who thinks he's seen me naked.

He looks at me in the rearview mirror. 'You don't want to complete the journey?' he asks. 'It won't change the charge.'

'Please. Now. Please stop the car.'

He taps the steering wheel a few times, then brakes and pulls over. 'I know who you are, you know.'

I fumble with the door handle.

'I'm not sure it's safe for you out there. A girl like you on her own at night.'

A girl like you.

'I'll be fine,' I stutter. I step out onto the sidewalk. He waits for a few seconds, then accelerates off, and I feel like I've both escaped a monster and been abandoned by an adult. I'm next to the highway, so it's not quiet or remote, but it is almost dark now. Cars rush past, but their headlights face forward, no one noticing the kid hovering with nowhere to go.

Except of course I do have somewhere to go, if I choose to. A bedroom with its own en-suite in a plush house in one of Provo's nicest neighborhoods. I'm lucky compared to so many girls my age. Girls exploited by disgusting men for real, like whoever's body is being used with my face on the dark web.

Because those photos come from somewhere. Even if they're AI generated now, the technology only works because someone took a picture of a naked child and made it public. And not one, but thousands. Children exploited by vile men all over the world.

Fucking, skanky, disgusting pedophiles.

Well, maybe I'm done with it. With feeling ashamed, and scared, and guilty, when it's not my fault. None of our faults. And I'm done with my parents too, for lying to me for fourteen years, then shouting the news out from the poolside because they've got some points to score. Like my feelings don't count.

Fuck them all.

And fuck risk too, because I'm going to Vegas. I'm going to find Ella and tell her that I know exactly how she feels, about all of it. Being sexually abused by thousands of men without even knowing about it, having parents who never put you first, trying to be the girl everyone else wants you to be, and feeling bad for hating it. And I'll tell her how badly I need her. That I won't be able to get through all this without her.

I open TikTok. Shit, I've only got two percent battery left on my phone. I quickly find Brandoninthesky and send him a message while I still can.

I'm coming to find Ella. I'll be on the first bus out of Provo tomorrow morning. Meet me at that bus station, like you said.

I press send and watch my phone die.

I stare at the dead, black screen. But instead of feeling scared of having no way to communicate, I feel free. Because no one can make demands on me now. No 'get ready with me' videos to record, or comments to respond to, or Mom making me feel guilty for never being enough.

It's just me, and a tiny glimmer of hope in Vegas.

I know the next bus is a Greyhound leaving Provo tomorrow morning at 7.50 a.m. because I checked the schedule after Brandon messaged me earlier. Before Mom and Dad sent me spiraling. It means I'll have to spend the night at Provo Central Station, which isn't ideal, especially without a working phone. But I'm not doing this because it's easy.

I turn in the direction of the main bus station and start walking.

Chapter 76

Maple

@Richboy25_rn, TikTok
Hey, I've heard that Netflix are making a documentary about the Harts and it's going to destroy them. Can anyone confirm or deny??

I hand over one hundred and twenty dollars to the tired-looking woman at the Greyhound desk, then take the slip from her like it's Willy Wonka's golden ticket.

When I first got to the station waiting room last night, I felt good. I bought a sandwich and a hot chocolate from the kiosk, then found a magazine someone had left behind and lost myself in that for a while. But as it got later, and the station got quieter, the staff started looking interested in me, like they were questioning why a kid my age was there on my own so late, and I knew I couldn't stay.

Provo Central Station is a sprawling place, a transport hub for trains as well as buses, with a huge parking lot for cars and bikes, so it was easy enough to find a place to hide. But the shadows still freaked me out. And the noises. Scratches and scuffles. A few distant screams, which could have been human or animal, I couldn't tell. And it was so cold. I curled up underneath a bench with my knees inside my hoodie, but I didn't shut my eyes. I just waited for night to be done, and tried not to regret my decision.

When the sky finally turned a dirty gray color, I uncurled myself and came back inside. But I haven't slept, and even with the sun warming things up, I still feel cold in my bones.

'Oh, also,' I say, turning back to the ticket lady. 'Is there anywhere I can charge my phone?' I might have been happy with a dead battery last night, but today I need to be able to communicate.

'Sure,' the woman says, pointing at a bank of chargers in the far corner of the waiting room.

I walk over, but as I reach for a cable, I pause, remembering how Mom tracked me to the maple tree last week. I can't have her screeching over here and demanding I go home, so as soon as my phone lights up, I cancel sharing my location on Find My iPhone and turn the Map function off on Snapchat. Next, I check TikTok and it's there, as I expected, a message from Brandon. This one's short – just confirming he'll pick me up – and I delete it along with mine.

An hour later, with a fresh supply of snacks, I finally climb aboard the Greyhound bus and choose a window seat halfway down. I look out as the familiar streets of south Provo fly past, but I'm desperate for sleep, so when we leave the city, I rest my head back against the cushion and close my eyes. Except that brings on a weird sensation, like exhaustion butting up against panic. I shift in my seat a few times, but nothing helps, so eventually I open my eyes again.

Of course I can't sleep. I'm all alone, heading out of state on the advice of a stranger, to save a girl I've never met. And I've told no one about it. I know the holy trinity of online safety rules – don't believe what someone you meet online tells you; always think twice before meeting up with them in real life; if you do choose to meet them, make sure a friend or family member knows about it. I'm breaking all of them.

I pull out my phone. I can't cope with talking to anyone, to hearing someone tell me how stupid I'm being. But I could send Coco a voice note. Then at least someone will know what I'm doing. I hold the microphone close, then talk at low volume, explaining why I'm taking the risk, hoping it will play into Coco's own fight for justice. She opens the voice note straight away. But shit, now she's video-calling me.

I cut the call. And again a second time, and a third. Dammit, why doesn't she get the hint that I don't want to speak?

Then she swaps to audio. Her fourth attempt to get hold of me. Her fifth.

Fuck this.

I pick up.

Chapter 77

Maple

@TommyInfluenza, TikTok
I've checked, and Maple has never tagged Coco in any of her posts. Think about it, people! That's supposed to be her bestie. I guess Coco's numbers have never been good enough for Princess Maple.

'Shit, babe, this is crazy,' she says, her serious voice making the words sound worse.

I close my eyes. 'I need to do this, Coco. For every girl who's been abused. For girls like Sophie Lyle.'

'But what do you even know about this Brandon guy?' she continues. 'I don't want to sound like I'm judging you, or telling you what to do, but his story about Ella might be complete bullshit. If he's really a pedo on the hunt, what then?'

'He isn't,' I say, mainly because I need to hear it. 'And my instincts feel so strong on this. I'm certain he's a good guy, that he wants to help. And you've always believed in trusting your instincts, haven't you? Like that neighbor of Sophie's you interviewed, how you were pissed off that the police didn't take any notice of her gut feeling about that guy hanging around.'

'Why do you keep bringing up Sophie?' Coco asks, her voice quieter now. 'It's almost like you're using her tragedy as currency to win your argument.'

Shame spreads across my cheeks. Because am I doing that? It's the exact thing my mom would do. 'No, I'm not. It's just . . .'

'Although, maybe it's right to talk about her,' Coco interrupts. 'Because Sophie's murder shows exactly what men are capable of.'

'Some men,' I point out. 'Most men are good, like most people are.' God, I want to believe it. Believe there are more Dylans out there than men who give children chocolates, or demand selfies, or stare grossly, or watch child porn.

'I'm scared you're wrong' Coco says.

'Listen, I get why you lowkey hate all men,' I say quietly. 'Because the man who killed Sophie really is evil, and he's always front of mind for you. But that doesn't mean Brandon is going to do the same to me. I have to think there are good men out there too, and that I'm smart enough to know the difference.'

'But it's so risky.'

'It's brave. And that's what you called me.'

I listen to her sigh heavily. 'You're going to do this, aren't you,' she says. 'Whatever I say, you're still going to go.'

'I promise I'll keep in touch,' I say, like some crap peace offering. 'How about I message you every hour, tell you what's going on?'

'And what am I supposed to do if the messages stop? I'm in Miami; that's over two thousand miles from Vegas.'

'The messages won't stop,' I say.

'For fuck's sake, Maple! Come on!'

'Okay, okay,' I mutter. 'Well, if you think I'm in trouble, you can call my parents.' *The man she calls Dad is just some schmuck who fell for her pregnant mom's fake charm!* 'Actually no, not them,' I continue. 'But you could tell Dylan. Or even call the police. There are loads of options.'

'So you get to do this massively reckless, possibly heroic but probably dangerous thing, but it's my responsibility to save you.'

'I didn't mean it like that.'

'And what if I can't?' Coco continues, her voice sounding desperate now. 'And then I have to live with that for the rest of my life? It'll be hell; I know it. And that's not fair, babe.' Her voice cracks, and she sucks in a breath like she's trying not to cry.

I think about Coco's obsession with finding Sophie Lyle's killer. I wish I'd asked more about why she's doing it. But not now. I can't risk it knocking me off course now. 'Listen to me,' I say, trying to sound like an adult. 'This is not on you. You've told me not to go, and I've ignored you. Whatever happens to me, you did your best to stop it, okay?'

'But, Maple,' she breathes.

'Okay?' I repeat, like a parent might.

'I guess so,' she finally murmurs, defeated.

'And I will be fine,' I say. 'I promise.'

'You know, I wish I believed in God,' she says. 'Because then I could pray for you.'

I bite my lip, close my eyes. 'You know what, pray anyway.'

Chapter 78

Kirsten

@Greenyflypodcasts, TikTok
We're launching a podcast next week to discuss the ins and outs of the Maple Clark and Ella Hart story, and we would love you all to get involved! Follow us for more details #findElla #findMaple

I've wiped my tears, brushed my teeth, and reapplied my makeup. I've also found a photo of Maple, one taken at Garrett's parents' house last Christmas, which I think strikes the right balance between wholesome and pretty.

But when I head back to the kitchen, my carefully constructed demeanor cracks on impact because there are two strangers – a man and a woman, both younger than Officer Browne, but with the same air of authority – leaning against the counter next to him. Garrett has retreated to the couch and is now staring at the backyard, maybe replaying our poolside argument in his head. I hope he's hating himself for it.

'Mrs. Clark?' the woman says, taking a step forward. She's tall and blond, with freckles, and long hair tied back in a low ponytail. 'I'm Detective Nicholls and this is my colleague,

Detective Martinez. Is that Maple?' She gestures toward the photo.

I nod, smile, pass it to her.

'Thank you. To be clear, while we are here to investigate Maple's disappearance as a potential kidnapping, that doesn't mean it's our primary line of inquiry – still the most likely scenario is that she's run away. But Officer Browne has those protocols in hand – he's issued a BOLO locally and has added Maple's details to the NCIC's Missing Persons File amongst other things. But are you okay for me to ask you a few questions?'

I nod again. I should probably speak at some point, but my throat is too constricted.

'Great,' Detective Nicholls continues. 'Now, I understand you have access to Maple's social media accounts. I appreciate Maple has a lot of followers, but have you noticed anything of particular concern lately? Like followers who've shown a heightened level of interest in her? You know, messaging her a lot, asking for private photos or to meet up in real life?'

I think of Blake. The invite to Vegas. The two requests for photos. 'No, nothing like that,' I say, finding my voice at last, even if it is croaky. 'I mean, there are always some unsavory comments on her posts, but I just delete those and block the account that left them, and that's the end of it. I'm very vigilant about this stuff.'

'I'm sure you are,' the detective says in a voice that screams the opposite. 'And what about messaging apps like Snapchat and WhatsApp? Do you have Maple's login details for those too?'

Heat rises in my cheeks. 'Maple is nearly fifteen. We felt she deserved some privacy.'

'Privacy, yes, of course.'

I narrow my eyes. Was that a dig?

'Mr. Clark said there was an incident at school a few weeks ago,' the detective continues, looking over toward Garrett then back at me. 'But you didn't report it.'

'The man with the chocolates?' I raise my eyebrows. 'I didn't report it because Maple asked me not to. She said the guy seemed harmless and she didn't want to make a fuss.'

'Okay.' The detective draws out the word. 'And there have been no other incidents?'

'Nope.' I shake my head.

'Mrs. Clark, I understand Maple has recently started a new YouTube channel.'

I turn toward Detective Martinez. His voice is lower than his colleague's but also softer. 'You mean this thing she's doing with Dylan?' I ask. 'They've got it into their heads that Ella Hart, she's another influencer, or was anyway, part of the Hart family – you probably know of them. Anyway, Maple and Dylan think she's gone missing and they're trying to track her down.'

'So two teenagers set up a channel to find a missing girl, and then one of them goes missing herself,' Detective Martinez says slowly. 'This definitely isn't a publicity stunt?'

'Maple wouldn't do that to us,' Garrett mutters from the couch. I'm not sure I agree – I imagine hurting us is very high on Maple's agenda right now – but I don't think she's doing this for likes either. I also don't think Dylan's capable of it; he's too green, too naïve to try anything that smart.

'It's not Dylan you should be suspecting of helping Maple,' I say. 'It's her friend Coco, a girl who I think might be more of a bad influence on Maple than I realized.'

'Coco who?' Detective Nicholls asks.

'Well, that's just it, we don't know,' I say. 'Dylan's trying to track her down through his TikTok fanbase, but with all your police resources, I imagine you can beat a fifteen-year-old kid to that kind of information? I mean, you could stay here and chat to us some more if you prefer, but that might be a better use of your time?'

Chapter 79

Him

He looks at himself in the bathroom mirror.

Carpe diem. That's what people say at times like this. Or maybe fortune favors the bold. Who dares wins. It's now or never.

He should have a shower first though. Sort himself out.

He pulls his T-shirt over his head and drops it on the floor. His bathroom is more like a closet, but there's a toilet and tiny sink, plus a shower unit with enough hot water for him. He unzips his jeans, removes his boxer shorts, and steps naked under the measly jets of spray.

Then he closes his eyes and conjures up Maple. That first time he saw her in the flesh, she was all dressed up. Makeup, fancy clothes. Posing in a glass box in the sky, of all the crazy ways to meet. He doubts she'll be looking that way now; she'll be tired, pensive, scared maybe. And that thought causes some undefinable emotion to hollow out his chest.

He uses soap, then watches the grimy water circle down through the plughole. He gets a certain satisfaction from it, but it doesn't make him feel clean. Except he knows from experience not to expect that. Not after the things he's done in his life.

But there's no point dwelling on those. Not now he has Maple to think about.

He gets out of the shower and rubs himself dry. But as he stares at his face in the cracked mirror, he senses it's not enough, so he strides into his bedroom, finds his old pair of clippers at the bottom of the closet, then goes back to the mirror. Ten minutes later, the beard has gone and the hair that reached his jawline has been replaced with a neat buzz cut. He finds a clean shirt – fucking miracle of miracles – and a pair of jeans that aren't stinking or stained and puts them on. From the outside he looks like a new man.

He heads out of the trailer and fires up his truck. He's ready.

Chapter 80

Maple

@7Harts<3, TikTok
We just want to put on public record that we are devastated for the Clark family about this terrible news. No parent should have to go through losing a daughter, even temporarily. We will hold Maple in our prayers until she's safely back home. God bless you all #findMaple

The bus driver pulls up against the sidewalk and shouts that it's the downtown stop, so I grab my things and head off the bus. I should probably feel sick with nerves right now, four hundred miles from home, my best friend thinking my life's in danger. But actually, I feel excited. I just might find Ella Hart today.

I can see the Bonneville Transit Center across the street. It's bright and modern, with lots of glass and angled roofs like sails. It gives me a good feeling, like nothing bad could happen in there. I wait for the Walk sign to appear – no point taking any unnecessary risks – then cross over and head inside.

It's busy, and as I walk to the seating area under the clock, like Brandon told me to, I start wishing I'd asked what he looks like. I knew he'd recognize me, and I guess I thought that would be enough for us to find each other. I reach the red plastic chairs, but I'm done with sitting down today, so I lean against a pillar and scan the space instead.

I see a man looking over at me. He's younger than I imagined Brandon to be, early twenties, but then Brandon never told me his age, so I don't know why I assumed that. I smile at him, but it's like it jolts him out of a daydream, because instead of smiling back, he looks embarrassed for a moment then turns his head away.

'Maple?'

I twist around. 'Oh, hi.'

'I'm Brandon,' a man says. He's wearing jeans, a light blue shirt, and a Las Vegas Raiders cap. I was right about him being older than the other guy, but his eyes are bright, and he looks what Mom would call well groomed. I give myself an internal high-five for reading this right. 'And I'm going to take you to Ella,' he adds.

'Thank you,' I murmur. I smile at him, and he smiles back. 'And thanks for finding her too.'

He shrugs, almost apologetically. 'We drink in the same bar, so I got lucky, I guess. I'm just really happy I can help.'

'And you have her address too?'

He nods, then looks at the clock on the wall. 'Listen, could we talk about this on the way? The neighborhood she's living in isn't exactly friendly. The earlier we get to her, the safer it will be.'

My stomach flips. Except what I was expecting? A penthouse apartment in Spanish Hills? 'Yeah, sure,' I mumble. 'But I might just message my friend first; tell her I've arrived.' I know I'm not being fair on Coco, that by messaging her, I'm making her part of this, the one thing I promised not to do. But she's the only person who knows I'm meeting Brandon, and now I'm here, I realize I need that lifeline.

His smile fades. 'Your friend?'

'Yeah, Coco. She was a bit stressed about me meeting a stranger by myself, so I promised to message her heaps.'

I wonder if he'll take offence, but the smile is back now. 'Of course,' he says. 'Coco sounds like a good friend. But would you mind doing it once we're on the move? I'm a little nervous about leaving things too late. For you more than me, with you being a girl, and famous.'

'Oh, right.' I've focused so hard on whether Brandon's a bad guy, I haven't thought about the danger that finding Ella might put me in. 'I guess, yeah.'

'Great,' he says, looking relieved. 'My truck is just outside.'

He starts walking toward the exit. I hold off for a moment, but I know if I lose him, I'll lose my chance of finding Ella too. I just need to be brave one more time.

'Coming,' I call out, and scurry to catch up.

Chapter 81

Maple

@JackMonroe1997, TikTok
This is totally a scam; those publicity whores are fine and y'all are so dumb for falling for it.

Brandon drives a dusty red pickup truck. It's less luxurious than Mom's, but more comfortable than Dad's, and my heart rate doesn't spike too much when the doors lock automatically. Brandon seems like a good guy, almost familiar in a crazy kind of way.

'You thirsty?' he asks. 'Or hungry? I was conscious it was a long bus ride for you, so I brought a few supplies.'

The aircon is blasting, but it doesn't seem to be having much of an effect because the cab is still roasting hot, and I can already feel my forehead starting to sweat. 'Maybe some water,' I say. 'If you have some.'

'Sure.' He nods toward my footwell, and I follow his gaze. There's a small black cooler bag wedged in at the back. 'There's some cold water in there,' he says. 'Or a Pepsi if you'd prefer that, and I got some mango. I figured teenage girls like fresh fruit; sorry if that's me stereotyping though.'

'No, I love mango,' I say, wanting to reassure him, and because it's true. But I don't think my stomach could cope with digesting any food right now, and I've always been more of a Coke girl. 'But water is good, thank you.'

I reach down and unzip the bag. There's a glass bottle of Voss water inside, and it's ice cold, like it's been stored in a freezer. I unscrew the wide lid and take a few long gulps.

'So, did you want to message your friend?' Brandon asks.

'Oh yes.' I open Snapchat and start typing. My fingers feel a bit chaotic – nerves, I guess – but eventually I get the basic facts down and press send. I imagine Coco sitting in her second-hand gaming chair receiving my message. Will she be relieved? Pleased? Or mad with me for involving her?

'And your parents,' Brandon continues. 'They're okay with you coming out here?'

'Oh, yes, they're cool with it,' I say. The last thing I need is him insisting I message them. 'They know how important this is to me.'

'They must be very proud of you,' he says. 'Putting so much effort into finding Ella.'

I manage half a smile, but Brandon's words make me want to cry. He's a stranger, but he already seems more decent – and more complimentary – than either my mom or my fake dad. 'So you said you knew it was Ella for sure from her tattoo?' I say, wanting to take the focus off me.

'Yeah, it's striking, isn't it? Although I had no idea what it symbolized until you explained it on your channel. That must have been awful for her, finding out that her image was being used on illegal porn sites.' He shifts in his seat, like he's suddenly uncomfortable. 'But it explains a lot, I guess.'

'Like what?' I ask. The cab is still too warm, and after missing a night's sleep and barely napping on the bus, my vision seems blurry. I try to focus on his face. 'You said she'd been mistreated by a man, I think?'

Brandon sighs. 'Listen, I don't know that for sure, but there's a big drug scene in Vegas. Fentanyl, methamphetamine. And whenever I've seen Ella, she looks wasted. She's always at the bar with this one guy, and I think he's her dealer. He's pretty rough with her, and I wonder if the porn stuff has made her think she's not worth more.'

I try to process what he's saying, but my brain feels sluggish. 'Are you saying Ella's an addict? And that she's sleeping with her dealer?' I finally ask.

He doesn't answer, but I take his silence to mean yes and it makes me feel sick. Ella was one of America's most popular teens a few years ago, an amazing dancer, always so bubbly and confident. How could she have sunk so low?

Except that's a bullshit question, because I know exactly how fake that whole smile-for-the-camera life is. I mean, wouldn't I be categorized as super popular right now? And look at me. Dealing with a pile of shit almost as big as Ella's.

'Are we nearly there?' I ask, still trying to swallow down my nausea. The streets do look rougher here, like Brandon warned.

'Almost,' he says. 'Just rest your head back and close your eyes. I'll tell you when we're close.'

I nod. I don't know why – his answer doesn't make sense – but still, the suggestion sounds so welcome that I let my eyelids drop. And darkness claim me.

Chapter 82

Kirsten

@RealRyanB14, TikTok
Hi everyone, my name's Ryan and this is my first TikTok. I cleared four three at high jump today. Oh, and I've just sent Dylan Dope a message with the name of Coco's YouTube channel #findMaple

I collect the bottle from the pantry and place it on the kitchen countertop. Then I reach for a glass and pour a generous measure. The wine's blood-red color provides a satisfying contrast in my white kitchen, a visual *fuck you* to the world.

I have held on to my biggest secret for over fifteen years to protect my daughter, and in one argument, Garrett has ruined everything. And now Maple's gone, either by choice to punish us, or taken by force because she was vulnerable.

Either way, it's his fault. So I'm done with caring what my husband thinks of me.

I take a long gulp, then brace myself as he walks into the room.

'The twins are asleep, finally,' he says, then his words dry up as he sees my glass. 'What are you doing?'

‘Numbing the pain,’ I say, taking another mouthful.

‘Drinking alcohol is a sin,’ he reminds me. ‘You know that.’

‘And you lost your right to judge me when you told our children our darkest secret.’

He flinches, and I celebrate the moment by finishing my glass. Then quickly pouring another.

‘I stood by you when I had no reason to,’ he says through gritted teeth. ‘My ex-girlfriend, pregnant with another man’s child. Not many would take you in, but I did. And I have been a devoted husband to you, and father to Maple, ever since.’

‘Devoted? What have you done, Garrett? Because I’m the one who’s raised this family. Raised the kids, raised our finances, raised us up to be better.’

‘Better than what?’ he throws back.

There’s silence while I finish my second glass, pour a third.

Then he finally speaks. ‘Even now, with Maple gone, the twins traumatized, everyone on social media bitching about us, you still have no regrets, do you?’

‘Oh, I have a few,’ I say. I mean getting pregnant at the wrong time, settling for Garrett, giving him enough rope to hang us both. But the image that springs up alongside those words is something different. It’s Blake’s message – *Could you possibly send some photos of Maple growing up? Unfiltered, natural.*

I shake the image away and wonder if one bottle is going to be enough.

‘And you lied to the police about that freak with the chocolates,’ Garrett goes on. ‘Maple was petrified of him; it was you who convinced her it was nothing.’

‘Maple is a child. Children get scared of lots of things that won’t hurt them. It’s our job to educate them on what’s dangerous, and what’s not.’ I like how confident I sound; how solid my argument is. I’m not stupid, I know this is the alcohol working its magic. But I don't care. It's been a shitty day, and it's good to feel in control again.

'And how do you know the man wasn't dangerous?' Garrett asks. 'Or the thousands of other sick men who watch Maple's content?' He shakes his head in disgust, even though he's a fucking hypocrite because it wasn't me who tried to bribe Maple back online with dirty sodas. 'Do you know who I spoke to this afternoon?' he asks.

'No, I don't know. God?'

'The Uber driver who picked Maple up. I figured I wasn't going to wait for the police to do it, so I bounced between a dozen chatbots until I found him. And he admitted that he didn't drop Maple home. That she demanded to get out of his car only a couple of minutes into the journey. So she was out there, alone, in the dark. A fourteen-year-old girl who two million strangers think they know, who have seen her bedroom countless times. Does that make you feel differently? Do you regret making her famous now?'

Dammit, those messages are back behind my eyes. Blake blowing hot and cold, manipulating me into giving away too much of Maple. I shake my head. My glass is empty again too, so I reach for the bottle. But when I pour, I just get sediment. Tears burn my eyes. Am I missing Maple or mourning the empty wine bottle? I drop my face into my hands, and suddenly I'm crying. Loud, ugly sobs.

Incredibly, Garrett reaches for me. And even more surprisingly, I let him.

And it feels good, resting my head against his broad, warm chest. Because I'm tired. Tired of pretending life is always good; of repeating the mantra that Maple's fine when she might well not be; of trying to believe that this isn't my fault when everyone else thinks it is. And tired of holding on to all this guilt about Blake when the truth is I was manipulated by him. I'm a victim too.

'Do you think she might have been taken?' Garrett whispers into my hair. 'Because if she has, you're right; it is my fault. For upsetting her, putting her at risk.'

'I'm scared she might have been,' I confess into Garrett's sweater. 'Because I've been tricked, I think, by this nasty liar. I thought it was a woman at first, but I'm not sure I think that now. And I sent him photos of Maple; he even wanted ones when she was little.'

I feel a coolness on my cheeks as Garrett steps away from me but I don't hear the coolness in his voice. 'Tell me more,' he whispers.

'His name's Blake,' I murmur. 'He said he ran a modeling agency.' I try to move closer again, but Garrett holds my arms, so I look into his eyes. 'And why would I think any different? I mean, I guess the Telegram thing could have been a red flag,' I mumble. 'But he sounded so genuine.'

Garrett turns toward the window for a few seconds, but when he looks back at me, his eyes are soft again. 'Can I see the messages?'

I stare at his outstretched hand. Has my imperfect husband finally become an ally? I open Telegram and slowly hand him my phone, instantly feeling its loss.

He smiles at me, hesitates a moment, then leaves the room. I listen to the soft clink of the study door closing.

Chapter 83

Kirsten

@CharliiKnoxville06, TikTok
What the fuck is going on with these kidfluencer moms? They should all be locked up for how they use and abuse their children imo. And where the fuck are the dads?? #findElla #findMaple

God, my head hurts. Again. What is happening to me? I have spent years enjoying a clandestine glass of wine in the pantry when the mood suits, but only one, with zero consequences attached. Okay, there have been occasions when I've been tempted to have a second, but never a third glass. And definitely not in public. But now I've done it three times in a fortnight.

Except, my daughter is missing. No one can expect me to function properly now.

I kick back the duvet, roll onto my side, and push up to sitting. My brain judders inside my skull for a moment, but settles, so I risk standing up. So far, so good. I walk into my bathroom, run the shower, then force myself to step under a stream of cold water. It takes my breath away, and makes me shiver, but it helps. I feel a wisp of energy seep in, my mind clear a degree or two.

Oh God.

I choke on some spray.

I told Garrett about Blake last night.

My heart bursts into a sprint, the new energy morphing into panic as I replay the moment. My head on his chest. His arms around my back. Feeling like a team again. At least he didn't get angry when I told him, like he might have done. He just calmly asked to see my phone.

He's got my phone. My very most private thing. Another lurch of panic grabs my insides. My stomach roils and I retch, spit out a dribble of red-tinted vomit, watch it snake down the drain. I feel dirty now, so I switch the shower to hot, close my eyes, let it burn my skin.

Last night Garrett blamed himself for Maple's disappearance. Has he switched that blame to me now? I don't remember him coming to bed last night, but I would have fallen asleep quickly, a bottle of wine on an empty stomach. And it's not surprising that he got up before me this morning.

I need to see him. To work out exactly how mad he is with me and find a way back into his good books. Garrett has disappointed me so many times over the years, but last night I realized that I still love him, in my own way. And now, with Maple missing and the whole of social media hating on me, I need him.

I pull on a yellow sundress – his favorite – and head downstairs as fast as my hungover body will carry me.

'Garrett?' I call out, listening for noise. 'Aspen? Ash?' But I feel the emptiness as much as I hear it.

They'll be at the park, I think. Garrett giving me some time to recover. Hopefully he'll have left my phone somewhere obvious too.

And yes, it's there in the kitchen. Exactly where my wine glass sat last night, except the contrast of the black handset against the white surface doesn't have the same impact. In fact, it looks completely normal.

Except for the piece of paper next to it, folded, my name scrawled on the side facing up. I reach for it with a trembling hand.

Kirsten,

I know I'm not a perfect dad. But I have never used our kids to chase my own dreams like you have. I should have stopped you years ago, but you wouldn't let me near Maple, always finding silent ways to remind me how she wasn't mine, that I had no jurisdiction. Then you made me feel so worthless when I lost my job that the twins suffered from my indecision too. It took other people – child psychologists, anthropologists, investigative journalists, survivors – on those podcasts you hate so much to make me realise what should have been obvious. Children shouldn't be on unregulated social media, period. And they definitely shouldn't be expected to earn their family income.

I wanted to convince you, not fight you. But what you told me last night – how you abused Maple's trust, her image, and her safety in such an abhorrent way – made me realize that there is no hope for us, or for you. So I'm taking the twins, and when Maple gets in touch – because I have to believe she will, that your disgusting pedo buddy Blake hasn't taken her – I will make it clear that she will always have a home with me. And that she should never live with you again.

Goodbye, Kirsten. As a Christian, I hope you find redemption.

But as a father, I hope you suffer.

Chapter 84

Maple

@mimilittleponyyy, TikTok
I had a horrible dream last night about Maybe Maple. I'm really scared for her #findMaple

I blink. It's dark. My heart thuds.

Where am I?

Brandon. I was in his car; we were going to find Ella. It was hot but comfortable. He was nice, gave me water. And I was so tired.

I fell asleep.

But why can't I remember what happened next? How I got here? Wherever here is.

My body shivers. My hoodie's gone; I'm just in a T-shirt. My sneakers are off too.

There's a bed beneath me; I can feel the mattress. But there's something hard against my wrists. I lift my arms. There's a loud chiming, then my arms stop midair. I try again, and again, more violently, but I can't get them past the same point. Metal digs into my skin. Handcuffs on a chain, attached to the bed.

I try my legs next, but they're in shackles too, and as I try to move them, I realize they're even more restricted.

Panic rips at my insides. I twist, roll onto my side. The chain on my right wrist resists, wrenching my shoulder, but I have just enough flex to curl up to sitting. Except I'm too dizzy upright, too nauseous. My head spins, I drop back down, feel my eyes burn. My heart races.

What have I done?

Why the fuck did I think I could trust a stranger?

Why didn't I listen to Coco?

Tears bubble and burst. I need to get out of here.

'Help!!' I scream into the black void. 'Help me!!'

The door flies open. Bright light floods through the doorway, blinding me. I scrunch my eyes half shut, but I can't let them close completely because there's a man walking toward me, a looming black silhouette.

'Hey, calm down, it's going to be okay.'

I recognize the voice. Brandon. Soft and friendly like when he picked me up, but it sounds repulsive now. Another scream forms in my belly, then blasts out. Brandon's hand clamps over my mouth. Hot and sweaty. I want to bite him, but there's too much pressure for me to move my jaw.

'I get why you're mad,' he whispers, turning on a lamp. 'But I promise you'll feel better soon. Once you've had time to get used to things.'

I try to shake my head, but I can barely move it. I can't breathe either, my nose too full of snotty tears.

'Now, if I take my hand away, will you be nice and calm?' he asks.

My vision's blurring; my lungs are burning. I need oxygen. I nod, and as his hand lifts, I gasp for air.

'No one can hear your screams anyway,' he says. 'Or maybe

I mean no one would care. But I don't *like* to hear them. If you give this a chance, we could be friends.'

His words make me want to vomit. 'I want to go home,' I whisper.

'I don't think you do though, not really,' he says, stroking my hair. I try to pull away, but he just leans further over me, keeps stroking. 'I mean, I feel bad for you, but your mom is not a good person. And she's a terrible mom, dollar signs in her eyes instead of love. And your dad? Why doesn't he look out for you? No, you deserve better than them. But it's okay because I'm going to take care of you now.'

I twist my head away. Feel tears slide down my temple. He's a monster. He tricked me into coming to Vegas. He must have drugged me to knock me out. Then he chained me to this bed. How dare he act like my parents are worse than him?

Except Mom does care more about making money than protecting me. And Dad has sat by and let her. Probably because he's not my real dad.

'I'm going to take you to the bathroom now,' he says, pulling something out of his pocket. I think it's keys. But no, shit, it's a gun first. Then keys next. My body starts to shake. 'And if you're a good girl,' he continues, 'I'm going to make us your favorite meal. And don't worry, I've watched all your Maybe Maple videos, so I know exactly what you like. I know everything about you.'

He fumbles with the chains on my legs, and they drop away. The chains on my hands go next, except he replaces those with regular handcuffs. I imagine swinging my fists into his face and making a run for it. But every muscle feels like Jell-O, my vision's too blurred to see straight, and I need to pee so bad. So instead, I let him drag me out of the room and lead me into his tiny, dirty, disgusting bathroom.

Chapter 85

Maple

@Tabitha.Penrod12, TikTok
I go to school with Maple and I used to wish I was her. Until I found a video of her in a shitty diaper on her YouTube channel. I mean, that's embarrassing, right? But I feel bad about that now #findMaple

This room smells of dirt and decay. There are windows, but they're covered in so much newspaper, it's constantly dark. When Brandon took me to the bathroom, he let me close the door, thank God. But there was nothing in there to help me. No window to jump out of, no soap to squirt in his eyes.

So I peed, then I took the water he offered, too thirsty to care if it was spiked, and when he flicked his gun toward the bed, I lay back down and let him re-chain my limbs.

And now I'm in darkness again, with nothing to do but think. Like thinking about the water bottle I drank from in his truck, how I was impressed by the Voss label. The seal on those fancy bottles is small, so it would be easy not to notice if it was broken. I guess that's why Brandon chose it. And if he has watched all my videos, he'll know I don't like Pepsi either, so I wouldn't have taken the can.

I close my eyes. Part comfort, part shame for being so stupid. So convinced that I knew best. Why didn't I tell Dylan about Brandon, ask him to come with me? We're supposed to be a team; that's what he called us. I was so arrogant, thinking that only I could save Ella. I told Coco, then didn't listen to her warning. I was too desperate to be the hero, to prove that I'm worth something. I feel a hollowing in my chest, like my lungs are shutting down.

The only tiny slice of hope is that I messaged Coco from Brandon's truck. I don't have my phone – I guess the pedo freak took it – so I can't check whether she read it. But I can't believe she'd ignore my messages. Yes, she was pissed at me for coming here, but she wouldn't abandon me.

And if she told the police, or Dylan, or maybe my parents, there must be a good chance they'll find me. The bus station will have CCTV, and Coco will be able to give them pretty accurate times. Brandon was wearing a cap, another red flag I didn't pick up on, so maybe he won't be easy to recognize, but they must be able to track his truck.

But I have no idea where we are now, or how long I spent unconscious on the road. Maybe we traveled too far out of Vegas for cameras to continue picking us up.

Fresh tears start to build, but I rub them away because I need to have hope. Mom and Dad might not be the best parents, but they'll have called the police in Provo when I didn't show up on Thursday night. And I missed Friday's show, so Dylan will be stressing too. Maybe he's using our channel to find me, like we've been doing for Ella.

And Jesus, I have nearly two million subscribers of my own. How can anyone disappear with that many friends?

Except that's exactly what happened to Ella.

I also deleted all my messages with Brandon. I thought I was being clever, keeping it a secret, but it means Mom won't see them when she checks my TikTok. And I bet the twins have told Mom and Dad what we overheard. They'll think I chose to leave, that I needed to get away from them.

Which I did, but shit, how could I be so fucking dumb?!

I look at the thin line of yellow light slinking under the door and feel a drowning sensation. Coco might well be my only chance to get out of here.

And I told her not to be responsible for me.

Chapter 86

Nikki, West Virginia

@hereforthedrama09, TikTok
Did anyone track down Coco yet? #findMaple

Nikki Herrera scoops up a mouthful of yoghurt, berries and granola. She doesn't actually like yoghurt – it's somehow both too sour and too creamy – but she follows so many wellbeing influencers on Instagram that it's impossible to avoid the hype. She shudders slightly as she swallows, then dunks her spoon and goes again.

It's Saturday, which means she can take as long as she likes to eat her breakfast. She takes a slurp of coffee. It's her amateur attempt at a flat white, not quite Biggby quality, but still. She picks up her phone and starts scrolling Instagram, always her go-to social media. She watches a few cute dog memes, which sets off her daydream about having her own Frenchie one day. Then she gets lost in pickleball content, transfixed by a forty-seven-shot rally from this year's Minto Open.

Eventually she moves on, flicking away adverts for bikinis and supplements, trying not to get jealous over her friends' sickeningly beautiful vacation shots. When she reaches a *New*

York Times post about a new article, she slows down, her brain whirring with something like recognition.

> A SECOND KIDFLUENCER GOES MISSING
>
> Maple Clark revealed the truth behind Ella Hart's disappearance. Now she is missing too. What's going on and who's to blame?

Nikki stares at the post, curling her hair around her ears, her unruly brown mop always impossible to tame. Wasn't that kid at camp yesterday talking about someone called Maple going missing? Nikki narrows her eyes, taps her fingernails against the glass screen of her phone. Yes, Ryan with the TikTok addiction. He called her Maybe Maple. And a boy called Dylan Dope who's trying to find her.

Nikki doesn't have a *New York Times* subscription, but she's invested now, so she opens TikTok and searches for 'Maple Clark goes missing'. A ton of videos come up. Mainly teenagers, but some older people too, all shouting into the camera, like their opinion is the only one that matters. She sighs. How can she be too old for something already? She's only twenty-seven but TikTok overwhelms her half the time. She rolls her eyes in self-reproach, then switches her search to look for Dylan Dope's profile on the app instead.

A lot of his content is skateboarding, but his most recent TikTok is a direct-to-camera piece. And as she plays the video, Nikki realizes that this is what Ryan must have been watching curled over himself on the bleachers yesterday. Dylan talking about Maple being missing and asking for help to find her friend Coco. Nikki thinks back. Wasn't that why Ryan was all excited? Because he knew the name of Coco's YouTube channel?

Suddenly the yoghurt feels extra heavy in her stomach as she replays their exchange. Ryan was eager to tell Dylan what he knew, but she just ignored that and gave him ten seconds to sort his shit out. She didn't give the TikTok plea a moment's thought. Even though it was a plea to find a missing child.

She pushes the bowl away, drains her coffee.

She's being ridiculous. Ryan is a twelve-year-old boy from West Virginia. He is not the lynchpin in this investigation. More than that, he'll have told Dylan Dope – and possibly the whole of TikTok considering how amped he was – what he knew as soon as he got home, which was over eighteen hours ago. And Nikki can't even remember the name of the YouTube channel he mentioned anyway.

A new WhatsApp message appears on her screen, and she looks down, grateful for the distraction. It's from her friend Emily.

SOS call! Marla pulled out of pickle. Says it's her ankle – it is SO NOT her ankle (and SO IS a guy). Court paid for. Can you make up a 4 at 10 a.m.?

Nikki checks her watch. Shit. That gives her ten minutes to shower and get dressed. But she's not going to miss a chance to play her favorite sport for free. She sends a quick thumbs-up and leaps off the stool.

Chapter 87

Kirsten

@Verityslamdunk, TikTok
Anyone notice how Maple's little twin siblings have disappeared from YouTube too? #justsayin #findMaple #findthetwins

Garrett has left me. Taken my babies.

How could he do that when our daughter, my daughter, is out there, somewhere, and I'm fighting to get her back?

That letter – *there is nothing left for us; I hope you suffer* – was brutal. And epically hypocritical, after he's lived off the spoils of my hard work for years. It's like he hasn't considered for one moment how I might be feeling after being tricked by a perverted fraudster.

I pick up my phone, open it, but then pause. It's such an involuntary action, but what do I want it for? I am not calling Garrett, feeding his self-righteous energy by begging for him to change his mind. And I can't bear to read all those sympathy messages either. Family, friends, church people, internet people. All fake in their own way, pretending to care about Maple when they're at least fifty percent excited by the drama.

But I don't want to check my social media either. All those

comments, reels, TikToks, criticizing how I raise my children. Of course I'd love to respond to every piece of scathing content, tell those toxic trolls that they don't know us, how close Maple and I have always been. But I know these posts are like locusts. For each one I stamp on, there'll be a hundred more buzzing around my head.

Maybe I should phone the police for an update. Prove how much I care. Detective Nicholls left a business card, so I have her direct number. But she might ask more awkward questions about Maple's work. And I also don't know what Garrett might have told her since he found out about Blake.

There's a voicemail from Stu Miller that I could listen to. And maybe I should be keeping him sweet, talking to him about Maple even. But I can't think straight right now, especially with my own mistakes being thrown in my face on repeat.

As I contemplate what to do next, a message from Garrett pops up on my screen. I read it and instantly feel out of breath.

Drove through the night to get to St George.
Just about to go live with Dylan.
I'm sorry but it needs saying.

Please do not let that message mean what I think it means.

My phone shrills. The sudden noise makes me jerk so hard I almost drop it. I expect it to be Garrett, but the caller ID comes up as Provo PD. Shit. I cut the call on instinct. It rings again, but I can't talk to the police right now, not after what I'm increasingly certain Garrett has told them. I turn my phone off completely, usually such an alien move.

Then with my hands shaking like they've been possessed by a twerker, I slide my laptop toward me and open YouTube.

Chapter 88

Maple & Dylan

@BrookebabeNYC, TikTok
Oh my fucking Goddddddd!!

Dylan: *So you guys probably all know by now that Maple's missing. She was last seen on Thursday afternoon, so nearly forty-eight hours ago now, and I really need your help to find her. Because today, this morning, about an hour ago, I found out something really bad. Something that means there's more chance that she's been taken by someone who means her harm. But this isn't my story to tell, so I'm going to pass you over to my guest today, Mr. Garrett Clark. Maple's dad.*
Garrett: *Um, hey. You know, I don't normally do this kind of stuff, so sorry if I don't come across that great.*
Dylan: *You're doing fine. No one expects you to be word perfect when your daughter's missing.*
Garrett: *You know, just on that, could I say something direct to Maple? In case she's watching?*
Dylan: *Of course. The floor's yours.*
Garrett: *Okay, thanks. Um, Maple, first of all, I hope you're*

safe. Off having fun somewhere, flipping the bird to me and your mom, because we deserve it, no question there. But I also really hope that you'll come home soon, forgive me, let me show you just how much I love you. Because you're my daughter, Maple. My firstborn. I haven't always been there for you, not in the way I should have been, but that all changes today. Because you're my daughter. You hear that?

Dylan: *You know, I think Maple will appreciate that, Mr Clarke. But that's not the only thing you came here to say, is it?*

Garrett: *No, it isn't.*

Dylan: *Sorry, do you need a moment?*

Garrett: *No. It's just hard, you know. It feels like I'm betraying the woman I'm supposed to love. But I know deep down that she doesn't deserve my loyalty. And if telling your subscribers about Blake, and what he's been doing, if that might trigger some recognition, and get me one step closer to figuring out where Maple might be, I'm gonna take it.*

Dylan: *And I appreciate that; we all do. But now of course everyone wants to know who Blake is.*

Garrett: *Yeah, okay, here goes. My wife, Maple's mom, Kirsten, has been talking to a guy called Blake on Telegram, at least I'm assuming it's a guy, although I doubt that's his real name. He says he runs a modeling agency in New York, but he hasn't given any other details, so I'm pretty sure that's bullshit too. And he's asked for photos of Maple. Recent ones, and . . . and past ones. From when Maple was a little girl.*

Dylan: *Did Blake ask for anything else?*

Garrett: *Yeah. He said he was in Vegas for work a few weeks ago, and he asked if Kirsten would take Maple there* *to meet him. Except not a proper meeting. He wanted to take Maple to see a show, just the two of them. She didn't go, and I'd love to think that's because my wife prioritized Maple's safety. But then she sent the holiday photos after that, so I guess not. The comms stopped then, but I'm scared that's because he got to Maple a different way. Men like that don't suddenly grow a conscience, do they?*

Dylan: *Our gut is shouting loud that Blake is not a good guy, and that he wanted Maple's photos for gross reasons, to jerk off to or whatever. We're also really worried that he's involved in her disappearance. So if any of you know who this dude is, or if he's ever slid into your DMs asking for similar things, please, please get in touch. And just to remind you, he may have connections to Vegas.*

Garrett: *My daughter's missing. And now I find out that some sick pedo has been chasing her for weeks. I don't know for sure if it's connected – and I hope with all my heart that it's not – but if you've got any info that might help, anything at all, we'd really appreciate if you could let us know.*

Dylan: *And of course, if you've seen Maple in the last two days, let us know that too.*

Chapter 89

Kirsten

@JackDwight888, TikTok
Just watched Maple's dad totally destroy his wife on YouTube. Man, that family is fucked up. And I bet this is just the tip of the iceberg. Get the fucking popcorn in, guys

The room spins around me. I grip the kitchen countertop to stop myself from falling, but it's pointless. Because I'm already falling. Hurtling down a treacherous ravine toward hell on Earth. A lonely divorcee. A social media pariah. Canceled.

How could Garrett do this to me? At my most vulnerable, I trusted him with my terrible secret. But instead of offering sympathy, he took my children, then told the world about my one mistake. Without telling them how much I love Maple. How desperately I want her back.

The video has finished uploading now. There for anyone to watch, now and forever. Unless I can convince Dylan to take it down. Or Maple, if she ever comes back to me. The comments are multiplying too. Tens, hundreds, soon there will be thousands. Thousands of people who will blame me for this. Not Blake, the sick freak who started the conversation, but me. A mom who just wanted the world for her daughter.

I shouldn't read the comments. But, like some form of self-torture, I do.

WTAF? Some women shouldn't be allowed to have kids

I thought we'd peaked with psycho influencer moms, but clearly not

Sending photos of a child on Telegram? Isn't that a crime?

I used to love their Mom & Maple content. Can't believe it must all have been fake

That vile bitch deserves to die for this

I slam down my laptop screen, then eye my phone. I can't remember the last time I turned it off completely. There might be a message from Maple on there, asking for me to go collect her from wherever she's been hiding out.

I grab it, turn it on, almost certain now that there'll be something from my daughter.

But no; there's nothing from Maple. Just a new voicemail from Provo police department.

This is Detective Nicholls. Mrs. Clark, my colleague Detective Martinez has spoken with your husband about an individual called Blake who we believe could be central to our investigation. I appreciate this is a difficult time for you, especially as you're also dealing with, um, domestic tension. But it is vital that we speak to you about this, so please call me asap.

Panic twists my insides. I don't want to call her. To explain, again. Hear judgment and damnation in her voice. How is it that when lonely cat ladies are duped by Nigerian fraudsters pretending to love them, everyone feels sorry for them, but when I get deceived, I'm the one at fault?

I had such big dreams. It was supposed to be Mom and Maple forever. Now Maple's gone, and I'm being canceled. And all that's left is a YouTube channel that nobody's watching. Nobody except pervs and pedos and podcasters hunting for ever more content to hang me with.

The doorbell rings, and I just know who it will be. I imagine her, leaning against our front door, peering through the glass side panels, her hair neatly tied back and gun holstered. I wonder for a moment if I should hide upstairs. Or escape through the backyard.

But I'm Kirsten Clark. I don't run away.

I grab my emergency lipstick from the cutlery drawer, touch it up in the fridge's reflection, and go to greet Detective Nicholls.

Chapter 90

Kirsten

@JuliaCartwrighttherapy, TikTok
Listen up, guys. The National Center for Missing and Exploited Children gets nearly forty million reports on their tipline every year. It's a sad fact that we can't stop the predators, which is why we need to stop the moms

'Thank you,' Detective Nicholls says in a clipped voice as I gesture toward the kitchen.

'Sorry I didn't get back to you,' I say as we lower onto the barstools, not quite facing each other. 'I guess this morning has been a lot.' Honesty sounds strange after years applying positive spin, but I'm too exhausted to try anything else. And as I watch her face soften, I decide telling the truth has its uses. Occasionally.

'I can't imagine what you must be going through right now,' she says. 'But we are doing everything we can to find Maple.'

'And I appreciate that, I really do.'

She smiles, but her face tightens again, like the goodwill is already used up. 'Mrs. Clark, could you tell me about Blake?'

I sigh. 'Blake runs a modeling agency in New York. At least

that's what he or she said. You know, I always assumed it was a woman, like Blake Lively, that's why my guard was down, I suppose. But maybe I was wrong. Anyway, Blake noticed Maple from a digital advertising campaign she starred in a few weeks ago and was keen to sign her.'

'I understand this person asked to correspond through Telegram,' the detective says. 'And provided no details about their modeling agency, even after you requested them. And that he, because we believe it is a he, requested photos of Maple, both professional shots and family pictures – which you sent. And he also tried to organize a private meeting with her. We have alerted colleagues in Las Vegas about this development, but there's not much for them to work with yet.'

I swallow. 'Look, I know it sounds bad. But Maple had just started out on her modeling career. It all added up.'

'Even his choice of communication channel?'

I decide to remain silent.

'I have a form I'd like you to sign, Mrs. Clark,' the detective continues. 'So that I can take your phone for analysis.'

'What?' My eyelashes reach my eyebrows. 'No.'

'And I'd like you to know that I've escalated Maple's case to the FBI. Sexual exploitation and the luring of a minor is a federal offence.'

'How do you even know she's been exploited?!' I blurt out, my pitch reaching an unattractive high note. 'Blake might be an innocent modeling agent!'

'That's possible,' she says in a voice that doesn't agree. 'Having your phone will give us his IP address and other relevant metadata, which will help us determine that.'

'But I need my phone!' I know how I sound, like I don't care about finding Maple. But the thought of being without my phone, of strangers in suits trawling through my content, is too much.

'Then I'll get a warrant from the magistrate,' she continues. 'This is inevitable, Mrs. Clark, and the sooner we can look into Blake's digital footprint, the faster this investigation will progress. Isn't that what you want?'

'No! I mean, yes! But you're not taking my phone.'

Detective Nicholls' expression sours, but then her own phone rings, distracting her. She accepts the call and I watch her nod a few times, then say goodbye.

'Was that about Maple?' I ask.

She hesitates for a moment but then must remember who I am. Mom and Maple forever. 'Your husband called the station again,' she says. 'One of Dylan's followers has given him the name of Coco's YouTube channel, so we'll be able to get in touch with her via that.'

'Really? That's great,' I say, feeling a tiny sliver of optimism. 'Because Maple might be with Coco, right? I mean, there's no actual proof that Blake has taken her. What's the channel called?'

'Coco's Cold Case,' Detective Nicholls says, while pushing to standing. 'It seems that she's interested in a serious crime that took place out in Miami a few years ago where the perpetrator has never been caught.'

'And Coco wants to find him,' I murmur.

'Something like that,' Detective Nicholls says. 'Look, I need to go now, but I'll be back very soon with that warrant.' She pauses for a moment. 'Unless you want to make life easier for everyone and give me your phone now?'

'How about I show you out?' I choose as my answer.

Chapter 91

Kirsten

@MaisieMDanceTX, TikTok
Watching Maple's dad on Dylan's YouTube show gave me goosebumps because Ella talked about wanting to dance in a Vegas show once. I'd hate her to have met someone like Blake #findElla #findMaple

As soon as the detective's car drives away, I reopen my laptop and look for Coco's channel on YouTube. I know I can't stick around for long, that I need to be elsewhere when she comes back with a warrant. But I don't imagine Provo magistrates are fans of weekend work, so I'm guessing I have a couple of hours to figure out a place to lay low.

Compared to most teenagers, Coco doesn't have that much content on her page. Plenty of shorts, but only six long-form videos. I watch her latest, filmed a couple of months ago. It's mainly a voiceover and images with Coco talking very earnestly about a girl called Sophie Lyle, like she thinks she's Kendall Rae.

So this is Maple's best friend. They're the same age, and Coco is pretty too, I suppose, dark curly hair and big brown eyes. But she lives thousands of miles away, she's obsessed with a murder victim, and she's got less than five thousand followers on YouTube. What does Maple see in her? And would she really have chosen to leave me to go to her?

But if Maple's not with Coco, or Dylan, or any of her friends in Provo, does that mean that Garrett and the detective and half the internet are right? Blake has taken her?

My phone buzzes again. This time it's Garrett's mom so I let it ring out, then wait a full two minutes before a double beep tells me she's left a voicemail. I'm not listening to her sermon about my absent mothering skills, so I hit delete. But as I do, I notice the voice message from Stu Miller again, the one I still haven't listened to.

I was so proud of myself when I first thought about contacting him. Yes, I had the optimism of inebriation on my side, but I really believed I'd figured out a solution to our problem. I would hire a private investigator to find Ella Hart, and he would accomplish Maple's mission for her. She'd go back to being Maybe Maple, Maddie would forgive her, and we could put the whole sorry episode behind us. Of course, I had no idea then that Maple would disappear before my plan had a chance to crystallize.

I drum my fingernails against the countertop. Narrow my eyes.

Maple's mission remains unaccomplished.

I push off the barstool. How have I been this stupid? This blind? Maple is obsessed with finding Ella Hart! She hasn't been taken by a pedophile, or found solace with a YouTube nobody. She's found a clue – Dylan even told me this, a new piece of information Maple was reluctant to share – and gone on a hunt. And of course she'd want to do it solo, because she's my daughter. Brave, independent. Ambitious.

I grab my phone, hit play on Stu Miller's message, and feel my chest swell, like my heart is literally fixing itself in real time. And as I listen to Stu's soft Utah twang, I thank God for agreeing to pay him in advance too. Because not only has he found Ella, he's sharing all her details, including her address.

This is where Maple will be. Not with Coco in Miami, or Blake in New York, or wherever the hell he really lives. But out there, finishing the task she set herself.

And maybe the most exciting bit is that I'm the only one who's figured it out. So I get to be the one who finds her. The heroic mom, with the most finely tuned instincts.

I need to book a flight.

Chapter 92

Maple

@JoelMTBchamp, TikTok
Remember Selena Hart made up a bullshit story about Ella going to dance with the Royal Ballet. This Blake dude might just be more clickbait fantasy cooked up by the Clarks

'Come on, eat.' Brandon's voice is quiet but intense. 'I made it specially for you. Mac 'n' cheese with ham, your favorite.'

I look down at the plate of food. Thick creamy sauce, yellow pasta, pale pink slivers that look like kitten tongues. He's right that I've called this my favorite meal before, but I don't know how because it looks disgusting now. He reaches out, curls his hot, sweaty hand around my neck. It's not painful, but it's intimate, which makes it worse.

'Maple, don't let me down after all the effort I've been to.'

His hand slips away, and the relief gives me just enough energy to lift my fork. But that's it. My hands are in handcuffs – my legs too this time – and the chain between them is short. As it pulls taut, I want to scream. How does he think me sharing a meal with him like this is normal behavior? I'm his prisoner, for fuck's sake. I lower the fork again, swallow a sob.

He leans toward me, his hot, damp breath landing on my cheek. 'Listen, we can do this the easy way or the hard way,' he says quietly. 'I'm a reasonable guy; I know you need a bit of time to settle in. But if you don't make any effort, well, that's gonna rile me, you know? And then I'll start wondering why I'm being so patient.'

He takes my chin, gentle but firm, and pulls it round until our eyes meet. His are a faded blue, more tired than alert, I see that now. He's clean-shaven, short-haired, with nothing special about his face. He looks like a regular guy, not the kind of man who drugs girls and then chains them up. Except what do those men look like?

'Why do you want me here?' I whisper, my heart booming, just for asking a question. Then it slows, maybe even stops, when his eyes move down my body.

'From the moment I first saw you,' he says, 'I had a feeling that we'd end up together. Like it was our destiny. I thought it might happen differently, more mutually, you know. But sometimes one person needs to take the initiative, don't they?' He sighs and his eyes go hazy. 'I imagine it was a little scary for you, waking up in a strange house. But I promise I'll make it up to you.'

He leans closer, nuzzles his face into my neck. I jerk away on instinct. I'm scared he'll get mad, hit me or something. But he just laughs, like he gets off on humiliating me, and it causes some anger to flicker in my belly. 'But I don't want you to,' I say. 'I don't want to be here.'

The laughter dies. He clicks his tongue. 'Well, spoilt influencer brats don't always get what they want, Maybe Maple.'

I blink away his warning. 'The bus station will have heaps of CCTV,' I say. 'And my friend Coco will have called the police too. They'll find your truck, run your license plate. There's no way they won't find us.'

'You think so, huh?' His voice is so calm; I want to scratch at his throat. 'Do you remember anything about getting here?' he continues. 'The different routes we took, how I changed my plates, where we even are?'

Acid swirls in my gut. I look away, will myself not to cry. Because of course I don't.

'No one's coming for you, Maple,' he continues, smug now. 'Just like no one looked for Ella.'

I jolt. The name hits like a firework exploding in my ear. When I woke up here, I figured Brandon claiming to know where Ella lived was bullshit, just a way to coax me to Vegas. But is that wrong? Is taking girls what he does?

Or maybe I'm being stupid. Ella has been gone for eighteen months, and thanks to Dylan and me, the whole world knows that she's still missing, that no one has cared enough to look.

'Do you know where Ella is?' I murmur. 'Please, I just want the truth.'

'Oh come on, Maple. The truth doesn't exist anymore. You know that just as well as I do.'

Chapter 93

Kirsten

@MollyMarch14, TikTok
If there were naked photos of me on the dark web, I think I'd want to hide away too. Maybe we should let Ella be? #findMaple #dontfindElla

I pull into a space in the airport parking garage and unfurl my fingers from the steering wheel. This Lexus was supposed to be a symbol of my success, but today it feels more like a getaway car. Helping me escape Detective Nicholls' clutches.

I climb out, zap the lock, and take the elevator to departures. Judging by Ella's address, a penthouse apartment in LA's Century City, she's clearly not in need of saving, but it sounds like an awesome place to hang out, so I'm praying that's what Maple's doing. Enjoying the fruits of whatever labor is funding Ella's luxury lifestyle.

And that everyone else – Garrett, the police, the internet – has got it wrong.

I shake off an uncomfortable sense of foreboding, a whispering voice telling me my mother's instinct is off, and head to airport security. I flash my driver's license and the boarding pass for my Delta flight to LAX at the TSA officer, then drop my bag into the plastic bin. I have to remove my phone, expose it to people in uniform, which makes my neck bead with sweat. But it slides through the X-ray machine without anyone showing an interest, and I arrive at the gate just as the screen above the desk flashes, *Boarding*.

It's late afternoon by the time the Uber pulls up outside Ella's address, and I instantly realize that this isn't going to be as easy as I hoped. Park Place is a sprawling, gated community, with a gatehouse that doesn't look easy to slip past.

I take a deep breath, find my best smile, and walk up to the gate attendant. 'Hey there,' I say breezily. He's young, dark and beautiful, so looking doe-eyed and grateful isn't too much of a stretch. 'I'm here to see Leah Tarl in apartment 106.' That's the fake name Stu Miller told me about in his voice message. And maybe Ella thought she was being clever, but frankly, it doesn't take a genius to work out an anagram of her own name.

'Of course,' the attendant says, with the requisite Californian smile. 'Is she expecting you?'

I shake my head, max out on my demure look. 'No, it's a surprise,' I say. 'I guess surprises are allowed here?'

His sparkle dims. 'We actually value privacy a little more here at Park Place. How about I call Ms. Tarl, check she's cool with your visit. If you could give me your name?'

I sigh silently. Here goes. I lose the smile. 'Detective Nicholls. With the Provo police department in Utah. I'm investigating the disappearance of a minor in my jurisdiction and there's strong evidence to suggest that Ms. Tarl has information that could help us locate her.'

This can only work if he doesn't ask to see my badge, so I

nod at the gate, like he's obstructing my investigation now. But he holds his ground.

'Let me call her,' he finally says. He disappears back into the gatehouse, then re-emerges a minute later. His arm is lifted at a weird angle, and I think for a moment that he's holding a pistol, that the City of Angels' reputation for gun violence is playing out in front of my eyes. But then I realize it's a phone. Except my relief doesn't last long because he takes a photo of me. 'What the hell?' I splutter. 'You can't do that without my consent! I thought you valued privacy?'

He shrugs. 'More for residents than guests, I guess. And Ms. Tarl requested a photo.'

Damn; that's my cover blown. Ella Hart was a kidfluencer for eighteen years. There's no way she won't recognize me. How the hell am I going to get into her apartment now?

'She says it's fine.'

I narrow my eyes. 'What?'

'Ms. Tarl says you can go on up.'

Chapter 94

Kirsten

@GracieMiaAdams, TikTok
You know, I think I met a modeling agent called Blake in New York once. I mean, it could be legit, right?

My heart booms as I wait for Ella to open the door. I can't believe she fell for that detective story, so this must mean Maple's inside, that I'm about to be reunited with my daughter. Excitement and nerves and hope and impatience all fizz together like a sour cocktail.

The door swings open.

'Hi!' I exclaim, then fall silent as I take in Ella's new look. The blond hair has gone, but so has the awkward emo look. This Ella is slim, manicured, poised, with a mane of chestnut brown hair that contrasts strikingly with her blue eyes. But there's something missing from her perfect face; I can't quite work out what. 'Is Maple here?' I continue, a little breathless now.

Ella stares at me for a moment, then steps back. 'You better come in.'

I tumble inside, then pull up. Because the apartment is

incredible. White walls, three sets of French doors leading onto a sun-drenched balcony, stylish furniture in light, natural tones. Every wall hung with stunning artwork that looks expensive and not a luxury item out of place.

But no sign of Maple.

'Where is she?' I ask, refusing to let the hope die. 'In the bathroom maybe?'

Ella sighs. 'I'm sorry but I've no idea where your daughter is, Mrs. Clark.'

'Oh.' I drop into a fawn leather armchair. She knows exactly who I am; of course she does. But that doesn't make much difference now. I was so convinced that Maple would be here, doing something brave and intrepid, the sort of thing I would have done when I was young. Like finding a father for my child when I didn't have one. But if Maple didn't come to LA, then where is she? Is she with Coco in Miami? Or do I need to accept the worst possible truth?

'Can I get you something?' Ella asks. 'A glass of water? A Xanax maybe?'

'Xanax?' I say it as a question, but Ella must take it as an answer because she walks over to a white Baroque-style table in the corner of the room and picks up a pill box. There's a laptop on the table too, and it's like Ella's shocked to see it there, because she stares at the screen for a moment, then slams down the lid.

'Here you go,' she says, handing me a small white pill. I watch her take one for herself and dry-swallow it. And for some reason – grief, loss, shame, utter hopelessness maybe – I do the same.

Ella looks pleased, like she hasn't self-medicated in company for a while and it's good to mix things up, then she walks over to the huge cream chaise longue and lowers onto it, curling her feet underneath her. As I watch the careful movements, I sense that missing part of her again. And decide it's mass. She looks hollow.

'I am aware of the YouTube show Maple's been hosting with her skater-boy friend by the way,' she says. 'Trying to work out where I disappeared to.'

I imagine Ella watching the show, laughing at Maple and Dylan's earnest, childish, naïve attempts to save her. An arrow of annoyance stabs at my sternum. And not just for our lost earnings. 'But you didn't think to tell them you're okay?' I ask. 'That they didn't need to worry about you?'

Her face falls a notch, which brings a degree of comfort. Unless that's the Xanax kicking in. 'I felt bad keeping quiet,' she admits. 'But it was too much of a risk. I don't want anyone to know I'm here.'

'But I know you're here,' I remind her. 'You let me in.'

'Which may turn out to be a mistake,' she murmurs, looking away. 'But you came a long way to find your daughter. When it came to it, I couldn't turn you away.'

I'm a good mom. See, Ella thinks so. But then I think about Selena Hart, and what a low bar she will have set. 'So your mom didn't come then?' I ask gently.

'I don't need her.' Ella drifts her arm in a circle with the grace of a ballerina, which reminds me that she is one. Or at least she used to be. 'See?' she continues. 'I'm doing fine by myself.'

I look around the apartment. 'It is beautiful,' I concede, but I feel a strange sense of sadness, like I'm not sure it is such a great home after all. Which is odd, for a million-dollar-plus penthouse. 'Do you live here alone?'

'As I said, I don't need anyone.'

'It can't come cheap,' I murmur. Because I can't help

wondering how this nineteen-year-old recluse can afford such luxury.

She lifts her hands and stares at her beautifully manicured nails. 'I model. And you know, if you need any life hacks, it's a crazy-easy way to become a millionaire.' She smiles but it doesn't reach her eyes, and it makes me think about Blake's offer of a modeling contract for Maple, how it felt like a dream come true at the time. But it wasn't.

Then I think of how ashamed Ella looked about whatever was on her laptop screen. And her swallowing that pill like it was sustenance. And I think that maybe I do know where those dollars are coming from after all.

Chapter 95

Kirsten

@Vicsecretsspilled, TikTok
Maybe Maple must have made thousands of dollars over the years. But I bet her greedy bitch mom hasn't let her have a cent #findMaple

'Are you an OnlyFans model?' I ask Ella, trying to hold eye contact.

She blinks, turns her head. 'YouTube, Instagram, TikTok, OnlyFans; it's all the same really. Looking pretty so that sad incels can jerk off over you. At least OnlyFans doesn't pretend to be something different.'

I place my hands on my knees. My motto has always been to post and let post, but I've never considered whether that extends to soft porn, an even bigger sin than alcohol in our church. But more than morality, Ella was such a great dancer, and she had dozens of brand deals. It feels like such a waste. 'But you were one of America's favorite teenagers,' I remind her. 'Aren't you worth more than OnlyFans?'

She scoffs. 'Worth more? When I was *also* one of America's favorite child porn stars? And of course you know about that because your daughter told everyone on YouTube.'

'It's not you though, is it?' I manage to say, although my voice has weakened, like my argument, I'm sensing. 'I mean, I know it's your face, but the rest is AI.'

'You think that makes a difference?' she throws back, shaking her head. 'Everyone assumes it's me so it may as well be.' She uncurls from the chaise longue, then walks over to one of the many windows. She turns her back on me and stares out. She's wearing a sleeveless silk top, and I can see that lotus flower tattoo Maple talked about peeking out above the neckline.

'Then I don't understand,' I say. 'Isn't OnlyFans a tamer version of the same thing?'

'I guess. But now I get to show my body and not my face, so no one knows it's me.' She says this without turning, but her voice still rings clear. 'And I take all the money, control everything, and those faceless bastards on the dark web don't make a dime. Smart, hey?'

Not really that smart at all, I want to say. But does that make me a hypocrite? I think about my argument with Garrett by the pool two days ago, him accusing me of enabling child abuse and my response. *The twins are the winners, the ones earning money, getting famous.* Isn't that the same logic that Ella is using on me now? Logic I'm completely rejecting?

'But what about your life back in Texas?' I ask instead. 'Don't you miss your friends? Your fam—'

'How did you find me?' she interrupts. 'Because everyone knows me as Leah here, and I don't get out much.'

'I hired a PI based in Provo,' I say. 'He found you for me.'

'Right. And how long did it take him to get the address?'

'A couple of weeks.'

I still can't see her face, but her voice changes. 'I've been gone eighteen months,' she murmurs. 'If my family wanted to see me, they'd have tracked me down by now. You know, all I did was refuse to go to London for an audition Mom somehow swung for me at the Royal Ballet. An audition I'd never have passed, by the way. But that caused a huge fight, and now it seems like they've disowned me. So do I miss them? What do you think?'

'But you can't hide away forever,' I try. 'I mean, what's the point of having all this money if you've got no one to share it with?'

She stands still for a while. Until finally, she twists away from the window. Her eyes are a little red but her makeup still looks perfect, as though she knows from experience to use waterproof products.

'You know, I haven't figured everything out yet, Mrs. Clark. But I'd love to hear any advice you've got. Because from what I've seen online, it's not just me who's going to be spending the rest of their life alone.'

Chapter 96

Nikki, West Virginia

@Annie.Matthews98, TikTok
Does anyone else think Maple's dad looks like Chris Hemsworth? He's hot, right?? And single now I guess?

Nikki swings the fridge door open, leaning on its heavy frame for balance. She's starving, but as per usual, the options are limited. She decides on her late-night staple, cheese and crackers, and grabs the half-eaten packet of Tillamook. As she pushes the door shut, she tips forward slightly, but manages to right herself, and even stretches onto her tiptoes to grab the crackers without toppling over. *Good job, girl,* she thinks, proud of herself.

Pickleball was so much fun that the four of them decided to celebrate with an al fresco lunch, washed down with mimosas, of course. Lunch morphed seamlessly into Aperol Spritz sundowners, and then Emily suggested they go drunk bowling. It was hysterical, trying to hold on to a five-kilogram ball by her fingertips while cantering down an over-polished runway in a straight line, and still try to hit the target. But she managed it better than her friends – even got two strikes by some miracle – and topped the leaderboard in all three games.

But now she's home alone at nine p.m. on a Saturday night, with a hangover starting to kick in. She needs food, water, and to not drunk-call her ex again.

She cuts a few slices of cheese, fills a pint glass from the tap, and takes her supper through the back and outside. When she could finally afford to buy her own place, she chose a run-down 1950s terrace because it had a yard, and she spends as much time out here as possible. She sinks into the lounger her parents gifted her last birthday and – on autopilot – pulls out her phone.

The first thing she sees is a TikTok notification suggesting a new friend, @RealRyanB14, and she rolls her eyes as she recognizes the profile photo – it's that kid from the sports camp. Yeah, TikTok, spending a few minutes in close proximity to a twelve-year-old on his phone – presumably claiming to be thirteen to pass age restrictions – definitely means she wants to connect with him on a deeper level. No wonder she's single if this is the help she gets from one of the world's smartest algorithms.

Except for some reason, she can't help clicking on the notification, and letting TikTok guide her to Ryan's profile in the app. He's only uploaded five videos in total, and when she narrows her eyes to get rid of the blurred vision, she sees that they've all been uploaded in the last two days. This must be his new hobby.

Ryan's first TikTok is from Friday night, which, now she thinks about it, is only a few hours after he got all excited about knowing that girl's YouTube channel. Maybe that's what prompted him to start creating content. Intrigued, Nikki presses play.

Hi everyone, my name's Ryan and this is my first TikTok. I cleared four three at high jump today. Oh, and I've just told Dylan Dope what Coco's YouTube channel is called. And he was SO happy. You know, Coco who's Maybe Maple's friend? I watch both their content all the time, and I didn't even know they were friends. Isn't that crazy? I like Coco's channel best though because I love true crime, especially violent murders. It's called Coco's Cold Case in case you want to check it out. Okay, and um, thanks for watching my first TikTok. And yeah, bye.

Nikki smiles. She can't help feeling a waft of affection for Ryan and his awkward sign-off. She wonders if this will be it for him, a few amateurish posts before he finds some other way to waste his time – Call of Duty maybe, Minecraft hopefully. Or if he'll be sucked in by the dopamine rush of likes and follows, plus the omnipresent belief amongst teenagers that creating content is the easiest way to make millions.

But then again, what does she care. He's an affluent white boy with the swagger of the privileged and above-average sporting talent. Whatever way he spends his youth, he'll be fine.

But that same inevitability doesn't feel quite so clear cut for the YouTuber he's talking about: Coco. Because posting about violent murders doesn't feel very appropriate for a teenager. Nikki wonders what kind of parents she has: the liberal type who believe children should be free to experiment, however risky that experiment might be. Or the absent type, the ones who don't have a clue what their children are doing online.

Curious now, Nikki opens YouTube and searches for Coco's Cold Case. It comes up straight away, and she clicks on the page.

But then her heart starts to beat a little faster. She blinks, and when that doesn't work, she rubs her eyes. But nothing changes.

She sits up straighter, spreads her fingers across the screen to enlarge the image.

That's Coco? But it can't be. Jesus, is this because she's drunk? Or is something really fucking weird going on?

Chapter 97

Maple

@JonnieMather.ss, TikTok
It's been 50 hours since Maple went missing. Sorry but it doesn't look good #findMaple

It's too dark in this room.

Nothing to do but think.

I think about my little brother and sister, their muddled faces when Dad blurted out the truth about me. And the last time I saw them, when I told them I'd be back soon, that they shouldn't pause the movie for me. I know that was Thursday morning, but I'm not sure what day it is anymore. I wonder if they're missing me. If I'll ever see them again.

But no, I can't just vanish. There must be people looking for me, finding clues that will lead them here. But if that's true, why did Brandon sound so certain that he's covered his tracks? And he talked about Ella. Was that bullshit to scare me, or is he some kind of serial kidnapper?

I might never be found. And being here is hell now, but it could get even worse. He already touches me in a way that makes me want to vomit. He holds my hand, strokes my hair.

So far, when I pull away – which I always do, I can't not – he lets me go. But will that change at some point? He's not a big guy, but he's bigger than me. Stronger. And he's got a gun.

The thought makes my face crack with fresh tears. I have to believe that I'll be rescued before then, that Coco will come through for me, like she always does. That any second now, the door will be rammed so hard it breaks off its hinges; a group of feds will run in, throw Brandon to the floor and tell me everything's going to be okay.

The door flies open, smashes against the wall.

But it's not the feds. It's him.

'Hello, my sweet girl,' he says. 'It's late; shouldn't you be asleep by now?'

My skin crawls. He either treats me like his girlfriend or his child, and both disgust me. Every cell in my body is screaming, begging for me to find a way out of here. But how? This sick, fucked-up human has chained me to a bed and locked me in a blacked-out room.

He sits next to me on the bed. I shuffle away, toward the wall, but he leans over me. My body starts to shake. 'Oh, Maple,' he murmurs. 'I don't know why you're fighting it. You and I could be best friends if you just let it happen.'

'I hate you,' I murmur. 'You're twisted.'

'I could be like Coco,' he goes on, as though I haven't spoken. 'Telling each other our secrets. Sharing photos all day long.'

'You're nothing like Coco,' I whisper, wanting to defend my friend, even though I can barely breathe.

'Needing each other so desperately that we get a one-hundred-day snap streak. That would be fun, wouldn't it?'

I stare at him.

'Ha! You look so confused,' he continues, grinning. 'I love it.'

'You're insane,' I manage.

'Me?' he asks in mock outrage. 'But I thought I always gave the best advice?' His eyes glint like he's said something funny. 'And that I'm brave and righteous and compassionate for investigating a girl's murder.'

'That's . . .' I'm almost panting now; short, rapid breaths. What the hell is he saying? 'That's Coco,' I stutter, even as invisible sirens blare in my brain. 'Not you.'

'Oh, your face!' Brandon giggles like a kid. 'Who knew AI could be so much fun.'

'I don't know what you're saying, but you're not Coco.'

He sighs, but the grin stays. 'So here's the thing, Maple. That's exactly who I am.'

Chapter 98

Nikki

@RealRyanB14, TikTok
Hey, what's happened to the Coco's Cold Case YouTube channel? There's just a message saying, 'this account has been terminated'. I loved her content

Nikki has her phone on the kitchen counter, on speaker mode so her hands are free to check her laptop. Her head is throbbing and she feels sick, but she doesn't know if that's down to the booze she drank yesterday, or what she saw on YouTube last night.

She's also struggling not to throw her phone across the room because Tom – one of her oldest friends, and more relevantly, the only person she knows who works in cyber security – is not freaking out as much as she is. Last night, drunk, she managed to label what she saw as fucking weird and go to bed. But when she woke up at dawn – hungover but sober – she realized that a serious crime had taken place. So she called Tom every ten minutes until eventually he picked up.

'Yeah, it's fucked up,' he says now. 'But it happens a lot. Identity theft.'

'But I don't get it!' Nikki cries out, sounding more like a dramatic teenager than she intended. 'It's me, all of me, but from when I was a kid, and in clothes I never wore. Modern stuff that teenagers wear now, not twelve, thirteen years ago when I was that age. I mean, how did this Coco even get hold of my image?'

'Were your parents into Facebook when you were growing up?'

'Sure,' she says. 'We used to do big road trips to Florida in summer break. Mom would take a gazillion photos of us and then do a kind of travel log on Facebook.'

'That's probably it then. Back in the day, a lot of people didn't get the importance of keeping their page private, which meant photos became fair game for everyone on the internet. And now, with AI, you can scrape an existing photo off a random page – or a bundle of photos to make it more accurate – and make infinite new ones in the same image.'

'God, I guess I knew that, but why would she choose me?'

'I don't know. I guess you're kinda photogenic.'

A flash of a memory from junior prom, Tom's hand on her back as they danced like wooden soldiers to Justin Bieber's 'Love Yourself'. But Nikki swallows down the awkwardness. She's got something way more disturbing to deal with right now.

'And, sorry to freak you out even more,' Tom goes on, 'but I doubt it is a "she".'

Nikki straightens her spine. 'What?'

'Well, it's my professional opinion that this Coco chick is actually a dude. Probably a middle-aged white guy who lives alone and can't form genuine social bonds, if you believe the profilers.'

Nikki drops her forehead into her palms, feels tears burn her eyes. 'Tom, can you do me a favor and stop treating this like another day at the office? This is my face staring back at me, attached to a website I knew nothing about until it was linked to the case of a missing child. And I still don't really have a clue how I'm involved in all of this.'

'Shit, sorry,' Tom says, instantly contrite. 'Because yeah, that's exactly what I'm doing. As soon as AI-image-generation models became open-source a few years ago, this problem of fake images exploded, so the sad fact is, this kind of thing has become normal for me. But you're right, each time it happens is still horrific.'

Nikki takes a long, slow breath. 'So you're saying that Coco is most likely some kind of online predator?'

'I'm sorry, but yeah, that would be my guess. That Coco is a whole fake persona using your image to befriend kids.'

Nikki shudders, breathes. 'This channel though, it's not your average teen content,' she says, still clinging to the hope that Tom's somehow wrong. 'She – or he – says they're investigating the murder of a teenage girl.' Nikki searches through her hungover brain for the name. 'Sophie Lyle,' she spurts out, suddenly remembering. 'And that's pretty niche, isn't it? So why would they do that?'

The line goes quiet for a while, and Nikki finds herself suddenly desperate for Tom's blasé office voice. 'I don't know,' he finally says. 'Maybe it's a fetish thing. Or maybe he thinks vulnerable teenage girls are more into true crime than makeup or whatever these days. But you said a girl's gone missing . . .'

'You think he could be the one who killed Sophie Lyle?' Nikki asks, her voice breaking.

'No. I mean, how would I know?' Tom says quickly. 'I guess it just feels like a creepy coincidence.'

'Fuck,' Nikki spits out. 'What is it with these kids who make their besties on Snapchat?'

'Well, if the guy's tech-savvy, and can afford hardware with the fastest processing speeds, he'll be able to do a lot more than send snaps.'

'Like what?'

'Voice notes, video messages. Even live video calls.'

'Live video calls as me? How can that be possible?'

'AI makes the gap between virtual and reality microscopically narrow. Too narrow for the naked eye basically. You know, a finance worker in Hong Kong was persuaded to transfer twenty-five million dollars of company money to a fraudster presenting as his CFO in a video conference. It's crazy.'

Nikki closes her eyes. 'So what do I do?' she whispers.

'Report it to the Cyber tip line. And if there's a missing child involved, call the police.'

Chapter 99

Maple

@ChrisJBrent02, TikTok
So yeah, I've been off grid since Friday, camping with Lola in the Nevada desert. It was epic, but I'm back online now. So what's been happening in TikTok land?

I stir, reach consciousness. I don't know how I'm managing to sleep in this hellhole. Maybe my brain is forcing some time-out on me because the reality is too terrifying. But when I open my eyes, Brandon is staring at me. I scream.

'Shush,' he hisses. 'Or I'll gag you again.'

I remember the panic of not being able to breathe and ram my lips together. I contract my chest muscles, plead with my body to relax. When Brandon told me that he was Coco – last night I think, because there's a dim sense of morning seeping through the layers of newspaper on the windows now – I couldn't think straight. My brain felt like a drill, shooting sharp pieces of debris around my skull. So I shut it down, went mute. He hated that, not being able to get a reaction out of me. And eventually he gave up trying.

But now he's back. To try again.

'You still look shocked, babe,' he says, tipping his head to one side, in a way – some sick, horrific way – that reminds me of Coco. 'Which is a surprise because I thought you Gen Alpha kids were savvy about fakes.'

Fake. Coco is all fake. Just a sick pedophile, the lowest form of human, pretending to be my best friend. I think about all the snaps we've sent each other. How good it felt to be totally myself with Coco, not Maybe Maple the influencer, or Maple Clark, the student navigating popularity. Just me goofing around, talking about boys, getting sad one minute and crazy the next. Me trying on new outfits, confessing my darkest secrets, like my dad not being my real dad. This freak knows it all.

Does he still paw over all the pictures I've sent him?

Then another thought hits me. It was Coco who told me my image was on the dark web, naked pictures of me using AI, the same fate Ella suffered. But was it him, Brandon, who created them in the first place?

'Not that it was all fake, you know,' he says, his expression becoming earnest. 'Yes, I had to use face-swapping technology, and voice cloning, and a little synthetic media to make sure you'd like me. But the person behind Coco is the real me. I'm who you became best friends with, Maple.'

My eyes blur with tears while my cheeks burn with fury. 'I would never be friends with you.'

'Sorry, babe, but that's what we are. Best friends, in fact.'

I think about my last conversation with the girl I knew as Coco, how concerned she'd sounded about me traveling to Vegas to meet a stranger. How could she also be that stranger? 'But Coco told me not to come,' I say. 'Why would you lure me here, then try to stop me? It doesn't make sense.'

'You know, Maple, I love to observe people, and record the

moment, one way or another. Did you know I was at your photoshoot in Vegas?'

'What?' I stare at him through the gloom. Is he the man who dropped the diffuser? That guy had long hair and a thick beard, but of course those can be shaved off. I don't recognize him, but then maybe I wouldn't; I only looked at the guy for a few seconds. Couldn't stomach his disgusting stare for longer than that.

'You don't recognize me, huh? You know, it's amazing what you miss if you don't look properly. Just as it's amazing what you see if you do. And trust me, you learn a lot about reverse psychology from observing people, especially if they're on the edge of something, whether that thing is the worst thing possible, or the best.'

'You mean you told me not to come to make sure I did?' I say, trying to make sense of his words.

'Aren't I smart, Maple?'

'And Sophie Lyle? I suppose that's a fake story too?'

His face suddenly changes. Darkens. And then I feel his hand whip across my cheek.

Chapter 100

Maple

@Lois.Studio88, TikTok
I worked with Maple Clark on a photoshoot in Vegas. She was a star, but I remember thinking her mom was a lot; she took more photos than we did. Poor kid. God, I hope she's okay #findMaple

I gasp. My neck snaps. Pain ricochets around my head. I close my eyes. I want to curl into a ball, wrap my arms around my knees, but I can't even do that in these chains.

'Of course Sophie Lyle is real!' he shouts.

'I'm sorry,' I whisper, trying to defuse his anger. I want to hold my cheek. But that means shifting toward him to allow the chain on my arm to reach, and I'm not doing that.

'Sophie Lyle was very important to me,' he says, his voice quieter now, but somehow even scarier. 'She shaped my life.'

'How?' I whisper, thinking of the different ways a dead teenager might shape an old man's life. None of them good.

'You know, the world talks about social media being fake,' he says. 'That we put content on there that makes our lives look perfect, when the reality is completely different. But that's bullshit. It's not just on social media that we do that. We pretend that we're happy, that life is wonderful, all the fucking time. Even as that voice in our head screams at us that we're worthless, we still smile, act like we've got this. People are so fucking scared of being themselves, of owning up to their own shit.'

Despite everything he's done to me, his words kind of land. Because I moan about always having to create more content, to smile for the camera. But I'm not that different when we're not filming. Still desperate to be liked. By my friends, by Theo and Dylan, my mom and dad.

Brandon must see the understanding on my face, because he smiles like we're in this together, Coco and Maple reunited. I look away, disgusted with myself.

'It's not often that we show our real, true selves, is it?' he goes on. 'Mask removed, raw feelings on display. But Sophie showed me hers, and I'll always be grateful for that.'

Then he pulls my chin around and gives me that weird, gross smile again, part little kid, part senile old man. 'And now I want to see the real you, every part of you.'

His words crawl over me. 'Did you do it?' I whisper, my need to know suddenly urgent. 'Did you make those pictures of me for the dark web?'

His face tightens. 'Oh that. No, I made that up.'

'Huh?'

'Well, it was all Dylan this, Dylan that,' he goes on, flicking his hand left and right. 'How gorgeous he was, what a great team you made. It was gross, babe. Embarrassing. I needed to take the clippers to your ego.'

'Wait, are you saying my images aren't on the dark web?' I ask, my heart thudding. 'You only said that because you were jealous?'

'It didn't work though, did it? You and Dylan got tighter, if anything. That's why I had to separate you permanently.' He clicks his tongue, like he's bored of the conversation. 'Anyway, I don't want to talk about Dylan.'

Suddenly, he's grabbing my legs. He drags me down the bed until my arms are above my head, taut against the chains. And now his hands are on my torso, pushing my T-shirt up, above my belly, above my chest, exposing my bra. I kick out, but my feet don't get close to reaching him. I writhe, but he pushes me down.

'Stop being difficult,' he says, in a voice that makes him sound more like a teacher than the sadist he is. 'Otherwise, I'll have to punish you. I'm just going take a few photos. And don't worry about not looking your best because that's the point. I want to capture the real you, Maybe Maple raw and exposed.'

His words make me want to vomit, to lash out at him. But I'm trapped. He reaches for a boxy black camera on the side table, holds it chest height. I screw my eyes closed, try to block out the nightmare. But I can feel his hands on my body, hear the click of photos being taken.

Then he moves me again. And again. Until he's taken hundreds of them. And in the blackness, it feels like there's nothing left of me that's mine.

Chapter 101

Dylan

@LolaLollipop182, TikTok
My boyfriend might just turn out to be the hero in this story #findMaple

His dad's only been back from church for five minutes, but there's clearly no peace or goodwill on his mind as he slams his open palm against their living room wall. Dylan tries to hold eye contact with him, but he can't, so he looks away, toward his mom. But she's just staring at the floor, like she's praying for an escape. He hates how his dad does this, uses fear to win every argument, never willing to listen. But Dylan's only fifteen; he has no choice but to ride it out.

'I have been so accommodating these last few weeks, Dylan!' his dad shouts. 'Even with all that shit you've been pulling, creating content I never agreed to, neglecting your riding and your brand work. And you repay me by bringing a stranger into my house, and his disrespectful kids who tear up the place?!'

'He's Maple's dad,' Dylan tries. 'And her little brother and sister.'

'I know who they are, for Chrissakes!' his dad throws back.

'My point is that I didn't invite them, and yet here they were when I got home from a very busy Saturday morning at work.'

'They're staying in a motel; Garrett just came to record some content.'

His dad's eyes blaze with a new level of fury. 'Yes, content about pedophiles, you making comments about sexual acts in front of thousands. You are disgusting!'

He raises his hand, takes a step forwards. Dylan flinches. His mom gasps.

'I'm sorry, okay!' Dylan splutters, lifting his hands to protect himself. 'I wasn't thinking straight. I'm worried about Maple. She's my friend and she's missing.'

'You should never have gone there in the first place!' His dad turns to his mom, shifts his anger. 'And that was your fault, getting charmed by a woman who converses with deviants. Agreeing for Dylan to stay with strangers. How could you be so stupid?!'

'I don't know,' Dylan's mom stutters. 'I don't understand how I didn't see it.'

Dylan's phone buzzes in his back pocket. He's used to that, more so since he started his channel with Maple, and tenfold more again since she went missing, but he's still itching to check it. Yeah, most of the comments are dross, but that's social media; he read somewhere that you have to wade through the churn to find the pearls, and that sounds about right.

Like that kid who told him about Coco's YouTube channel, the DM he found in his TikTok requests on Saturday morning. That was helpful. Although it's been twenty-four hours now, so it's a bit weird that Coco hasn't responded to his email. And Garrett hasn't heard anything from the Miami police. Why is real life always so much slower than online life?

His phone buzzes again. God, it's almost painful. The

thought that it might be another decent piece of intel. 'Can I go now?' he risks asking.

'You can go and clean my barbecue!' his dad hollers. 'While I think of a ton more chores for you. And don't even think about leaving the house!'

Dylan nods, finds a weak smile for his mom, and backs out of the room. As soon as he's out of sight, he opens TikTok, goes straight to the message requests where he found that kid's DM. There are thirty-four new ones. He scrolls through them, slower now, not wanting to miss something important.

He stops on a message from someone called Chris Brent. Holds his breath as he reads.

Hey, I'm pretty sure I saw Maple Clark at Bonneville Transit Center in Las Vegas on Friday afternoon. I did that double-take thing when you think you know someone you actually recognize from Instagram or whatever. It was around 3 p.m. and she met up with a middle-aged guy. Seemed friendly enough. Sorry for not messaging earlier – I've been camping with my girlfriend for the weekend, off grid you know. Hope you find her.

Dylan grips the phone, feels a jolt of excitement – Maple has been spotted in Vegas. But the feeling quickly morphs into dread. Vegas is where that guy Blake wanted Maple to go. And the message says she walked off with a middle-aged guy. Two days ago.

It has to be him. But why would she go willingly? What line did he feed her for that to happen?

All Dylan knows for sure is that he needs to be in Vegas. Fuck his dad. He's done with worrying about when that asshole might throw the next punch. He calls Garrett, his hands shaking.

'Hey,' Garrett says, sounding crushed. 'I've just heard some terrible news.'

'Well, let me go first because at least mine's got a positive side,' Dylan interrupts. 'Maple's been spotted in Vegas, so can you drive us there?'

Chapter 102

Kirsten

@Kaiathecatlady, TikTok
Everyone gets drawn to the glitz and glamour of Vegas, but trust me, I spent five years there, and what you see isn't what you get. #findMaple

I love Los Angeles! Why have I never been here before? Why have I wasted my life in puritanical Provo when the City of Angels is just two hours away? I mean, there are karaoke bars here that never close! Basement speakeasies with disco balls and microphones. What more could a girl want?

I've sung Beyoncé, Ariana Grande, Rhianna, even Madonna. If I didn't need to replenish my drink, I'd still be on stage now. Well, that, and those plastic women in leopard print telling me I was hogging the mic.

But I can't help who I am, a natural performer; of course the stage is like a magnet for me. It reminds me how much I loved singing at Kilby Court, back when I didn't have anyone's happiness to think about except my own.

Just like now, as Ella pointed out this afternoon; or maybe yesterday, it's hard to keep track of time down here. Because being alone is just negative speak for doing exactly what you want.

I pick up my – seventh? Eighth? – mojito and say a silent toast to Ella, a thank-you for pointing out my new beginning, my chance to be blissfully in charge of my own destiny and not responsible for anyone else's. Because those days when I was single, they were the absolute best days. No question.

And now I am free to do it again. Lucky, lucky me. I take a gulp.

'Hey, I heard you singing up there. You've got a great voice.'

I turn toward the compliment, like a sunflower opening to the sun. 'Why thank you.' The man isn't gorgeous, not like that gate attendant from Ella's apartment block, but he's not bad-looking. And I need to celebrate my newfound freedom somehow. 'I'm just taking a break,' I purr. 'But I'll be going back up soon; I love to sing.'

He nods. 'Well, it's good to see you looking so happy. It feels like that doesn't happen often enough these days.'

Ha! Even this stranger can tell that I'm on top of the world.

'You know, you look kinda familiar,' the man continues, tipping his head. 'Are you a regular here?'

'Not me, I'm a Utah girl,' I say proudly, which is weird because I've never been particularly proud of that. Except for how damn good we all are at social media, of course.

'Huh,' he says, still staring, still trying to figure it out.

The warning bell screeches in my head at the exact same time that he gets it.

'Hey, you're that girl's mom!' he exclaims, tensing up like a surprised cat. 'The one who's gone missing. What the fuck are you doing in here singing? Oh my God, what is wrong with you?'

I twist off the barstool, drop onto my feet. Damn, the floor is slippery. I stagger, find my balance.

'Jesus, I was feeling sorry for you, all that online abuse being hurled in your direction. But you deserve it all, and a hell of a lot more!'

I turn away, drop my eyeline, push through the crowd. I need to get out of here before anyone else recognizes me, or that guy stops shouting long enough to get his phone out. I trip on the first stair, so take the rest on my hands and knees, shame licking like flames as the doorman watches on. He pushes open the front door for me, but I recoil, screw my eyes closed. It's so bright. What time is it? How the hell can the sun be so high in the sky?

I skitter onto the sidewalk, try to make sense of my surroundings, how different it looks without the dark sky and neon signs. But then my phone starts dinging and buzzing like its own electronic orchestra. It must be finally picking up a cell tower after hours spent underground.

Panic grabs me. Maple. My beautiful Maple. I miss her so much! I grab my phone out of my bag, swipe and scroll, check for anything important.

How could I have spent the night in a bar when my daughter is out there, in trouble? But I've been under so much pressure! And that Xanax stopped me thinking straight!

My stomach lurches. There's a message from Garrett. When it lurches again, I realize I'm going to be sick. I race into the Starbucks opposite, head straight for the restroom, and throw up in the sink. Liquid vomit that swills down easily, thank God. A woman walks in – mid-thirties, smartly dressed – and I freeze, pray she can't smell sick, or white rum. But she ignores me, the best outcome for once, and disappears into a cubicle.

I splash my face with cold water, dry it with paper towels, and open Garrett's message.

Maple spotted in Vegas on Friday p.m. Main bus station.
Met a man there and left with him.
Also, friend Coco is a fake. FBI on it.
Maybe a pedo with two fake profiles. Maybe two pedos.
Either way, ONE SHIT MOM

My hand trembles. The phone slips from my grasp. And I listen to it smash on the tiles.

Chapter 103

Him

He stares at the bottle of tequila. He hasn't surrendered yet, but he still might. Yeah, he's been sober for five years, but he can still remember the bliss of intoxication like he'd sunk his last bottle yesterday.

Why the hell wasn't Maple where he told her to go? His first message was strong. And he'd class his second as a thing of fucking beauty. She didn't respond, but she didn't need to. She just needed to read it. And when he saw that she was missing, he assumed that's exactly what she'd done, and that she'd acted on it.

So like a schmuck, he drove for five hours straight. Excited, making plans; his palms sweaty on the steering wheel. He waited three hours in that place, asked around as best he could, but she wasn't there. She'd never been there. He'd fucked up again. And the only thing left was to drive the miserable five hours back to his trailer.

He thought things couldn't get worse, Maple missing and him not having a clue where she is, but now he's being labeled a pedo on YouTube. Accused of sickening acts of depravity without an ounce of proof by a dude who claims to be her father but still fucking lost her.

The only good thing is that no one knows he's Blake, including the feds. Fake name, untraceable VPN; it's easy to cover your tracks these days.

He sighs and curls his fingers around the bottle of tequila. He knows it'll be a step into hell. He'll give up eating, stop washing. Work will dry up. He'll sell the truck, his laptop, anything he can get a few dollars for. And he knows this because he's traveled that road before.

But why not? It's not like he's got anything to stay conscious for.

A jolt of anger, of hope come and gone, spikes his bloodstream. He pushes the bottle away, grabs the four-pack of Dr Pepper beside it, suddenly needing the sugar rush that has saved him so many times before. He releases one, cracks the ring pull, and lifts it to his lips. As he gulps down the sweet, medicinal liquid, the fizz lodges in his chest, and he uses the pain to ground himself. He needs to believe there is still hope.

He picks up his phone, flicks through the different apps, fast, content blurring. Not sure what he's looking for. Then he sees there's a new TikTok from that kid, Maple's friend. Dylan. He's filming in a car, driven by that fucked-up father, Garrett. Dylan says they're heading to Vegas. What the hell?

He crushes the can, sits up straighter. Maple was spotted at the Bonneville Transit Center downtown on Friday at around three p.m. with a middle-aged man.

Maple is in Vegas. While he was heading north to meet her, she was in his city. But not with him. With another man.

No, that can't be.

Anger bursts out of every pore like flames.

He slams his palms against the table.

No! He won't allow it. Maple is his. He needs to find her.

He pushes to standing, grabs the keys to his truck. Storms out.

Chapter 104

Dylan

@BillieEsuperfan16, TikTok
I know it's great that Maple's family can narrow down their search to Vegas, but do you guys know that sex traffickers use bus stations to recruit vulnerable women and girls all the time? I hate to say it, but I don't think they're finding her anytime soon #findMaple

Neither he nor Garrett talked much on the drive to Vegas, both too shellshocked by Detective Nicholls' news. Coco isn't a real person. Maple's best friend is a fake. Her image belongs to a woman from West Virginia called Nikki Herrera, except Nikki is twenty-seven now, which makes the stolen images over a decade old. The FBI believe Coco is an older man, a pedophile trying to befriend kids online. Possibly the same person who pretended to be Blake. Possibly, but not definitely.

Because Blake raised one red flag after another – Maple's mom was just too greedy to notice – while the man behind Coco has proven himself the perfect liar, able to deceive Maple every day for months. And highly skilled in AI technology.

It's hard to believe there could be two predators hunting

Maple. But Maple has two million subscribers, which would make it one sicko per million. And looking at it that way, it feels like an underestimate.

'So is Maple here then?' Aspen asks, as they walk into the bus station. Dylan's noticed that she seems pissed at her dad, which feels wrong, with Garrett so stressed about Maple. But Dylan is permanently pissed with his own dad, so maybe he shouldn't judge.

'Um, no,' Garrett mumbles. 'But she was here, and now we're going to find out where she went next.'

'How?' Ash asks.

'By checking CCTV,' Dylan says, gesturing toward the customer service kiosk. 'Come on.' He walks up and gives the old dude behind the desk the kind of smile he usually saves for his bishop. 'Hi, sir,' he says. 'This is Garrett Clark, and these are his kids. Their sister's missing, and she was last seen here, on Friday, and we were hoping—'

'Yeah, I know about Maple Clark,' the guy interrupts. 'Feds only left thirty minutes ago, once we'd copied the CCTV for them.' He turns to Garrett. 'I feel for you, man. I have four kids myself.'

'So there is CCTV of her then,' Dylan says. 'Can we see it?'

'Ah, you'll have to ask the police or the FBI about that. It's officially evidence now.'

Garrett lifts his palms. 'Please. I just want to see her. And see the guy who took her, the whites of his eyes, you know?'

'Honestly, man, I get it. I'd be raging too if I was walking in your shoes. But it's more than my job's worth, you know? Talk to the feds. I'm sure they'll let you see it.'

'Were you working here Friday?' Garrett asks, changing tack. 'Did you see her?'

The man shakes his head. 'I was here, yeah, but this place is busy. Especially on a Friday afternoon in summer, people going a hundred different places. I didn't see anything.'

'What about other people who work here? Could we talk to them?'

The guy sighs, like he's starting to get impatient. 'The police have already interviewed everyone. I promise your best bet is to go see them.'

Dylan mutters 'thank you' and guides Garrett away from the desk. 'How about we film a TikTok here,' he suggests. 'It might jog someone's memory.'

'I'll do the filming,' Aspen says, flipping down her hand. Dylan drops his phone into her open palm then walks to the seating area where the guy, Chris Brent, said he saw Maple. He waits for Aspen to set up, then starts talking.

'So we are here, at Bonneville Transit Center in Las Vegas, close to the spot where Maple was last seen, and she was talking to a man we're almost positive is very dangerous.' He pauses, the thought of not knowing who that man is, two possible suspects, hitting his gut harder than his dad's punches ever have. He takes a breath. 'So please, if you were here on Friday afternoon around three o'clock, think about what you might have seen. And get in touch. My DMs are open.'

'Hey, man. You're Dylan Dope, right?'

Dylan turns toward the voice. It belongs to a young skinny guy with cropped ginger hair, wearing the same uniform as the guy behind the customer service desk. 'Yeah, that's me.'

'I'm Sam. I follow you on TikTok. Your riding's sick, man.'

'I appreciate that, Sam, thanks.' Dylan can sense the guy's got more to say, so he waits, praying that it's to do with Maple and not skateboarding.

'Listen,' Sam finally says. 'I'm sorry about your friend. You know, I saw her, and the guy she left with.'

'You did?' Garrett takes a step forward. 'That guy behind the desk said—'

'Shit, no,' Sam interrupts, his eyes widening. 'I wasn't even here on Friday. What I mean is I saw her on the CCTV; I copied the footage for the feds. And I just thought you should know that she seemed okay with things. Maybe a little nervous, but he didn't drag her out or anything.'

'Right.' Garrett's shoulders slump.

'Can you tell us anything about the guy?' Dylan asks. 'What he looked like, what he was wearing? Anything at all, man. We're kinda desperate.'

Sam's face flushes beetroot. 'Well, he was wearing a Raiders cap. Sorry, I should probably go.'

'Do you have a photo of him?'

Dylan turns toward Ash. The kid barely speaks, but his stare is pretty intimidating now, and Sam's face flushes under its scrutiny. And it makes sense, Dylan supposes, for this guy to take a keepsake with all the drama Maple's disappearance is causing. Clout for his socials.

'Listen, man,' Dylan says, reaching out and touching the guy's arm, just gently. 'If you have something you could share with us, I would be so grateful. We all would.'

Sam bites his lip, looks at the guy behind the desk for a second, then exhales. 'Bring your phone closer,' he murmurs.

Dylan does as he's told, and a moment later, sees the familiar ripple of an Airdropped file. Sam gives him a tiny nod, then slopes off behind a door marked Private.

Chapter 105

Him

He stares at the boy standing by the red plastic chairs, talking like he thinks he's some kind of news reporter, except the cameraman is a little girl with an iPhone. Then he zooms out, clocks another short kid, and that asshole Garrett who called him a pervert.

He's not surprised they're here, following Maple's scent, just like he is. But it irks him all the same, like they're trying to claim Maple when she belongs to him.

He watches a kid in uniform walk up to Dylan, and there's something about their furtive conversation that makes him curious. So a minute later, with the kid gone, and the others heading out, he's not sure what to do. Stay at the bus station a while longer, talk to the people the police never bother with? Or follow that family and find out what they know?

But then it hits him. Whatever Dylan has discovered, it'll be on TikTok in minutes. Sharing their lives on social media is ingrained in kids like him.

Decision made, he turns, walks toward the smaller, dingier back exit, his head down and pace steady. There will still be police around, asking questions, looking interested, and he'd prefer to stay out of their line of sight.

He leans against the outside wall and checks his phone. There it is. A new TikTok from Dylan Dope. But his hands get sweaty as he watches it, hearing Dylan call the guy Maple left with very dangerous. Could Dylan be talking about him? Are the police stupid enough to think that him sending the mom a few messages, scheming a little, means he stole Maple from a bus station?

Or is there someone else in the frame?

Dylan's face disappears from the screen, but it's replaced by a photo of CCTV footage, with text overlaid asking if anyone recognizes the man. He pushes his forefinger and thumb to take a photo, then spreads his fingers across the screen to zoom in.

There's Maple, looking tired, but also beautiful, because she is so damn beautiful. And there's the guy. The bastard who took her. He's wearing a Las Vegas Raiders cap, which feels like a weird coincidence, except not really, because half of Vegas supports the local football team like he does. The cap's down low, so even magnified, he can't see much, but maybe there's something about the guy that looks familiar. Maybe.

'Got any change, man?'

He looks down at a man in dirty jeans, and a Hawaiian shirt, sitting against the wall, his legs splayed out in a V. Then he crouches down. He's not rich by any count, but now he's kicked the booze, the drugs; he's got enough spare cash to bribe a homeless man. He gives the guy a ten-dollar bill. 'Do you hang out around the bus station a lot?' he asks.

The guy shrugs, takes the cash. 'Most days, yeah.'

He holds his phone out. 'Do you recognize this man?'

The guy peers at the screen, scrunching his face. 'Nah, don't think so. Who is he?'

He considers his answer, decides on the truth. 'He kidnapped a girl. She's fourteen.'

'Fucking cunt,' the guy mutters. 'Sorry I can't help.' Then his eyes narrow. 'I don't know him, but I feel like I know you.' He scratches his chin. 'Have we met before?'

Heat rises in his cheeks. Fuck. He needs to cut the guy off, because yeah, there's a chance he has. 'I doubt it,' he says. 'I've not been in Vegas long. But I appreciate your sentiment, because that's exactly what the guy is.'

The homeless man nods like he's processing, then finally speaks. 'Yeah, okay. Message received. I'm Todd, by the way.'

'Nice to meet you, Todd.'

Todd nods a bit longer, then pushes to standing. 'You know what, come with me.'

'Where are we going?'

'The one thing being homeless gives you,' Todd says, 'is plenty of time to watch the world go by. If your guy lives in Vegas, one of my buddies might recognize him. Come on.'

Chapter 106

Him

Todd leads him downtown and through Fremont Street, its crazy big video canopy dazzling neither of them while the groups of tourists agitate them both. Once they get through, Todd carries on up toward North Main Street and West Bonanza, the sprawling encampments set up for Vegas's homeless. The area known as the corridor of hope without an ounce of irony.

He knows it well.

It's mostly men. Young dudes with missing teeth, high on methamphetamines. Older guys, some sleeping, plenty with bottles of spirits in their hands. But there are women too, some so young and desperate it makes his skin sizzle.

Todd gets plenty of nods and half-smiles as they walk through the encampment, and he uses their goodwill to his advantage, showing his phone to every guy who's conscious. A few won't engage, but most do, screwing up their faces, shaking their heads.

'Got to be patient, man,' Todd says as they walk on, seeming to enjoy this new job he's carved out for himself. 'Someone will know him.'

'Hey, what's on that?' A woman crawls out of a makeshift

tent made of tarpaulin and plastic bags. She's wearing a denim skirt and stars and stripes T-shirt. Her dark hair is hanging loose on her shoulders and there's a yellowing bruise on her cheek. She might be in her thirties, but she looks about fifty.

'A guy I'm trying to track down,' he answers. Keep it simple.

'A fucking pedo,' Todd adds. 'Taken a kid.'

'Let me see,' the woman says.

He lifts his phone. She leans over until her nose is only an inch from the screen.

'You know, he looks kinda familiar,' she says. Then she turns toward her tent. 'Hey, kiddo, come out here!'

A face appears out of the shadows, and jeez, she looks so young. He pushes his palms together, rubs them. The girl's wearing pink velvet yoga pants and a silver cropped top, like she's ready for a night out. Except the outfit's filthy and frayed, and her face is grubby and gaunt. 'What?' she says.

'Come look at this.'

The girl stumbles over.

'This guy,' the older woman says, pointing at the screen. 'I feel like I know him, but I don't know why.'

The girl barely hesitates before answering. 'Yeah, he's that photographer,' she says, her voice monotone but certain. 'Remember, he took pictures of me for a thing he was doing about Vegas streets or something.'

'Ah, yeah, course it is.' The older woman smiles like she's won a prize. 'He couldn't stop staring at your tits. Fucking creep, I remember now.'

A jolt of anger surges through him – this fucking freak has got his Maple – but it must also jump-start his brain, because a flash of something rips through his mind. A memory maybe.

The girl said he was a photographer. That he took pictures of her.

Why does that make sense to him? Why, on some level, was it not a surprise to hear her say that?

'Did he tell you his name?' he demands, everything more urgent now.

'What? No.' The older woman shrugs, defensive. 'He gave us twenty bucks.'

'He said he made good money from his photos,' the girl pitches in. 'And he had a fancy camera. Big boxy thing. Said it cost him fifteen grand.'

A fancy, boxy, expensive camera.

Fuck, that's it! That's where he's seen him before!

'Gotta go,' he shouts, even though these people don't give a shit what he does. Then he runs back down Fremont, toward the bus station, toward his truck. But as he's running, he takes his phone out and calls his ex-boss, the grumpy fucker who fired him for dropping one diffuser.

'Paul,' he says, breathing heavy. 'It's Brandon.'

Chapter 107

Him

'Brandon? What the fuck do you want?'

Brandon feels that spike of anger again, of injustice. But he needs to find some self-discipline, a skill he's never excelled at, so he slows to a walk, sucks in a long breath. 'That last gig I worked on with you,' he says finally, cool as ice, because it really matters now. 'The Azione photoshoot. You had an assistant with you.'

'No I didn't. I never work with anyone else; Christ, have you forgotten that already?'

Brandon closes his eyes, tries again. 'A guy taking photos then, stood right next to you. He was shooting with a Fujifilm GFX 100 so he must be a pro.'

'Oh him,' Paul mutters. 'Like a handheld could ever outperform a Hasselblad. He was nothing to do with me, part of Maple Clark's crew, filming content for her socials.'

Brandon frowns. 'You're sure?'

'That's what he told me.'

'But the mom does all that,' Brandon continues. 'Maple's always saying so on her posts; and I remember her crediting her mom for the content she posted from the photoshoot.'

'Well I don't fucking know,' Paul shoots back. 'I don't follow teenagers on TikTok.'

The accusation is there, in the silence. Brandon moves on. 'Do you know his name then? Where he lives?'

'He introduced himself as Jake. That's all I know. Although now I think about it, he asked for your name too, right after you pulled that weird face and broke my diffuser. And actually, I'm pretty sure he took some pictures of you as well. Like he was really into you. Maybe he thinks you've got modeling potential.' Paul cracks a laugh.

'So did you tell him my name?' Brandon asks, his heart beating faster now.

'Of course. Why? You got something to hide?'

Brandon sits in his truck. He needs to make sense of it all, but it's tough, too many brain cells killed by alcohol to cope with shit like this.

A man called Jake has taken Maple. But he got her to meet him in Vegas, which is his, Brandon's, hometown. And he was wearing a Raiders cap, which is his, Brandon's, team. And the fucker knows his name because he asked Paul for it. And he took photos of him. Brandon grinds his teeth. Is he being set up for this? Expected to take the fall for Maple's disappearance? Then it hits him. He slams his palms against the steering wheel and blinks with the effort. There was that guy Dylan mentioned on their channel. Brandon in the sky. He thought it was a freaky coincidence at the time; he didn't get the sky reference at all. But that must have been Jake, pretending to be him, luring Maple with bullshit about Ella. And of course Maple would go with him; her dumb teenage brain labeling it a risk worth taking.

He was happy to take a risk when the spoils were high, but go down without the prize? No. He's not doing that.

He needs to find her. Find him.

But how?

A photographer called Jake isn't much to go on.

Except Maple didn't have much to go on when she started looking for Ella. Nor did Dylan when he put out that plea to find Coco. Brandon prefers to lurk on social media, not post or comment, but if it will help get him to Maple, that's different.

He opens TikTok, creates a new profile – Paul.Evans32 with a photo of his ex-boss because fuck him – then follows twenty random people and prays they follow him back, make his profile look more legit. Then he opens Dylan's latest post and comments.

I recognize this guy. He's called Jake and he's a pro photographer but that's all I know. Anyone else got any ideas? Man, I really want to help Dylan find his girl.

Dylan's girl. He's not comfortable writing that, but if it makes people more likely to help, it's worth it. And maybe it works, because the responses start coming through straight away.

This is awesome! I hope someone knows more.

Photographer? That figures. Taking indecent images of children, I bet.

This account only has seven followers, got to be a bot.

Wait, @codybriarsss could this be the guy taking photos of your sister up close when she was mugged in Venice Beach?

Yo, I know this dude. He hangs around Watts with a sigma camera, like he's got a death wish or something.

Omg there's a guy that does that here in North Town! Same guy maybe?

Guys, this is definitely a bot. Ignore.

So I bought a picture of the Mojave Desert online from a photographer called Jake who had dozens of that area. I'm not saying more on here in case it isn't him, but @Dy1anD0pe, DM me.

Brandon grinds his teeth. Of course the TikToker would trust Dylan more than him. No one ever trusts him with the truth, do they? Not when it really matters anyway. He clicks his tongue. The Mojave Desert is fifty thousand square miles of dying land. He'll never be able to find Maple in that vast nothingness.

But then a new comment appears.

My dad did the Route 66 centennial road trip a few weeks ago and he got talking to a local guy with an aura camera in Bagdad Café and I just asked him AND IT IS THIS GUY!

Brandon stares at the message for a second or two longer than it requires to digest. Then a smile spreads across his face. Bagdad Café, from the movie.

Fucking hell, has he almost found Maple?

He rams the truck into gear and accelerates onto the highway, heading for Newberry Springs.

Chapter 108

Dylan

@LeonieMeadowsLA, TikTok
I heard from a guy that Maple's mom was doing karaoke in a dive bar in north Hollywood on Saturday night WHILE HER DAUGHTER IS MISSING!! So gross #findMaple

Dylan shuffles restlessly in the uncomfortable plastic chair. Jeez, this is painful. Why are they even here? If they wanted to sit around in a soulless police station, they could have stayed in Utah.

'What's taking so long?' he mutters. 'How hard can it be to find a detective working on Maple's case?'

'Maybe it's a good sign,' Garrett murmurs, the hope in his voice so obviously fake. 'Maybe they can't talk to us because they're out looking for Maple.'

'But isn't that what we're supposed to be doing?' Aspen says, with the accusing pout of a professional eight-year-old. 'Isn't that why we're in Vegas?'

Dylan's face burns. Because she's right. When they left St George for Vegas, they were convinced they had enough intel to kick-start their search for Maple. But it only took one dude in uniform to direct them to the police station, and they deferred responsibility like dogs around poop.

'What about your TikTok?' Ash asks.

Dylan shakes his head. 'Nothing helpful, not last time I checked anyway.'

'And how long ago was that?' Aspen asks, in a tone that matches her expression.

Dylan suddenly realizes it's been a while, maybe more than ten minutes. He opens the app. There are over fifty new comments, so he scrolls as fast as he can, speed reading, wishing his brain could process stuff as quickly as ChatGPT.

'Hey wait,' he suddenly calls out, his thumb breaking like rigor mortis has set in. 'Some guy called Paul Evans says he knows him, or at least that he knows he's a photographer called Jake.'

'Really?' Garrett twists forward in the chair. 'How does he know? Does he say anything else?'

Dylan turns back to his phone. 'No, but there are some replies,' he says, his voice still too loud for the hushed waiting room. 'People saying he looks like a guy who hangs out in dodgy areas of LA and Vegas. Someone's sister being mugged. And then someone called Claudia says I should DM her about a photo she bought online.' He scrolls further, looks up. 'Holy shit, a kid says his dad met him in some café, and the dad's actually IDed him!'

'What café?' Garrett demands, his eyes wide, sweat beading on his forehead.

'He says it's called Bagdad Café. I'll message him for more info.'

'No need.' Garrett pushes off the chair. 'I've seen the movie. I know exactly where that is.'

Chapter 109

Dylan

@Taylrtrix666, TikTok
Jeez @Claudia.Anstey99, serious killjoy asking Dylan to DM you. We all deserve to know who this Jake guy is. Come on, spill!!

A few minutes later, they're on the I-15, driving south. It doesn't take long for the glitzy hotels and condominiums to give way to desert plains and a horizon that seems to go on forever. It's getting late, and the sun is low and fiery in the sky. It feels apocalyptic to Dylan, like they're heading into hell. But he knows that's crazy. The sun sets every night, still wakes up fresh in the morning.

'You should message that Claudia too,' Garrett reminds him from the driver's seat. 'See if the guy she bought the picture from is our guy.'

'Yeah, you're right,' Dylan says, finding Claudia Anstey's profile and tapping out a DM. She must be waiting for it too, because her reply is instant.

Hey Dylan. The photographer we bought from is called Jake and his website is rawdreamsphotography.com, but there's no photo of him on there, so he might have nothing to do with this. Don't jump to conclusions on my watch, you know? But good luck.

It's him, Dylan knows it in his gut. He opens the website, scrolls through the various pages. But it's just photographs, nothing helpful about the photographer except his first name, Jake. He tries to work out if the photos tell him anything, but they're all landscape shots, moody desert plains encroaching on abandoned buildings. One house holds his eye – half of it is blood red, like the owner bled out while painting it, and there are iron square windows that remind him of prison bars. But it doesn't help him work out where Maple is.

'Anything?' Garrett asks grimly, like he knows the answer already.

'Nah,' Dylan manages.

'Bagdad Café it is then,' Garrett mutters, staring at the road ahead. 'And I'm pretty sure only a handful of people live in Newberry Springs these days, so we just need to pray that Jake's one of them.'

It takes them nearly two and a half hours to reach the café – two hours pushing the truck to its max speed limit, then twenty minutes cursing and doubling back after missing exit 206. They've been mostly quiet on the journey, but Garrett has explained that Bagdad Café is a cult movie from the 1980s – *Stranger Things* era – with an epic theme tune, so Dylan is surprised when they pull up outside a rundown, one-story roadside café.

But then again, they're not here for movie nostalgia.

Dylan throws open the truck door and races toward the café, the others in step behind him. Closer up, he can see hundreds of stickers in the windows, flags from dozens of different countries stuffed in flowerpots or stuck to splintered wooden beams. He pulls on the main door, but it only rattles. He tries it again, then realizes it's locked.

'Shit,' Garrett mutters, pointing to a sign with the opening hours. 'The café closed half an hour ago.'

'So what do we do?' Dylan asks, scanning the desolate landscape. The sun has disappeared over the horizon now; it'll be dark soon. How the hell are they going to find Maple in this? He rattles the handle again, but in frustration this time, so he almost falls over when the door opens.

'Jeez, can't you read a sign?' a man in denim shorts and a grubby white T-shirt mutters. 'I've been on my feet since dawn, broke my own record for flipping flippin' buffel burgers for German tourists. I really don't need kids trying to break my door down too.'

Dylan raises his hands. 'I'm sorry but we really need your help.'

'Oh yeah?' The man looks at him suspiciously, then shifts his gaze to Garrett and the twins and visibly softens. 'What kind of help?'

'Do you know someone called Jake who lives around here?' Dylan asks. 'He's a photographer, has an amazing camera apparently. He was in here recently. I mean I guess you have visitors from all over but . . .'

'Yeah, I know him,' the man interrupts. 'Jake Carter. Lives out on Aleppo Lane.' He frowns slightly. 'You know, I always had him down as a loner, but you're the second person who's asked about him tonight.'

Dylan's eyes widen. 'Was it the police asking?'

The man screws his face up. 'I don't think so.'

'Okay, let's go!' Garrett shouts, already running back to his truck.

'Get the police down there, please,' Dylan begs the man. Then he turns and runs too.

Chapter 110

Maple

@Unicornsarereal<3, TikTok
I'm really scared for Maple #findMaple

I guess I'm going to die here. Yeah, Brandon gives me rations. Bottles of water I gulp down, food my stomach still refuses. But my soul is dying, I can feel it shriveling up like roadkill in the sun, and I don't suppose my body can survive without that.

I squeeze my eyes closed. Fuck, why did I think my life was so bad before? Mom might not be perfect, but all she asked of me was to make a few videos, create content worth clicking on. And in return I got an amazing home, cool stuff for free, so many friends. Endless fun. But still I threw a teenage tantrum, refused to do what Mom asked. Then one bad thing happened – I found out my dad isn't my dad – and even though he's been an awesome father really, I ran off. Thought I knew best.

But then again, I also called Coco my closest friend in the world, which shows how messed up my brain is.

I lift my legs as far as they will go, then ram them down, kicking out, not caring about the pain that explodes as my heels make contact with the iron bedframe. I want to scream too but

I daren't in case he storms in, gags me again. So I create fists instead, punch the mattress, almost die from the futility of it.

But then, something.

A noise.

I stop, listen. It's not coming from the door, but from the other side of the room, beyond the window covered in newspapers. Outside. I freeze, listen as hard as I can.

There. Again. Rustling and scratching. The thud of a footstep maybe. It could be an animal, I suppose, but it sounds more purposeful than that. Like a person trying to get in.

My heart races.

Have the police found me? Am I going to be saved? Do I get to go home after all?

I want to shout, beg for help, make sure whoever's out there knows I need them. But I force myself to stay quiet; I can't risk Brandon hearing me. I know the smart thing is to wait it out. And I need to start acting smart.

More scuffling. My heart rate gets even faster.

I jerk at a higher-pitched crack. A window breaking. But it's not that loud, like a tiny window, a small single pane. Was it loud enough for Brandon to hear? I tense, prepare for him to rush in, pray that whoever broke the window has their gun locked and loaded.

A hand appears at the window, a man's hand, ripping at the newspaper, feeling around like a spider hunting moths. I hold my breath. My brain short-circuits.

Then there's a thud, a snap, a creak, and the window swings open.

'Hello?' I whisper. It's twilight outside, minutes from darkness, and all I can see is a man in the shadows. I feel petrified, but I'm being stupid again. He must be police, or FBI. He's here to save me.

He climbs through the window, then turns. I can see him clearer now, his face, his eyes, the sweat glistening on his forehead. He walks toward me, his forefinger at his lips, telling me to stay quiet.

But how can I stay quiet?

Because it's him.

My body starts convulsing with fear.

He might have shaved the beard, cut his hair, but I realize now, I'd recognize him anywhere.

It's the gross man from the photoshoot. The freak in the scissor lift who broke a diffuser because he was staring so hard at me.

When Brandon told me that he was at the photoshoot, I assumed he must be the man with the freaky stare. Even though I didn't recognize him. But there were dozens of people there that day. Security staff, agency people, hangers-on. He could be any one of those.

There were two sickos watching me.

Two men who think they have rights over me.

How could I be so unlucky?

Except that's stupid. I've heard the stories, the sickos who hang out together in private chat rooms. Share disgusting content. Of course they can be friends in real life too. Partners in crime.

I scream.

His hand lands on my mouth, pushes hard. 'Shush,' he hisses, his face scowling. 'You need to be quiet.'

My eyes erupt with tears. I thought someone was coming to save me. I thought there were good people out there, stopping the bad people.

But there's just more bad people. Bad men.

'I'm gonna rescue you,' he whispers, like a slithering snake. 'Take care of you.'

I shake my head, frenzied. I don't want to stay here, but I can't bear to go with him either. I want to die; that's what I want. I moan, like a cornered animal, and some of the sound seeps through his fingers.

'Shush, Maple, please!'

The door flies open; artificial yellow light floods in. Brandon in silhouette, his arms high, a gun wrapped inside his fingers. But it's pointed at the man, not me.

The man twists, his hand falls away from my mouth as he pushes to standing. He stares at the gun for a moment, then turns back to me and there are tears in his eyes. 'I'm sorry,' he murmurs. 'I've fucked up again, haven't I? I just so wanted to be a good dad for once.'

Chapter 111

Maple

@TarotCaro92, TikTok
I have this horrible feeling that Maybe Maple is dead

A good dad? What the fuck does he mean?

'Get away from her, or I'll shoot you both!' Brandon shouts from the doorway.

My body wants to fold in on itself, as though that might protect me from the gunfire, even though that's bullshit, and the chains make it impossible anyway. I try to lie still, but my body shakes, the chains clink.

A good dad. Oh God, please no.

Brandon takes a few steps forward, the gun barrel swaying between me and the intruder now, his finger hovering over the trigger. Then suddenly, he bursts out laughing.

'Oh Jesus Christ, it's you. Brandon with the sweaty hands. The man I stole my cover name from.'

Wait, what? My eyes dart between them. I've been calling my captor Brandon because of his social media handle. But of course that could be fake. Jesus, ninety percent of social media is fake and this guy's been pretending to be Coco for months. He flicks the gun in the intruder's direction. The man who must actually be called Brandon. Who might actually be my real dad. Fuck.

'I knew you were obsessed with Maple,' my captor goes on. 'I saw it in your sad little face when you dropped the diffuser that day, but I never thought a loser like you would do anything about it. Maybe I'm even a little impressed, you finding my home out here in the desert. Shame you fucked it at the final hurdle, hey?'

'You gave Paul a fake reason for being at that photoshoot,' Brandon says, his voice a whole lot steadier than mine would be if I dared to speak. 'The rest of us thought you were his assistant. Then you set me up. And it wasn't just stealing my name, my favorite football team. It was my job too. Because I suppose you're Brandon in the sky, the YouTube subscriber who pretended to know where Ella is. I guess that's how you convinced Maple to meet you. Hey, Jake?'

Jake. Is that my captor's real name? Or just another lie?

'Well, I had to protect myself,' he throws back. 'Yes, the feds are still embarrassingly analogue, but there was always the chance they'd work out who I was, so I needed to give them a sacrificial lamb. When Maple told me she had a photoshoot in Vegas, I wasn't going to miss out. Two hours from my home. Maple pouting in not many clothes. And of course I was going to take my camera along, immortalize the moment. It was easy to pretend I was part of Maple's team.

'Then I saw you there, dribbling over Maple like a baby craving milk. I soon realized that fate had dealt me a lucky hand. I created a couple of profiles in your name – TikTok, YouTube – you know this anyway. And the rest was easy.' He sniggers. 'Gullible, these kids.'

‘So you don’t know where Ella is then,’ I murmur. ‘You never did.’

He laughs again, shakes his head, like I’m the stupidest girl ever, which he’s right about. ‘Of course not.’ He licks his lips, winks. ‘You know I only have time for you, babe.’

A loud noise suddenly explodes out of the real Brandon’s mouth, like a wild animal warning its prey of an imminent attack. Then he surges forward, barreling toward Jake like he doesn’t give a shit about the gun. But he doesn’t reach him in time.

The gun goes off.

BANG!

BANG!

And I scream. And keep on screaming.

Chapter 112

Maple

@mimilittleponyyy, TikTok
Please can someone just save her already?

Jake slumps to the floor. Brandon rears backwards. Blood seeps out of Jake's chest. Brandon stares wide-eyed.

Wait, no! That doesn't make any sense!

My ears buzz like a million angry bees. My vision blurs. But there's a new shadow in the doorway. Another man. Another gun.

'Dad?!' I scream.

Dad's whole body is shaking, and his eyes are wild, like the big cats he loves. But he's holding a rifle, the one he hunts with. That's why Jake is bleeding out and Brandon is alive. The double shot was from Dad's gun. Dad shot the man who was about to kill someone else.

'Maple!' he shouts, running in. But then he pulls up. His eyes dart to Brandon, and he lifts the rifle again, aiming it at him.

'No, wait!' I cry. 'He came to help. I mean, I think he did. It's so confusing! I think . . .'

'She's right,' Brandon says, scrambling onto his feet and taking a few steps backwards, his hands high and shaking. 'Listen, I know it looks bad, and I should probably have called the police rather than act the hero, but it all just felt too urgent, and I didn't think they'd believe me,' he babbles. 'I don't always make the best decisions.'

Same. Fuck. Am I like him? Is that because he's my real dad?

'But I couldn't let Maple down,' he goes on. 'Not again. Not after I'd just found her.'

Dad shakes his head, screws up his face. 'What do you mean, just found her?'

'Maple!'

I turn toward the familiar voice. 'Aspen! Oh jeez, Ash. Dylan, oh my God, you're all here.'

'I told you to stay in the car,' Dad says. But he doesn't sound mad, like he knew they had to come. His rifle is aimed at Brandon, but the guy still risks moving, stepping in front of Jake's body to hide the dead perv's injuries from the twins. It's more thoughtful than I'd have expected from the sweaty man with the gross stare.

'There were some keys in the kitchen,' Dylan says, his voice low and stuttering. 'Maybe they're for the cuffs?' He disappears, then returns a few seconds later. He tries to smile like he's got this as he pushes the different keys into my handcuffs, but his eyes are wet and his fingers tremble.

I mouth 'thank you' as the cuffs finally open. I want to say more, but I don't know what. *I owe you my life? Thinking about you helped me get through all of this?* But I can see in his eyes that he already gets it. So I just squeeze his hand for a second and let him gently guide me up to sitting.

'How did you find me?' I ask. My eyes dart between them all, not sure who I'm asking.

‘Mainly TikTok, I guess,’ Dylan says. ‘Then a local guy knew Jake, and I recognized this house from his photography website. That half-painted red wall is freaky.’

‘This house?’ I repeat, realizing I don’t have a clue where I am.

‘A creepy building in the middle of the Mojave Desert,’ Dylan explains. ‘But I guess it’s the perfect home for a freak who can pretend to be a teenage girl for months on end.’

Shame scorches my cheeks. ‘You know he’s Coco then,’ I murmur.

‘I know he’s a disgusting, lying pedo,’ Dylan responds. Then he turns to Brandon and gives him an accusing glare. ‘But I’ve no idea who this dude is.’

Brandon looks at me like he’s asking for permission. I force myself to keep eye contact, to try and find something good in his face. Then I take a breath and say it out loud. ‘I think he might be my biological father.’

Chapter 113

Maple

@Amelieeeetalking, TikTok
So is Jake the photographer also Blake the modeling agent? I'm so confused #findMaple

'What?' Dad's eyes widen – the man who's always been my dad, who saved my life, and the life of this man who might also be my dad. He looks at me, then at Brandon. Color drains from his face. 'Is that why you're here?' he asks. 'Did you really come to save her?'

Brandon nods, but his face cracks and he drops his eyeline to the floor. 'My life has mostly been a car wreck,' he admits quietly. 'Big dreams about making it in Vegas, all crushed. Lost nearly ten years to booze and drugs. Finally got myself sober, but all I've really got to be proud of is volunteering at a homeless shelter once a week. It's not much, is it?'

He goes quiet for a while, then finally lifts his head and looks at me. 'But then I pick up some work on a photoshoot, and everything changes. I recognized your mom first; she hasn't changed that much in fifteen years. Then I looked at you in that glass box, really looked. And yeah, the math worked out, but it wasn't that. It was like I'd seen you before, but in photos of my mom when she was a kid.' He bites his lip. 'The likeness is crazy.'

'That's why you dropped the equipment,' I murmur, remembering the moment, how I laughed to hide my discomfort. Then I think about his mom. I have sat at my vanity so many times wishing I had honey blond hair like Mom, or strawberry blond like Dad and the twins. When all along there was someone out there who I did resemble. Another grandma.

'Then of course I had to know everything about you,' Brandon continues. 'And it was so easy. Your whole life was right there on YouTube. And when I realized you were this smart, beautiful, funny girl who cared about people you'd never met . . .' He smiles and there are tears in his eyes now. 'But I went about it all wrong. Pretending to be a modeling agent called Blake, getting family photos that didn't make it online, trying to meet you without your mom there. I guess I thought you'd refuse to see me if I was honest about who I was.

'I even messaged you direct a couple of times,' he admits in a gruff whisper. 'Asked you to meet me at Kilby Court in Salt Lake City, where I watched your mom sing on the night we . . . Anyway, I shouldn't have done that either, pretending I had intel on Ella to convince you to come. I would have helped you find her though, I promise you that. I'm not like him.'

I think I remember those messages now, alongside so many others from strangers. How I read them as bullshit and deleted them straight away. I wonder how I would have reacted if I had gone to meet him, if he'd pointed to the stage Mom sang on, then told me he was my biological father. Would I have given him a chance?

But who knows because that's not what happened. What

really happened is that he drove out to the desert to rescue me with no weapon and not much of a plan. He was brave and stupid and hopeful and unprepared. Just like me.

Brandon looks at me for a moment longer, like he finds it hard to pull away, then turns to my dad. 'And I owe you an apology.'

'Oh yeah?'

'I hated you calling me a pedophile on YouTube, I felt disgusted to be given that kind of label. But you were a dad looking out for your kid; I should have recognized that.'

'Especially now I've saved your life, you mean?'

Brandon's face spreads into a sheepish smile. 'Yeah, especially now.' He takes a few steps toward Dad, then holds out his hand. Dad looks at it for a moment, then reaches for it.

Chapter 114

Kirsten

@FBIpressrelations, TikTok
Maple Clark has been found unharmed at a private dwelling in San Bernardino County and the alleged perpetrator in her kidnap is deceased. We are not looking for anyone else in relation to this matter. Please do not speculate as this is a live investigation.

I slam the door of the Uber X and take a moment to reset. It's been a terrible day – worst of my life, for sure – but I know no one inside this building will care about my problems. The online hate, the hours it took to replace my broken phone, the migraine that has cursed me all day. And the final straw: finding out that Garrett made himself the hero without even giving me the chance to get to Maple first.

Well, I'm here now, ready to step in. To remind everyone that it's Mom and Maple forever.

I run my fingers through my hair, pray that my reapplied makeup hides the dark circles, and walk inside the San Bernardino Sheriff's Office. It's only a small place, and I can see Maple sitting in the open-plan office beyond the glass screen of the reception area. She's surrounded by a pile of empty snack packets that would normally make me shudder. Still do, to be frank.

Garrett is there too, and the twins, bless them, plus Dylan of course, Maple's limpet. And a man I don't recognize, although there's something vaguely familiar about him. As I stare at them all, I feel a little like Patrick Swayze in that film *Ghost*, watching life go on without me. But I shake the feeling away. My marriage might be over, but those are my kids.

'Can I help you?' the officer behind the reception desk asks. She looks suspicious, like she has one expression that goes with the uniform and isn't prepared to mix and match.

'I'm with them,' I say, pointing at my family and giving her my sunniest smile. 'I'm Kirsten Clark, Maple's mother.' She doesn't look impressed, but she presses a button somewhere under the desk and nods at the door. A low buzz sounds and I push it open.

'Mom!' Maple calls out as soon she sees me.

My eyes instantly blur with tears. She looks so bedraggled. Gaunt and tired. Greasy hair and pimples on her chin. 'My poor Maple honey,' I murmur, taking her in my arms. She smells terrible, but of course she would. She's been gone for three days. Chained to a bed for more than two. 'Thank God you're safe.'

'I'm sorry I ran away,' she mumbles into my chest. 'I was so stupid, trusting some random guy online. I was just desperate to find Ella; I wasn't thinking straight.'

'Oh yes, about that,' I say, pulling away slightly and trying not to look too smug. 'I found Ella for you.'

Maple's eyes widen with such a heady mix of shock and joy that all the stresses of the day melt away. 'You did?' she asks. 'But how?'

I take a moment to give Garrett my most triumphant look, then turn back. 'You know me, Maple. You wanted to find Ella, so of course I was going to help with that. I hired the best PI in Utah.'

Maybe there's hint of disappointment in Maple's face, a lone expert doing a better job than a hive of Gen Alphas, but her expression quickly clears. 'Where is she?' she asks. 'Is she okay?'

'Well, she's living in Century City in LA, in the most opulent penthouse I've ever been in.' I decide not to mention the OnlyFans work, or the pills she dry-swallows.

Maple beams, then turns to Dylan. 'Did you hear that? Ella's alive, and she's doing great off grid, all by herself.'

Dylan looks at me suspiciously. 'And you're sure this isn't another one of your fake stories?' he asks.

'That would be my guess,' Garrett mutters.

'Of course I am,' I say. God, those two deserve each other. I turn to Maple. 'She apologized for not contacting you, but her privacy is very important to her; she didn't feel like she could risk it.'

Maple nods but she looks sad, like she assumes Ella not wanting to talk to her must be her fault. Which is funny, because I'm pretty sure it's really because Ella doesn't believe she's worthy of Maple's concern. But Maple would never understand that because she's never made a shameful decision in her life. Stupid, yes. Very, very stupid. But stupidity is easy to forgive because it's an imperfection. Shameful is different. Shame is knowing what you're doing is bad but doing it anyway.

Like stripping for men and choosing to believe that anonymity keeps you pure.

Or having unprotected sex with a man you barely know.

'Mom, you know, you should probably meet Brandon.'

'Sorry?'

'Brandon,' Maple repeats. But then her pale face glows beetroot. 'Shit, that's stupid. Of course you've met him before.'

Brandon. Why is that name familiar?

Oh God.

Chapter 115

Maple & Dylan

@7Harts<3, TikTok
Bodi and I have been praying for the safe return of Maple Clark to her family, and our hearts are warm, knowing those prayers have been answered. However, due to several credible death threats over the last few weeks, we have decided to step back from social media now and concentrate on raising our beautiful family in private.

Maple: *Hey everyone, yep, I'm back.*
Dylan: *Alive, healthy, and even smiling.*
Maple: *Which has a lot to do with Dylan, and my dad, and my little brother and sister, for rescuing me. But it also has a lot to do with you guys. For following my story, sharing it, and giving Dylan the clues that meant he knew where to look. So thank you, from the bottom of my heart.*
Dylan: *We've also got some special thank-yous to make. Thank you Ryan, and Chris, and Sam, and Claudia, and Tyler, plus Tyler's dad. Without your intel, we wouldn't have found Maple. There's a couple more thank-yous to make, but that comes later.*

Maple: *So you might have seen that I've shut down my Maybe Maple channel now – I guess I'm done with acting the squeaky-clean little girl when half my followers are dirty old men – but we wanted you to hear how my story ended. Except some of this stuff isn't easy to talk about, so Dylan's helping me out.*

Dylan: *I guess that's what friends are for. Will I start with Coco?*

Maple: *No, let's start with my mom.*

Dylan: *Hmm okay. Well, on our last show, you probably remember that Maple's dad told us about Blake. Well, it turns out that Blake was lying – he isn't a modeling agent – but he isn't a pedophile either. And you could say, at a stretch, that he was lying for the right reasons.*

Maple: *So my mom probably doesn't deserve all the hate she's getting. She's not perfect, jeez, I know that, but she's sorry. So if you guys could lay off her a little, I'd appreciate it.*

Dylan: *While Coco does deserve all your hate.*

Maple: *Except not Coco, because Coco doesn't exist.*

Dylan: *And luckily neither does Jake Carter now, the fifty-one-year-old man who used the latest AI technology to pretend to be a fourteen-year-old girl, just so he could get close to Maple.*

Maple: *And then got so jealous of me being friends with Dylan that he decided to kidnap me. He chained me to a bed and he . . . well he didn't do that, what you're thinking, but . . .*

Dylan: *He treated Maple like she belonged to him, to do whatever he wanted with. Like take photos of her when she was chained up. And it turns out that Jake Carter has been obsessed with watching girls in distress since he was a* *kid. Some of you might know that Coco's YouTube channel was about a girl called Sophie Lyle who was raped and murdered in her home. Coco made out that it happened three years ago in Miami, but the FBI told us that it actually happened in 1986, in Phoenix, Arizona.*

Maple: *And the reason Jake was hung up on the case was because he was there. An eleven-year-old witness. He lived next door to Sophie's family and was obsessed with their cat apparently. He'd climb out of his bedroom window at night and go into their garden to look for it. And he was there the night Sophie was killed.*

Dylan: *I mean, we're thinking that he was a weird kid already, fixating on a cat like that. But then he sees a girl attacked, terrified, probably screaming, begging for the guy to stop.*

Maple: *And he kinda loves it. Gets excited by it.*

Dylan: *The FBI found thousands of images on his PC of women and girls in trouble. Women being mugged by strangers or pushed around by boyfriends, girls being hassled by groups of guys. He was addicted to seeing women in pain.*

Maple: *And as well as thousands of images of me, the FBI also found photos of a woman called Nikki from when she was a kid. And he used her image to become Coco, and trick me into trusting him. Nikki discovered this, and reported it, which meant the FBI knew where to start looking. So if you're watching, Nikki, thank you so much.*

Dylan: *AI has given child abuse a whole new look, and it's a disgusting one.*

Maple: *Which brings us to Ella Hart, the reason we set this show up in the first place. It's awkward, because we have to respect Ella's wishes to stay hidden, but we know how invested you guys have been in Ella's story, so . . .*

Dylan: *So yeah, we found her. Or Maple's mom did anyway. And apparently, she's fine. More than fine, doing great, living her best life.*
Maple: *But my mom isn't always the best at judging these things. It's not her fault; her brain just isn't wired that way. So, Ella, if you're watching, we just want to tell you three things and then we'll let you be.*
Dylan: *Firstly, the ICAC Taskforce have made a heap of progress on getting those fake images of you taken down, and they say they're committed to finishing the job.*
Maple: *And secondly, whatever you're doing right now, we hope it's dancing. Because your talent at that – we think it's unreal.*
Dylan: *And yeah, thirdly.*
Maple: *Thirdly, I want to say thank you. Because when Jake Carter told me, as Coco, a bullshit story about there being pictures of me on the dark web, all I could think about was you. And how I knew you'd tell me not to be ashamed of something that wasn't my fault.*

Chapter 116

Maple

@CaseyTylerNJ, TikTok
Have you seen Ruby True's new content on YouTube? Those challenges are wild! What is it with Utah producing the best kidfluencers?

I watch him ordering me a dirty soda and a slice of cherry pie. The conversation with the server goes on longer than seems necessary, so it's not a total surprise when he turns around and there's a candle pushed into the pie, its flame flickering in the draft sneaking under the door of the oldest diner in St George.

'Happy birthday,' he says, a little awkwardly as he sits down opposite me. My birthday was actually last weekend. Dad took me to see a mountain lion he's been tracking, and even though he was technically just taking me to work with him – he's got a new job as a ranger in Zion, his dream job at last – I still loved spending the day with him.

'Thanks,' I murmur, blowing out the candle. 'And thanks for the pie.'

Brandon shrugs. 'Thanks for agreeing to see me. I mean, we didn't exactly meet in the best circumstances.'

I think about the last time I saw Brandon, three months ago, saying goodbye to him at the sheriff's office. We were all there for hours, the twins eventually falling asleep in the sheriff's dog's bed. Luckily it was an Alsatian, so the bed was pretty big. The officers interviewed us individually, and got the local doctor to check me over, but eventually we were free to go. All except Brandon, who had to wait for the FBI from Vegas to arrive. They had some questions for him, about soliciting child images.

He asked for Dad's number before we left though – not Mom's; she was too mad with him, although whether that was down to him tricking her with the modeling bullshit, or just him still being on the planet, was hard to tell – and he messaged Dad the next day to say he'd been let go without charge. And that he'd love to see me again, when I was ready.

So here I am.

'Not the best,' I agree. 'But I know you had good intentions. And you distracting Jake gave Dad the chance to shoot him.'

'I thought he was going to kill me,' Brandon admits quietly. 'I was an idiot, running straight at him like that. But I couldn't stand how he was talking to you.' He smiles at the table, an embarrassed smile. 'You know, it's funny. I'd never met you, not properly, and yet I had this urge to protect you so strong, a fire in my belly that wasn't going out. It's crazy what biology can do.'

I think about my mom, the other half of my DNA. Would she have put herself in the line of fire like Brandon did? I mean, it's hard to picture.

'I don't think it's just biology,' I mumble, also finding something interesting on the table to stare at. 'I guess it also shows that you're a good guy. You know, deep down.'

'Yeah, very fucking deep.' Then Brandon's eyes widen. 'Shit, sorry for swearing. Shit. Oh jeez, I'm not used to being around kids.'

His discomfort makes me laugh. And then he laughs, and it feels pretty good to be laughing with him. 'I've heard worse, I promise,' I say. 'Like when Dad told Mom he was moving to St George and taking us kids with him. She cried and cursed and threatened a million things over that.'

'I'm sorry; no one likes to hear their parents fighting.'

It's funny. Brandon has a certain look. Gruff, worn down, rough around the edges. But he keeps coming out with stuff like that.

'She says she's turned over a new leaf,' I tell him. 'That she'll do whatever it takes to get us back.'

'And do you think she will?' he asks. 'That she can? I mean, take it from me, changing your spots isn't the easiest thing to do.'

I think about the messages Mom sends me every day. The apologies and promises and inspirational Instagram quotes (because people can only change so much). 'I know she's trying,' I choose. 'And maybe I'm ready to give her a chance.'

Chapter 117

Maple

@EllaHartisback, TikTok
Loving being on tour with Florence + The Machine! Being a backing dancer is a dream come true. So grateful to the band for the opportunity and to @_MaybeMaple_ and @Dy1anD0pe for inspiring me to give real life another shot.

Mom pulls off the copper-red, bobbed wig and shakes out her hair.

'That was fun, wasn't it?' she says, dropping onto a barstool and removing her scuffed white trainers. Apparently Mom dressed as a *New York Times* reporter this Halloween. 'You know, I'm so glad you came, my Maple honey. Don't you think our street puts on the best Halloween parade in Provo?'

I peel off my Spider-Man mask – I chose it to celebrate how I'm not scared of spiders anymore, not now I've survived being kidnapped, but it's also a great way to stay incognito. When Mom first invited me for the Halloween weekend, I assumed she had an ulterior motive – pictures of us in costume together would make great content – so I chose an outfit with a mask to ruin her plans. But actually, Mom didn't take one selfie, or mention social media at all.

'I guess,' I say, reaching for a glass and holding it under the fridge water tap. Candy always makes me thirsty. 'And it's cool being back here, in my old house. I wasn't sure you'd be able to keep it with, you know . . .' I feel my cheeks flush pink and wish I could put the mask back on.

'With you all abandoning me, you mean?' Mom says. But then she smiles. 'It's fine. I'm not one to hold a grudge – you know that. You're here now, and I seem to be making a ton of money without you.'

'You are?'

'You know Maple, it's amazing how many ambitious moms there are in Utah. I guess it's in our DNA.'

'Wait, you're helping other moms make their kids famous?'

'I explain the dangers to them, obviously,' she says, like she's offended I might think otherwise. 'But if they're willing to take the risk, far be it for me to judge. Post and let post, that's always been our motto, hasn't it? This way, I can cover the mortgage for when you're ready to come home, and you don't have to . . . stick to a schedule,' she finally chooses.

'I suppose,' I murmur, wondering if she's right, or if she's still managing to twist my thoughts. 'You know, I'm pretty tired,' I say, suddenly feeling like I need some distance. 'I might head upstairs.'

'Oh. Okay.' Her face drops and she looks so forlorn and defeated – two very alien expressions for Mom – that my stomach lurches.

'Or I could stay with you a bit longer,' I hear myself say.

The familiar beam returns in an instant. 'Oh, Maple honey, that's so sweet. How about I get us some snacks as a thank-you? Something savory after all that candy.'

Wow. Mom never used to let me eat snacks unless they came attached to a paycheck. 'I guess I could eat,' I say, wondering if requesting cheese is a step too far.

'Great!' She beams again, then twists off the barstool and disappears into the pantry. She returns with a big bag of chips. 'Have you tried these? They're called Shell Shocked. Chips made from egg whites. So tasty, but also really healthy. Great name too, isn't it? Here, try them.'

She empties the bag into a bowl and I take one. I'm not expecting much – egg whites are basically slimy water – but actually, it tastes pretty good. So I take another, and another. 'Wow, these are crazy moreish,' I say between mouthfuls.

'They are, aren't they? So moreish.'

I drink in Mom's beaming face. Return her smile as best I can. Crunch another chip.

Then I shift my gaze.

And spot the tiny camera perched on the shelf.

Epilogue

Another Him

She's perfect, he thinks. A perfect, precious thing. Like a peach. A sweet peach, ripening just for him.

He watches her crunching the chip, wonders whether she really likes it, or if it's just for show. For money.

Not that it matters.

He's just glad he can see her again after all these months. Her smile. The way she tips her head when she laughs.

Bliss. Pure bliss.

He taps his belt buckle, curls his fingers around the smooth leather strap.

And he supposes he's got Mrs. Clark to thank for bringing the girl back online. Yes, gratitude is due.

'Thank you, honey,' he murmurs at the screen. 'You've made an old man very happy.'

Acknowledgements

I didn't give kidfluencing much thought before I wrote *The Tradwife's Secret* – I mean, where was the harm in children making fun videos for YouTube? But if Tradwife influencing can be a mirage, it makes sense that 'kids having fun' can be too. And it's worse, because these are children – a demographic universally accepted as vulnerable. With governments across the world asking whether we're doing enough to protect our children from social media, I knew I wanted to explore these issues in a fictional book.

The role of AI came about more organically. As I carried out my research, I realised how big a game changer AI is proving to be in both the accessibility and execution of child abuse. When X introduced the Grok-2 functionality as I was mid-draft – literally handing would-be abusers the tools to create explicit images without consent – I felt even more determined to show how damaging this 'victimless' crime is.

However, slightly awkwardly, my first thank you must go to those channels who also fuel the kidfluencing industry. Because I consumed all the Netflix shows, listened to dozens of podcasts, and spent too many hours watching unboxing videos on YouTube (you should see my Santa list). I also listened to privacy advocates dissect the dangers of children having an online presence, like Sarah Adams via her @mom.unchartered Instagram account. All this content helped me refine my own opinions, as well as understand the arguments on all sides.

My next thank you goes to my publisher, HQ. There was a changing of the guard for this book, which effectively meant I had double the number of people tell me that they loved it – to note, I will be expecting this level of affirmation going forward, Team HQ! Thank you Cicely Aspinall for your initial excitement, Francesca von Krauland for your early feedback, Seema Mitra for picking up the reins so capably, and Najiyah Begum for making sure the book actually made it to print. Thank you to the wider team too. To Rhiannon and Lou for working so hard to promote my books, and to everyone in the rights department for negotiating *The Tradwife's Secret* so successfully.

Thank you to my agent, Ed Wood. I'm so happy that Kirsten Clark waltzing through Harry Reid airport caught your attention, and very excited to see what comes next.

I couldn't do this job without support from my fellow authors, with a special shout out for Katy Brent. Thank you all for being at the other end of a WhatsApp message – the jury is out on whether your lightning-fast responses are down to your eagerness to help, or your enthusiasm for a distraction. As ever, thank you to my friends and family for continuing to get excited about my books. And of course, thank you to my readers for making all this possible – your reviews, comments, posts and messages make me smile every single time.

And the biggest thank you goes to my family. Scarlett and Finn – I love you completely, despite you never earning me a penny. And Chris, no one can get me off social media like you can.

Another twisty thriller full of secrets and suspense . . .

'A gripping thriller about deception and self-discovery'
Woman & Home

Madison March is the perfect wife,
with the perfect family and the perfect life.

She spends her days baking sourdough and picking vegetables from the garden while watching her children play in the fields surrounding her Montana homestead.

Dinner is always on the table for her husband, and they end their days sitting on the porch, watching the sun go down.

It's a life anyone would dream of.

And it's all a lie.